the exalted

Books by Kaitlyn Sage Patterson

The Diminished
The Exalted

KAITLYN SAGE PATTERSON

the exalted

ink
yard
press

ISBN-13: 978-1-335-01757-4

The Exalted

InkyardPress.com

Printed in U.S.A.

For Iya, always in my heart.

Part One

"Let the burden of vengeance rest solely on my shoulders, for what has passed cannot be undone. I am the wrath and the fury. I am the fire and the brimstone. I am the hammer and the sword. Seek justice in each choice you make, for no one is safe from my watchful gaze."

—from the *Book of Dzallie, the Warrior*

"From death, new life is born. The ashes of our loss fertilize my earth, turning dust to soil and loam to life. The lives of all my people, twin and singleborn alike, pass in the blink of an eye. With each breath, you grow closer to me, and to your eternity in the halls of the gods. Take comfort in death, for each passing feeds the cycle, bringing forth new life."

—from the *Book of Teuber, the Earthbound*

CHAPTER ONE

Vi

"It's strange, to remember a time before I met you, before I knew you were there at the other end of this connection. For most of my life, I assumed it was my twin, pulling me toward the afterlife, but now it gives me a comfort I'd never imagined, even as you travel across the ocean, even as the light between us grows fainter by the day. Deep in my heart, I harbor that flicker of you, and I know that I'll never be truly alone again."
—*from Vi to Bo*

For days after my brother's ship disappeared over the horizon, I watched the sea. I spent hours on the balcony of Mal and Quill's house in Williford, staring out over the rooftops at the vast span of open water that swelled between my twin and me. Though I'd once again upended their lives, Mal and Quill had made space for me, had taken care of me with a generosity so fierce, I teared up if I thought too much about it.

As the sun set on the fifth week since my brother's departure, I leaned back in my chair, bare feet up on the railing as the sun sank below the horizon. The air buzzed with a chorus of cicadas, and somewhere down the street a fiddle sang, harmonizing with a chorus of trilling birds. Sweat pooled irritatingly in the crook of my elbow. Mal and Quill's housekeeper, Noona, insisted that the shoulder I'd pulled out of socket wouldn't heal unless I kept the arm strapped to my chest in a sling for another two weeks. My shoulder hardly ached at all anymore, but it was easier to argue with a stone wall than with Noona when her mind was made up.

I froze as a flash of white by the gate sent my heart racing. The Shriven, the knives in the temple's belt, prowled the streets in greater numbers every day, but I was safely hidden in the Whipplestons' house. Safe, at least, until the governor granted the temple the right to begin ransacking folks' homes.

Then one of the puppies I'd brought with me from Plumleen, the house Bo and I had barely escaped from with our lives, tumbled out of my bedroom and onto the balcony, yipping and shattering the illusion of fearful stillness on the balcony. A moment later, Quill appeared, the lamp he carried bathing us in a golden glow.

"Learned how to read in the dark, have you?" he asked, grinning down at the open book in my lap.

I flipped the book closed and treated Quill to a sharp glare, tempered by a smile I couldn't keep from my lips whenever he was around. No matter how upended and useless I'd felt as my shoulder healed, Quill's presence always brought a shine of joy to my days. "It wasn't dark until a few minutes ago."

He leaned down and kissed the tip of my nose. "I knew you could see in the dark. Part bat, part girl, just as I suspected. Next thing I know, I'll come out to find you hanging from the rafters by your toes."

"Hush," I said with a laugh. "Is Mal back?"

"He and Curlin are playing brag in the sitting room. Supper's almost ready. Do you want to come down?"

I made a face at the mention of Curlin's name. I wasn't entirely convinced that I'd been right to insist we not leave her in the woods behind Plumleen Hall. Quill set the lamp down and leaned against the railing, crossing his arms over his broad chest and studying me intently, as if he could see into my treacherous heart.

"She's trying, Vi. And she's lost just as much as you have. More, even."

I bit the inside of my cheek, frustrated. "Trying doesn't erase what she's done. The promises she's broken. Trying doesn't bring back the dead."

"Curlin used to be your best friend," Quill insisted. "You can't keep punishing her for her desperate choices. She's remorseful. She wants the same things you do. You both want to see the temple fall."

"It's just not that easy to trust her again."

Quill knelt next to my chair and cupped my cheek in his warm hand. I leaned into his touch, despite my irritation. He was right, and I knew it. "It'd be easier if you spoke to her. If you tried, Vi."

"I'm not the only one who could make an effort," I sniped, then immediately felt a spike of guilt at the expression on Quill's face. Before he could open his mouth, I put up a hand. "I'll try. Promise."

"Good. Then come downstairs. Noona's made a feast." Quill scooped up the puppy and the lamp and I followed him inside, glancing one last time over my shoulder at the gate. I didn't see anyone, but I knew better than to feel safe when I'd spent so much of my own life hidden in shadows.

We found Curlin and Mal in the sitting room, glaring at one another over a table littered with coins and cards.

"Who's winning?" Quill asked.

Mal's smile lit the room. "I don't think Curlin understands that the game's about lying. Or if she does, she's truly terrible at it."

Curlin huffed and threw her cards down on the table. "I fold. This game is aggressively pointless."

I crouched just inside the threshold to pet the mama dog, awkward and unsure where to look. Thankfully, Noona appeared a moment later, wiping her hands on her apron.

"Food'll get cold if you lot keep dillydallying," she chided. "Let's go. You girls won't heal if you don't feed those bodies of yours."

My eyes slid to Curlin and found her looking back at me with a small, tight smile. Noona's tone was so like the one Anchorite Lugine had used to berate us when we'd taken too long to clean our plates as brats. The smile I returned was half-hearted at best, but it was something. It was a start.

After a supper taut with long silences and weighted looks exchanged between the Whipplestons, Curlin caught my eye and raised an eyebrow. I could have pretended not to see the look, ignored the question painted across her face as clearly as her tattoos, but I knew it was time. The moment we'd cleared the table, after Noona and her brother retreated to the kitchen for their evening pot of tea, I blocked the door before Mal and Quill could escape.

"Maybe the four of us could go out to the garden—"

Curlin cut me off with a sharp shake of her head. "Upstairs. One of the rooms at the back of the house."

Mal furrowed his brows, shooting quizzical looks around the room, but Quill seemed to understand immediately.

"We've got time," he insisted. "The both of you still have weeks of healing ahead of you, and we still haven't made contact—"

Mal heaved a deep sigh and ran a hand over his face. "Quill. They're right. It's time."

"Well past time, I'd say," Curlin agreed.

"Fine," Quill said, snagging a bottle of wine off the bar cart. "Upstairs, then. Mal? Glasses?"

Mal, frowning, collected four long-stemmed crystal glasses and followed his brother, refusing to meet my eyes. Curlin tugged absently at the bandage covering her bicep and the wound that had nearly killed her. "You know what it is your sweetheart's been keeping so close to the chest?"

I shook my head, wary, as my mind churned with the possibilities. Had he found the rebels and kept it from us? Or could he have heard from Bo? What was he hiding behind that perfect smile?

"He's got secrets, Vi. I can promise you that."

I rolled my eyes, but my stomach was in knots. "I'm sure he'll tell us what we need to know."

Curlin shrugged and followed me up the stairs. At the end of the hall, lamplight spilled from Quill's bedroom door. I walked past my room and down the corridor, hopping over the squeaky boards between Quill's room and mine without thinking. Behind me, Curlin snorted, and the hot flood of a blush washed up my neck and burned bright spots on my cheeks.

Mal stood at the window as we entered the room, lifting the edge of the curtain to peer out into the dark night. Quill was perched on the corner of his bed, but hopped up to hand Curlin and me each a glass of wine the same gold as his eyes.

I sank into one of the two overstuffed armchairs that flanked Quill's bookcase, and Curlin leaned against the wall just to my right, positioning herself so that her injured arm and mine were side by side. I didn't think she even realized she was doing it, putting the two of us in a defensive position like that—the instincts earned from years of the Shriven's brutal training would probably never leave her, though I hoped the haunted look would someday fade from her eyes.

"Well," I started, "what've you got to tell us? Have you found the rebels?"

Mal crossed the room and locked the door, reaching out to give Curlin a reassuring pat on the shoulder as he passed. She danced out of his reach, glaring. "Out with it," she spit.

"Finding the resistance has never been a problem," Quill said, staring down at his hands, knotted together in his lap. "I've known where they are all along."

I narrowed my eyes at him. "What do you mean?"

Quill took a deep, shuddering breath and met my searching gaze, his golden eyes glitteringly bright in the light of the sunlamps.

"Several years ago, when my brother and I first started coming to Ilor with Uncle Hamlin, I saw the way that the laborers here were being treated, and it grated at me. But when I learned that the temples were contracting laborers to grow philomena, I knew I couldn't stand by and watch. Like everyone else in the colonies, I remembered what'd happened the last time folks farmed philomenas. I had to do something."

"Do what, exactly?" My mouth went dry. I knew what was coming. I could feel the anger burbling in my belly, ready to erupt just as soon as he said the words.

"I had the resources and the ability. I knew I could make a difference. And I'd started to. Dealing in contract labor gave me connections in places I wouldn't have had access to otherwise, and I made sure that the folks I placed were either well cared for and happy or got away clean." Quill paused and gave me a small, sweet smile that I could not—*would* not—return.

"And then you came along. You turned me on my head. Gods, you turned the whole of Ilor on its head. There's not a soul in the colonies who doesn't know your name. And then, when you stayed behind after Bo—"

"You lied to me." I cut him off. Frustration bubbled up in my chest, threatening to set me alight. I wanted him to come right out and say it. Tell me what it was he'd been hiding from me all these weeks.

Quill, to his credit, kept his eyes on mine, though a muscle in his jaw twitched, betraying the sting in my words.

"What, might I ask, are they saying about me?" I spit.

Crossing his arms over his chest, Quill glanced at his brother, whose eyes were on the toes of his boots, offering him no help at all. With a deep breath, Quill said, "That you'd hardly been in Ilor for a moment when the man who'd bought your contract was dead and his estate razed. There are rumors that you harnessed some kind of power from being diminished and have turned that rage and hate into magic. They say that you've taken over the leadership of the rebellion and that you plan to end Alskad's grasp on the governance of Ilor."

I snorted, and laughter spilled out of me. It was absurd. All of this was absurd.

"I know the truth," Quill said, "and it was hard even for me not to get caught up in the rumors."

"What's the truth, then?" Curlin asked, her voice steady, far more measured than I could manage at the moment. I shot her a grateful look.

"I know where the rebellion is camped. I've always known." Quill hesitated. "I'm one of its leaders."

I blinked back furious tears. "Why didn't you tell me this sooner? Don't you trust me?"

"Because it's not just about me," Quill said. "There are hundreds of people whose lives depend on my keeping their existence secret. If I'd just shown up in camp with you, they'd have panicked. I have to convince the rest of the leaders that you're a useful asset."

"They think we're a liability," Curlin said bitterly, and my heart wrenched at the truth in her words. How I could've been so clueless before was beyond me. I was no one. I was utterly useless to the people I wanted to help, and the Whipplestons had spent weeks trying to protect me from that truth.

Mal nodded. "We've been going in circles for weeks, trying to figure out how to keep you safe. To keep them safe."

"It's not your job to keep me safe," I spit. "If I'd wanted to be wrapped in cotton wool and put away on a shelf, I would've gone back to Alskad with Bo. I'm here to do something. To make a difference. And if you can't see that, then maybe it's time for me to leave."

I shot out of my chair, flung open the door and, before any of them could say another word, stalked down the hall to my room. Hot, wrathful tears spilled down my cheeks. Just when I'd finally felt the burden of being a dimmy lifted from my shoulders, I'd come to realize that I had just as little say in the direction of my life as I'd ever had. Less, even.

It seemed I was of no use to anyone.

CHAPTER TWO

Bo

"Despite having trained rigorously for a position of political power almost every day of my life, not a day goes by when I feel entirely confident that I've managed to do the right thing, or even the adequate thing, in a given situation."

—*from Bo to Vi*

I paced the length of the council chamber, in part to keep from shivering, but mostly because I simply couldn't sit still and wait any longer. Despite the fires roaring in the large hearths on either side of the long table, the council chamber was one of the coldest rooms in the palace. Its bank of windows faced north, and no effort had been made to insulate the stone walls and floors with rugs or tapestries. Runa didn't want the councillors to be comfortable here. She wanted them on edge, the better to see the holes in their armor.

In fact, the whole chamber was uncharacteristically bare compared to the rest of the palace. The only decorations were a collection of ancient, ornately decorated rifles tarnishing on their hooks over each fireplace. Undyed, moth-eaten sheepskins hung over the high backs of the chairs on either side of the table, and the thrones that sat at the head and foot were plain, cushioned affairs draped in furs only slightly less worn than the sheepskins.

The table was the most beautiful thing in the room by a long stretch. Old as the empire itself, and with the scars to prove it, the table had been made from a single slice of a tree trunk that must've once measured more than ten feet around when it stood.

"They won't expect to see you." The low, measured voice of my grandmother, Queen Runa, effortlessly filled the council chamber. "Some of them will be thrown off guard by your presence here. Allow them the time they need to adjust."

Swinton, who'd returned to Alskad with me after helping me find my sister, laughed. "He isn't nervous—are you, Bo?"

I bit the inside of my cheek and studied the spread of smoked fish, soft cheeses and fresh shoots of bitter greens on the table. I wasn't nervous; I just…felt out of place. I'd come back to Alskad changed, and having seen more clearly into the lives of the people I was meant to rule someday.

But Alskad was the same. The same people, the same parties, the same endless political scheming that did nothing to better the lives of the people of our empire. Though I had never enjoyed it before, now that I was back, I found that I had no patience for the lies and manipulations of the court—and even less than none for the Suzerain, the treacherous leaders of the temple who'd been poisoning our people.

Runa tapped out a rhythm on the table as she studied the collection of gilded perfume bottles that sat, innocuous as a nest of vipers, in the middle of the table.

"Let's finish reviewing, then," she said. "The boy in the basement. Which details will you use to convince the royal council that this part of the story isn't heresy?"

It was the third time she'd asked me about the boy my twin sister, Vi, had seen in the temple basement back in Ilor. Every time I repeated the story, my heart broke a little more for his poor soul. And each time, I grew a little angrier.

In a fair imitation of my accent, Swinton said, "His name was Tobain. He was nine years old. The only thing he'd ever harmed was a chicken…"

Runa cut him off with a glare, but Swinton merely waggled his eyebrows at the queen, grinning, and slid into the nearest chair.

It had taken no small amount of doing, but the moment we'd landed in Penby three weeks ago, Swinton had set his sights on finding every remaining drop of the philomena perfume that had inspired the Suzerain's horrifying experiment in Ilor. He'd bought two bottles off noblewomen who'd kept them as reminders of investments gone awry. Another turned up in the poorest section of town, the End, purchased for no more than a few *twilling*. The fourth was a vial Runa herself had locked away in a cabinet after she'd shut down the perfumeries in the wake of the Ilorian tragedy.

We knew that the perfume wasn't exactly the same concoction the temple was using to poison the diminished, but I certainly felt better knowing it was safe in our hands. Furthermore, it was all the proof we could procure without storming the temple itself. Swinton, wary of the fact that he might have been secretly dosed at some point in his life, had stayed well away from the stuff, but both Runa and I had each taken a single, cautious sniff. It had a light, almost citrusy scent, like sunlight and greenery and the first bloom of spring. It didn't smell like violence distilled in a bottle.

I picked up where Swinton had left off. "Tobain's mother had made him wring the chicken's neck for supper. He had eyes like cherrywood knots. The temple in Ilor was a nearly exact replica of the temples here in Penby, which is, to be frank, remarkably impractical. The people in Ilor build their houses with wide windows and fans to cool the rooms for a reason—the temple there trapped the heat of Ilor like an oven."

"Good," she said. "Now, just remember—sit up straight. Don't fidget. Try not to let them rattle you."

Since my return from Ilor, my grandmother had kept up a near-endless soliloquy on the ideal behavior of a monarch. I must dress with care and richness, but never gaudy vanity. I must walk more determinedly, but less quickly. I must speak at a softer volume in a loud room and with greater volume in a quiet one. I mustn't eat with too much enthusiasm or too little. And on and on and on.

But when we'd spoken about this meeting, this conversation, her only requirement was that she be the one to actually inform the council of the temple's crimes. She insisted that, were I to bring the news before the council, I'd be laughed out of the room. Any respect I'd gained as the future leader of the empire would be shattered. I must function only as a witness.

Swinton swung his feet up onto the table, one ankle over the other, and leaned his chair back, studying his nails. I bit back a smile and watched Runa out of the corner of my eye. She'd immediately warmed to Swinton upon our arrival, charmed by his outright refusal to treat her with the same obsequious, pandering respect that she got from nearly everyone else in the kingdom. They'd settled into a playfully antagonistic rhythm over the past few weeks; a rhythm that I would have enjoyed immensely, had I not been so nervous about the meeting of the council that was set to start in less than an hour.

It was truly a thing of beauty, watching the scoundrel I adored tease and chivy the most powerful woman in the world.

Runa looked up from her papers, and her face paled in horror when she saw Swinton's boots propped on the ancient table. It didn't take her long to regain her composure, though, and her eyes were twinkling when she said, "Young man, do you know anything about the history of this table?"

Swinton looked at the table and yawned. "Can't say as I do."

"Perhaps you will consider removing your feet and allowing me to enlighten you."

The story of this particular table and the tree it came from was one I'd been told a thousand times or more—as had every child in the Alskad Empire—but I'd never heard Runa tell it. I leaned in, unrepentantly excited to hear the history of my nation recounted in the queen's own words.

Long ago, in the earliest days after the cataclysm, the first empress and her people journeyed north, camping and scavenging what food they could manage. So little of the earth had been habitable then, and the empress had led her people over miles of devastated land, searching for a place where they might settle. Somewhere safe from the earthquakes and floods, the hurricanes and tsunamis, and the shards of the fractured moon that still rained from the sky.

One night, having walked as far as they could, the group set up camp in a clearing in the woods, beneath an enormous old tree. One of the children was sick, and in hopes of keeping the disease from spreading, the empress gave her tent to the mother and child so that they might isolate themselves from the rest of their family.

The empress nestled her own blankets among the roots of the ancient tree and quickly fell asleep. Her rest was not peaceful, however, for in the middle of the night, she was startled awake by a resounding crash and a hair-raising jolt of electricity.

The tree had been struck by lightning. The empress got to her feet, and as she stood, looking up into the branches, the tree swayed and heaved. Before she could call out a warning to her people, the tree crashed to the ground. But rather than falling on the hundreds of souls who'd survived their long journey, the tree fell away from the group, harming no one. And instead of sending the empress, standing at the base of the trunk, toppling head over heels, the roots lifted her high above the crowd.

From her high vantage point, across a path cleared by the enormous tree's fall, the empress saw the Penby harbor for the first time.

The palace was built on that very spot, the forest around it cleared and the wood used to build the city. And the tree that had cleared the first empress's way to the ocean was used to build furniture for the palace, furniture that has been used by generation upon generation of Alskad's queens. The trunk was fashioned into the council chamber's table, where the most important decisions in the kingdom have been made since the settling of Alskad. The throne was carved from the roots of the tree, and the dais on which it stood from the branches— turned upside down, just as the tree had once been.

When Runa finished the story, Swinton glanced from the table to me, to Runa and back to the table again. Grinning, he said, "Well, aren't we a sentimental bunch? All that for an old, battered table?"

"You feel no call to respect the history of our empire?" Runa asked.

Swinton gave her an indulgent smile. The kind of smile

you might save for a precocious child. "*Your* empire, Runa. Not mine. Not my home, either."

A knock at the door interrupted the queen's sharp response, and she gave Swinton a wry smile as she shuffled her papers back into place.

"We'll continue this conversation later. Have no doubt about that," she said, plucking her crown from the table and settling it onto her head. "Now, if you'll excuse us, I would hate to keep the council waiting."

Swinton got to his feet and crossed the room. He wrapped his arms around me and gave me a kiss, his scruff rubbing my freshly shaved cheek. "You can do this, Bo."

I smiled at him, hoping that his confidence would bolster me into someone who might be mistaken for a future ruler, at least in the low light of the council chamber. At Runa's nod, I pressed a switch hidden on the side of the fireplace. The stone wall sank back, revealing a dark landing and a narrow set of stairs that led directly to the rooms I'd been given on my arrival. The suite of the heir to the throne. I assumed there was another such passage that led to Runa's rooms, but though she'd entrusted me with many secrets in the weeks since I'd returned from Ilor, I knew that for every truth she trusted me with, she kept three more hidden.

Swinton gave my hand a final quick squeeze and dashed up the stairs, and I closed the secret passage behind him, steeling myself for the trial that lay ahead of me.

CHAPTER THREE

Vi

"Over the past few weeks, I've realized that I never really learned how to trust. I've spent my whole life guarding against people bound and determined to hurt me, so much so that I don't know how to let those guards down. Now that I see it, though, maybe I can find a way to change."

—*from Vi to Bo*

I slammed my bedroom door closed behind me with no regard for the Whipplestons' feelings or for Noona and her brother, who were likely already asleep in their rooms downstairs. Tears coursed down my cheeks as I whipped a satchel from its hook on the back of the door and set about awkwardly tearing clothes out of the chest of drawers one-handed, flinging them onto the bed. I couldn't stand to be in this house for another minute, the Shriven hunting me be damned.

For weeks—*weeks!*—I'd been twiddling my thumbs, waiting idly as Quill told me he was searching for the resistance, when he'd known exactly where they were all along. I'd waited through half-truths and lies while he and his brother tried to decide what was best for me.

Me, a woman grown. A woman who'd been fending for herself while Quill had tried to hide behind a forest of excuses.

The audacity, the sheer gall it must take to think himself so much more capable than me, was infuriating. I didn't need his help or anyone else's. I would end the temple's stranglehold on Ilor myself, even if it meant tearing each haven hall down, stone by stone, with my bare hands.

There was a soft knock, and I flew across the room, throwing the bolt down. "Go away."

"Vi, don't be so ram-skulled," Curlin called through the door.

Ignoring her, I dug through the thin blouses and undershirts in one of my drawers, feeling around for the small leather pouch that held my pearls, my only real wealth, my last remaining connection to Alskad. The pearls I'd spent years cultivating and harvesting back in Penby harbor, hoping they'd someday buy me a life away from the temple. A life of peace. I double-checked the knot that held the pouch secure and looped the long cord over my head and around my neck, tucking it between my breasts.

"If you could look past your pride for a tenth of a second—"

"This isn't about pride," I seethed, even as the words left the tinny taste of lies on my tongue. "Now go away. You wouldn't understand."

Outside, Curlin heaved a heavy sigh and slid down the door like a wave being pulled back by the tide, blocking the dim lamplight that filtered beneath the crack in the door. "What wouldn't I understand? Promises? Truth? Sacrifices? At some point you're going to have to hear my side of things, you know."

Rolling my eyes, I grabbed a handful of socks and stuffed them into my bag. I didn't need to hear her excuses. I'd been there the day she promised, with me and Sawny and Lily, the best friends of our childhood—now cold in their graves—that none of us would ever join the ranks of the Shriven. That nothing in the world could make us walk away from the one thing that had kept us from losing hope in the bleak landscape of our shared childhood: our friendship.

And I would never forget the day I came back to the room I'd shared with Curlin all my life to find her things gone, her side of the room bare, as if she'd never been there in the first place.

Curlin rapped on the door again. "Vi. Come on. Let me in."

Sawny might have, in time, forgiven her for joining the Shriven. But I couldn't. Wouldn't. Even if she'd once been the person I trusted most in the world. And if Mal and Quill could lie to me for all this time, I couldn't rightly see much use at all for trust anymore. My throat tightened, and I closed my eyes, reaching for the tiny flicker of comfort and stability that tied me to Bo, no matter how far away he was. I didn't want to cry anymore. My heart was cracking, crumbling in my chest, and the only thing I could think to do was seal it up, pack it away in ice and clay until I'd accomplished what I'd set out to do. Until I'd broken the Suzerain's death grip on the people of Alskad and Ilor once and for all.

I scanned the room, looking for anything I'd forgotten, and perched on the edge of the bed to pull my boots on. I wasn't entirely confident I could saddle my horse, Beetle, one-handed, but I couldn't stand to be in this house another night. If Quill refused to help me find the rebels, I would find them on my own.

And if they didn't want my help? Well, then, I would just have to find another way to stop the temple.

I slung my bag onto my good shoulder, flipped the lock and opened the door. Where I probably would have tumbled backward into the room if I'd been in her position, Curlin was on her feet in an instant, her sharp eyes assessing every detail and narrowing as she realized what I had planned.

"You're not leaving."

I tried to shove past her, but she was quicker and a great deal stronger, and her wounds had healed much more quickly than mine. With one hand on the doorframe, she cornered me, trapping me inside my room. "See if you can stop me," I hissed, aware of Mal and Quill just down the hall.

She pushed me gently backward, careful to avoid my shoulder, and closed the door behind her. "You're just going to walk out into the night, with the Shriven combing the town for you? Have you lost all good sense? Mal and Quill want to help you. They're *trying* to help you. If you'd just stop being such a stubborn ninny, you'd see that."

"They're trying to wrap me in cotton wool and stick me in a drawer to rot," I snapped. "I didn't decide to stay behind when Bo left so that I could lounge about drinking tea and eating Noona's pastries for the rest of my life. I stayed to fight. And if they're not going to help me take down the temple, I'm going to find someone who will."

Curlin studied me, eyebrows knit together. "Well, if you're going to insist on leaving, I'm coming with you."

"Forget it. There's no way."

"Your shoulder's not healed, and you haven't got the fog-giest idea how to conceal yourself from the Shriven, not to mention the fact that you don't have any idea where you're going. I, at least, have overheard things in the temple that might help us."

I crossed my uninjured arm over my sling, gripping my elbow as pain radiated out of my still-knitting joint. She wasn't wrong, and I kind of hated her for it. "I don't trust you."

Curlin grinned, a roguish smirk so familiar and so surprising, I took a step back. She snorted a laugh and rolled her eyes. "And why would you? You've not talked to me in years, aside from the two days the anchorites made me watch you before they sent you here, and the one when I threatened you with the most horrifying side of the temple's many misdeeds. You've no reason to trust me. Not yet, at least."

"I'll douse Gadrian's flames in my own spit before I'll ever trust you again, Curlin."

She sighed and ran a hand over the auburn stubble that'd sprouted from her scalp over the past few weeks. "Don't be so dramatic. Now, if you're serious about leaving without a word to the two people who've done more to help you than anyone else in this godsforsaken world, fine. But at least let me come so that you don't get yourself killed."

I'd gotten so used to struggling through life on my own that I didn't always see the times when I needed help. Curlin's betrayal had cut me deep, but somewhere deep in the recesses of my brain, I knew that Sawny would have been right to forgive her. We didn't know why she'd joined the Shriven, but we did know how manipulative and how utterly without conscience they could be.

So I resolved to do as Sawny would have, had he been here, and try to forgive her. Someday.

"Fine," I said with a sigh. "Meet me in the stables in ten minutes. But if you breathe a word of this to Mal or Quill, I'll skin you alive."

Curlin smiled and reached out to squeeze my hand. "I'll be as silent as the grave. But on the off chance I did say something, you know you couldn't manage it even if you caught me in a net and knocked me out first."

A moment later she was gone, and I was left in the middle of a room that felt more like home than any other ever had, readying myself to go to war with the one person I trusted least in the world guarding my back.

Sweat rolled down my back, beaded on my upper lip and trickled, stinging, into my eyes. The jungle swarmed with gnats and mosquitoes, a horde of millions bound and determined to pepper my skin with tiny, itching welts. I ducked forward over and over again, burying my face in Beetle's thick mane to avoid being scraped off her back by one low-hanging branch after another.

I wasn't entirely convinced that we were still on the right path—or even on any kind of path at all—but I wasn't about to face Curlin's ridicule by pulling out the map she'd swiped from the Whipplestons' study for what would probably be the tenth time since we'd left our first campsite at dawn.

We'd crept out in the middle of the night, and despite my boiling fury at Mal and Quill and the unsteady truce Curlin and I had forged, a thrill had run through me as we rode away from the coast toward the moon-washed mountains. Now, though, away from the ocean breezes and Noona's endless snacks and glasses of cool tea, I was having a hard time remembering why I'd been so anxious to leave.

I twisted in my saddle to see Curlin clinging to her ancient gray mule's sparse mane, like the plodding beast was bound to start bucking and rearing any second.

"All right back there?"

Through clenched teeth, Curlin said, "We could've walked up this mountain a cursed lot faster if you'd agreed to leave these damned beasts behind."

I wiped the sweat off my face with a handkerchief and forced myself to take a deep breath. She wasn't going to get any less irritating, and since throttling her wasn't a real option, I would have to find a way to cope. Curlin had been one of my best friends in the world when we were children, one of my only friends, and her intense need to control every situation had been a challenge even then. Her years with the Shriven hadn't improved her temper one bit.

"You really think we could have carried this lot up and down these mountains, with your arm only just out of stitches? To say nothing of my Rayleane-damned shoulder." I jerked my chin at our bedrolls and saddlebags stuffed with pilfered food, clothes and weapons. Quill's door had been closed and the twins' voices raised at one another when I'd snuck down the stairs and raided the kitchen on the way out to the barn. The pang of sneaking away without a goodbye hadn't been painful enough that I was willing to leave empty-handed, and there was no way in all of Hamil's tumultuous seas that we would've been able to carry all of it.

Curlin's lips tightened, and the tattoos over her cheekbones glistened with what could have been either sweat or tears. It was hard to tell. If I had to put money on it, I'd guess sweat. Details of the Shriven's training were a well-guarded secret, but one so closely held that even as a wee thing, I'd known that the worst I could imagine didn't come close to the horrors of the truth. More than a few brats who'd grown up in the temple with me, dimmy and twin alike, had been recruited by the Shriven over the years.

And once they'd gone for training, they, like Curlin, had become almost entirely unrecognizable.

The Shriven moved with the languid, dangerous grace and speed of predators. I'd heard folks say that one of the Shriven could be across the room in a second, and by the time the clock had moved on to the next, they'd have cut your throat and disappeared, and not a person in the room the wiser. Not, at least, until you fell to the floor in a puddle of your own blood.

The only thing on the planet more dangerous than one of the Shriven, they'd say, was a dimmy. That word still rankled me. Even after learning about the temple's awful experiments with the philomena extract, even after finding Bo…the word still sent me into a tailspin.

Dimmy. Diminished.

I'd lived my whole life with that word hanging over my head. And even though I knew it didn't define me—didn't define anyone, really—it still wrapped around my neck like a vine, threatening to choke all the life out of me.

If I had my way, not another soul would be manipulated by the Suzerain and their temple lackeys the way I had been. If I had my way, no one else would be controlled or fall victim to the violent grief that was supposedly the burden of the diminished.

The path widened, and I reined Beetle in, waiting for Curlin to catch up. Our mounts walked docilely together, Curlin's doing its best to pull the reins out of her grip in order to graze at the long grass that lined the path. Beetle, thankfully, seemed somehow aware of my tender shoulder and continued to march stoically along.

I rolled the question that'd been plaguing me for weeks around in my head, looking for a way to shape it that wouldn't get Curlin's hackles up. It didn't take me long to realize that it wasn't Curlin who'd positioned herself on the defensive— it was me. She'd gone out of her way to help me, to keep me safe, and I'd met her with barbs and shields because I couldn't wrap my head around the one decision she'd made that'd shattered me so many years ago. I'd never understood why she'd joined the Shriven. And I still wasn't brave enough to ask.

CHAPTER FOUR

Bo

"I feel as though I am a hen living in a den of foxes. I need to find my claws if I am to survive the machinations and scheming that are the bread and butter of this court. Be grateful that your only foes are the Shriven. At least they are straightforward in their attacks."

—*from Bo to Vi*

When the passage door was fully closed behind Swinton, Runa swung the enormous doors of the council chamber open. I watched her, studying the subtle change in her expression as the council members filed into the room. Each of them stopped before her, bowing to kiss the gold cuff she wore around her wrist, almost identical to my own.

A servant pulled out the throne at the foot of the table, and I took my seat. The members of the council whispered among themselves, largely ignoring me, apart from the occasional glance. My distant cousins Patrise and Lisette were the last two to swan into the room, and as soon as they'd observed the proper niceties with Runa, they were at my side, petting and praising me.

"Oh, darling, you've grown into a proper young man, haven't you?" Lisette crooned. "I am so very sorry for the loss of your mother and cousins. It's just devastating, isn't it? You do know that Patrise and I are here for you, yes?"

Patrise ruffled my hair, but his reassuring grin didn't quite reach his eyes. "Of course we are, cousin. We both know how difficult it is to be singleborn, but you mustn't think of yourself as being all alone. Lisette and I are here to guide you."

I gritted my teeth and gave them a tight smile. "Thank you, cousins. I'll certainly keep that in mind."

The queen's voice cut through the noise of the room. "I will now call this meeting of the council to order. Please take your seats." To my chagrin, Lisette and Patrise chose the chairs on either side of me.

As soon as the creaking of the old wooden chairs settled, silence fell over the chamber, and the queen began the story we'd rehearsed. It was, in its essence, the truth of what I'd learned while in Ilor, but we'd removed Vi from the narrative, shaping her pieces of the story so that they might've come from my perspective rather than hers.

I listened intently, my nerves frayed and my stomach sour from too much kaffe and not nearly enough to eat, as she told them about the philomena farms, the tincture the temple used to make the diminished lose themselves to grief and the horrifying neglect and mistreatment of the laborers in Ilor. She outlined everything Vi and I had learned in our short time in the colony.

I shifted on my throne at the foot of the table, the chill of the stone chamber creeping into the soles of my feet, in spite of the thick boots and wool socks I wore. I wanted desperately to stick my hands beneath my thighs to warm them, but I kept them clasped on the table in front of me.

I had to appear strong, focused, unflappable. I had to take up space, to have a true presence here.

When Runa finished, the only sounds in the room were the crackling logs in the hearths and the wheeze of Dame Turshaw's breath. I looked from face to shocked, calculating face, searching for some sign that the council members believed what the queen had told them. Of the six members of the council, there were only three I knew beyond their reputations and years of formal interactions at court: Patrise, Lisette and Rylain, the singleborn, who were more or less in my generation, though I was by far the youngest of the group.

It'd taken some getting used to for me to stop counting myself among them. Among the singleborn. Until I'd learned about Vi, my sister, my twin, I'd thought of them as the three *other* singleborn of my generation. I must, in their minds, still be neatly filed away in that category, as well. Each time I considered what would inevitably happen when they—and the rest of the empire—learned that I was a twin, the thought tightened like a noose around my neck. I knew we couldn't hide the truth forever, but I always felt like I was betraying Vi by wishing for more time.

Lisette yawned, breaking the silence. "Please don't tell me that you believe the little fool. I was there not five years ago, and I saw nothing of the sort then."

I tried not to glare at Lisette. She, like the other singleborn, had an innate ability to command the attention of a room without moving a muscle. She was in her early thirties and wore her mass of auburn hair loose over her shoulders. Her heavy-lidded brown eyes glittered like agate chips over her high cheekbones and bow of a mouth. Just before she spoke, her mouth had twitched into something more akin to a snarl than a smile as she exchanged an incomprehensible look with Patrise.

Patrise was talking before Lisette's words had settled in our ears. "Honestly, Runa. You called us all here to talk about this boy's nonsense? I'm surprised at you. You know, just as we all do, that he's been wild with grief since the deaths of his mother and cousins. Surely he snatched this whole ridiculous story line from one of his novels."

Runa scowled as she saw the irritation I betrayed on my face. "Patrise, you *will* address me by my proper title, or you'll spend a week locked in a cell with nothing but bread and water. I don't give two shits rubbed together whether you believe the information Ambrose provided or not. I've seen the evidence, and *I* believe him. As the monarch of this country, my judgment trumps yours. Do I make myself clear?"

"Yes, Your Majesty," he muttered.

Patrise and Lisette were hardly ever apart, so close they were almost a matched pair. More siblings than cousins. Patrise was one of those unnervingly handsome men who, unlike me, never allowed his face to betray his emotions. He and Lisette had always been on the periphery of my life, alternately scheming against me and doing their best to spoil me rotten in hopes of garnering the queen's favor. Patrise had tried more than once to have me killed, and I was sure that, at the very least, Lisette hadn't been ignorant of those plans. She may have even had a hand in orchestrating them.

But the two of them had also seen to it that the presents they sent for my birthday were more extravagant by half than anything else I was given. They'd planted spies in my household. Spies who, in addition to the work of learning all of my habits and watching my every move, had ferried lascivious gossip to my cousins Claes and Penelope, which they'd then used as blackmail on my behalf. Or at least they had, until their untimely deaths. Despite Claes's betrayal of me on his deathbed, I dearly missed them both.

The others around the table shifted and murmured among themselves, beginning to process what the queen had told them. The other members of the council were also singleborn, representing the handful of families that had borne singleborn children since the founding of Alskad. Each of the people around the table was, by some complicated means or another, related to each other. We could all trace our lineage back to the first empress of Alskad and her singleborn children.

A clear contralto voice cut over the rising tide of the council's worrying. Rylain. "Your Majesty, if I may ask— why have you brought this matter to our attention?"

My relationship with Patrise and Lisette was much more complicated than what existed between Rylain, the eldest singleborn of our generation, and me. Rylain had always done her best to separate herself from the council and the other singleborn. Her estates were even farther north than mine, at the very edge of the border between Alskad and the Arctic waste. Refusing to engage in the backstabbing complexities of court life, Rylain only came to Penby when a direct order from the queen required the trip, and she had always been vocal about her lack of interest in the politics of the empire or the throne.

Needless to say, of all my singleborn cousins, I felt the most kinship with Rylain. Unlike Patrise and Lisette, she was never a threat to my ascension, and any time I tired of the end-less politicking of the other singleborn, she was always there, ready with a conversation that had nothing to do with the machinations of court life.

The council's voices rose again, echoing Rylain's question and calling out more queries in increasingly shrill tones. Rylain never schemed or postured like the others—she quietly observed, just as she did now. With wide-set brown eyes so dark as to be almost black, she studied each face in the room, watching the slight changes in their expression and cataloging them as she would the books in her library.

After a few minutes of this, the queen stood and slammed her hands down on the wooden table with a loud *bang*.

"Quiet!" she roared.

Rylain's eyes met mine, holding my gaze for just a moment before turning her intent stare on Dame Turshaw, who was seated on the queen's left. The ancient woman's deeply wrinkled forehead creased as her eyebrows knit together in a furious expression, and she tossed an imperious glare at the queen.

"Your Majesty, Rylain asked you a question," she said. "And a good one, at that. You've obviously gathered us here for a reason. Without the evidence you claim to have received from the crown prince—" she spit the word like a foul bit of spoiled fruit "—and with no clear purpose, all you've done here is defame and defile the good name of our temple and the Suzerain."

I cleared my throat. "Your Majesty, if I may—"

"Son, you are here as a courtesy and a courtesy alone," Dame Turshaw snapped. "Despite your status as heir, you've not yet been given a place on this council, in part because of your ill-advised and unapproved trip to Ilor. A trip, I might add, that is the entire cause of this disruptive and inconvenient meeting. You've no right to speak."

Lisette nodded at Dame Turshaw. "You make a good point. Without membership on the royal council, the crown prince is present as a guest and is without a vote. Therefore, I move that Crown Prince Ambrose be voted onto this council."

"If we allow him to join the council, our number will be seven. It's against our bylaws for the table to exceed six," Olivar, a rotund man in his late middle age, countered. "Someone will have to step down."

My jaw tensed. I knew the bylaws. Runa and I had discussed the issue at length, and who should be asked to step down. In my ideal world, it would be Patrise or Lisette—ridding myself of those awful, conniving power-grubbers would please me to no end—but such a choice wouldn't be wise. Better to keep danger in plain sight than shove it off to the side where it might fester and grow into something nastier.

"I second the nomination of the prince to the council," Patrise said, his eyes holding mine in a long stare. He surely thought that this move would buy him my favor, or at least a bargaining chip at some point in the not-too-distant future. I wondered if he had any idea how much I loathed him.

Lisette rolled her eyes so dramatically that no one at the table could have missed it, and then raised her hand. "A third nomination carries it. Your Majesty, will you consider calling to vote the nomination of Crown Prince Ambrose Oswin Trousillion Gyllen to the royal council?"

"We must first discuss the implications of such a decision." The queen nodded. "Prince Ambrose, please adjourn to the antechamber while the council goes into private session."

I rose and left the room, feeling the pressure of the council's eyes on me as I departed.

I was prepared. I was ready. I was the picture of kingly calm.

Runa had warned me that the council would refuse to accept my testimony unless I was sworn in and thus bound to protect the secrets I heard in that chamber. And without the testimony of an eyewitness, they would dither and refuse to act against the temple until it was too late. We had to force them into action. I didn't quite see how it mattered that I become an official member of the council, given that the oaths I'd taken when I was declared heir were far more binding than those I'd swear to sit on the council. But, as Swinton and Runa had endlessly reminded me over the course of the last three weeks, tradition meant a great deal to these people, and it would be hard for them to break with it.

In the end, the true challenge wouldn't be allowing me to sit on the council, but deciding who would have to step down in order to give me that seat. I was confident that Runa and I had chosen the right person to ask, though it remained to be seen whether the other members of the council would agree.

The guards ushered me through the little antechamber and into the hall, where I wouldn't have even the faintest chance of hearing the council's discussion. I paced up and down the hall, the heels of my boots echoing like drumbeats. Snow fell in quiet drifts on the other side of the casement windows, and icy air seeped through the ancient stone as shadows climbed like ivy up the walls.

On my sixth lap of the hall, I stopped in front of the guards. "Do you have the time, Tibbaux?"

I wasn't positive that the woman's name was Tibbaux, but I was fairly certain it started with a *T,* at least. Runa knew the names of each and every person who served the crown—from the boy who turned the spit in the kitchen to the captain of the guard, no one was too small or unimportant for Runa. I hoped to be the same when I wore the crown.

Tibbaux—Theeo?—patted the pockets of her uniform's trousers and, coming up empty-handed, looked at the guard standing next to her. With an ill-concealed smirk, he pointed at an enormous gilded clock ticking in an alcove just to his right. I pressed my lips into a thin smile, feeling a bit sheepish.

"Thank you. Waiting like this makes me skittish as a newborn foal, wouldn't you agree?"

The guards nodded, their feelings once again hidden behind impassive masks, and I wanted to cram the words back into my mouth as soon as I'd finished speaking. Their whole lives were spent waiting—waiting for people like me to make decisions for people like them, for people like me to finish whatever secret task I'd accomplish behind one closed door before being escorted to another. Waiting for something to happen, for some attack or action that would never come.

I paced and watched the minute hand creep around the clock's gilded, midnight blue face. Eventually, my legs like jelly, I sank onto a cold, hard bench and picked at my cuticles—though I knew Runa would scold me for it—listening to the ticktock of the ever-slowing seconds passing.

A loud bang yanked me out of my sullen reverie, but before I could scramble to my feet, Rylain swept past me in a rush of somber rust-colored silk and thunderhead cashmere.

"Rylain, wait!" I called down the hall.

She turned on a heel and faced me, her cheeks flushed deeply red. "Magritte keep you from that nest of vipers, cousin. You don't have a single true friend in that room."

Without another word, she slipped through the heavy doors and was gone. A moment later, Lisette appeared at my side and threaded her arm through mine. "It was…not unanimous," she announced. "But you've been approved, nonetheless. The queen asked Rylain to step down to make a place for you, and we voted you into her seat. I've honestly no idea why she even cares. It isn't as if she ever willingly engages in the running of the empire unless she's forced to come down out of her hiding place in the North."

"She seemed upset," I said, wondering if our choice had actually been the right one. Runa and I hadn't expected Rylain to be so put out.

Lisette tittered. "Of course she's upset. She just lost the last modicum of influence she ever had. But come now, let's not keep the others waiting. It's been a long enough day already, and everyone's ready for their suppers and their beds."

Since she was still clinging to my arm, I escorted Lisette back into the chamber, taking in each of the council members' faces as we entered. I nearly laughed. It was painfully obvious who in the room had voted against my joining the council. Dame Turshaw and Olivar looked as though they'd each been given a spoonful of rancid cod-liver oil.

I stopped at Runa's throne and bent to kiss her bracelet.

"Crown Prince Ambrose Oswin Trousillion Gyllen, the council has voted in favor of granting your petition to be inducted into our ranks. Will you swear, in the name of your chosen god, to hold the secrets of this council and its members until your death?"

"I swear on my honor and in Gadrian the Firebound's name."

"And will you, on pain of imprisonment, death or removal from your throne, swear that all words you utter within the four walls of this chamber be true?"

I did everything in my power to control the horrified expression that threatened to fall over my face like a mask. The queen hadn't prepared me for this part of the vow, but given that I'd just watched her tell a story to the council that was really only half-true, I managed to school my features into a kind of knit-brow concern.

"Certainly," I said, my voice more of a squeak than the confident affirmation I'd intended.

"Lovely," Runa said, gleeful. "The council will hear your testimony tonight, and tomorrow we will reconvene in order to discuss the issue. I ask that you all hold your recommendations until that time. And, of course, I would like to remind you that nothing we say here may leave this chamber."

The councillors nodded their assent, and I took a deep breath, trying to collect my racing thoughts and focus on the story I was meant to tell. I would have more than enough time to ask Runa questions later.

CHAPTER FIVE

Vi

"I certainly hope that wherever you are right now, it's cooler than this blasted Ilorian heat. I feel like I may dissolve in a pool of my own sweat if it doesn't let up soon."

—*from Vi to Bo*

We stopped for the night just as the sun was setting over the mountains. A small waterfall tumbled into a deep, rock-cluttered pool just at the edge of the clearing, and a screen of trees provided some cover from the path.

Once we'd fed and hobbled the horses, built a fire and erected our tent, I pulled a set of spare clothes, a towel and a net bag from my bedroll, tucking my little bag of pearls into the center of the roll for safekeeping.

I set the clothes and the towel on a rock near the water. Then, with my back to Curlin, I shimmied out of my sweat-soaked clothes, looped the strap of the net bag across my chest and waded into the cool, fresh lap of the waves. All of the stress and terror and confusion of the last few months washed away in the familiar pull of the water. I wasn't ten steps in before I was up to my shoulders, and I took a few deep breaths in preparation for a dive.

I picked up a couple of stones to weigh me down and kicked hard toward the bottom of the pool. The fading light of the day cast the depths in shadow, but the water was clear, and tiny, bright fish darted around me in waves of silver and bubbles. The huge, rounded rocks that littered the bottom of the pool were smoother and larger than any I'd seen in the harbor back home.

The water here didn't sting my eyes the way that the salty ocean had, but I found the same kind of tranquility in the pounding crash of the waterfall that I'd loved in the rhythm of the waves. Long, dark green leaves danced and curled up from the bottom of the pool, and pearlescent shells glittered in the cracks between the stones.

Diving had the same comforting familiarity as walking into a dark room I knew by heart, avoiding every shin-knocking table corner and jutting doorknob by habit. It was easy, peaceful. Each moment underwater brought me closer to myself. I dug my fingers into the sand and felt around until I found the smooth, hard shell of a mollusk. I dug and dug, loading my bag with as many clams as I could find before I ran out of air. As I fingered through the sand, I ran through my mental inventory of the food in our saddlebags, and an idea for our supper came together quick as anything.

I'd spent a lot of time in Noona's kitchen while Curlin and I recovered, and I'd picked up a thing or two. Turned out, after a life of living on stolen scraps, I'd a bit of an affinity for cooking and more than a little appreciation for good food. Every time I stirred a pot or seasoned a sauce, I thought of

Sawny. And every time, the balance between grief and sweetness swung just a little further from tears.

I was out of practice, and it couldn't have been more than a few minutes before I started to feel the burning need to breathe again. When my aching lungs finally forced me to the surface, I broke through the water, smiling contentedly. My grin faded when I heard Curlin screaming my name, her voice high and shaking with panic.

"What the blasted hell is wrong?" I snapped, just as soon as I'd caught my breath.

Curlin was crouched by the rock where I'd left my clothes, long knife drawn and muscles tense. The tattoos on her cheeks drew stark lines against her cheekbones, and the short stubble of her auburn hair was like a smudge on her scalp in the growing darkness.

"I thought you'd drowned or had been pulled under by some horrible beast. What would possess you to go swimming in a pool you know nothing about just as the sun is setting? Furthermore, don't you think it would've been considerate to tell me what you'd planned on doing? I could've at least made sure you didn't drown…"

I swam back to the shoreline, half listening to Curlin's rant, half reveling in the burn of the long-neglected muscles in my chest and arms and legs as I swam. When I got close to the shore, I slid the bag off my shoulder and lounged, neck-deep in the cool water, reveling in the silky familiarity of it.

I finally interrupted her. "When you finish cataloging my faults, do you think you might be willing to hand me that towel there?"

Curlin stopped her tirade, but fixed me with a long glare. Finally, just before I'd decided to get the damn thing myself, she grabbed the towel and thrust it at me.

"I don't know why you're acting like you're the only one making sacrifices in this thing, Vi. I've been doing everything in my power to show you that I'm still the same girl you grew up with, the same girl who held your secrets and protected you for years. The anchorites—Sula, Lugine, Bethea—they pushed for me to be sent to Ilor, to watch out for you. Why can't you even try to trust me?"

I whipped the towel around myself and waded out of the water. The sun had disappeared over the horizon, taking with it the heavy heat of the day. I shivered, angry at the frustration I felt both with myself and with her. I didn't know how to say that she'd broken my heart. There weren't words for the emptiness that'd grown inside me that day when I'd come back to a room stripped of her things.

I wanted to sink back into a familiar friendship. I wanted to mourn Sawny and Lily with her, but the truth of the matter was that I didn't know how. I had no idea where to even start.

When I didn't immediately answer her, Curlin stalked back to the fire, leaving me to dress in peace. As I wrung the water from my hair and slipped into my clothes, I chewed over what I might do to unknot some of the tension that snarled between Curlin and me. I knew I had to let go of her time with the Shriven. I needed to find my way back to the friend I'd known for as long as I had memories. She'd once been nearly a sister to me. Holding on to a grudge over something she'd not even wanted to do in the first place wouldn't do either of us a lick of good.

Truth be told, I knew it would be more than a little useful to have someone by my side who'd gone through the Shriven's training and knew their habits and tactics, if we ever came up against them in a fight. I didn't know what to expect when we found the resistance, but we were both counting on Curlin's knowledge of the Shriven and what I'd learned about the philomenas to win us acceptance into the rebel fold. We didn't need Quill to prove our worth for us—we could do it ourselves.

I left the sack of clams weighed down by a rock in the shallows of the pool, scooped up my boots and went over to the fire. Curlin sat beside it, staring gloomily into the flames and poking the embers with a long stick.

"I'm going to give my clothes a rinse and see if I can't dig up a few more clams. Want me to wash yours, as well?" I offered.

Curlin nodded, stood and unbuckled her belt. I turned to give her a bit of privacy. I hadn't really let myself think about it, but just then, staring up at the stars glittering like crushed pearls sprinkled over velvet, the weight of what I'd done to Quill settled on my shoulders. After everything he'd given me, every sacrifice he'd made for me and all the patience he'd shown me, I'd left him, without a word, in the middle of the night. If that didn't make me into something horrible, I didn't know what could. Why did I always walk away from everyone who loved me?

Curlin's clothes landed in a pile at my feet, breaking my reverie. "Are you sure we can eat the clams you're spending so much energy gathering?" she asked.

"I don't remember you ever being one to turn down a free meal," I said, bending to gather up her clothes. "I've never gotten sick from anything I've plucked right from the water, but you go ahead and have sausages and stale bread if it'll please you."

Curlin's huff chased me to the edge of the pool, and I was shin-deep in the cool water, digging clams out of the sand, when she called after me.

"Tell me what to do to hurry this along. I'm ravenous."

I hid my smile in the curtain of my damp curls and tried to keep the mirth out of my voice as I told her to brown chopped onion and sausage in one of our pots and set a bit of water to boil. When I'd filled my net bag near to bursting with clams and had rinsed the sweat and road dust from our clothes, I wrapped the clothes in my towel and lugged everything back over to the fire. Curlin, in a burst of uncharacteristic thoughtfulness, had strung up a line between two trees at the edge of the clearing. She took our damp clothes from me and hung them over the line to dry while I finished making our supper.

I quickly cleaned the clams and dumped them in with the sizzling onions and bits of sausage, covering the whole thing with a generous glug from one of the jugs of beer I'd swiped from the Whipplestons' kitchen. That done, I set to toasting the stale heels of our remaining bread and brewing tea in the boiling water. By the time Curlin joined me at the fire, the whole clearing was rich with the smells of our decadent supper, and my stomach was growling loud enough that folks back in Williford could probably hear.

We ate amid a raucous symphony of jungle noises, all buzzing insects and faraway growls, passing the jug of beer between us. When we'd finally slurped the last bits of juicy meat from the clamshells and sopped up all the pot liquor with our bread, Curlin took the dishes down to the edge of the water to clean. I poured our tea into the now-empty beer jug, corked it and took it down to the pond where it could cool overnight.

"Thanks for cleaning," I offered, trying to bridge the gap between us.

"Sure," Curlin said. "Thanks for supper."

"No problem. Sorry I scared you. I really didn't mean to."

I stole a glance at Curlin, the moonlight bringing out the subtle knot along the bridge of her nose—a break that must have happened in her time with the Shriven.

"I know." She stood and carried the pot back toward the campfire. I followed her.

"I've been a swimmer for as long as I can remember. You know that. I didn't even think about there being some kind of danger down there I couldn't handle. I mean, at least there aren't freshwater sharks, you know?"

"You were just under for a really long time."

"I used to be able to hold my breath for more than ten minutes." I grimaced. I sounded like a puffed-up novice anchorite. "You could've just stuck your head under and looked."

Curlin unrolled her bedroll with a violent flap. On the edge of the clearing, Beetle and Curlin's gray mule startled out of their drowse with a whinny and a bray, their ears pricking up. Thank Dzallie I'd remembered to hobble them, or we'd have had to walk the rest of the way to the rebel camp.

I unrolled my own bedding, slipped the bag of pearls back over my head and wadded a sweater into a pillow, settling in to wait for her response. I pulled a package of taffy wrapped in bits of waxed paper from my saddlebags and handed one to Curlin, taking another for myself before I stowed the package away again. She took the sweet from me, unwrapped it and threw the paper into the fire.

Finally, barely louder than a whisper, she said, "I can't swim."

I rolled onto my elbows to look at her, my mouth glued shut with the sticky candy. When I finally managed to swallow, I gaped at her. "You can too! You must've learned when you were a brat. We all did."

Curlin shook her head. "The summer you all learned was the summer that I had the violet pox. Now, are you taking first watch, or am I? Because if you are, I'd like to get some sleep."

I'd argued with Curlin about the need for a watch enough our first night on the road to know that this was a fight I wasn't going to win.

"I'll wake you in a few hours," I said, and pulled myself to my feet, much to the dismay of my screaming muscles. I was bone-tired, but I knew the only way I'd manage to stay awake until the end of my watch was with the help of strong tea and the occasional shock of dipping my feet in the cool pond. So I trudged over to the shoreline, took a deep swig from the jar of tea and leaned against one of the rocks by the edge of the water, trying to unknot the tangle of feelings I'd put between myself and every person who'd ever had the audacity to care about me.

CHAPTER SIX

Bo

"Truth be told, I don't think there's ever been a group of people so dedicated to the art of subtle insults as the singleborn of Alskad."

—*from Bo to Vi*

The next day, the council meeting dragged on through three meals and so many pots of kaffe that I lost count. Despite an endless series of subtle digs and fruitless accusations, Runa managed, with her imposing intellect and blunt speech, to force the council to grudgingly admit that there might be some truth in the story we'd laid before them.

Watching the queen marshal her council into formation was inspirational, a thing of beauty. The moment one of the councillors' eyes began to glaze, Runa was in their face, knotting strands of their life story into the narrative she wove about the Suzerain's horrifying corruption of the temple and exploitation of the people of Alskad. By the time Runa called the session to a close, we'd voted unanimously that the Suzerain had created a problem that was the duty of the crown to solve.

It was, perhaps, too ambitious of me to have expected that the council might actually begin to chew over the multitude of ways we could address the Suzerain's injustices and the growing power they held within the empire.

"I know that you all have lives of your own, but I would like to see this matter resolved as quickly as possible," Runa said, rising from the table. "To that end, I will call another session of the council to order at noon on the day after tomorrow."

Dame Turshaw huffed and scowled at Runa. "If you're so set on putting into place a plan of action, why not set the meeting for tomorrow?"

The thin veneer of control slipped from the queen's face, and Runa gave Dame Turshaw a look so withering, it could have scoured the light from the sun. A moment later, the queen's ferocity had been replaced with cool disdain, but I was certain that not a soul in the council chamber had missed the exchange.

"As you well know, we cannot hold a meeting tomorrow," Runa said, all ice and thunder, "because it is my birthday, and I will be otherwise occupied with the annual parade and celebrations that the crown has always held to uplift the spirits of the citizens of Alskad."

Dame Turshaw's lips disappeared into a thin line, but she continued to meet Runa's steady gaze. It was clear to everyone in the room that she'd "forgotten" the queen's birthday as a thinly veiled jab. Lisette hid a smile in her kaffe cup and Patrise gave me a lazy grin. I looked around the table to see all the other councillors wearing looks of amusement that ranged from well concealed to recklessly overt.

Foxes, the lot of them. They'd each be as furious at being called out as Dame Turshaw was now, but they reveled in her shame, nevertheless.

When Dame Turshaw kept silent, Runa gathered her papers and pushed her throne back from the table. "If there are no further objections, I suggest that we resume this discussion, as planned, the day after tomorrow. You are dismissed."

The queen stood, and the rest of the council stood and bowed deferentially to Runa, ignoring me, as the doors swung open. Everyone followed her silently out, leaving me alone in the cold room. I sank back into my throne and wrapped my hands around my swiftly cooling cup of kaffe.

To preserve the secret of the passage to my suite, I'd have to go the long way, but I wanted to give the councillors every opportunity to meander back to their own rooms before I left. The well of my patience had long since run dry, and I was tired enough that I was barely clinging to civility. I watched the fires crackle for a time, my body shifting and settling like the logs, releasing the tension of the day and moving toward sleep.

Hamil's teeth, but sleep sounded like heaven. I tried not to think about the short hours I'd spend in bed before the servants appeared to help me ready myself for the queen's birthday revelries. I drained my kaffe and stood. With a last glance at the old, scarred table littered with kaffe cups and crystal wineglasses, picked-over platters of fish and pickled vegetables, the crumbs and heels of loaves of bread and hard knobs of butter kept cold in the chill of the room, I left.

I'd not even made it past the council room's antechamber before Lisette swooped in beside me and laced her arm through mine. Through my haze of exhaustion, I wondered where Patrise had gotten off to. I almost never saw the two of them apart.

"Darling, do tell me what the queen is aiming at. You must realize that we all know this is a power play," Lisette said in a conspiratorial whisper. "Despite what the old bat believes, we aren't stupid. I know there's more to this story than you're letting on. Patrise and I can help you get your way with the council."

"Thank you, Lisette, but I believe Runa has nothing but Alskad's best intentions in mind. The Suzerain have simply overstepped the bounds of their duties and must be checked."

With a delicate snort of laughter, Lisette shrugged. "You know that I'm here to be of use to you, Bo. And you've grown into quite a strapping young man. Perhaps I can help...relieve some of your tension. Take your mind off your troubles."

Lisette tucked a curl behind my ear and traced a finger along my jawline. The woman was anything but subtle. It took every ounce of self-control I had not to shudder and take off down the hall at a dead sprint. Lisette was beautiful, certainly, but her beauty was like that of a pit viper—something I wanted to stay far, far away from.

"A generous offer, I'm sure," I said, "but one I'll have to decline."

Lisette twined her long fingers with mine. "Use me, little princeling. I can be very...obliging."

I bit back my irritation and disentangled myself from her grasp. The guards at each end of the hallway wore looks of studied disinterest, but their eyes flicked quickly away from us when I glanced at them.

A person was never truly alone in the palace. It'd taken me by surprise, how much I missed the decadent solitude of a life without servants when Swinton and I had returned from Ilor. My whole life had been spent in the company of servants. Karyta, the head of our staff, and her brother, Jasper, the head cook, had been as much parents to me as my mother and father.

Myrella. A twinge of grief and regret washed over me each time I thought of her—the woman who'd wanted a child so badly that she'd accepted me into her home and worked past my father's infidelity. Never one for cuddles and kisses, she hadn't exactly been a warm mother, but she'd loved me in the best way she could, with all her ambition and cunning and accumulation of resources.

I hadn't been to see Ina, the woman who'd given birth to Vi and me, since returning to Penby. Perhaps it was cowardice, or perhaps I didn't want to be somehow disloyal to the woman who'd raised me, my mother. Either way, I couldn't quite bring myself to face her, even if Runa would agree to it.

"You know, I am quite well connected," Lisette said, trying to regain my attention. "Even if you're not interested in the *other* diversions I excel at, you could make use of the information I can provide for you. A king must use all the tools available to him in order to succeed, my dear cousin."

I studied Lisette's sharp, elegant features, her olive skin and glossy auburn hair glowing in the dim light of the solar lamps. She could hardly hold back her glee.

"Honestly," I said, crossing the hall toward the stairs. "If your other spies are even the least bit as useless as Birger and Temperance were, then I think I'll do better collecting my own information. Now, if you'll excuse me, I must be getting to bed. I've a long day tomorrow. Good night."

Lisette hurried to catch up with me, refusing to be dismissed. "I'm quite the history enthusiast, you know, and I've never seen your quarters. I heard that you have some of the first empress's things in your rooms. Artifacts." She draped herself over my shoulder and twirled a finger in one of my curls. "Perhaps you'd like to show me?"

A blush crept up my neck, but I shook her off and kept walking. She was nothing if not persistent, and her hints weren't even the least bit subtle anymore. Swinton would collapse in a heap of laughter the moment I told him about this nonsense.

The staircase that led to the royal wing of the palace was tantalizingly close, and the guards at the base of the stairs wouldn't let anyone pass. Not without explicit permission from Queen Runa or myself. As I opened my mouth to issue an order to the guards, Patrise appeared at the top of the stairs, stopping me in my tracks.

I stared at him, baffled. Where'd he come from? Perhaps the queen had invited him to her chambers? Lisette's proposition still souring in my throat, I wondered if Patrise had tried the same tact with Runa, and shuddered at the thought.

"Our Ambrose doesn't like girls, Lissie. You should know that by now. Haven't you seen the great hulking peasant he's been toting around since his return?" Patrise glided down the staircase, his slow smile opening like a trove of horrifying secrets. "I bet your young man wouldn't mind if Lissie and I showed up in your bed, would he, Ambrose? His preferences run the gamut, I believe."

Patrise's voice was all velvet and venom, making my temper burn. I was done—with *both* of them. I turned on a heel to face them, letting my fury cut blackly into my eyes and voice.

"Shove off, vultures. I'm not a child you can pet and spoil for secrets anymore." I was shouting, but I couldn't bring myself to care who I disturbed. "I am *done.* Do you hear me? I am done with your games. I am done with your manipulations. Neither of you will ever bear the weight of the crown. *Never.* So you can stop with your lies and your power plays and stay the hell away from me."

Patrise raised an eyebrow at me, and Lisette smiled her sly, charming smirk. I took a deep breath, nodded stiffly at them and fled up the stairs without so much as a good-night.

When the guards pulled open my sitting room door, I was surprised to find the room already occupied. I'd assumed that Swinton would've retreated to his bedroom in the suite we shared hours ago, but instead I found him sprawled over a settee, chatting with Runa. The queen's feet were propped on a pouf pulled dangerously close to the fire, and she had a huge fur blanket wrapped around her, making her look like nothing so much as a surly bear. They didn't so much as look up when I entered the room, but Swinton pulled himself into something that vaguely resembled a sitting position and patted the settee beside him.

"We expected you ages ago," Runa said. "What took so long?"

"I was held up," I said, curling up next to Swinton and pulling a thick blanket over myself.

"Get the boy something warm to drink. It's just impossible to shake the chill of that awful room, isn't it, Bo?"

Swinton pecked me on the cheek and went to the sideboard. He came back with three steaming porcelain cups. He gave one to the queen and passed another to me. The sharp, boozy tang of ouzel punched into my nostrils, nearly obscuring the herbal tea's floral notes. Swinton settled next to me, nudged my elbow with one socked foot and, when I lifted my teacup out of the way, swung his legs up onto my lap. Runa watched us, amusement playing in her amber eyes.

"It went well tonight. The council has begun to respect you."

"I'm glad to hear you think so," I said. "I'm worried about Rylain, though. She seemed genuinely angry." I took a sip of my tea, savoring the sweet, honeyed warmth as it poured down my throat and into my belly.

"That woman's never been interested in anything beyond her histories, her wine and her birds. Don't worry about her," Runa said dismissively. "Her feelings were hurt, is all."

"Runa's told me how badly those nattering idiots wanted to paint you a liar, as expected," Swinton interjected. "How long do you think until we're able to start burning temples to the ground and the Suzerain with them? I suppose we can spare some of the anchorites. Send them to work in Ilor in place of the poor, exploited laborers? How about that? They're sworn to a life of service, after all."

I sighed and took another sip from my teacup. It didn't matter how many times we had this conversation; we always landed in the same place.

"We can't just tear down the temples, bully," I said, the pet name hanging in the air between us like a white flag of truce. "They're not *all* bad, after all. It's the Suzerain's corrupt leadership that's the problem, not the religion and everything that goes along with it. No matter what our own personal beliefs are, we can't tell anyone else what they ought to believe. Not through words *or* actions. Besides, we have a plan—we expose the Suzerain's corruption to the people. Alskaders are, after all, a discerning lot. They'll see the truth if we do the work to set it before them. Runa—"

"Gran," she interrupted. "We're alone. I insist that you call me Gran when we're alone, and enough of this talk about politics. We've done enough work for today. On to brighter things. Yes?"

"May I call you Gran, too?" Swinton asked, his face a picture of innocence and mischief all at once.

I reached under the blanket and pinched his thigh. He grinned at me.

"That depends," Runa said, not missing a beat. "What are your intentions toward my grandson?"

Swinton's brows shot up his forehead, nearly to his hairline. He pressed a hand over his heart and looked from Runa to me and back again.

"Madame, you cut me to the core. Why, even after all these weeks, even after I have bared the depths of my soul to you—to think that you could possibly begin to imagine my intentions are anything less than honorable! Do we not follow every rule of your household? Do we not sleep in separate beds and refrain from expressing our extraordinary fondness for one another in public? Do I not allow your dim-witted lords and ladies to travel through your palace, their pockets unpicked? Do I not tell you each time I see one of your honorable and well-trained guards snoozing in your hallways? What more need I do to prove myself to you?"

Midway through this soliloquy, laughter began to burble in my stomach, and by the time Swinton had finished, I was gasping for breath. Runa's eyes glittered, and she chuckled as she raised her glass to Swinton.

"A solid, if rather unusual, argument, my dear. You may call me Gran, in private, if you pour me one more of these. And then it's off to bed for all of us. Tomorrow will be a very long day."

CHAPTER SEVEN

Vi

"I don't know if you noticed in the short time we were together, but I have a bit of a temper. It's so strange, though—the farther away you are, the more quickly my feelings flare. I can go from elation to ire in a matter of moments. It's exhausting."

—*from Vi to Bo*

I woke to the pop and crackle of potatoes roasting in the embers of our fire. The sun, peeking from between the trees, painted the sky in pink and orange and globe-thistle blue. Throwing off the rough blanket covering my legs, I sprang to my feet and looked around the campsite, fumbling for the knife in my boot. I didn't remember falling asleep, and I certainly hadn't fetched my blanket from its spot by the fire before doing so. And yet, inexplicably, morning had come, and Curlin was nowhere to be seen.

I didn't think she'd leave without waking me, but I'd fallen asleep on my watch, and there was no telling what kind of danger lurked amid the jungle trees. What if the Shriven had been following us? What if a wildcat had hauled her into the woods? Dozens of terrifying possibilities flew through my mind.

Gritting my teeth, I sprinted across the path to the clearing where we'd hobbled Beetle and Curlin's gray mule. They were grazing peacefully, just as they'd been the night before. The mule—the sweet creature desperately needed a name—whinnied a greeting at me, then swiveled its head to look down the path. Following her gaze, I saw Curlin coming up the path, and with her, a sight that made my heart beat in my chest like a drum.

Beside her, leading a mule and a small cart, was Mal, and a ways down the path behind them, on a tall buckskin gelding I recognized from the Whipplestons' stable, Quill. His reins were caught, dangerously, between his teeth as he studied a map, and his brown skin glowed in the growing light of the rising sun. As much as I was still furious with him, seeing his face made me feel as though I'd finally exhaled a breath I didn't know I'd been holding since I'd stormed out of his room and then his house.

"I don't know if you know this, Vi, but leaving without saying goodbye is considered rude in most civilized societies," Mal called, laughter playing around the edges of his words.

I stared down at my boots, the heat of a blush sweeping across my cheeks as thoughts flew through my head like a flock of gulls swooping and calling for my attention. Glad as I was to see them, if Mal and Quill tried to convince me to abandon my plans, I might scream. And though it had taken me ages—plus the panic of waking up and thinking her gone—to realize it, I knew now that I needed Curlin. If she took their side, I might as well give up and take the next sunship back to Alskad. At least then I could help Bo.

"The word you're looking for is *sorry*," Curlin teased.

"What're they doing here?"

"You really think you'd be able to find a group of people who don't want to be found?" Mal asked, flabbergasted. "And even if you managed to walk into their camp, bold as anything, do you think you'd live to make your case? And you with one of the Shriven by your side? No offense, Curlin."

"None taken."

Mal reined in his mule and looked back at Quill, whose eyes were trained on me. We stared at each other, and for a moment, I felt like we might just stay that way, stuck in a stubborn impasse, until we turned to stone and then to dust. But then Quill kicked his foot out of his stirrup and dismounted with a sigh. He led his horse across the clearing to me and reached out to take my hand. "I'm sorry. I never should have tried to dictate decisions that are yours to make. I let my desire to see you safe get in the way of what I knew you wanted."

I pulled my hand back and glared at him, jaw tensed against the tears that threatened to come. "You know you can't do that, right? You don't get to make decisions for me."

"I understand. I promise. I rode through the night to find you. To help you. Please let me."

He seemed so sincere, so repentant. And though I'd never admit it to a living soul, I knew that he'd been right to try to protect me. I wasn't a warrior. I didn't have any skills that would be useful in a real fight. And, to make matters worse, I had a target on my back. I couldn't just push my way into this established rebellion and expect to be hailed as a savior. I needed an inroad if I wanted to be of use, and Quill had that on offer.

"I think Curlin's right," I said. "I owe you an apology."

Curlin slapped Mal on the calf, grinning. "You hear that? She said I was right."

The tension in the clearing shattered like ice, and we all laughed.

"But don't think we're not going to talk about your falling asleep on your watch," Curlin scolded.

I groaned, and Mal hopped down from the cart. "I'm starved. You two have anything to eat?"

Curlin, still smiling, looped her arm through Mal's and led him toward our camp, already conferring with him in low, mischievous tones.

By way of apology, I took Quill's hand and pulled him into a hug. He waited a long moment before wrapping his arms around me, but as his body relaxed into mine, I felt a tension inside me relax for the first time since our argument. I nestled my face into the curve of his neck and breathed in the warm, masculine scent of his skin; spices and soap and salt air. Asking for help would never be easy for me, but I was grateful that I had people in my life who were willing to push me in the right direction from time to time.

We stayed in the clearing by the waterfall for a few more hours so that the Whipplestons could sleep a bit and let their mounts rest. I went for another swim and tried to coax Curlin into the water, but she anchored herself firmly on the edge of the pond. When the sun was at its zenith, we packed our things, saddled our mounts and set off down the trail together.

On his buckskin cob, Quill could travel a great deal faster than my lazy pony, Beetle, or the mules. He rode ahead to warn the rest of the resistance's leadership that we were on our way while Mal, Curlin and I made our slow, plodding journey up the mountain. The sun was sinking below the trees and I was sticky with half-dried sweat when the trail came to an abrupt end. I twisted in my saddle to look at Mal.

"You get us lost, Whippleston?"

He grinned at me. "Not a chance. We'll just have to hike the last little bit. Help me stow the cart?"

Curlin and I swung down from our saddles, hitched our mounts to a couple of saplings and went to give Mal a hand. I'd just unloaded the last bag of grain from the cart when I heard a familiar voice.

"Surprise!"

I turned, bringing a hand up to shade my eyes from rays of the setting sun, and found the last person I expected to see, standing in front of me, grinning wildly.

"Aphra?" I asked, shocked, forcing myself not to check the bag of pearls around my neck. Its weight was still there and heavy between my breasts, just as it had been when I fled her burning house.

It would be impossible to mistake the woman for anyone else. She was an amalgam, feared and hated for their supposed power almost as much as the diminished were feared for their murderous fury. She stood straight and tall in the glaring sun, one half of her body deeply tanned, the other far more freckled than the last time I'd seen her. Her long hair was tied in a knot on top of her head, the coppery red and golden halves twining together like a crown of precious metal. Her face was thin, too thin, but both her green eye and the violet one sparkled, and she looked positively overjoyed to see me.

Aphra, who'd saved my friend Myrna the night of her whipping.

Aphra, who'd murdered her husband, Phineas, the cruel sociopath who was responsible for the death of my best friend.

"Yes, darling! Of course," she said. "Quill said you were on your way, and I couldn't help but come to greet you myself. I see that you've brought one of the Shriven. The others will have words for you, I'm sure. Introduce us?"

"Former Shriven," I corrected. "Curlin, Aphra. Aphra, Curlin."

I looked from one woman to the other, from Curlin's short stubble and the black tattoos coiling all over her sweaty, heat-reddened skin, to Aphra's coolly composed, linen-clad form, thinking just how terrified most of the folks in Alskad would feel to be standing between one of the Shriven and an amalgam. The two women sized each other up, visibly flexing and bristling in the presence of another person whose power so clearly came close to equaling their own.

Thankfully, Mal managed to break the tension. "If you don't mind, Aphra, these creatures need a good rubdown and a place to stretch their legs. Think you can show Vi where the pasture is while Curlin and I haul these supplies up to camp?"

I shot Mal a look, but he was already busy piling bags and bundles into Curlin's waiting arms. I'd trusted Aphra with my life at one point, but that had been before she'd left my brother tied up in a barn next to her burning house. Before she'd slit her husband's throat. Not that she'd been without reason—Phineas had been a monster—but even a defensible murder was still murder.

As if she could read my mind, Aphra said, "Quill told me that you know what happened to Phineas. I'm not sorry I did it, but you should know that you're safe with me. I would never do anything to hurt you."

I untied Beetle's hitch from the tree and forced myself to smile at Aphra. "I know," I lied. "I'm happy to see you look-

ing so well. You'll have to catch me up on everything that's
happened since that night."

"Let's see to these animals first, and then I'll catch you up."

Aphra took the mule that'd pulled Mal's cart and slipped
through a dense cluster of vines. I followed her with Curlin's
gray mule and Beetle. The path picked up again on the other
side of the foliage and, just a short ways down the trail, the
trees opened up, revealing a large, fenced clearing. Horses,
mules and donkeys grazed alongside goats and chickens. A
small, dilapidated chicken coop sat on one end of the pasture
next to a shed and a wide shelter where the animals could
weather a storm.

As soon as we'd untacked the horse and mules and seen to
their needs, Aphra told me to wait in the clearing, then disappeared into the woods. She reappeared a moment later with
a green glass bottle. She leaned against the fence, pulled the
cork out with her teeth and took a big swig before offering
the bottle to me. The glass was cool with condensation as I
took a tentative sip. It was makgee, the milky, semi-alcoholic
rice wine that was so popular in the taverns of Ilor. I'd had my
share of the stuff while recovering at the Whipplestons', and
still wasn't sure what the Ilorians liked about it so much. But
it was cold, and I was hot, so I took another sip as I waited for
Aphra to speak, taking in the sounds and sights of the jungle
around me.

Birds sang to each other from the branches of the verdant
trees overhead. Great cats yowled across valleys while cicadas
droned. Bright orange-and-purple flowers bloomed from hanging vines and bushes along the edge of the creek, and the setting sun cast everything in a pink-gold light.

"After the fire at Plumleen," Aphra began, "I hid in the woods
to avoid the Shriven. I didn't—still don't—know why they were

there that night, but I've enough sense not to let a bunch of the Shriven find me without some kind of protection in place. So after they left, I went looking for Myrna. I figured that I could take shelter with the resistance and use Myrna and Hepsy as go-betweens for seeing my affairs settled. If everyone in Ilor thought I'd fled after a rebel attack on our estates, all the easier for me to disappear, see?"

I nodded, and Aphra continued. "Myrna wasn't hard to find, and when we finally managed to convince Hepsy that the fire had been started by the Shriven and not the resistance, she reluctantly agreed not to go to the temple for help. They gathered up all the servants who'd had the good sense not to be snatched by the Shriven or run off into the jungle un-prepared and unarmed. Meanwhile, I combed through what was left of the house and pulled out everything that might be of use or be sold."

"But surely, with access to all of your wealth, you had more than enough to get away from the Shriven. You could've gone to Samiria or Denor," I said. "It's one thing to lend financial support to a cause. It's another thing entirely to risk your life."

"And there, my dear, is half the trouble. With Phineas dead, I no longer have the protection of his reputation. Further, my banks won't just hand over the contents of my accounts to anyone. My insurers refuse to settle my accounts with Hepsy, even with my sealed letters asking that they do just that."

"Then why not just go into Williford, empty your bank account and claim your insurance money? Wouldn't that solve most of your problems?"

Aphra sighed and handed me the bottle of makgee. "You don't know?"

"Know what?"

"The towns are crawling with the Shriven. The banks, especially. Myrna and Hepsy say there're at least two inside and another four outside every bank in Williford, Cape Hillate and Southill. There's no good way to disguise what I am. I'd be seized in a moment, and no one would ask questions until I'd long since disappeared. My money, at least for now, is no more than an idea. It can't help me escape, and it can't be used to help fund the resistance any longer."

I wrestled with her words, trying to unknot all the strands Aphra had shoved at me as the sun set behind the trees. Her very existence taunted the temple. Amalgam children weren't allowed to live—the fact that Aphra's parents and then Phineas had managed to keep her safe for so long was a miracle. She had as much, if not more, of a reason to fight against the Suzerain's violent hold on the empire as anyone.

Sweat trickled between my breasts, and I was suddenly aware of the bag of pearls hanging there. I'd cultivated and coveted this little treasure for so long, thinking that it would, at some point, be my ticket to freedom. I knew that Bo wouldn't hesitate— he'd hand over the stash, find a way to get Aphra to safety, then roll up his sleeves and do what he could to help the resistance.

That kind of generosity wasn't easy for me. I'd not been raised with the kind of abundance that Bo had been accustomed to, and while I wasn't dense enough to think that our parents' choices hadn't been hard for him, too, there were just some things that were simpler for him than they were for me.

I gritted my teeth, thinking of the little cottage by the sea that'd always been my quiet dream. I knew that I had money, in theory, and that Bo would find a way to give me whatever my heart desired. But the thought of parting with the only physical wealth that'd ever been mine was painful. But it was what Bo would do. What I *should* do.

"I could get you the money," I offered. "And the Whipple-stons could put you on a ship. Let me help you."

Aphra reached out and squeezed my hand, giving me a small smile. "No. Thank you, but no. It's too late for me. These last weeks, staying with these people, I've realized that I can't run anymore. I can't hide behind my wealth and priv-ilege. I have to do something. So I'm here to stay. I'm here to fight."

"And Myrna and Hepsy?" I swallowed another mouthful of makgee and passed the bottle back to Aphra. Of every-one I'd ever met, those two were the most dissimilar. Back at Plumleen, I'd taken to Myrna as quickly as her sister had developed a distaste for me. They had, far and away, the most contentious relationship of any pair of twins I'd ever met. "I can't imagine Hepsy coming around to taking part in a fight against authority. Especially not against the temple."

Aphra shot me a wry look. "You're right. Hepsy's not ex-actly come around to it, but the fire at Plumleen shook her, and she knows as well as anyone how badly some contract workers are treated by people like Phineas. She's beginning to see that there needs to be some change."

"Do they accept you?" I asked suddenly. "The people here?"

I looked up from the dusty toes of my boots and forced myself to meet Aphra's gaze. Her mismatched eyebrows were so closely knit together that they'd nearly met in the mid-dle of her tanned and freckled forehead. I forced myself to wait for her to say something. She'd killed Phineas—slit his throat, Bo'd said. But despite that fact, Aphra was someone I'd come to respect back at Plumleen; a woman who always stood up for her people.

I hoped that the people here were able to see that part of her.

After another long swig from the bottle, Aphra took a deep breath and said, "There was some—tension—at first. But I've made my worth clear to them."

"What do you mean?"

"There are a number of wildly exaggerated tales about the powers of the amalgam," she explained. "I only know what's true for myself and the one other amalgam I've met. From time to time, my dreams show me one possibility among many for how my future might play out. The dreams are more warnings than anything—they're complex and convoluted, and it would take a lifetime of study to learn how to interpret them."

Aphra hesitated for a moment, then added, "And there's something else. You may have noticed that I can be a bit more…persuasive than the average person. It's not a coincidence. I've learned, as I've matured, that if I speak certain combinations of words, people will do almost anything I ask of them, and the ability is only growing stronger as time goes on."

I plucked the bottle from Aphra's hand and took three long gulps. "That seems like a dangerous amount of power for one person."

Aphra's red eyebrow climbed her forehead. "I'm aware. As are the others." Her eyes flicked up to the sky overhead. "But it's getting dark. We should get you back before Quill comes looking for you."

I pushed myself off the fence with a sigh and stretched. My shoulder was still sore, but most of my muscles screamed with every movement, so it was hard to tell if I'd done any extra damage to the tender joint. A thought niggled at me, and I paused as I shut the gate behind me.

"Aphra, will you promise me something?"

She turned, fixing her eyes on me. "Maybe?"

"Promise me you won't use your powers on me." My voice hitched in my throat, squeaking on the word *powers*.

"I promise I won't ever do anything to hurt you." With that, Aphra turned on her heel and strode up the path.

"That's not the same thing," I muttered, but I followed her anyway, curious to see what the resistance really looked like and trying to ignore the fear curdling my gut.

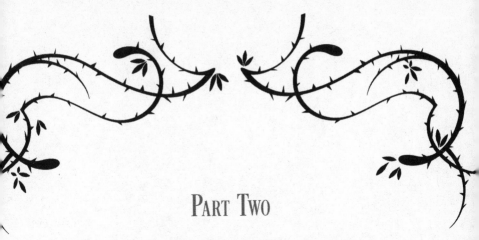

PART TWO

"My children, bow before no altar but truth, for those who worship wealth are always unsatisfied, those who sing of power are always alone, and those who seek escape are always trapped. Only truthseekers may truly be exalted."

—from the *Book of Magritte, the Educator*

"We, the firebound, stand strong in the flames of desire. We are unmoved by denigration and adulation. We march forward through the flames, together. I am your guide and your witness. I am your power, the flames are your strength."

—from the *Book of Gadrian, the Firebound*

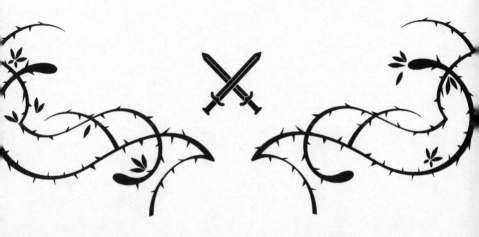

CHAPTER EIGHT

Bo

"The queen's birthday celebration promises to be a welcome respite from the endless insults and bureaucracy that have occupied my every moment since I came back to Alskad. I wish you were here to enjoy it with us."
—from Bo to Vi

I felt like I'd closed my eyes for less than a minute when the servants stomped into my room to wake me for Runa's birthday celebrations. I pulled a pillow over my head and willed myself back to sleep. I wasn't fond of mornings to begin with, but coming back to a life of being pried out of bed and fussed over by bowing, obsequious servants after so much time tending to myself drove me to fury.

I missed the quiet prodding and familiar chiding of Gunnar, who'd been my personal servant since I was just a boy. When I'd returned to Alskad, however, Runa had demanded that I move from my father's town house to the palace, where the guards could better protect me, and I'd elevated Gunnar to a position as head of my staff—half out of the sheer joy of seeing him, and half out of guilt for sneaking off to Ilor without a word.

I'd regretted it every day since. He'd made sure of it.

After so many years of service, Gunnar knew me almost as well as I knew myself. Unfortunately, his degree of familiarity with me and my habits meant he knew just how to subtly chivy me to the edge of fury. Every morning was the same. It began not with the scent of kaffe wafting out of a cup set gently on my bedside table, but with draperies whipped open to wake me with the glare of the morning sun, fire pokers and grates ceaselessly clanging and unbearably formal requests that I get up and dressed and on my way.

This morning was no different. The servants—a mind-bogglingly unnecessary seven of them—banged and clattered and "please, Your Higness'ed" me out of bed. I scowled and swore silent revenge on Gunnar, and the moment I managed to get a word in, I sent them scurrying away to find jewels that I had no intention of actually wearing. As soon as the door closed behind them, I shrugged into the formal silks and furs they'd laid out for me. I was pulling on my boots when Swinton swept into the room, the picture of a good night's rest, and dressed in the formal uniform of the royal guard.

"Where'd your minions get off to, bully?" He went to the side table, made a face and poured kaffe into a cup, doctoring it with excessive amounts of cream and sugar. "I honestly haven't got a clue how you folks stomach this stuff."

"Sleep well?" I asked. I kissed him on the cheek, stole his cup and drained it.

"Wicked princeling," he grumbled, smiling. He refilled his cup and poured another for me.

I sat down at the dressing table, accepted the cup and assessed myself in the mirror. My curly black hair was in desperate need of a trim. The bags under my eyes were like smudges of blue-black ink, and after my time in Ilor, my freckles stood out more than ever against my tanned skin. I didn't look like much of a prince at all. I picked up two crowns—one a plain gold circlet, the other white gold and studded with chunks of raw diamonds and citrine. It was a slightly smaller version of the Crown of Alskad that the queen would wear.

"Which one?" I asked.

Swinton considered, his lips pursed and his face comically serious. He set one after the other on my head, then switched them back and forth until I swatted at his hand.

"Both," he said. "One on top of the other."

"Be serious!"

He rolled his eyes. "Wear the Circlet of Alskad. It's expected, and you can hardly afford to be anything less than overpoweringly formal. You should wear as many jewels as you can. Dress like you're begging a pickpocket to stumble across your path and rob you blind."

I made a face. He wasn't wrong, but I didn't think I'd ever be comfortable with calling that much attention to myself, especially when I had so much to hide. "Why are you dressed like a guard, by the way?"

"Runa's idea. I'll be able to ride beside your carriage and entertain you with my witty commentary on the idiocy of your nobility."

I wrapped my arms around his neck and kissed him, pressing myself into the hard lines of his muscular form. There was a knock at the door, and I broke away from Swinton just as Gunnar strode into the room, followed by my three servants, each carrying a jewel chest.

"Your Highness. Master Swinton," Gunnar said.

A blush exploded up my chest and neck, blooming over my face. I cleared my throat. "You've trained your people well, Gunnar. They're more, erhm, efficient every morning."

Gunnar's face remained impassive, though from the twinkle in his eyes, I was sure he'd caught the barb in my words.

"I'd not realized you'd joined the guard, Master Swinton," Gunnar said.

Swinton tugged on his sleeves and brushed the front of the jacket. "A present from Runa. An up close ticket to the show, you know?"

Gunnar merely raised an eyebrow and opened one of the chests, displaying a glittering array of jewels.

A half hour later, I was dripping with wealth and stuffing a flaky salmonberry pastry into my mouth as quickly as I could while being bundled into the open-top birchwood-and-gold royal carriage. Queen Runa appeared a moment later. She was a far cry from the grandmotherly figure who'd sat laughing by my fire the night before. This Runa was larger than life, intimidating and regal. The Crown of Alskad glittered on her forehead, and she sported a white fox cloak over a steel-gray silk suit.

A servant settled a bearskin rug over her lap and another over mine. I surreptitiously brushed the crumbs off my jacket and waited for her to speak as she studied me, one eyebrow raised.

"Your circlet is crooked."

I put a hand to it, but she waved me away and leaned across the carriage to adjust it herself.

"You know what we're to do today?"

"Smile? Wave?" I shrugged. "Is there much else to it?"

"You must learn to take this more seriously, especially with what we face," she admonished. "The people mustn't think that you're just another stuffed-up, lazy nobleman. The fact that you're my grandson may not be public knowledge, but Alskad must see you as my heir."

I nodded, not sure how I could possibly demonstrate to people who'd see me for only a moment that I had their best interests at heart. Suddenly I was horribly embarrassed by the quantity of jewels I wore. I unfastened one gaudy necklace and stuffed it deep into my jacket pocket, blushing, and started on the other jewels around my neck and wrists. I was suddenly very glad I'd not let Swinton pierce my ears.

Runa reached across the carriage just as it started to roll and cupped my cheek.

"You're a wonderful young man, Bo. All you need to do is let them see your heart."

Our carriage rolled out onto the snowy street outside the palace just as I stuffed the last of the jewels into my pocket. All that was left was the cuff on my wrist and the circlet around my head, the two undeniable symbols of my status as heir to the throne. The procession stretched out before us: royal guards and cavalry surrounding our carriage and those of the nobility who joined the procession, and the Shriven, in stark, formal black, ringing the carriage of the Suzerain. My eyes flicked away from their coal-black carriage, not yet ready to prepare myself to face them today.

People lined the road, waving and smiling in the dim or-angey glow of the midmorning sunrise. It was nearly ten o'clock in the morning, and the sun had just begun to peek over the horizon. It would be dark long before we saw the palace again.

Swinton rode up beside the carriage on a large bay geld-ing and saluted the queen with a wink. Despite the crisp uni-form and the effort he'd made to tame his tawny waves into a passable braid, no one who looked twice at him would believe Swinton was actually a member of the guard. His posture was too relaxed. He looked at ease with himself and his surroundings in a way that no guard could manage.

He was lovely. Maybe later, in the confusion and busyness of the celebration, we could sneak away for a few moments alone...

Something sharp prodded me in the thigh.

"Stop daydreaming about your sweetheart and look sharp. We're nearly to the first pavilion."

The carriage rolled to a stop, and liveried servants hurried to place the ostentatious gilded step stool and open the carriage door. I followed Queen Runa out of the carriage and down a rope-lined walkway, glancing back to see Swinton joining ranks with the guards who trailed behind us at a respectful distance. I took a deep breath and steeled myself for the first event of the day.

The crowds surged forward against the barrier, calling Runa's name and, to my great surprise, my own. They tossed flowers over the heads of the royal guards, who stood at intervals along the path. Following Runa's example, I stopped every few feet to shake hands with the people, to coo over babies and to press hard candies into the hands of children.

When we reached the pavilion, a hush ran through the crowd and silence fell over the park like a blanket of snow. The Suzerain stood on the edge of the pavilion, surrounded by the Shriven, beatific looks on their nearly identical faces as they inclined their heads to the queen and me.

Runa stepped forward. "It is my very great honor to share my birthday with the people of Alskad, and with my great-nephew and heir, the Crown Prince Ambrose."

A blush crept up my neck, and I fought the urge to look away from the crowd as Runa continued.

"Believe me when I tell you that Prince Ambrose will be a leader that you will be proud to follow. A leader who will uphold and honor the traditions of our great empire, while looking to the future and the good of his people."

A ripple ran through the audience, and whispers grew like waves. Someone in the back of the park shouted something, and a moment later, guards swarmed in that direction. Queen Runa's face remained impassive as the guards hauled several people out of the park. Swinton stood just in front of me at the bottom of the pavilion's stairs, his spine ramrod-straight, and I could almost feel the electric energy of his attention on the crowd.

"Now, though it is customary to receive gifts on one's birthday, I much prefer being the one to give gifts. So today, I ask the people of Alskad to indulge me and share in the extraordinary talents of the palace bakers."

Behind us, the walls of a large white tent were rolled up, and the scents of buttery, yeasted pastries, cloud buns rich with bacon jam and brown sugar cakes spiced with candied ginger wafted into the icy air. Long tables inside the tent were piled high with boxes, each tied with a bright red ribbon. Samovars held tea and spiced cider, and servants in crisp white aprons stood ready to distribute the boxes of treats and cups of warm drinks.

The crowd cheered as they formed lines outside the tent. Queen Runa celebrated her birthday this way every year, and the people knew the routine well at this point. I followed Runa into the tent and took up my position beside a table. We'd hand out the first few boxes before moving on to do the exact same thing at the next pavilion.

I was relieved to be away from the Suzerain and their guard

for a moment. They always hung back on these occasions—present, but allowing the queen to hold the people's attention.

People filed into the tent one by one. Swinton prowled around the room, all languid watchfulness, like a predatory cat. I pasted a smile onto my face and handed the first box to a little girl with a giant pouf of hair tamed only by a pair of colorfully striped earmuffs tied under her chin.

"I like your earmuffs," I said. "How old are you?"

The girl pursed her lips and looked up at her mother standing behind her. The woman squeezed her daughter's shoulder and said, "Go on, tell His Highness how old you are."

Still clutching the box in one hand, the girl held up four fingers. I grinned at her and handed a box to her mother.

"Well," I said. "You have excellent taste. I hope you enjoy the queen's birthday."

The girl and her mother filed past me toward the samovars, and I spoke to the next few people in line behind them, distributing boxes and doing my best to be the picture of a kind and caring future monarch. My eyes darted over to Swinton as I handed a box to an elderly woman in a bright knit cap. He leaned against a tent pole, a paper cup steaming in his hand as he laughed with one of the guards. The man could make friends with anyone.

"You don't look like one of the singleborn."

I jerked my head up, surprised, and the sharp tang of tafia hit me like a brick to the face. I struggled to find my placid smile and erase the shock from my face. The man standing in front of me wore a ratty wool coat the color of bile and scuffed, cracked leather boots. His salt-and-pepper hair hung in oily hanks around his ears, and his deep brown eyes were unfocused with drink.

"You just look like a boy playing at being a prince. The

whole city's talking, you know," he slurred. "The whole city's talking about how the princeling is back from Ilor. You know who isn't talking, though? My wife. For the first time in her goddess-damned life, my Ina's keeping her mouth shut."

I looked frantically around the room, smile plastered to my face, searching for someone to help me. I caught Swinton's eye and jerked my head as I took the man by the elbow and steered him toward the back of the tent. A servant stepped smoothly into my place at the table.

"Where're we going?" the man slurred. "I needa talk to you about my Ina and my Vi. I needa talk to you."

Swinton crossed the room to whisper in Runa's ear, and with a grace I could never hope to achieve, she extracted herself and followed Swinton through the crowd as I yanked the man through the back flap of the tent.

"I would be ever so pleased to speak with you as well, sir." I gave him a tight smile. A carriage pulled around the corner and rolled to a stop just down the path. Though most of the people who'd come to the pavilion were in the tent already, stragglers ranged over the snow-dusted grounds. Anything we said here would surely be heard.

"It's just that the day is busy," I added, trying to stay calm. "I can't possibly ask you to wait in the cold. I'm going to send you back to the palace with my most trusted confidante. You'll be fed and given a place to rest, and I'll make time to speak to you this evening. How does that sound?"

The man grunted as Runa bustled up to us. "Who is this?"

"You know what they're sayin' about your princeling, Majesty?" The man gave an extravagant bow and toppled over onto his knees. Swinton hauled him back up by the elbow. "They're sayin' as he aren't really singleborn at all. They're sayin' he got him a twin hidden away in Ilor."

My heart rate sped up to a gallop. The blood drained from Runa's face. She gestured for us to follow her, then turned on a heel and stalked toward our carriage. We scrambled to keep up, Swinton and I propping up the drunkard between us.

"Take him to the palace, Swinton," I said, pleading in my voice. "I'll get there as soon as I can. Just keep him out of sight until then. Please?"

Swinton's jaw tightened. "Bo—"

"*Please.* This is the worst time for secrets to start spilling from the woodwork."

The driver hopped down from his seat and came around to hand Runa, her mouth a thin, angry line, into the royal carriage.

"Fine." Swinton wrapped an arm around the man's waist and held him steady. "I'll see you soon."

"Thank you." I gave Swinton's hand a surreptitious squeeze and stepped up onto the carriage's first step.

"You look just like her, you know, princeling. You look just like my Vi."

The carriage shifted as Runa stood bolt upright and I jumped back down, terror and fury warring within me at the thought of someone overhearing. If the man was right, and rumors that I was a twin really were circulating the city, the council might see fit to contest the queen's decision to name me heir. I took a step toward Swinton, glancing around for anyone who might be within earshot.

And then my heart stopped, along with time and my breath. My fury melted away, leaving only fear in its place as a line of palace guards, their uniforms the color of moss and black fur collars gleaming in the stark light of the morning, raised their rifles in our direction.

A shot cracked through the air. I froze, but Swinton sprang

into action. He shoved the drunkard past me and into the carriage. I watched in horror as the guards reloaded their weapons. Why would the people sworn to protect the queen and me raise their weapons against us? It didn't make any sense.

Someone screamed, and I turned to find Runa slumped in her seat, hands clutching her throat, looking at me with wild eyes. The drunkard huddled on the seat across from her, head buried in his hands and rocking back and forth.

For the longest moment, I waited, terrified, for the sear of a bullet to wrench my soul from my body. My thoughts flashed to Vi, halfway across the world and unwittingly in mortal danger. Then another thunderclap of shots shattered the ice that had held me in place.

In that moment, I made a choice. I could collapse, or I could fight. I swung myself into the carriage, ripping the silk stock from my collar, and knelt on the floor in front of Runa. Swinton leaped over me and into the driver's seat. I pressed the fabric to Runa's neck as Swinton spurred the horses into a reckless gallop, careening through the streets of Penby as shots and screams echoed off the buildings around us.

I watched my grandmother's life-force seep between my fingertips, staining my fingers red with her blood. Tears cascaded down my cheeks as she took her last, shuddering breath. Then her eyes went blank, and she began her journey to the afterlife in the halls of the gods.

CHAPTER NINE

Vi

"I seem to spend a great deal of time convincing people that I am capable of making my own decisions. I don't know what I've done to seem so incompetent, but I know my worth, and I'm determined to prove it."
—*from Vi to Bo*

I followed Aphra up a path and into a large clearing. A number of ramshackle bungalows were perched on stilts around the edge, and the clustered stumps of freshly hewn trees declared the settlement's very recent construction. Dogs lounged beneath the bungalows while chickens and peacocks pecked at the loamy earth. A large garden, newly tilled and surrounded by a tall, spiked fence, took up nearly a third of the clearing. A girl knelt by a firepit, slowly turning a spitted goat over the embers.

As I took in my surroundings, I began to notice how few people were in the camp. A ragtag group of maybe ten gangly teenagers was draped over the railings of one of the bungalows, and a cluster of six or so swung their legs between the slats of another building's porch. Their eyes followed me, curious, as they picked at plates of food. A pair of Samirian twins, olive-skinned and covered in lean muscle, raked at the embers of the fire, skewering blistered root vegetables from the ashes and depositing them onto a long platter.

"Is this everyone?" I whispered to Aphra, suddenly afraid that the so-called rebellion I'd sought out was nothing more than a few kids no older than Curlin and me.

She threw back her head and laughed, a raucous belly laugh that turned the heads of everyone in the clearing. Still chuckling, Aphra looped her arm through mine and led me farther up the path to a pavilion, bright with torchlight and fizzling with activity. A series of long tables and benches were set in lines beneath the roof, and people swarmed around them. I spotted Mal, Quill and Curlin seated at a table in one corner, their faces grim and intensely focused as they spoke to two women I didn't recognize.

There were stacks of bowls and plates on every table, a bizarre collection of crude wooden pieces and fine china in mismatched patterns. A young man walked past us, carrying a basket of bread that perfumed the air with its heavenly, yeasty scent. My stomach growled, and I realized that it had been hours since I'd eaten. Just then, someone let out a loud whoop and, fast as you know it, I was wrapped in a ferocious embrace. When I was finally released, I found myself face-to-face with Myrna, her face alight with excitement. Behind her, Hepsy stood with her arms crossed over her chest, glaring.

"You sneak!" Myrna cried. "Rayleane's knees! How'd you find us? We thought you'd been snatched up by those awful Shriven thugs after the fire."

I cringed, thinking of Curlin just a few yards away.

Hepsy pinched her sister's arm, but before she could say anything, Myrna laughed. "Yes, yes, I know. Don't curse."

Hepsy's stern expression faltered, and she nearly smiled as she said, "Gracious. You've only just arrived. Has anyone even offered you somewhere to wash up?" When I shook my head, she sighed disapprovingly. "There's water in a basin in our bungalow. Go get yourself cleaned up. We've words to say to Aphra, anyhow."

Aphra smiled at me. "We're sharing the first bungalow on the left, just down the path. Think you can find your way? It looks like supper should be ready soon, so don't take too long. Feel free to borrow something clean from my trunk."

Nothing sounded better than a rinse, so I nodded and hugged Myrna again, thrilled to see her safe. Hepsy handed me her lamp with a look that might have been mistaken for a smile, and I set off to make myself presentable.

The bungalow was sparsely furnished with a simple writing desk, three large trunks and an eclectic assortment of chairs. Six hammocks were strung up, one on top of the other, climbing the walls on two sides of the room. Walls may have been a bit of an overstatement—the bungalows weren't much more than raised platforms with tall roofs and half walls. The breeze through the trees cut the heat a bit, and the space didn't feel too crowded, though it was a great deal more rustic than the luxury that had surrounded Aphra back at Plumleen Hall.

I hurriedly stripped off my clothes and scrubbed the sweat and dirt away with a rag and a bit of fine soap I found beside the basin of cool, fresh water. Then I dug through the trunks in search of a pair of loose trousers and a shirt. Once I was dressed, I rubbed a little bit of oil into my hair and began to work a comb through my snarled curls.

I wondered what the rebel leaders would say when Curlin and I asked to join them. Had we climbed this mountain in vain? I wanted to do something to make a difference, but now that I saw the hopelessness of this so-called rebellion with my own eyes, I didn't know if I really had anything to offer beyond my determination—and frankly, that didn't seem like enough.

A bell rang, and somewhere in the camp a clear, high voice called, "Meat! Come and eat before it's gone."

Suddenly the smells of cooking food—fire-licked meat, fresh bread and some sharp, unidentifiable tang—hit me like a wall, and all I could think about was my growling stomach.

Leaving my dirty clothes bundled in a corner, I climbed down the bungalow's ladder and hiked back to the pavilion as fast as I could manage with my sore, exhausted muscles. Quill met me on the path, wearing fresh clothes and a smile. "The others are willing to give you a chance," he said. "But you'll have to answer some questions. Just be honest, yeah?"

I squeezed his hand, giving him a tight smile. "I'll do my best, but do you think I can eat something first? I'm so hungry I can barely think."

"Of course," he said, and we walked the rest of the way in comfortable silence.

The meal I found spread over the trestle tables was impressive. I took a thick slice of well-spiced goat and scooped a generous portion of some kind of shredded green vegetable dressed in eye-watering vinegar onto my wooden plate, then plucked a soft, golden roll from a basket. Quill and I joined Curlin, Mal, Aphra, Myrna and Hepsy at their table. I sat beside Myrna and gave Curlin, perched on the far end of the bench next to Mal, a tentative smile. The longer I was around her, the more I began to see the girl I'd grown up with behind her tough shell—even as she watched the other women suspiciously, her right hand lingering near her knife. I rolled my eyes at her, exasperated.

"Myrna, Hepsy, I assume you've met Curlin. She and I grew up together back in Alskad. Curlin, Myrna and Hepsy."

Aphra picked up two delicate purple teacups I recognized from Plumleen and filled them with cool, milky makgee, which she handed our way. Myrna passed over horn cups and poured spring water for each of us before settling back into her place. Hepsy eyed Curlin warily while Mal and Quill watched the whole awkward scene with twin looks of bemusement.

Aphra raised her own teacup to us with a nod. "It may not be Denorian wine and elegantly served courses, but we are so grateful to you for showing up to fight alongside us. Here's to you both, and to a new beginning for us all."

"To a new beginning," I said, and drained my teacup. Out of the corner of my eye, I saw Curlin gulp hers down, as well.

"So," Myrna said. "Tell us literally everything that's happened to you since we last saw you."

I smiled, and as I ate, I filled them in. Not on everything—I'd promised Bo that I'd keep his identity a secret—but the bits and pieces I couldn't tell them, I embellished with the half-truths Bo and I'd come up with together. I told them that Bo was my half brother, come to Ilor to bring me news of my inheritance after our father's death.

Curlin kept her eyes on her food, refusing to engage in the conversation even when I tried to pull her in. I talked about the poison and the Shriven, and the horrors I'd seen in the basement of the temple. The children who'd lost their lives to the Suzerain's sadistic experiments. I told them about how the current Suzerain and their predecessors had used the poison to control Alskad's citizens. As I spoke, I caught sight of a boy, maybe eleven or twelve years old, inching around the pavilion toward us, his eyes trained on Curlin.

"I, for one, am glad that you're here, but you're going to have a hard time convincing the leaders to take you on," Myrna said. "We've too many mouths to feed already, and not enough of them fighters."

The boy edged closer to Curlin, stopping just outside of arm's reach. Curlin wrapped an arm around her plate and glared at him. Ever so tentatively, he extended a cluster of grapes toward her, his hand shaking. Her eyebrows shot up in surprise, and she plucked the grapes from his hand, nodding to the stool across the table. He shot a look at Quill, who didn't even seem to notice, and lowered himself onto a stool.

"Speaking of," Quill said. "It's time. Vi? We should get this over with."

I followed Mal and Quill across the pavilion to a table where two people sat together. They rose as we approached, and I took the opportunity to study them. They appeared to be twins, both in their middle age with deep, russet-brown skin. One was a woman, with thick black hair braided away from her face. The other was tall and lanky and appeared nonbinary, with very short brown hair curling tightly against their skull.

"This is the girl?" the woman asked.

Quill nodded. "You've already met Vi's childhood friend Curlin, but I'd like to introduce you to Vi herself. She's the one I've been telling you about. Biz, Neve, this is Vi. Vi, Biz and Neve. We lead this effort as a team."

I extended my hand. "It's nice to meet you both. I'd like to do what I can to help."

Biz eyed my hand with one eyebrow cocked before reaching out and shaking it. "Quill's filled us in on your background. We just have a few questions. Sit, please."

I sat across from Biz and Neve while Mal and Quill took chairs at the head of the table.

"So, I'll dive right in. Am I to understand that you gave up the possibility of a cushy life at a country estate in Alskad with a wealthy brother who came all the way here to find you, so that you could traipse into the jungle at first opportunity? What was your plan? Find an army and a heap of trouble?" Skepticism was writ large over Neve's face. "Do you know one damn thing about fighting? What good did you think you could do?"

"I honestly don't know," I said, taken aback at the hostility in her voice. "I thought that having information would help, and Myrna seemed to think I'd be of use when we were back at Plumleen. I suppose I thought you could use me here, too. I grew up in the temple with Curlin. I can't claim to've seen everything she has, but I've seen a lot, and I want to fight with you. I want to stop the temple from hurting anyone else."

Neve and Biz exchanged a long look, and I glanced to the other side of the pavilion to find Curlin and the boy engaged in a whispered conversation. They wore twin expressions of serious determination and were oblivious to everyone around them.

Neve cleared her throat. "You're clearly invested in our cause, but I can't let you believe that we'll soon make any kind of impact against the Shriven. We simply don't have the numbers, the resources or the training. We won't get anywhere unless we find someone who knows a thing or two about combat, and more importantly, about the Shriven."

"You said you'd already spoken to Curlin? She's been

through their training. If anyone can get a group into fighting shape, it's her."

"But you're a liability," Biz said pointedly. "Surely you know that."

"The Shriven have been swarming all over Williford for weeks now. If they couldn't find her in plain sight, what makes you think they'll be able to track her here?" Mal asked.

I cleared my throat, all of the fury and fear and frustration of my life swimming through my head. "I don't want to put anyone in harm's way. But if I can do some good? If I can help? I'd put anything on the line to see an end to the temple's choke hold on Alskad."

"You really want to do this?" Neve asked. "You really want to risk your life for a bunch of people you don't even know?"

"I think I have to," I said.

Quill raised his eyebrows at Biz and Neve in a silent question. The two of them exchanged a glance before nodding, and everyone at the table grinned. "Then you're welcome here," Biz declared. "To stay and to fight, just so long as your friend is willing to put in the work to see the rest of the group trained alongside you."

Under the table, Quill's hand reached for mine, and as I laced my fingers through his, I returned the council's smiles. I didn't relish the fact that my worth was so closely linked to Curlin's participation and goodwill, but I had to remind myself that even this chance was a whole lot better than being kicked off the mountain and forced to go back to Alskad with my tail between my legs, forced to rely on my brother's patronage.

Before I stood to leave, I pulled the leather strap that held my bag of pearls over my head and set it gently on the table in front of Biz and Neve. "I didn't want to try to buy my place here, but I think you could use these more than I can."

I opened the little bag, letting the incandescent glow of the pearls speak for themselves. I pulled one out and said, "For luck," then slipped the single pearl into my pocket. All that would remain to remind me of the years I'd spent dreaming of my escape from the temple.

"Are you sure?" Quill asked. "That's a fortune."

"I'm sure," I said, pushing myself to my feet. I left Biz and Neve wearing matching stunned expressions and went to find Aphra.

I had given away my safety net, and now I was ready to jump. I would find the fire within myself to burn the Suzerain to the ground. I would make myself into the spark that would set the world aflame.

CHAPTER TEN

Bo

"When I was younger and imagined being king, I pictured lavish parties and secret passages and horses wearing golden bridles. That illusion has been well and truly shattered since my return from Ilor."

—*from Bo to Vi*

The carriage slowed as the horses' hooves clattered to a halt in a narrow alley. Their snorting, heaving breaths swelled like an orchestra, filling my ears and constricting my throat even as my hands continued to press against Runa's wound, her blood settling in my cuticles, seeping between my fingers, rolling down my wrists. Stone buildings rose up on either side of us, blocking out all the light from the dim midwinter sun as it began to set. It would be dark before long.

I felt blank. Hollow. I closed my eyes, but the image of my grandmother's still face had been burned into my memory. I couldn't shake it.

A cool hand on my wrist forced me out of the cocoon of

denial. Swinton gently pried my fingers away from Runa's neck, wrapped his arm around my shoulder and pulled me to my feet. He led me down the steps and out of the carriage. I leaned back against a stone wall and let the damp cold seep through my skin and into my bones as I waited numbly to be told what to do next.

"I need a damned drink," the drunkard whined.

"The last thing you need is a drink. Just hold the damn horses," Swinton said. "Bo, I need to take a piece of your jacket. I'm going to rip it, yes?"

I nodded. My heart thundered. A tug on my shoulder. I tried to focus on my breath. Tearing fabric. The steady whisk of horses' tails.

Runa was dead. Gran. My grandmother was dead. Shot by her own guards.

"We need to make a plan, Bo. This man here is called Dammal. He says he can take us back to his place. Give us a moment to catch our breath. To get our bearings."

"His place?" I asked. My eyes kept drifting toward Runa's body. "Why? We have to get the queen back to the palace."

Dammal's voice was tight. "She's long gone, Magritte take her. All hail the king."

I flinched. I couldn't be king. I couldn't even think about it right now. "There will be things to take care of. We must see that her body is prepared for the funeral. There will be documents to sign. Arrangements to make."

Swinton put a hand on mine. "Bo. Someone tried to kill you."

"We don't know that." My voice was shaking, near hysterical. I felt like I was a step away from my body, panic pushing me outside myself.

"We're going to send the horses and the carriage out into the street," Swinton explained. "We're close to the palace. They'll make their way home and take Runa with them, Magritte take her soul. But we need to hide, and quickly." He lifted the Circlet of Alskad off my head and put it in my hands. "Put this in your inner pocket. We need to be as discreet as possible. Can you do that?"

I forced myself to nod. I trusted Swinton. He was thinking clearly. He would know better than I what we should do. His next move, however, shook me to my very core. He climbed back into the carriage and approached Runa's body, her limbs sprawled at careless and uncomfortable angles. He bowed his head for a respectful moment, then gently took the crown from her head. The soft gold was bent into an odd shape, and one of the gems was cracked.

"What are you doing, Swinton?"

"You'll need this someday. We shouldn't send it back with her."

My hands tightened into fists. I couldn't think about her lifeless body, about her teasing and prodding me just hours ago. I couldn't think about the godsdamned crown.

"Fine," I snapped, then turned to look at Dammal. "Before I go anywhere with you, I'll need to know who the hell you are."

Dammal, apparently somewhat sobered by the assassination and our hair-raising gallop through the city, fixed me with a hard stare. "My name is Dammal Abernathy. I've been married to Ina Abernathy these fifteen years."

"And?" I asked, glad the long sleeves of my formal jacket covered the chill bumps raising hair up and down my arms. I knew what his answer would be, but I needed to hear it from him. I needed him to tell me the truth he'd come to Runa's birthday celebration to confront me with. I needed him to tell me he knew about Vi.

"And my wife gave up a dimmy girl, Vi, to the care of the anchorites these sixteen years ago. For Vi's whole life, Ina's said her twin, Prudence, died when she was just a babe. She'd lament about the babes when she was deep in her drink, but these past few months, that story's disappeared, and Ina's been lurking around the cushy parts of town. Watching a solicitor's office. Spending hours staring at the palace gates."

Dammal licked his lips and glared at Swinton, who was knotting the long reins onto the driver's pommel.

"Weren't til I went to visit Vi—she's like my own, despite being a dimmy doomed—and learned she'd been shipped off to Ilor that I got curious. And then our crown prince swans back into town, and that gets my head going real good. But it weren't til I saw you with my own two eyes that I knew it were true. I don't know what Ina got up to all those years ago, but Prudence ain't dead. He's standing right in front of me."

I groped for the words to voice my grief and fury and the overwhelming fear that had settled in my belly, spreading its rot to my very bones. Swinton sidled up to me and whispered, "Are you sure you want him to be voicing this out in the wind where anyone might overhear?"

"I had to know."

"And now we need to hide."

"I'll take you to our place," Dammal offered. "Ain't no one from the palace going to come looking for you in the End."

"Fine," I said, unable to think of another option. Not with my head swimming the way it was.

"Do you want to say goodbye?" Swinton asked. "Before we go, I mean. Do you want to say goodbye to Runa?"

I shook my head, eyes on my boots. The memory of my grandmother's lifeblood draining out between my fingers, her last shuddering breath, her terror-filled eyes turning slowly glassy… Those images would stay with me for the rest of my life. I made a silent vow that I would never forget my grandmother as she was in life, but I knew it would be her death that would always haunt me.

"It'll feel more real if you look at her, Bo."

I shook my head again and, though I could feel Swinton staring at me, I started walking. I didn't want to look. Didn't want to layer another memory of my grandmother's lifeless corpse atop my memories of her life. "My hands are damp with her blood. I am soaked in it. Her death is real enough."

Swinton took my hand and squeezed. "As you wish, bully. Dammal? Lead the way."

Dammal walked around the carriage, buttoned his coat and slapped one of the horses' rumps. Already spooked by the smell of blood, the animals thundered down the cobblestone alley and careened out onto the street. Dammal pulled a flask from an inner pocket, took a gulp and waved it toward Swinton and me. Swinton shook his head, but I grabbed the flask and took a long, burning gulp before handing it back. Dammal gave me a crooked grin and took off down the alley opposite the way the horses had gone.

Dammal led us on a winding path through back alleys and down narrow streets half-blocked with rotting refuse and broken furniture. Eventually, he wrenched open a rusty iron gate and climbed the stairs of a ramshackle house. We were on the farthest edge of what had been a very fashionable area of the city a century before: the End. Vi had spent her childhood haunting this neighborhood, whereas I'd lived my whole life without setting foot in places like this.

I looked up and down the street, lost in a spiraling current of what-ifs broken only by the memory of gunshots fired by palace guards. The lawns were crowded with junk and the skeletal remains of bushes. At nearly every house, the paint peeled and flaked down onto the snow like colorful ashes. A shutter on the second floor of Dammal's house hung precariously from a single hinge, and tall weeds poked through the gray snow that lay in drifts across the lawn. The crooked stairs looked like they could collapse at any moment.

Swinton took my hand. "In we go, bully."

I needed to steel myself, pull myself together. Runa was dead. I was the king. My responsibility was to my empire now, and I didn't have time to indulge in grief. "I think we should go back to the palace. Runa didn't want me anywhere near these people."

"Your family?" Swinton's fingers tightened around mine.

Dammal was peering into the front door's lock and jiggling the handle. The man's hands were clumsy, likely from years of too much drink. Nothing about him invited even the tiniest measure of confidence—for all I knew, he could be luring me into some kind of trap of his own.

"I can't hide here, Swinton. I have a duty to the people." My concerns spewed from my mouth like angry bees spilling out of a hive, but I kept my eyes on the toes of my boots, stained with the blood and grit of our escape. I wanted, more than anything, to put the events of the day behind me and move forward, away from this too-familiar place of grief and despair. "I have to go back to the palace. I'll need to make a statement to the citizens, meet with the council, see to the funeral arrangements...make sure the people who did this come to justice."

Swinton cupped my cheek and gently turned my face, making it impossible to avoid looking him in the eyes.

"Bo, the guards sworn to protect you *fired* at you. They killed the queen. Until we know who's behind this scheme, you can't go back to the palace. Your position is incredibly weak, and whoever it was that set those guards to murder is sure as rain to try again. Runa set the pieces in place to see you on the throne, but you'll have to play a smart game until we can see her plans through."

I'd just opened my mouth to argue when a shutter on the first floor screeched as it was thrown wide and a boy, maybe eight or nine, stuck his head out. His bright auburn hair glinted like copper in the afternoon light. He scowled at Dammal, yelled something into the house and then disappeared. A moment later, another boy, this one a bit older, appeared at the window.

"You drunk, Da?"

Dammal, who'd been obliviously trying to open the front door, shot up straight and stumbled back a few steps, nearly falling backward off the porch, his appearance of sobriety obliterated by the flask that clattered out of his pocket as he fell.

The boy shook his mop of dark brown curls in disgust. Then a girl pushed him out of the way, and Swinton took in a sharp breath as she came into full view. The girl looked like Vi—a *lot* like Vi. She had the same high cheekbones covered in freckles, the same jetty tangles, the same ferocity in her features.

"You ain't got food or money, you can go straight to hell, Da," she yelled. "We ain't none of us got the time nor the inclination to put up with your drunk ass. Go find somewhere else to sleep it off."

"Aww, come on, Brenna. Open the door. Let your da in. Ma'd be fair steamed to know you'd locked me out in the cold."

"Ma can take it up with me when she starts putting food on the table more regular."

"Still think they're no relation?" Swinton asked, a bit of amusement in his tone.

Brenna's head jerked up at the sound of Swinton's voice, her skull banging against the windowsill. As she took in the sight of us, her expression went from irritation to openmouthed horror. I realized I was still wearing the rich silks and furs I'd chosen for the parade, and Swinton was dressed like one of the royal guard.

There was no question in my mind now. This girl was Vi's sister. *My* sister. And it'd been stupid for us to follow Dammal. Stupider still to come here, to endanger all of the queen's careful planning and the secrets she'd so carefully tended for so many years.

"And just who the hell are you?" she asked.

"Well—" I started.

Swinton interrupted me. "It's a long story. Let us in?"

The girl looked us up and down appraisingly. "Got any cash?"

I dug through my trouser pockets. Having not really left the palace since we'd arrived, I hadn't had much need for money, but I thought I might have a few *tvilling* on me. Swinton sighed and stuck his hand into my jacket pocket, dug around and pulled out a ring, which he held up for Brenna's inspection. The light danced along the clusters of fat rubies and diamonds that adorned the gaudy thing, and her eyes went wide.

"That'll do."

A moment later, the door swung open, and I followed Swinton and Dammal into the house.

Lamplight from the street filtered in through dusty, faded curtains, casting long shadows in the dim foyer. Three kids clustered on the stairs in the entryway, staring at us with wide eyes.

The girl, Brenna, held out her hand to Swinton, who dropped the ring onto her palm. She examined it closely, hunger ill concealed beneath her dark lashes. Dammal grabbed at it, but she swatted his hand away.

"Go find yourself somewhere to sleep it off, Da."

"I've just as much a right to sleep in this house as you, you ungrateful brat," Dammal grumbled.

"You and Ma'll have a right to this house the day you start paying bills."

"Come on now, Remembrance. Aren't you supposed to remember some respect for your father? Give me a bite to eat and let me rest. It's been a long day."

Brenna rolled her eyes. "Empty your pockets and don't call me Remembrance."

"I've not got a *tvilling* to my name, child, or it'd be yours."

"Empty your pockets, and I'll let you have supper tonight."

Dammal groaned and dug into a pocket, coming up with a few linty coins. "Fine, but you'll give me a bed."

"Come up with a *drott*, and I'll let you sleep on the sofa for a few hours. I'll even make the little ones give you a pillow."

"Fine." Dammal handed Brenna another few coins, and she nodded toward the back of the house. "There should still be a fire going in the den. Go on, then. We'll take it from here."

Dammal gave Brenna a last hard look, clapped me on the shoulder and ambled down the hall.

"Fern," she yelled, "get down here."

A girl of about eleven appeared at the top of the stairs and deftly hopped her way over her sisters to the landing.

"What?" she spit.

Brenna held the ring up, and Fern's eyes went wide.

"That'll fetch a price," she said, awe in her words. "Meat for weeks."

"Will she be able to sell it?" Swinton asked. "Without someone pinching her for theft, I mean."

The girl laughed and snatched the ring out of Brenna's hand. "You ain't from here, are you? It's what? Six? Merk'll be opening up soon, and if we make tracks, I can get to the shops before they close. I'll bring Trix to help carry."

"Be sensible." Brenna caught Fern's jacket before the smaller girl could take off. "We can celebrate tonight, but the rest'll have to go to staples and savings. Hear me? Flour, lard, peas. Food we can stretch."

The girl's eyes kept cutting to the door. She was like a horse in the starting box before a race, itching to run.

"You can take Trix, but you're taking Pem and Still, too. I need someone to keep you in check."

Two of the children on the stairs scrambled down to stand behind Fern. One of them, a girl in layers upon layers of too-big knit sweaters, looked at me, brows furrowed. Fern scowled at her older sister, and the little girl kicked Fern hard in the shin. Brenna, still holding tight to Fern's jacket, plucked a wool cap from the stair rail and tugged it low over the little girl's brow, somehow releasing all the tension from her small body, which had been coiled like a spring.

Brenna said, "You can go to Mr. Bleckson's and get as many roasted pigeons as you can carry on your way home. Fair?"

Fern's face lit up, and as soon as Brenna let go of her jacket she bolted past us to the door, two of her siblings close on her heels. But the little girl stopped beside me for a moment, tugging insistently on my sleeve. I leaned down, and she whispered in my ear.

"Hi, Bo. Don't leave before we get back, hear?"

Before I could stammer out a response, she'd disappeared and slammed the door behind her with a gust of frigid air. Brenna hustled us down a long hallway and into the kitchen, where three other teenagers sat around a battered kitchen table. The boy with auburn hair who'd first opened the window regarded me from the head of the table, his freckled hands fisted on his knees.

"So." He jerked his chin at me. "This is him?"

I traded a look with Swinton. *Which version of the truth should I tell them?* Swinton bit his lower lip and shrugged. He'd never liked that Runa and I had chosen to hide my twin, but he saw the reason in it. I had to gain the favor of the people, find power in the loyalty and respect of the nobility and the citizens of Alskad. Their trust would help us take down the temple and their lies with them.

Being singleborn didn't make a person all-knowing. Being diminished didn't make a person violent. Being an amalgam didn't make a person evil. Violence, intelligence and power existed in every one of us—how we cultivated and controlled ourselves was up to each individual. We knew it, the temple knew it, and I'd made it my mission to show the world the truth when the time was right.

But all of our careful plans were shattered by the bullet that took Runa's life. I had no idea what to do now, no idea what the new plan should be. But looking into Swinton's eyes, I knew one thing for sure.

I couldn't lie to my family.

So I offered the boy my hand. "I'm Vi's twin, Bo."

CHAPTER ELEVEN

Vi

"I think Curlin is actually trying to end my life with her training plan. I've never been so sore. I never knew it was possible to be so sore. My muscles scream from morning until night, and when I'm finally allowed to fall into my hammock, I dream of sore muscles. I wouldn't wish this on my worst enemy."

—*from Vi to Bo*

Mal and Quill had left all sorts of things untended in Williford, and so, after waiting a day to see that Curlin and I were well settled, they made the trek back down the mountain with a promise to return as soon as they could. Biz and Neve took the seasoned fighters—the old guard of the rebel contingent—to a camp closer to New Branisford, where they could do some reconnaissance on the temple there and plan their next move.

And then, suddenly, Curlin and Aphra and I were alone, unsupervised, with a group of gangly half-grown brats we were supposed to turn into a squadron of capable fighters.

The moment Biz and Neve disappeared into the jungle, Curlin climbed onto a table and called the camp to order.

"You want to fight?" she asked. "Why?"

The full heat of the sun beat down on us as we waited to see how the recruits would respond. My black hair, piled on top of my head, was as hot as a coal about to burst into flames. Slowly, the others in the camp pressed forward, each pushing to be closer to Curlin. Beside me, Aphra watched her with narrowed eyes, while I gazed at the young people gathering around Curlin's table in the pavilion. I saw the faces she'd captured, and I realized that Curlin was good at this. She pulled the crowd in to her and held them with just the simple force of her will.

There was so much about who she'd become that I'd missed these past years. A thread of excitement knit its way into my heart at the thought of rediscovering the girl who'd once been my best friend in the world.

From the back of the group, a thin voice called, "For our freedom!"

"Who's keeping you in chains?" Curlin asked. "You're free now. I need a better reason."

"To kill the folks what bought and sold us," another voice rang out.

"No good's ever come from revenge."

The crowd shifted in place, some of them looking at their feet, all of them searching for the answer that would break the intensity of Curlin's silent, unblinking stare.

"For change," I said.

"What's that?" Curlin asked.

I climbed onto the table beside her. "We fight for change. Not for ourselves, but for those who'll come after us. We fight so that no one else ends up in chains. We fight for our brothers and sisters dosed by the temple and made to become rabid. We fight against the folks who'd call me diminished and turn grief into something to fear. We fight because we want to make this world a better place, and to do that, we have to take down the temples. We have to take down the Shriven and the Suzerain."

I glanced at Curlin as soon as the word left my mouth, leaving a sour taste on my tongue, but she nodded, encouraging me to continue. "We fight to make the queen back in Alskad hear our voices when we say that it is wrong to buy and sell the life of another person, even if just for a few years. We fight to make our world better." I took Curlin's hand in mine. It was foreign and strange, and at the same moment, it collapsed the years between us, and we were brats again. "You were one of the Shriven. I've been called diminished all my life. If we can fight for the same kind of justice, I think anything might be possible."

I turned my face back toward the crowd. "So are you with us?"

They cheered then. The raucous, joyous sound transformed their young, hungry faces from a pitiable sight into something that stirred a ferocious hope deep in my gut. Curlin reached out and pulled Aphra up onto the table, as well. Taking my hand and Aphra's in each of hers, she raised our fists together and stomped her foot three times.

Quiet fell over the clearing. Curlin looked out over the group, her fingers still twined in mine. The littlest children fidgeted from foot to foot, looking to their elders to see what they ought to do next.

"We'll have to work hard and smart," Curlin said. "There's no telling how long we'll have before the Shriven find out where we are. We need to be ready to meet them when they come. To do that, we'll need to play to our strengths. Every morning, we'll gather here to train our bodies. You need to get fast and strong and learn not to be afraid. After our mid-day meal, we'll split into groups. The youngest of us will learn how to sneak and climb and spy from Vi."

She looked at me with a twinkle in her dark blue eyes and winked. "She's the most devious person I've ever met, and I know she'll train you well. You older ones will learn fighting from me. At night, Aphra will take over. She has the most real education of the three of us, and her particular skills lend themselves well to war games and strategy." Curlin's face turned serious as she cast her gaze over the crowd. "Anyone can back out of their training at any time. I am not in the business of forcing people to fight. Those whose work it is to keep this camp running, to feed us and clothe us and tend to our wounds, are just as important as the fighters. Just know that if you give up your training, you cannot start again. So make your decisions wisely, for you'll only make them once."

As I trudged up the mountain two days later, I caught sight of a fluttering piece of cloth out of the corner of my eye.

"You're caught," I called. "Come on out and give it up."

The broad, jewel-green leaves at the edge of the path rustled, and a dirty face peeked out into the dappled sunlight. I carefully lowered my buckets to the ground and waited for the girl to edge her way out of the undergrowth. Lei was maybe ten years old. Her hair was cropped close to her head, and leaves stuck out of her tight curls at all angles. Her clothes were streaked with so much mud that it hardly could have happened by accident.

I glanced down at her belt, where only two of her three strips of green cloth remained. "You don't watch out, you're going to be going without supper tonight. I wouldn't have seen you if you hadn't been moving at such a clip. Don't need to be fast if no one sees you, remember?"

Lei kicked at a clod of dirt and untied one bit of cloth from her belt. "I was going after Bren. He's fair poor at hiding. Gets distracted easy. I got two of his flags yesterday and an extra scoop of stew for it."

I took the rag and stuffed it in my pocket. I'd given them three strips of cloth each. They all had a task to accomplish by suppertime. Some were picking fruit, others collecting firewood and still others hunting for the waddling, flightless birds that congregated around the mountain's pools and streams. The challenging part was this: if anyone caught sight of one of the brats, they had to surrender one of their flags. By the end of the day, those who'd lost all their flags missed out on supper. If they managed to snag another youngling's flag, they got her share of food. These brats had been hungry for so long, food was a powerful motivator.

"Might need to focus on keeping out of sight for the rest of the day, don't you think? Better one serving at suppertime than none, and you've only got one flag left."

She nodded and turned to go back into the woods.

"Wait," I called.

Lei stopped and eyed me warily. These brats didn't seem quite sure what to think of me, and fair enough there. They'd grown up with stories about atrocities committed by the diminished. By people like me. By contrast, despite the tattoos that so clearly marked her as a Shriven, they'd begun to treat Curlin with a kind of awed respect. After all, the Shriven protected them from people like me, didn't they?

"Tell you what," I said. "If I find a dozen eggs in my hammock just before supper, and you still have your last flag, I'll see that you get a special treat after the meal."

Lei grinned.

"Go on now." I waved her away. "Get."

When Lei had disappeared back into the jungle, I squatted, settled the pole across my shoulders again and tried not to cringe at the ache in my muscles as I stood. The buckets swung dangerously on either side of the pole, threatening to splash onto the dusty path. This was only my third trip up the mountain, and already my thighs were on fire.

I wasn't quite to the top of the hill when Aphra appeared once again, humming as she headed cheerfully back down the mountain. I kept my eyes down and tried not to fume at the apparent ease and untroubled delight with which she'd approached the grueling training schedule Curlin had imposed upon our little camp.

"You're not losing a drop from that bucket, are you?" Aphra asked, her mouth quirked in a smile.

"Don't start," I grunted, keeping my pace steady as I hauled myself up the mountain. I wasn't in the mood to be teased.

Curlin and I had spent much of the last two nights stitching together every scrap of leather we could find to make a pair of large bags. By the time we'd finished, they were almost as tall as Lei. We'd waterproofed them by boiling water in the laundry kettle and dunking the bags into the water, tightening the seams, which we then sealed with beeswax.

It had taken most of both nights, but by the time we were finished, we had two bags big enough to hold water for the whole camp for several days. Just as important as our training was making certain that, if we had to hole up in the camp—or in the worst-case scenario, if we were surrounded and stuck—we'd be well supplied. Plus, Curlin claimed we'd use the bags for training. I didn't see how, but I also had no plans to ask her about it. Not with that dangerous, gleeful spark in her eyes.

The bags were hung from beams beneath the stilted bungalows. They were heavy with water, each about half-full and swaying in the hot jungle breeze. I found Curlin crouched beneath one of them, rubbing beeswax into a damp seam. I lowered the buckets to the ground, breathing hard. I rubbed my aching shoulder with one hand, rotating it to work out the pain. My shoulder had healed, technically, but the hard work of the past few days had shown me just how much strength I'd lost.

Curlin dipped a cup of water from one of the bags and offered it to me. Taking the cup, I tilted my head from one side to the other, and my neck gave a satisfying crack.

"Shoulder giving you trouble?"

I drained the cup and handed it back, nodding.

"We'll need to work hard to strengthen your muscles there when we have more time. For now, focus on knife work with the other hand. I'll guard your weaker side. I always will."

She clapped me on the back and took one of my buckets to the water skin she'd already lowered. I heaved the other up and followed her, dumping my bucket in after hers.

"There's no good reason we can't just go down to the spring for water every day, the same way these folks've been doing this whole time," I said. "Why go to all the trouble of making these and hauling endless buckets up the hill?"

"You said you wouldn't question my training tactics," Curlin said.

"Come off it," I huffed.

Curlin hauled on the rope holding the bag off the ground, heaving it up nearly to the beam. She tied the end of the rope to a post and, grinning, pulled it back a step, her lean arms trembling a bit with the effort.

I raised an eyebrow at her. "And?"

She gave the bag a shove, and it came hurtling toward me. I jumped, but not fast enough, and it caught my bad shoulder. The wind rushed out of me, and the next thing I knew, I was on my ass, dazed and gasping.

"I thought you, of all people, could dodge a hit," Curlin chortled.

"I didn't see it coming!"

Curlin snorted and then began to cackle as I picked myself up off the dusty ground. The bag swung toward me again, but this time I was quick enough to roll out of its way. Curlin caught the bag and steadied it, still laughing.

"That's the point. You won't always see what's headed your way in a fight. Everyone's reactions have to be faster, and these kids have to learn how to take a hit. Half of them were punching with their eyes closed this morning. These bags will teach them to dodge, and they can whale on them a fair bit. Toughen up their dainty little fists before we start letting them hit each other."

"Do we really have time for this? Even if the others decide to wait on attacking the temple, they won't wait long enough for us to do much more than cross our fingers and hope."

The words I didn't say hung in the air between us. *This is hopeless. These people can't possibly be trained well enough to have even half a chance of surviving the Shriven. What have we gotten ourselves into?* "We need to compensate for our weaknesses, not try to beat them into submission."

Curlin flew at me, and before I'd had time to set my feet, she'd knocked me off them, landing hard on my hips, one fist raised and a wicked grin spreading across her face. I just knew there was something clever on the tip of her tongue. But that was Curlin's weakness—she always had to say something clever before she broke someone's nose. I'd seen her do it too many times to've not learned my lesson.

I threw my knees up and into her back, where they hit with a satisfying thump on either side of her ribs. At the same time, I shot a hand up and jabbed it into her throat, more to startle her than hurt her. Curlin's smile collapsed, and the tattooed lines on her face went suddenly straight and hard. I wriggled like an eel, trying to free myself from the iron grip of her legs. Her punch landed not on my face, as she'd likely intended, but on the top of my arm. A spike of pain shot through me, and my arm went numb. I caught her in the back again, the shoulder this time, with a knee, and got an elbow under me.

It was enough to wedge my hips up and shove Curlin off balance. I flung myself up and on top of her. Curlin's fists went flying, and instinct kicked in. Rather than trying to block the flurry of blows, I forced one of her elbows to the ground and pinned it with a knee. Her fist pounded my thighs, but that was a hell of a lot better than my face. Ignoring her snarling, I planted another knee on her sternum and struggled to get hold of her other wrist. Curlin's muscles strained, and she was the color of berries beneath her tattoos, but I gritted my teeth and kept her pinned to the dusty earth. I finally managed to grab her wrist and twisted it at an awkward angle, crowing triumphantly.

A cheer went up all around us, and I snapped my head up, startled. We were surrounded by more than half the camp, their eager faces peering at us between the stilts that held up the little bungalow above us. Two brats' faces, one dark brown, the other bright red, hung upside down from the porch with wide white grins, looking like eager little bats. I smiled back at them, let go of Curlin's wrists and eased myself off her. I stood, knees and spine creaking all the way up, and offered Curlin my hand.

"See," I said to the gathered crowd. "It is possible to take on one of the Shriven."

Curlin took my hand with a smirk, and before I knew it, she'd yanked me off balance with one hand and swept my feet out from under me with a leg. I landed flat on my back in the dust, laughter filling the air like a thunderstorm. I groaned.

"And that," Curlin said, "is why you never call a battle won until you've burned all the bodies and found your way safe home."

CHAPTER TWELVE

Bo

"There's nothing I can say—nothing I can do—to alleviate the wretched state of my shredded heart. Nothing, except to march numbly forward."
—*from Bo to Vi*

There were eight of them, and they all had the same kind of virtue names that our mother had bestowed upon Vi and me all those years ago: Remembrance, Clarity, Amity, Chastity, Forbearance, Temperance, Patience and Stillness.

The woman certainly stuck to a pattern.

Brenna—the girl who looked so much like Vi—rattled them off with a shrug, then proceeded to introduce her siblings with the names they actually used. She and her twin, Lair, were fifteen. They'd been born just a year and a half after Vi and me, and from Brenna's description, it seemed like they supervised most of what happened in the family.

"Lair does odd jobs as they come to him. Sweeps chimneys, takes in laundry, does a bit of pickpocketing in the rich bits of town, that sort of thing." Brenna winked at me. Daring me to react, just like Vi would've done. "I've apprenticed myself to a welder down at the docks. We need a steady income around here, and the brats can only do so much."

Brenna went on. There were only two boys, Lair and Tie, and I found myself studying their faces, looking for a reflection of myself in them. I didn't have to look hard. Lair's curls were walnut to my soot, but they sprang away from his square-jawed face in the same unruly tangle. And he and Tie both cocked their heads to the side as they listened to their sister—something I might not have noticed, except that Runa had spent the last few weeks scolding me for the same habit.

The thought of my grandmother brought the ache of her loss rushing back, but I forced myself to focus on Brenna's introductions. On the half siblings I'd only just discovered.

The auburn-haired boy was Tie, and his sister was Chase. They were fourteen, tall and gangly in the way that teenagers who've only just grown into their limbs can be.

"Tie's too clumsy to be as good a thief as our Chase, but he's fair smart," Brenna said. "Finished his schooling and keeps the books for some of the shopkeepers down the road. We all pull our weight." A deep flush crept up Tie's neck, but his smile was full of shy pride.

Fern, Trix, Pem and Still were the girls who'd taken off to sell my ring and stock up on supplies. They all had jobs. Even the littlest ones, Pem and Still, who were barely eight, managed to bring in some income. As I listened, I began to realize that very little, if any, of the money my father's estate had paid Ina over the years had gone to supporting my siblings.

Recollections of my own privileged childhood burned me through with embarrassment. How could my father have let this happen? How could I, for that matter? I'd known about these children—my *family*—and still, I'd pushed them out of my mind in my single-minded quest to find Vi.

"What about you, then?" Brenna asked. "How's it that a brother of ours turns up here dripping in silks and jewels, anyhow?"

I cleared my throat. "It's a long story."

Tie raised an eyebrow at me, a gesture so perfectly Vi that it startled me. "Gathered that. Who's this, then?"

My eyes widened, and I made an apologetic face at Swinton. "Gadrian's nose! I've no manners at all, have I?"

Swinton's perfect lips quirked in a half smile, and his eyes sparkled in response.

"This is Swinton. My, erhm…" I looked to Swinton for help. We'd never really defined what we were to one another. We just…were. He gave me a wicked look, obviously enjoying watching me flail. "My…paramour?"

Silence hung heavy over the table. My siblings exchanged sidelong glances with one another until Swinton snorted. His snort turned into a cackle, and then raucous laughter that spread like wildfire to everyone else in the room—except me. I buried my face in my hands. What the hell else should I've called him? My lover? My sweetheart? I groaned, waiting for the laughter to die down.

Eventually, Swinton laid a broad hand on my shoulder and squeezed, still wheezing with laughter.

"Your paramour?" Brenna asked with a giggle.

"He's no idea what he's talking about," Swinton said. "I'm his boyfriend. Swinton. From Ilor. Pleased to meet you all."

"Ilor." Chase rolled the word around in her mouth. "When did you immigrate?"

"Do you know Vi?" Lair asked.

"What business've you got in Ilor that buys jewels like that for your sweetheart?"

Swinton pressed his lips together and looked at me expectantly. We'd told so many versions of the truth to so many different people, but we'd never anticipated this.

"Could you excuse us for a moment, please?" I asked.

Brenna barely had time to nod before I stood and pulled Swinton out of the room, down the hall and onto the front porch.

"Well, what'll you tell them?"

"I don't know," I said helplessly. "I don't know what to do. If I tell them everything, there's a chance that word will get out, and I'll lose the throne entirely."

"Half the city's already gossiping about the chance that you're not singleborn. Can they really take the throne away from you that easily?"

I rolled my neck, and a series of crackling pops ran up and down my spine. "I don't think so. I don't think the law explicitly states that the leader of the empire has to be singleborn. It's the Book of Gadrian that goes on and on about the power and supremacy of the singleborn, I think. But I'm not a scholar of imperial law. It could be in there somewhere."

"I think the bigger question is, do you trust them?" Swinton's green eyes, the color of fir needles, bored into me, and I did my best to hold his gaze.

"I suppose I should—they're my family, after all. But Claes and Penelope were family, too, and they couldn't have turned out to be less trustworthy." I bit my lip. The memory of Claes's deathbed betrayal still ached each time it came up, like a bruise yet unhealed.

He continued to stare me down. "It's a simple question, bully. Do you trust them?"

I ran a hand through my hair. "I don't know. I know that you're supposed to trust family, and it won't serve me to hold everyone at arm's length my whole life. But...they owe me no loyalty at all. Do I leap in, consequences be damned, and tell them everything? Or should I be more cautious?"

"Did you tell Vi everything all at once?"

I glared at him; he knew that I hadn't.

"And was your relationship stronger because you kept that information close to your chest?"

I sighed. "You know it wasn't. But what if they tell someone about Vi? About me?"

"What if they tell someone you're a twin?" Swinton's smile was patient and just a touch condescending. If I weren't so very fond of him, I would've had a hard time not hating him in that moment. "Weren't you planning to tell the whole world at some point? What's more, who on earth would believe a half-starved brat from the End?"

Swinton's words—an echo of Vi—hit me like a blow to the chest. I stuffed my hands in my pockets and looked away from him, down the frigid street lined with falling-down row houses. I had to force back the tears that threatened to well up in my eyes.

Swinton sighed. He pulled me into his arms, but I stayed stiff as a rod. "I'm sorry, bully," he whispered into my hair. "That was rough of me. You've had the worst kind of day, and I should've been gentler with you."

I let myself sink into his embrace and wrapped my arms around him in return. "I just don't know what to do. I feel like the world is collapsing in on me, and I've been tasked with holding everything in place. Any moment, it's all going to come crashing down, and it'll be all my fault."

Tears ran hot down my cheeks, dampening the wool of

Swinton's borrowed military jacket as he held me tight against his broad chest. "You have me. I won't let you stand alone, bully. Tell your family who you are. Trust them. You don't have to keep the world spinning all on your own."

Taking a deep breath, I nodded and wiped my face with the back of my hand. Swinton fished a handkerchief out of his pocket and handed it to me.

"It's astonishing that the future leader of the Alskad Empire manages to so often be without his handkerchief," he said. "Now. Give me a kiss before you go inside and properly introduce yourself to your family."

I wrapped my arms around his waist and did just that.

Lair poured boiling water into a chipped porcelain teapot and added yet another spoonful of tea redolent with spices. The warm scent radiated through the cozy little kitchen, simultaneously unidentifiable and comforting. This would be the third pot the six of us had consumed, and each had been stronger than the last. Lair poured the last of a jar of honey into the pot as well and stirred, regarding me with narrowed, thoughtful eyes.

"So now that the queen is dead, you'll be the king."

I nodded.

"Our brother, the king. Has a nice ring to it." Chase took the pot from Lair and poured fresh tea into everyone's mismatched teacups. "But you're afraid to go back to the palace because the guards who shot the queen were aiming for you."

"Swinton saw them with his own eyes," I said.

Tie plucked at Swinton's sleeve. "Ain't hard to come across a guard's uniform, is it?"

"I can't say as I've been impressed by the overall security at the palace," Swinton said. "But to be fair, it's not as though there's been much of a need. Even though the singleborn nobles have been out for Bo's throat since he was toddling around in diapers, no one's ever gone after the queen. It's a game of power and prestige. Anyone can be the heir, but it's the queen who does all the real work, and not many of the singleborn are willing to wrap their heads around the idea of actually working."

Brenna, who'd been studying me thoughtfully, said, "This isn't the first time someone's tried to murder you?"

"According to my mother—" I stopped myself. "According to my adopted mother, there have been at least seven attempts on my life. Seven that we know of, anyway. I suppose this makes eight."

"Rich folks really don't have anything better to do?" Lair shook his head. "So you can't go back to the palace?"

"He can go back just as soon as we figure out who's behind it," Swinton said. "There are some folks who owe me favors. I'll get in touch with them and see if we can't get to the bottom of all this soon."

I squeezed Swinton's hand and leaned over to kiss him on the cheek. "You've hardly been in Alskad a minute, and already you've people who owe you favors?"

"You've lived here your whole life and you don't?" Swinton teased, and the tourniquet of grief that had closed around my heart after I watched my grandmother die loosened ever so slightly.

A door slammed at the front of the house, shattering the camaraderie that my siblings and I had been slowly building since I showed up on their doorstep. The sound of booted feet came thundering down the hallway, like a whole regiment of guards. I shot to my feet, heart pounding.

Fern caught herself, panting, on the kitchen doorway and

heaved, "The queen is dead, and the crown prince with her. They say they'll name the regent in front of the palace tomorrow at dawn."

"Where are the others?" Brenna asked.

"Be here soon. They're pulling the wagon. I thought you'd want to know about the queen."

"Might need to check your facts, pal," Swinton said.

I stood and offered Fern my hand. "I'm Vi's twin, Bo. Ambrose Oswin Trousillion Gyllen. Crown Prince of the Alskad Empire, Duke of Nome and Junot, Count of Sikts, Baron of the Kon, Protector of the Colonies of Ilor and the Great Northern Waste. Nice to meet you."

Fern gawked at me. "You're shitting me."

With a twist of a smile, Lair reached over and lightly smacked Fern's shoulder. "Don't curse at your brother. Can't you see? He looks just like Vi."

I pulled up my sleeve, revealing the golden cuff around my wrist. "Really the prince. And really Vi's twin."

Fern's mouth pursed, and she gave me a look full of skepticism. "You can't be the prince if you have a twin. Only the singleborn get to sit on the throne."

"The queen believed that was a particularly ridiculous rule. What do you think?" I asked.

Fern shrugged. "Not for me to decide. If you are the prince, though, you'd best go tell those guards you ain't dead."

Swinton's head snapped up. "Guards?"

"Sure. A whole pack of them. Coming up the block, pounding on doors, riffling through folks' houses. Can't say as what they're looking for this time, but they might cut it out if you let 'em know you're alive, right?"

"How close are they?" I asked.

"They're at the Holgates' now. Three houses down."

Brenna pushed her chair back and stood. "When was the last time we heard from Dammal?"

"He's passed out in the front room," Chase said. "Right?"

Tie darted out of the room and was back in one breathless moment. "He's gone."

"Magritte's knuckles," Brenna hissed. "I'm going to kill him."

My breath caught in my throat. "You think Dammal told them?"

"I should've seen this coming," Lair said. "He's a swindler. Of course he went for them. Probably got a reward, too."

I rubbed a hand across my scalp, befuddled. Vi had spoken so highly of him, but the man I'd seen had been a drunk at best. And his children obviously didn't think much of him.

"Is there a back door?"

She shook her head. "Can't go out the back. They'll have guards on either end of the alley. At least, the Shriven post guards out back whenever they come raiding."

"Hamil's tongue." I looked at Swinton. "What do we do?"

"You can hide in the attic until they're gone," Tie said. "There's a hidden room up there. They ain't found it yet."

Brenna nodded. "Not a word of this, Fern. Go get the others and help them bring in the supplies. Make sure they keep their mouths shut. Chase, clean this up. Lair, stow anything valuable or breakable. You know the way of it. Tie, show these two where to hide."

Everyone burst into motion. Fern raced through the house, the sound of her booted feet on the hardwood more mammoth than child. Chase swept the chipped teacups into the sink. Swinton followed Tie out of the kitchen, but I stood frozen for a moment, overwhelmed by the flurry of the family, so practiced at taking care of each other.

My family.

Brenna's eyes met mine, and she smiled. "Come on, brother. Can't have you show up on our doorstep one minute, only to be carted away the next. Let's get you hidden."

I huddled close to Swinton in the tiny attic room, grief flowing through my veins, flooding my heart. The icy air cut through cracks in the roof and siding, and the memory of my grandmother's death, of watching her life seep out of her, looped through my mind, unwilling to be set aside any longer.

Swinton pulled Runa's ruined crown from the inner pocket of his thick military coat and stared at it. Below us, glass shattered and doors slammed as the guards tore through the already ramshackle house. It would be sundown soon, and across the city, in the palace, the council was surely gathered to choose who would ascend the throne as regent until the line of succession could be established. I took the crown from Swinton's cold fingers and reached up to wedge it between the rafters just over our heads. It should be safe here for now, and at least I would know where it was, should I ever have reason to wear a crown again.

I shivered, and Swinton wrapped his arms around me. "It'll all turn out, Bo. As soon as the guards leave, I'll go back to the palace and find out what's going on. Rumors will be flying by now, and if one of the other singleborn truly did order the assassin, they're sure to be strutting around like a cat licking blood from his paws, stomach stuffed with mice."

I grimaced. "That's quite an image."

"We'll have you back in the palace in no time."

I wanted so desperately to believe him, but nothing about this day had been as I'd expected. I should've been changing clothes for the queen's birthday supper, and instead, I was shivering in an attic, praying with every fiber of my being that the guards who were meant to protect me wouldn't find and possibly murder me.

I hoped Vi was having more luck than I was.

CHAPTER THIRTEEN

Vi

"I am learning that it is one thing to feel helpless, and another experience entirely to find that, in the face of something terrifying, my particular skill set is just this side of useless."

—*from Vi to Bo*

Curlin brandished a thick fruitwood staff as long as she was tall and planted her feet in a wide stance. I flipped one of my knives into the air and caught it in an aggressive grip, the long blade tracing the length of my forearm. We'd wrapped our blades in layers of rags so as not to do any actual harm to each other, so the balance was a bit off, but I'd have to make do. It'd be a real pity to lose our one real advantage to a stupid training accident— even if she did drive me to the edge of my patience.

I rolled my neck, watching Curlin through narrowed eyes. I'd studied the Shriven all my life, counting the days until they would inevitably come for me. More than a little of my life had been devoted to thinking about how I might survive a confrontation with one of their order. Some of the Shriven fought with mace-tipped chains, but Curlin claimed that those were more for show. I'd also seen them use the wicked-looking weapons they called charmers—terrifying double-bladed swords. They could kill a foe in front and another behind them in a single motion, but if a person could get close enough, quickly enough, they might have a chance to avoid the kiss of steel.

The weapons Curlin and I worried most about were the staffs. Every one of the Shriven in Ilor carried a long staff like the one Curlin wielded. They were more like extensions of their limbs than weapons to the Shriven, and even though they looked innocuous enough, one hit could cave in a person's skull faster than their eyes could follow the deadly blow. A body had to be fast to fight one of the Shriven armed with a staff. And not just fast—smart, too.

The moment Curlin glanced away from me to look at the others circling us, I threw myself into a roll and came up slicing. There were only two real ways to take down one of the Shriven armed with a staff, at least without years of grueling training: get inside their reach fast enough to surprise them, or kill them with ranged weapons. Our youngest recruits were practicing their skills with bows and arrows in the lower field under Aphra's watchful eye. Most of them had grown up hunting in the kaffe groves, so they were fair proficient already. They'd do fine.

I caught Curlin in the belly with one knife and in the armpit with the other.

"Gut wound!" I called triumphantly. "You're down."

Curlin's face curled in a snarl made twice as terrifying by the knotted lines of her tattoos. Her staff connected with my ear the moment before Curlin's fist smashed into my skull. Sharp pain raced down my neck and reverberated across my whole body. I tried to stay calm through the ringing in my ears and the flashes of color and blackness that threatened to take my vision entirely. I threw myself backward in a flashy, impractical round-off that I wasn't sure I could land. My bare heel grazed Curlin's jaw, but I'd planned for it and managed to land in a crouch, knives up and head throbbing.

Curlin slammed the staff into the earth and leaned over, hands on her knees, panting.

One of the young men in the watching crowd—Pluto—brought a bucket to me.

"Thanks."

I dipped the wooden cup into the water and offered it to Curlin. She took it, drained it and handed it back. I refilled the cup and drank deeply.

"Good fight," I said.

She nodded and clapped me on the back.

"What'd you see?" she asked the gathered crowd.

Pluto raised his hand.

"Vi got in close and went right for the deadliest hits. She was fast and stayed low."

I bit back a smile.

"But?" Curlin asked.

"She let herself think she'd won," a familiar voice called through the crowd, sending a thrill up my spine. "She didn't expect a blow from a dying foe."

It'd been only a few days, but Quill's absence had left a hole by my side and a constant pang in my heart. And even though I tried to keep my mind occupied with other things, I couldn't stop filing away stories and jokes to share with him. I ached with the desire to hear his sweet laugh, to feel his arms around me, to kiss him. Missing him was a weight that got heavier as each day passed, one that I'd carried in silence. The fact that he'd returned, and so quickly, made my heart sing.

At Curlin's nod, I flew through the crowd to Quill. I took his hand and led him away from the press of bodies straining to see the opening swings of the next fight. Curlin claimed that the others could learn a lot from these fights. She said that watching others succeed and fail over and over again gave a body far more ideas than drilling the same exercises morning, noon and night. Her theory was that drills in the morning and sparring in the evening would push our charges into fighting shape far faster than either one alone. I couldn't argue with her—I certainly learned something new from every fight—but each time my fist brought up a blooming bruise on one of the younglings' cheeks, I felt guilty.

When Curlin paused fights to talk about what was working and what wasn't, or when she dissected each move afterward, I was often taken aback by how much she'd learned from the Shriven. We'd grown up watching the other brats tussle in back alleys in the End. In those days, I'd been terrified that getting even a little angry would make me turn, so I'd run from any fight that came my way. But everything I'd seen must've been filed away somewhere, because bits and pieces came rushing back each time someone came at me. Curlin's knowledge, on the other hand, was encyclopedic.

Quill followed me up the ladder into the bungalow I shared with Aphra and Curlin. I settled on one of the plush cushions Aphra had salvaged from Plumleen and gestured for him to join me.

"I think I can scrounge up some tea if you want it," I offered, doing my best to quickly rearrange my messy curls and kick dirty clothes behind the furniture.

"No, thank you," Quill said, and I could hear the smile in his words. "We've some business to attend to."

"Business?" I asked, letting a slow, wicked smile play across my lips. "I have no idea what you might be referring to, Mr. Whippleston."

I closed the distance between us and slipped an arm around his waist, letting my hand come to rest on the slope of his hip. His long, lean muscles radiated heat. The air was thick as velvet around us, and Quill's sharp, spicy scent mingled with the green jungle smell and became an intoxicating perfume.

He raised an eyebrow at me and brushed a loose curl away from my face. "You know exactly the business I mean."

One of his hands laced its way into the curls at the base of my neck while the other snaked around my waist and drew me still closer to him. The tug of his hand in my hair, the thudding of our hearts—who could rightly tell where my heartbeat began and his ended, pressed against each other as we were—every inch of my body ached to be closer to his. I pushed myself onto my toes and kissed him.

Kissing Quill was like sinking into the ocean. Not the icy, harsh waves of Alskad's shores, but the warm turquoise waters of Ilor. His lips against mine suspended time, pulled the aches from my muscles and reset the rhythms of my soul. That kiss made me indestructible and sent waves of shivering heat down my spine. When we finally let each other go, we were both breathless.

"Oh," I said. "*That* business."

Quill's laugh was all summer thunder and mountain streams. "I do love you, Vi, but I did come back for a reason. We should find the others."

★ ★ ★

For most of the time I'd spent with the resistance, the inhabitants of our little group were spread across the mountain, tending to all the various chores that kept us limping along. But when I slid down the ladder, I found the camp swarming with activity. Rarely had I seen it so overrun with people scurrying from place to place. Each face was clouded with grim determination, and where just hours ago, most folks would've stopped to say hello or check in with Quill, not a person in the camp seemed to have time for more than a polite nod. Even Quill, who'd been on the mountain less than an hour, could sense the net of tension tightening over the camp.

"Tell me it's not been like this since I left," he said.

I shook my head, scanning the crowded clearing. "No. Something's wrong. Do you see Aphra?"

A calloused hand grabbed my wrist, and before I'd a moment to gather my wits, Curlin pulled me stumbling into a bamboo-slatted storeroom beneath one of the bungalows. Quill followed close on my heels. Aphra was perched on a barrel, waiting.

"I'm glad to see you all well," he said. "I'm sorry to skip the civilities, but it's imperative that we speak. As soon as Mal and I got back to town, we had a message from Biz and Neve." Quill grimaced. "Their camp was overrun with the Shriven, and they were forced to retreat deep into the mountains. I have an idea of where they're headed, but it's unlikely we'll hear from them again soon, and I suspect the Shriven are close on their tails. They need our help."

"And risk our own necks?" Aphra scoffed. "More than likely the Shriven have already caught up to them, and they're long dead and burned by now."

Curlin turned, the full force of her dark blue eyes glaring

in the torchlight. The sharp lines of her tattoos obscured her features and made her stare that much more intense. "I hate to say you're wrong, Aphra, but you can't afford to forget that the Shriven are human. They're smart and well trained, and they've had the fear wrung out of them, but they've faults just like anyone else. They can be beaten. They can be outwitted. This heat, these mountains, this terrain? They're all beyond the scope of what the temple trained us for. The Shriven will adapt, like anyone, given time, but if your rebels are holed up on a mountain they know well, I'd put good money on them over the Shriven, at least for a time."

Quill nodded to Curlin and continued, his voice weary. "It doesn't look good for them, though. They've no way to come or go. No way to get supplies in or messages out. I imagine they'll be able to pick off any of the Shriven who get too close to their camp, but it's only a matter of time before they either starve or the Shriven blaze a trail up the mountain, traps and lookouts be damned."

"So what do we do?" Curlin asked.

"We help them, obviously," I said. "We've been training. Not for long, but we're not completely inept."

Aphra picked up the thread of my thought. "We do have the element of surprise. We should help them. They're probably looking for Vi, after all. We've got a duty to them."

Quill cleared his throat. "That's not quite true, and you know it, Aphra. It was the Shriven's work at Plumleen, and the Shriven who shoved Vi into a place of notoriety. We don't know what their objective is, but even you know that Vi didn't ask for this."

I thrust my hands into my pockets and squeezed my eyes closed. "I'll go. I'll fight. But anyone who doesn't feel ready stays, and I'm not taking any of the brats. They don't have nearly enough training. They'll just end up hurting themselves or us."

"Fair," Aphra said. "But the others will want to fight. They've been itching for it. We'll need weapons, too, and as many mounts as we can spare. If we're going to make a difference, we'll have to move fast."

CHAPTER FOURTEEN

Bo

"Our grandmother loved you, even though you never knew her. She wanted
desperately to meet you and tell you herself, and I am devastated that you
won't get to hear from her lips how much she had planned for you. I am so
sorry that you will never know her. You were so alike, in all the best ways."

—*from Bo to Vi*

Hours later, in the frozen dark of early morning, the hidden
attic door swung open and lamplight spilled into the room,
rousing me from my fitful doze on Swinton's shoulder. Brenna
stepped into the room, face masked with exhaustion.

"How bad was it?" Swinton asked, and I turned to look
at him, baffled. Seeing my confusion, he explained. "People
in positions of power—the palace guards, the Shriven, the
city watch—they've no reason to care about people like us.
Poor people. They come into your house, they break whatever they want, they leave with whatever they want, they say
whatever they want. There aren't any consequences when

they harass people like us, because people like you will never hear about it."

Brenna nodded. "They got our honey and a handful of *tvilling* Fern had in a jar under her bed. Broke a few dishes and ransacked the pantry, but we'd managed to hide most of what the girls brought back. They've got plainclothes watching at both ends of the street and in the alley, but they likely won't come back into the house unless they've good reason for it."

Swinton pulled himself to his feet, groaning, and offered me a hand up. "I should go to the palace and see if I can't call in a few favors. We can't hide out here forever."

"Do you really think it would be so unwise for me to go, too?"

Brenna furrowed her brows. "Based on what those guards were saying, I doubt you'd make it past the front gate alive. Best lie low for now."

I wondered, for a moment, what they'd said, but my thoughts were rolling through my brain as slowly as cold honey, and Swinton was already speaking before I could ask.

"Think I can borrow some clothes? It'll look more than a little suspicious if I turn up in a bloodstained guard's uniform."

Eyeing him appraisingly, Brenna nodded. "The others should be able to find something for you—I'll have to leave for work here in a minute. Just because one of my siblings is apparently royalty doesn't mean the rest of us don't have to work for a living."

I blushed, horrified by my self-absorption. "Brenna, I promise I'll see you taken care of. If I'd known—"

"Please. I'm not asking for a handout from you just because we're blood."

"We'll talk about it," I said, but forced myself to stop when

I recognized how condescending I must sound. "What I mean is, I'd like to help. If you'll let me. We're family, aren't we?"

I looked from Brenna to Swinton and back, seeking some kind—any kind—of affirmation. They held each other's gaze, exchanging a steady, knowing look until Brenna snorted and reached out to knock me in the shoulder.

"Don't know why you'd want to claim bilge water scum like the lot of us, but you keep at it, and you'll have a right hard time getting yourself rid of us. Come on downstairs."

Swinton cobbled together a getup borrowed from my brothers while Brenna flew through the house, readying herself for work and peppering the younger siblings with instructions. I lingered in the front hall, unsure of where I belonged, where I ought to position myself in the unfamiliar, ramshackle house full of closed doors and flickering lamplight. The furniture was well-worn and patched in places, but the house was kept tidy, everything in its place.

Except, of course, me. There was no place for me in this house.

Brenna, Lair and Swinton tripped merrily down the stairs, laughing and wrapping themselves in layers of scarves and sweaters against the biting cold of the early morning wind.

"I'm off to the docks, brother mine," Brenna said. "I'll be home around suppertime. The brats should be able to keep you occupied and fed in the meantime. Just ask if there's anything you need."

"Do you think I might have a bit of paper?" I asked tentatively. "I should let Gerlene, my solicitor, know where I am, and I'd like to write to Vi, if I can."

Brenna looked at Fern and jerked her chin. "Get the writing supplies from my trunk, yeah?" Fern darted up the stairs, the rest of the little ones following her like ducklings. Brenna squeezed my hand. "What's mine is yours. I mean it."

I squeezed back, smiling. "The same goes for you, Brenna. Thank you for opening your home to me. I know the danger it puts you in."

Her twin, Lair, clapped me on the back. "I'll go as far as the square with your man here," he said. "See him safe out of the neighborhood, like. I plan to see what gossip I can dig up as they announce the new regent. Tie and Chase can run your letter anywhere in the city. Just tell them the way."

With a pair of identical tight smiles, Brenna and Lair slipped out onto the porch, leaving Swinton and me alone in the hallway.

"Promise me you'll stay hidden until I get back?" Swinton asked, lacing his fingers through mine. "Keep away from the windows, borrow some plain clothes, stay out of sight. Yeah?"

"I don't like sending you off alone like this."

Swinton cupped my cheek with his elegant, calloused hand and kissed me gently. "You aren't sending me anywhere, little lord, and it's not as though you could sashay into the palace yourself right now. Not after your own guards did their best to assassinate you. I'll be back as soon as I can."

I leaned into him, resting my head on his shoulder. My world had completely shattered in the space of a day, and I couldn't stand to lose Swinton, too. "Please be careful."

Wrapping his arms around me, Swinton took a deep breath and whispered in my ear, "I'll always come back to you, Bo. Always. I love you."

With that, the tears that had been building for the last day spilled down my cheeks. Swinton held me as I wept. I cried for my grandmother, for my father, for the mother who had raised me and the one who'd given me away. I cried for Vi and for the half siblings who'd had to raise themselves. I cried for Claes and Penelope. But mostly, I wept for myself, for the softhearted boy I would have to leave behind in order to become the king that Alskad deserved.

When I'd finally cried myself out, Swinton handed me his handkerchief and slipped away, promising to return as soon as he could. As the door closed behind him, I turned to find a cluster of my siblings staring down at me from the landing. Fern clutched a sheaf of paper in one hand and a pen in the other. Chase and Tie exchanged a knowing look and dashed down the stairs to my side.

"I know what you need," Chase said.

"Tea," Tie finished. "The answer is always tea."

"And a place to write?" I asked. "Brenna said you could take a note to Gerlene for me. Do you mind terribly?"

"Of course they'll take it," Fern said. "You can write in the parlor. There's no desk, but it's quiet, and there's a low table fine for writing. I'll show you."

I followed Fern into the parlor and settled myself on the floor next to an elegantly carved, but now chipped, table. Fern curled up in a corner of the sofa and watched me as I dashed off a note to Gerlene.

"How long have you known about Vi?" she asked.

I looked up, startled. "Not long. A few months? I went to find her as soon as I found out."

"It makes me sad."

"What does?"

Fern gave me a stern look, her hazel eyes sparking with the same intensity Vi showed when she was frustrated. "I feel a little sad for you, that you've been alone for so long, but you've had people who loved you and enough to eat and an education and just so, so much privilege. But Vi. Dzallie's spite, *Vi*. She grew up hated, cast out. Vi grew up with nothing, no one, no love. She didn't even really have us, her family. I could just kick myself."

"I know," I said quietly. "It makes me sick. But you can't blame yourself. You didn't know. And I promise you, I am going to use every bit of privilege and power I have to make sure that no one ever has to grow up like that again."

"Good." Fern nodded. "I'm going to hold you to that."

Tie and Chase came into the parlor and set an overfull tea tray on the table.

"You have that note ready?" Tie asked.

I nodded and handed him the folded slip of paper. My words weren't—couldn't possibly be—enough, but they'd have to do for now. "Thank you again for taking this. Gerlene and the queen were…close. I'm sure she's devastated, but if she could come here to talk to me, that would make things so much easier. Her house is—"

Chase cut me off. "We know where to find her. Gerlene's lent a hand to some folks in the End from time to time. We'll give her your message."

Tie nodded his agreement. "Fern, can you run out and see if you can find Ma? We don't want her surprising us here, and if you slip her some money, she'll disappear for a few days."

Fern made a face. "Can't you make Trix do it? I'm not exactly itching to cross paths with our ma."

"Both of you go. Let's give Bo some space. I imagine after the night he's had, he could use a few hours of peace and quiet."

"I'll still be here when you get back," I said. "Promise."

Rolling her eyes, Fern heaved herself off the sofa. "Fine. But all three of you owe me."

I mouthed, "Thank you," to Chase and Tie as they followed Fern out of the parlor.

I'd just started a letter to Vi when two little girls—my sisters, I reminded myself—came crashing into the room.

Their faces and hands were smeared with grease and spices. One of them gnawed on a pigeon leg, while the other carried a plate piled high with flatbread, some sort of green vegetable and what I assumed was more pigeon meat. The girls were identical, from their tangles of tawny hair down to the constellations of freckles that spread across the sharp hooks of their noses and the planes of their cheeks.

"We thought you might be hungry," one of the girls said.

"We had to hide it from the soldiers, so it's gone cold, but it's still good," the other added.

"Thank you," I said, taking the plate and pushing my letter to Vi aside. "Which of you is Pem and which is Still?"

The girl who'd handed me the plate said, "She's Still. I'm Pem."

Through a mouthful of pigeon, Still said, "Pleasure."

"The pleasure's mine. I'm sorry we've not met before now." I tore off a corner of the flatbread and used it to pinch up a little of the greens. Cautiously, I took a bite. Vinegar and peppers and garlic exploded across my tongue. The greens were startlingly spicy, and the buttery bread only barely served to tame their flavor.

Pem shrugged. "We've seen you a few times since you got back from Ilor."

Still whacked her sister with the pigeon leg. "Weren't supposed to tell him that, goon! What's he going to think of us?"

"You've seen me?" I asked curiously.

"Yeah. Few months back, Ma got pie-eyed drunk and told us 'bout you and Vi and everything."

Still glared at her sister, but Pem kept talking.

"Vi's always been our favorite. We used to go down to the docks of a morning and watch her dive. We weren't a bit surprised that she weren't really a dimmy. After all, she ain't half-frightening unless she's angry."

I laughed. "You're right about that."

"Anyway. Ma told us who you were, and we was curious. But we've not told anyone else. Not even Brenna. We knew it were important that no one found out about you and Vi."

"I'm lucky to have such excellent sisters."

Pem beamed, but Still's look was all cold calculation.

"What'd you figure on giving us for keeping our traps shut?" she demanded.

Pem glared at her, but, hoping to quell the tension, I asked, "What would you like?"

"Jobs. Good ones. In the palace. We need to start pulling our weight, and we ain't aiming to be petty thieves like Lair and Chase. We're hard workers, and we ain't afraid of doing the dirty work. We just need a chance."

I did my best to hide my smile. "I'll see what I can find for you. Do you know how to read and write?"

Still bit her lip. "Enough. We ain't fixing to be school-teachers or nothing, but we can get by."

"I'll tell you what," I said, running a hand through my tangled curls. I couldn't imagine a time when I might be able to offer these girls some stability when I had none of my own. The future seemed so incredibly uncertain, so unstable, that I was exhausted even considering it. The idea of sleep called to me. I wanted to disappear, embrace nothingness, just for a little while. "Just as soon as I'm in a position to hire someone, you two will be at the top of my list. But right now, do you think there might be somewhere I could take a nap?"

Pem's and Still's faces lit up with identical grins. They each took one of my hands, pulled me off the floor and led me upstairs to a dim bedroom. I took off my boots, shrugged off my jacket and crawled into the unfamiliar bed. But before I let myself sleep, I closed my eyes and prayed. I didn't know if I believed in the gods or in anything anymore, but I felt compelled to ask whatever was out there—if anything was—to watch over the people I loved. I prayed for my grandmother's easy crossing and for all the people I'd lost. I prayed for Swinton's safety and for Vi's. I prayed for my half siblings. And finally, I prayed for Alskad. For the empire I'd sworn to protect, and for the strength to uphold my promises.

And then, finally, I slept.

CHAPTER FIFTEEN

Vi

"However this ends, know that I love you, and know that our cause was worthy."

—*from Vi to Bo*

The dreary, gray sky was barely visible through the massive canopy of trees, and we had to fight for each breath in the damp, oppressive heat that hung over the mountain like a curse. I swung a leg over Beetle's back and hopped down, landing with a disconcerting squish in the leaves and mud. I handed Beetle's reins to one of the younglings who'd come to look after the horses when they'd take us no farther and strapped my long, curved kaffe knife into place.

The terror that laced its way through the quiet, shuffling crowd was palpable. These people were like me—desperate folks from poor, awful places like the End, who'd come to Ilor looking for a chance at something better. The fact that we were here now, posturing as warriors, armed with kaffe

blades and the few odd pistols, was absurd. We'd found ourselves backed into a corner with nowhere to go and nothing
to hope for but change.

Panic rose in my chest as I watched the others ready themselves for the final half mile of the hike that would take us to
our positions. With pastes made of ink and soot, they drew
lines on one another's faces that reflected Curlin's tattoos.
Aphra had insisted that the more we looked like the Shriven,
the greater our element of surprise would be, and Curlin
had agreed with her. I leaned against the gnarled trunk of a
tree, trying to calm my racing heart, and watched as Aphra
wound a black scarf tight around her bright hair, just as I had
done earlier.

Securing the last knot, she stepped up onto a rock and
raised her hands as though to quiet the already silent group.

"Listen to me," she called. Her spine was straight and every
line of muscle on her body stood tense and electric. She seemed
to glow in the light of the sun coming up behind her. "Hear
me. We are strong, but we do not fight because we are strong.
We fight for those who cannot. We fight because at some point
in our lives, another person looked at us or someone we loved
and called us unworthy. We are well armed, well rested and
fairly well-fed. But those are not the things that will win us
this battle. We will win today because we are *right*."

Anticipation ran through each of us. I could see it in the fists
knotted against thighs, in the anxious checking and rechecking
of weapons, in the gnawed cuticles of nearly every one of us.

"Our fight is not with the gods and goddesses, for they
stand with the righteous. Our fight is with the Suzerain and
their temple, whose emissaries sully the good names of our
gods and goddesses with their deceitful power grabs and re-
lentless persecution of the innocent. We will win today be-

cause we fight for the innocent, for the downtrodden, for the tyrannized and silenced. You know your roles, your places, and you have no reason to be afraid. We will find victory at the end of this day!"

A ripple went through the crowd, and the nervous energy suddenly evaporated. It was as though Aphra's words had washed the fear and anticipation away and left only focused determination in its place. I'd never seen anything like it. My own anxiety was smoothed over like a stone polished by endless waves, and I saw for the first time Aphra's true power. Her words, and nothing more, had changed the very fabric of the group's energy, pushing us from the edge of terror to a brilliantly honed anticipation.

I caught Curlin's eye, and we hung back as Aphra led the group into the trees.

"Have you ever seen anything like that?" I asked.

Curlin shook her head. "Never. It was like her voice sucked all the panic, all the fear, out of us. Even me. My doubts about this nonsense were just...wiped away."

"Am I right in thinking that's a bit terrifying?"

"More than a bit, but I think that's a worry for another day."

Curlin took a quick step behind me to walk on my other side. I raised an eyebrow at her quizzically.

"I told you I'd protect your weaker side," she said, rolling her eyes. "Don't make a thing of it."

I elbowed Curlin in the ribs, the same way I'd done hundreds of times when we were children, and walked with her into the forest, puffed with Aphra's false bravery.

We spread ourselves in a line throughout the trees, looping the Shriven's camp at the base of the mountain. We moved more silently than wraiths across the forest floor, and once in position, waited for our signal from the rebel camp. We hoped Quill had made it across the Shriven's lines and into the rebel camp to ready them for the fight.

Pots clanged and fires crackled in the Shriven camp. They were all focused forward, in the direction of Biz and Neve's camp. Their low laughter and quiet conversations drifted through the trees, and even with Aphra's false confidence, my heart began to pound with anticipation. Then a branch snapped behind me, the sound as loud as a gunshot, and I whirled around, drawing my knives.

Lei, her chubby cheeks and close-cropped curls dappled with mud, stood frozen just behind me. A bow and quiver were slung over one of her shoulders, and a kaffe knife as long as her forearm was strapped to her waist.

"Shit," I mouthed.

Before I could collect my thoughts, Curlin had crossed the distance to Lei without a sound. We were so close to the Shriven camp that any noise, any sound at all, could alert them to our presence. Curlin jabbed a finger into Lei's shoulder and glowered at her expectantly. Lei silently snarled right back at Curlin, brandishing the kaffe knife. I shook my head.

"No," I mouthed, gesturing emphatically with each word. "Go. Now."

Curlin shook her head and pointed up the mountain. There wasn't enough time for Lei to get safely away. She'd have to hide. Dzallie's toes, I could've throttled the little girl. Curlin bit her lip, scanning the clearing for somewhere we could stash her. Finally, my throat tight with fear, I pointed to a tree with thick limbs that started too high for anyone to climb without help. We could lift Lei into the branches. Most folks never looked up anyway, and it was the best we could do.

We waited in a tense clump at the base of the tree, watching the only visible patch of gray sky, our fingers laced together so tightly I could feel each of our thudding heartbeats in the small bones of our hands. Finally, an explosion on the mountainside sent sparks flying into the clouds, and we moved. Lei stepped into the cup of Curlin's and my hands, and we vaulted her into the tree. I waved emphatically, gesturing for her to climb to a spot where no one would see her. All around us, our rebel group surged out of the trees and ran, bellowing, into the Shriven camp.

"Climb as high as you can, and wait for us," I yelled up to Lei, and took off after the others.

Branches whipped my face, and I had to push myself hard to keep up with Curlin. All around us, bodies crashed into one another, screeching with rage and anguish as they tore at each other. The Shriven hadn't expected this fight—I'd never seen them in anything but their crisp black robes, yet here they were half-clothed, their tattoos fully visible, snaking round their limbs and across their chests. Their shorn heads weren't powdered black from crown to cheek, and half of them were barefoot. But even unprepared, they fought with the same frightening bloodlust that kept the entirety of Alskad in constant terror.

Our people hacked at the Shriven like they were kaffe bushes, but the Shriven were faster than wind, faster than light. They moved like liquid, their weapons as much a part of their bodies as their hands. They fought with the same intensity and ferocious zeal as Curlin, but even in the midst of the melee, I could see the difference their years of experience made. The Shriven were faster, stronger and much more vicious, and the rebels we'd trained so carefully began to fall all around me.

We were simply no match for them. The Shriven used their entire camp as a makeshift armory, blinding our people with flapping blankets and setting whole tents ablaze, heedless of the loss of their shelter. And even as Quill's rebels swarmed into the camp from the other side, the Shriven tripped them with their tents' guylines and flung flaming blankets over them like nets from hell. I searched desperately for Quill, but didn't see him anywhere.

Suddenly a blade flashed toward me, and I ducked into a roll, coming up slashing, the heat of a banked cook fire all too close on my left. One knife slid into my attacker's leg, and the other I thrust up, jarring my wrist as it hit bone. Bright blood spurted from the shocked Shriven's inner thigh, and I knew my cut had found home. I yanked my other knife free of his hip and hurtled over toward Curlin, who was locked in a furious exchange of blows with a man nearly twice her size.

Pain exploded across my back and sent me flying forward into the dirt. I landed hard on my knees, face-planting into the sodden earth with my arms wide to avoid accidentally skewering myself. As soon as I hit the ground, I rolled myself onto my back, despite the shocks of agony crisscrossing my body. One of the Shriven, a woman perhaps in her midfifties, stalked toward me, swinging a spiked iron ball from a long chain. Drops of blood—*my* blood—dripped from its spikes. A wicked grin spread across her face, turning the loops and lines of her tattoos into menacing spikes.

I scrambled clumsily to my feet, wanting to help Curlin, and at the same time knowing that I couldn't take my eyes off this woman for even a second. She studied me, her dark eyes traveling the length of my body with slow, measured assessment. All around us, the sounds of people dying flooded the air, along with the sharp iron tang of their blood. But the woman circled me like we were alone in the world, without a thought for the warriors fighting to the death all around us.

"Gray eyes, freckles, black curls," she purred. "What are you, sixteen?"

I adjusted my grip on my knives nervously. Aphra's confidence came through in my words, even as I thought it had long since left me. "If you wanted to court me, you started off on the wrong foot, bitch."

The woman's wicked smile finally touched her eyes. "That's no way for a princess to speak to a loyal supporter of the crown."

She knows who I am. But even as I realized this, my heartbeat began to thunder in my ears as the pain between my shoulders faded and my vision tunneled. Something was wrong with me. Dreadfully, horribly, wrong.

"Not a princess for long, though. Not once the Suzerain get their hands on you. With you in their power, there's nothing they won't be able to make your worthless, lying brother do. Even Runa will have to bow to their wishes. The people of Alskad will never trust a liar who wanted a twin on the throne—not in times like these." The woman smirked at me. "Now, I'm still working on the exact formula, but I imagine you ought to be feeling a bit woozy just now."

From the corner of my eye, I watched the trail of Aphra's red-gold hair as she ran past. It was so pretty. Like a river of treasure streaming past me in the sunlight. I was warm. So warm. And tired. I bit my lip hard, trying to force myself back to lucidity. Someone was yelling. Why were they yelling? We were supposed to be quiet. Where was Curlin? She was supposed to be with me. Next to my shoulder.

I cocked my head to one side and considered the woman who stood in front of me, her hands on her hips. "Do you know Curlin?" I asked. "She's like you. Shriven. Or she was.

She's supposed to be here." I pointed to the ground beside me. "She's always supposed to be here."

The woman's face was blurry. There was that yelling again. Someone needed to tell them to be quiet. We were sneaking. The Shriven woman was so blurry. Was she Curlin? My head spun as her eyes went wide, wide, wide, red blood cascading down her face as she crumpled to the ground.

Iron hands around my arms. A face—two faces—thrust into mine. Half one person, half the other. Hair like the sun. Like fire. So close to me. I tried to twist away. Shrank back. So tired. A body behind me, holding me up. A shock of pain on my cheek. Eyelids heavy. So, so tired.

A voice, garbled at first. "Listen to me, Vi. Hear me. You will wake up. You will get out of here. Run. Find a horse. Follow Curlin. You have to stay awake until we're safe."

The world snapped back into focus, and before I could think, I was running. One foot in front of the other, eyes on Curlin's back, I ran. We tore through the trees, all of my focus intent on keeping my body upright and moving forward. Nothing else mattered. Nothing was real except my feet pounding the earth, running toward safety. The pain that had traveled in waves up and down my body was now a memory so distant it was almost impossible to recall.

As we ran through a familiar copse of trees, I heard Curlin shout something, but it didn't have to do with me, and so it didn't matter. One of our people appeared, holding three unfamiliar horses. Curlin tossed me a set of reins and boosted me into the big dun's saddle.

"Can you ride?" she asked.

"We have to get away." My answer wasn't an answer, but it was all I had.

Her eyes traveled over me critically, but I was already dig-

ging my heels into the horse's flanks. I could hear them behind us. They were coming, and they were fast. I had to ride,
had to run, had to get away. Get away. Away.

CHAPTER SIXTEEN

Bo

"Stay safe, Vi. If you do nothing else, if you must abandon your cause and hide yourself on some distant mountain to do so…please just stay safe. I can't stand to lose you, too."

—*from Bo to Vi*

An earsplitting squeal jolted me out of the nothingness of sleep. I sat up in the unfamiliar room, looking around blearily as the memories of the last few days came flooding back to me. The sharp tendrils of a headache laced through my skull, prodding and squeezing. I let myself fall back on the lumpy pillows and pulled a quilt up over my head. The last thing I wanted to do was face whatever waited for me at the bottom of that staircase.

I wanted to go back to my cozy sitting room in the palace, drinking tea with Gran and Swinton as they ribbed and teased each other. I wanted to go back to a time when I had allies as powerful as my enemies. A time when I didn't have to battle giants armed only with my wits and the few people who knew the full extent of what we faced: Swinton, Gerlene and, far away fighting her own battles in Ilor, Vi.

"It's just us," a voice called up the stairs, and a moment later Tie and Chase stomped into the bedroom, followed closely by Fern, Trix, Pem and Still. Tie ruffled Trix's short hair and then blew into his hands, shivering. Pem and Still crawled onto the bed with me, nesting on a pile of pillows in the corner.

"What time is it?" I asked.

Fern and Trix exchanged a quick and nearly imperceptible look. "Around nine."

"In the morning?" I shot out of bed, panicked. "How long have I been asleep?"

Tie gently pushed me back to sit on the bed. "At night. Don't worry. You needed the rest."

"What about Swinton? Where is he?" I asked, heart thundering in my chest.

"He's not back yet," Chase said. "But it was chaos outside the palace. I'm sure he'll be back soon enough."

I took a deep breath and nodded. I had to trust them. I had to trust that Swinton could take care of himself. "And? What did they announce?"

Chase looked at me quizzically. "Oh, right. The regent. It's some person named Rylain? I've never even seen her mentioned in the papers or nothing. Seems like a strange choice. Do you know her?"

Thoughts whirred through my mind like hummingbirds. Why Rylain? Why not Patrise or Lisette? They were younger, more involved in politics, knew more about the running of the country. Chase was right. It *was* a strange choice.

"I do," I said. "She's my cousin. Older. A bit of a recluse.

She's not even on the council anymore. And what about Gerlene? Did you find her?"

Tie nodded. "Yeah. Caught her leaving her house to see the regent announced. Slipped her your note and told her where we live. She said she'd come as soon as she could get away without being noticed. I've not seen her that preoccupied before."

"How do you know her?" I asked.

"She's always been a fair decent advocate for folks in the End. Her sister runs a soup kitchen not far from here, and Miss Gerlene does a lot of legal work for folks who can't afford to hire someone. She's been an awful lot more involved the last few months, though. Makes sense now." He winked at me.

"Sometimes she brings us pastries," Pem added.

"I'm still sorry that Ina's been so selfish with the funds my father put aside for her. It was more than enough to take care of you. All of you."

Fern laughed. "Clearly you don't know our ma well at all. She spends every *twilling* on tacky junk and getting plastered. We do well enough for ourselves. And we manage to steal a fair amount from her when she passes through here."

I cringed. The front door screeched open, and I looked at Chase. "Not to tell you your own business, but have you considered oiling that thing? It makes a terrible racket."

Pem, who'd been scooting closer and closer to me on the bed, petted my snarled curls. "If it didn't squeal, how would we know when someone comes in?"

I took a deep breath through my nose and looked around the room at the tired faces of my strange new family. They might not have Runa's power, but they were resourceful, scrappy and surprisingly loyal. I was lucky to have found them. For that, at least, I could be grateful to Ina and Dammal. "Well, then, I suppose we should see who's come."

I waited on the landing as my half siblings ricocheted down the stairs, their voices loud and their boots louder. The seconds ticked slowly by, marked by my galloping heart. If the castle guard had come, or worse yet, the Shriven, I would have to hide myself again, and fast. And, like the thoughtless, pampered princeling I was, I'd left my jacket on the bed and my boots by the bedside. What if I had to run? What if someone found them and persecuted my siblings because of it?

Just as my spiraling worries began to take hold, a familiar voice called up to me from the bottom of the stairs. "Best come down here, bully. We don't have a lot of time."

Swinton. I closed my eyes and took a deep, shuddering breath. He was safe. He'd come back to me safe. But then a single, musical chuckle shattered my grateful reverie. There was only one person in the world who laughed like that, and she didn't belong here. Lisette wouldn't be caught dead in the End.

"Come on, Bo, darling. Show us you're not a ghost after all."

I groaned. Not only Lisette, but Patrise, too. Why, in Gadrian's flaming heart, would Swinton have brought *them* here? And at a time like this? I rubbed a helpless hand through my hair with a sigh, tucked my shirt into my trousers and padded down the stairs. There was nothing I could do but own my disarray and face my cousins despite it.

Patrise and Lisette, decked out in indigo silk mourning clothes and thick fur wraps, raised their eyebrows in twin expressions of amusement as I descended the stairs.

"The queen is dead," Lisette said, her expression and voice suddenly somber.

"Long live the king," Patrise finished, and the pair of them dropped to their knees just as I reached the last step.

My siblings looked from me to my cousins and back again before kneeling, as well. A blush exploded across my face as Swinton followed suit. I swallowed, fighting back tears.

"Please, you don't have to—"

Patrise cut me off. "It's the customary protocol, Your Majesty. We *do* have to." He raised one eyebrow. "Though I never imagined you'd be barefoot and in your shirtsleeves when we finally did it."

Everyone stood and stared at me, as though I might have some answer for this bizarre situation.

"Why are you here?" I asked, then looked at Swinton, pleading. "Why did you bring them?"

"You need allies, Bo. They want to see you on the throne. They can help. They helped me get the perfume I collected—the only proof of the Suzerain's wretched scheme that exists. They could have destroyed it, but I have it all here." He patted a hardened leather case he held.

"I hope you wrapped it carefully," I said, fear coming through my words clear as a bell. "I can only imagine what would happen if it broke."

Tie clapped his hands. "This isn't a conversation for the front hall. You lot settle yourselves in the parlor. We'll scrounge up some tea and something to eat."

Lisette smiled coquettishly at Tie. "You don't happen to have any kaffe, do you? Or perhaps something a bit stronger? Our Bo here has had a nasty time of it."

Chase, Tie and Swinton burst into peals of laughter. Swinton clasped Lisette by the shoulders and steered her into the parlor, still chuckling. "You *are* out of your depth, aren't you, Lissie? You royal lot haven't the faintest idea how the world really works. A single pot of kaffe costs more than most people earn in a week."

I took one of the parlor's overstuffed armchairs, and Patrise and Lisette perched on the edge of the sofa. Pem and Still positioned themselves on the floor on either side of me, and the rest of my siblings bustled in and out, carrying mismatched teacups and dishes.

Swinton settled into the chair beside me and fixed Patrise and Lisette with a hard stare. "Well? You two want to tell Bo what you told me?"

Patrise looked at Lisette, who pursed her lips and nodded. "Rylain has been planning this for a very, very long time, Bo. We have good reason to believe that she orchestrated your mother's death, as well as Penelope's. She was almost certainly behind the queen's assassination."

"Surely you're mistaken. Rylain would never do that. She couldn't. She has no interest in power. She barely even comes to court."

With a dismissive wave of her hand, Lisette continued. "Rylain tricked everyone into thinking that she didn't care about politics or court life, so she became the obvious person to leave the council when you were voted in. Everyone on the council voted for themselves to become regent, which triggered some archaic law calling for the regent to be chosen from the singleborn not serving on the council. And, as you know, she's the only singleborn not on the council."

"She must have some very smart people on her side. I don't think any of us had ever heard of that particular clause before, and from what I can tell, it's only been used one other time, generations ago," Patrise said.

"Before the vote, we managed to discover that she'd bought

the captain of the guard. We just don't know *how*," Lisette added.

Patrise shook his head, and an uncharacteristic look of frustration flickered across his face. "She's had us fooled for years. She's always seemed so preoccupied with her books and her faith, and neither of us thought to have anyone really watching her carefully."

"But then we put the pieces together," Lisette said. "It all makes sense. The Suzerain must have been grooming her, preparing her for this day. They've wanted the throne for years, and now they've put their very own puppet right where they want her."

"But," I sputtered, "Rylain loves me. She's the only one of the singleborn who's ever really cared about me. I *know* her. She doesn't want power. She'll step down the moment I appear."

Lisette bit her lip, an expression of hurt masking her face. "Bo, what do you think it is that Patrise and I have done all these years, if not love you?"

I stared at them, shocked. "You've spied on me. You've tried to have me killed. You don't love me. You want my throne for yourselves."

Patrise rolled his eyes. "You silly child. We've watched over you, yes. We've derailed *real* assassination attempts. Whose spies do you think distracted the shooter in the park all those months ago before your birthday? We would never let anything happen to you."

Lisette wrinkled her nose. "Neither of us wants to run a country, silly. Do you know how much *time* it takes to be queen? I've far better ways to spend my days, thank you, and you're far more suited to it. Not that that matters now. You'll be captured and killed immediately if you come within sight of the palace."

"But I'm the *heir*. They can't do that. There's documentation. There were witnesses at the ceremony. *You* witnessed the ceremony."

Swinton laid a gentle hand on my knee. "This isn't a minor misunderstanding that can be cleared up in private, Bo. It's a coup."

"But surely the council..."

Lisette shook her head. "As soon as they named her regent, Rylain cited some ancient law that allowed her to double the size of the council. She appointed a number of anchorites who're clearly only doing the Suzerain's bidding. The Suzerain have the controlling vote on the royal council as of this afternoon."

I couldn't believe what I was hearing. "But why? Why would Rylain do this?"

"Rylain has ordered that all the dimmys be rounded up and brought to the temple," Swinton said. "For the safety of the people. You know what that means?"

Horror washed over me. "With the temple's help, they can make anyone who opposes them a dimmy," I said slowly. "They could, essentially, commit genocide in order to take over my empire." I stood, and Patrise rose to meet me. "I have to go, Patrise. I can convince Rylain to stop this. I *have* to stop her."

Patrise, his expression somber, reached out and touched the golden cuff that ringed my wrist. "You made a promise to your people, Bo. You can't help them if you're dead, and if you charge into the palace demanding your throne back, you'll be executed in less than an hour."

I slumped back into my chair and put my head in my hands.

It was hopeless. It was all so, so hopeless. I should have seen this coming. I should have known by the look on Rylain's face when she stormed out of the council room. If I'd been paying more attention, if I hadn't been so self-involved, maybe I could have saved my mother, Penelope, Claes.

But if I had...would I still have found Vi? I hated myself for thinking it. For considering for even a moment that my twin was worth more than my mother, more than Penelope, more than my first love. Because even though Claes had betrayed me, even though he'd broken my heart, I *had* loved him once.

"Just tell him, Patrise," Lisette snapped.

"Tell me what?" I asked, looking from Patrise to Lisette to Swinton and back again. Their expressions remained neutral, but Patrise compressed his lips in a way that told me he was avoiding telling me something.

"There are rumors, Bo," he said finally. "Rumors that you...might not be singleborn after all."

"They're true," I said, simply and without thinking twice. "I have a twin sister, Vi. Our mother, Ina, owns this house. These are my sisters and brothers."

Lisette studied the various Abernathys spread around the room. "I see the resemblance."

"And Runa knew?" Patrise asked, incredulous.

I nodded. "Gerlene will be here soon. She has the documents. If you want to see them, all you have to do is ask. Runa knew what she was doing when she declared that I would be the heir."

Patrise waved his hand dismissively as Lisette nodded.

"That doesn't surprise me a bit. But it does complicate things," Lisette said. "You'll need an army if you want to take back your throne. And the only way you're going to get one is if you make nice with Denor. I have a ship in the harbor—you can be there in less than a week."

"I can't leave Alskad and go begging at the foot of a foreign throne!" I exclaimed. "Not when my country is in the hands of the Suzerain."

"I don't think you have much of a choice," Swinton said, his voice low and gentle. "You can't go back to the palace without enough muscle to take down the palace guard as well as the Shriven. You need help."

I scrubbed my hands through my hair. "There's no good option here. I leave my country in Rylain's grasp, and she hands all control to the Suzerain, who've done more to harm Alskad and its people than any two people since the cataclysm, or I stay and try to fight with no army."

"Denor is the right choice, Bo. We'll be back as soon as we can manage," Swinton said.

"Why Denor?" Trix asked, and I started. I'd almost forgotten that my siblings were in the room.

Patrise was quick to answer. "Their army is one of the most highly trained in the world, and they're far more likely to help Bo than the Samirians. No foreigner has set foot on Samirian soil in more than a century. Denor is a small nation, but their soldiers are ferocious. It's why they've never been swept up by the empire. The Denorian queen is only a few years older than Bo. Lisette knows her well."

"I've already written a letter to Noriava," Lisette explained. "You won't need it to get in the door, of course, but it might help plead your case if Nori knows you have friends among the singleborn here."

"I still don't like it," I said. "I can't possibly feel good about leaving my people in Rylain's hands. And what if I come back, and the rest of the council won't support my reign? I need them if I'm going to take the throne back from Rylain."

"Don't worry about them," Lisette said. "Patrise and I can handle the other singleborn. You get Noriava's support in Denor, and I promise you'll return to a council ready to put you back on the throne and set this right."

Biting the inside of my cheek, I reluctantly nodded. "Fine. Let's make it happen."

The trip south to the Denorian capital would take five days, and Lisette's ship would set sail on the morning tide. I had the hours until then to get my affairs—and my head—in order. At a table in one of the small side rooms, I finished my letter to Vi. The last letter I'd be able to safely send for some time. I poured every detail I could manage into it, and with a quick prayer to Gadrian, sealed it with a glob of candle wax.

Grief and anxiety rolled through me in alternating waves. I wished that Vi and Runa could have gotten to know one another. They were so alike that I couldn't decide if they would have bickered viciously or become an unstoppable force of nature. Either way, it was a great loss that they would never know each other.

The front door squealed open, followed by multiple sets of booted feet galloping down the stairs. A cacophony of voices began to echo from the kitchen. Steeling myself for the chaos of my family, I tucked the letter into my jacket pocket and opened the door to find Pem grinning up at me. I caught sight of Swinton at the end of the hall, waiting for me, and nodded at him before turning my attention to Pem.

"Looking for me, are you?"

Pem grabbed my hand. "Gerlene is here, and she's brought tea and cakes and pasties enough that we can all eat until we throw up. Two huge baskets stuffed so full they wouldn't shut. I was going to knock, but you said not to knock, so I decided to wait for you instead."

I fought back a laugh. "Go, go! Before you're left with only crumbs. I need to have a quick word with Swinton, but I'll be there in just a moment."

Nodding, Pem looked down the hall at Swinton, who was leaning against a doorjamb with his arms crossed over his chest. Even though the house was cold to the point of turning the end of my nose and my fingertips to ice, Swinton had discarded his jacket and rolled up his shirtsleeves to reveal the ropy muscles and deeply tanned skin of his forearms.

"Save me a pasty, will you?" I asked Pem.

Pem's mouth knotted, and she narrowed her eyes at Swinton before giving my hand a squeeze and darting off down the hallway. I crossed the squeaking, scuffed hardwood to Swinton.

"Thanks for bringing Patrise and Lisette. I was a little alarmed at first, but I feel better now, knowing that I've got the support of the two most conniving people in Alskad," I said, pecking him on the cheek.

"The solicitor's here."

"Pem said. Are you all right?"

"Those two, Pem and Still. They seem to be under the impression that they'll be coming with us to Denor."

My mouth dropped open in surprise, I glanced over my shoulder just in time to see Pem's head disappear into the kitchen.

"I...well, I did promise that I'd find jobs for them, when I was once again in a position to do so. I certainly didn't tell them they could come with us to Denor. Though—"

Swinton put a finger to my lips. "Don't even start. They'd be a liability, and you know it."

I swatted his hand away. "I don't think they would be. They're thieves, and good ones, and they can read and write. There's no one more invisible than a street urchin."

"Except a street urchin who doesn't speak the language. We can use them *here*—put the whole family to work if they're willing—but I'm not about to take two brats into a foreign country where they're as likely to lose a hand for stealing as they are to pick up a useful bit of information."

I saw his point. The Denorians, governed by a strict code of personal responsibility and ethics rather than the pedantic law of the temple, enforced extraordinarily harsh punishments for crimes that affected the well-being and livelihood of others. They valued education, and school, followed by an apprenticeship, was mandatory for every Denorian citizen through early adulthood. They were a society of scientists and philosophers, and the medicine that came out of Denor was the most advanced in the world. They'd constructed, from the ruin of the earth, a society in which two children, roaming about without supervision, were sure to be noticed and taken in by someone whose job it was to look after their community's youth.

"What about as valets?" I asked, unable to shake my desire to fulfill the careless promise I'd made to the twins.

Swinton scratched the back of his head and eyed me, the muscles in his jaw doing a wild dance. I gave him a smile that I hoped was both sincere and seductive at the same time and willed him to agree. After a long moment, he sighed and pulled me into his arms. I drank in his scent—wood smoke and wool and sweat and spice—and let some of my tension seep out of my body.

"You've got all the makings of a terribly effective king, bully." Swinton's whisper prickled the hairs on my neck. "Unabashedly manipulative and frighteningly smart, with the good looks and charm to mask it from your unwitting victims." He kissed the tip of my nose. "They can go as cabin attendants turned valets. It'll excuse some of their ignorance, and they're sure to've picked up a bit of knowledge about ships from Brenna."

Whoops of delight shattered the quiet. Pem and Still came barreling down the hallway and wrapped themselves around our legs, nearly knocking Swinton and me off balance. A reluctant grin spread over Swinton's face, and he kissed me deeply, to a resounding chorus of gagging noises and "Eww!" from the twins knotted around our legs.

"Off, brats," Swinton commanded. "I've a powerful hunger, and this wouldn't be the first time I've eaten a little girl for a snack. Might not've signed up to go off to Denor with us if you'd known I was a dimmy like Vi, would you?"

Disentangling himself from me, Swinton winked and reached down to tickle the girls, who scrambled away, screaming and giggling.

"You'd never eat me," Still said. "Bo wouldn't let you."

I grinned and waggled my eyebrows at her. "We'll see how useful you make yourself, little sister."

The girls took off toward the kitchen, shrieking. We found the rest of the family sitting with Gerlene around the kitchen table, which was piled high with steaming jugs of tea, the peeled remnants of citrus fruits shipped from Ilor, sandwiches wrapped in waxed papers and piles of flaky pasties, both savory and sweet. Gerlene, in olive wool trimmed with forest green fur, pushed back her chair as I entered the room and sank to the floor in a deep bow.

"Long live the king."

Swinton echoed her. "Long live the king."

My chin quivered as my siblings repeated the phrase a third time. "Long live the king."

To keep myself from losing control and weeping for what felt like the millionth time since the sun rose on this horrible day, I knelt and pulled Gerlene to her feet. "I don't forget that you lost someone you loved, as well. She adored you, Gerlene. I am so very, very sorry for your loss."

Behind her glasses, Gerlene's eyes shimmered with tears. She cupped my cheek in one hand. "She loved you dearly, Bo, but more than that, she believed in you. I hope you know that."

"I know. And I know that she loved you, too." I squeezed Gerlene's hand. "I'll see that her legacy is honored. I'll take care of this empire. I swear it."

She smiled at me and sat back down. "Your siblings tell me you've a journey planned," she said.

Before I could open my mouth, Pem and Still were off at a gallop, telling Gerlene everything that had transpired during the afternoon's visit with Lisette and Patrise. Swinton laced his fingers through mine, and I settled myself in one of the rickety wooden chairs. I took a deep breath, poured myself a mug of tea and watched my glorious, wild family in action.

CHAPTER SEVENTEEN

Vi

"I have known pain. I have known panic. I have feared for my life. But until now, I have never experienced the blind rush that comes when you are barely clinging to survival."

—*from Vi to Bo*

We streaked through the jungle, our horses' hooves pounding a confident rhythm on the packed, damp earth of the trail. Even though the world around me felt strangely distant, terror still pounded through my veins. I urged my mount onward, following Curlin when she left the trail and slowing to a trot as we wove between the trees. As much as I ached to go faster, it would be suicide on an unfamiliar horse in the dense greenery.

As we forged ahead, the sounds of the Shriven on foot began to fade. But there were at least six on horseback behind us, and they were gaining ground fast. They crashed through the trees behind us, pushing their horses past what was safe, past what was smart.

"Faster, Vi," Curlin called. "We've got to go faster."

I crouched low over my horse's neck, urging him onward. Branches lashed my face, my arms, my back, and trails of pain coursed across my skin. The light that filtered through the trees grew brighter and brighter until we broke out of the jungle into a wide, open field. The sun had burned away the morning's fog and was blindingly bright overhead. Curlin and I both kicked our mounts to a gallop, weaving across the open grass.

Gunfire cracked like a whip in my ear, and I glanced back. The cluster of Shriven rode less than a ship's length behind us, and their guns glinted like diamonds in the sun. A bullet whizzed by my head, and I ducked even lower, the dusty smell of the horse's sweat and leather saddle overpowering the sharp tang of my own fear and sweat.

I had to get to safety. Everything would be fine once I was well away and safe.

The clap of the Shriven's guns became like drumbeats, pushing us faster and faster across the open field. Accuracy was impossible at this range. Their shots went wide or dipped into the earth too soon, but that didn't seem to deter them. As they drew closer, bullets flew past us and slammed into the earth around our horses' hooves, throwing up clods of dirt and grass. Curlin shouted a string of curses, but my only focus was staying on the horse and keeping the pain at bay. My shoulder burned, and the wind rushing over the ravaged skin and exposed muscle of my back felt like a thousand tiny knives.

As we galloped onward, I suddenly began to recognize our surroundings. Just over the next hill, we'd come to a thick patch of woods, and, on the other side, a gorge. There was only one way across the gorge for a mile in either direction, the picture of it clear as spring water in my head: a sturdy wooden suspension bridge that led to the little clearing where we'd left our horses and the brats to look after them.

We just had to get to the bridge. There would be a solution on the other side.

The sound of hoofbeats grew closer, and I twisted in my saddle to see how close our pursuers were. But the hoofbeats I heard weren't the Shriven—instead, a horse burst from the underbrush in the woods at the right, cutting an angle between Curlin and me and the Shriven. Aphra's red-gold hair flew out behind her like a flag, and Lei clung to the saddle as well, her short, scrawny legs flapping wildly. At the sight of Aphra, the Shriven's voices rose in an angry cacophony, and they changed the direction of their fire, aiming their guns at Aphra and Lei.

Despite the pain shrieking up my back and the fog that clouded my thoughts, I knew I couldn't let them hurt Aphra or Lei. But just as I reined my horse to the right and began to gallop toward them, Aphra raised her hand and, to my great surprise, threads of golden light came pouring out of her fingertips, weaving together to form a moving picture over her head. Golden figures galloped in the sky above her, and I recognized myself, Curlin, the Shriven, Aphra and Lei.

The image sped up, and in a matter of seconds, I watched the golden light image of Aphra ride closer to us and put Lei on my horse before she sped off into the woods, drawing half of the Shriven away from us. They galloped down the gorge toward the next bridge, while Curlin and Lei and I rode on.

Then the golden light flashed away. I looked back at the Shriven, but it was as though nothing had changed. They'd seen nothing. One of them took aim and fired at me, missing me by just a hair.

I never made the decision to follow the unspoken command Aphra had shown me—with what? Magic? I simply did it, wheeling my horse back toward Curlin as though it were the only option. Curlin disappeared into the woods just moments before Aphra and Lei's path converged with ours, and they rode up alongside me. Lei leaped onto my horse, settled herself behind the saddle and wrapped her arms, vise-like, around my ribs.

"Listen to me, Vi," Aphra gasped. "Hear me. Get to safety. We'll meet back at the camp. You must stay safe."

With that, Aphra peeled off out of sight, leaving Lei and me on Curlin's heels. It was almost like I couldn't even see her; my whole brain was so focused on riding away from the Shriven. We wove through the trees, and bullets hammered into the trunks, sending chunks of bark flying. A slice of pain tore through my left arm, and I cried out in shock, dropping that rein, but my horse galloped on. I kept riding and riding as blood ran down my arm and screams echoed all around me.

I couldn't stop. I had to get to safety. I had to ride on.

Suddenly, we were past the trees, and Curlin's horse galloped across the bridge. I guided my mount onto the wooden planks, but the moment its hooves touched wood, the horse froze. I flew up, and nearly over the horse's head, but managed to stay on. Lei whimpered, but I felt her small weight settle against my back.

Even as I did my best to urge the horse forward, blood poured down my limp left arm, and bullets flew through the trees behind me. My horse backed up, whinnying and screaming in fear. I kicked my feet out of the stirrups and slid to the ground. Without my body to keep her there, Lei tumbled off the horse like a sack of grain, and I did my best to catch her with my uninjured arm. She was smeared with blood, but I had no idea if it was hers or mine.

Just as I got her down, my horse reared and bolted away. Lei moaned and slumped to the ground, her eyes fluttering. I could hear the Shriven's horses rushing through the trees, branches snapping and bullets flying as they came closer and closer to us. I paused, just for a moment, and though it took every ounce of my strength, I pulled Lei up and lifted her onto my shoulder.

It felt like I was trying to move through water—every fiber of my being protested, but I couldn't leave her behind. On the far side of the bridge, the brats were yelling over each other, over Curlin's head, urging me forward.

We weren't but halfway across when the first of the Shriven burst through the trees. Curlin had reached the other side and held a torch high overhead in one hand and a bucket in the other. There were brats on either side of the bridge, sawing at the suspension ropes. I kept going, each step a stab of pain in my spine. Heavy footsteps pounded onto the bridge, and my balance faltered, offset by Lei's weight on my shoulder. I stepped sideways, steadying myself against the rope rail and then stumbling forward again, knowing the Shriven were closing in on me. Blood dripped from my limp hand, my vision tunneled and all I could see was Curlin, standing at the end of the bridge, waiting.

I ran. The moment my feet touched grass, I eased Lei down and onto her back, gasping for breath, praying I'd been fast enough to save us.

Behind me, there was a loud crack and a symphony of screams. It took every last ounce of strength in my body, but I turned, and as I sank to my knees, I watched the bridge flap over the chasm. One rope had been severed, and the Shriven on the bridge were clinging to the slats, trying to climb back to safety. But the wood was slick with the jungle damp, and there were too many of them. Even as they heaved themselves back the way they'd come, the brats kept sawing away at the suspension cable.

A moment later, the last rope snapped, and with a great, shuddering heave, the bridge collapsed, sending the Shriven hurtling down into the gorge. The edges of my sight went blurry, and then everything faded into blackness.

Part Three

"Your lives are often wasted, distracted from your true purpose in endless pursuit of survival. Worship is the way to bring you back to your center, where you may experience and taste your full being."

—from the *Book of Rayleane, the Builder*

"Let there be no compulsion in your worship of me. Truth cannot be washed away by even the strongest wave. Whomsoever rejects falsehoods and believes in my strength will be unstoppable. I am the protector of those who have faith in the truth."

—from the *Book of Hamil, the Seabound*

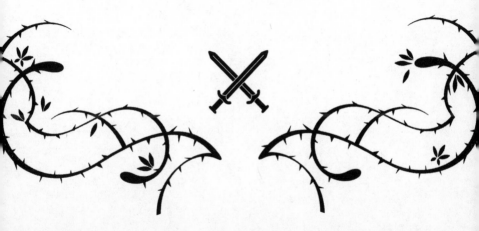

CHAPTER EIGHTEEN

Bo

"It's an odd thing to go from being an only child to a man with so very many sisters. I can't seem to remember a time without them, and yet, I can't imagine what it was like to grow up knowing them."

—*from Bo to Vi*

The icy chill of Alskad fell away as Lisette's small sunship made its way down the coast, carrying us toward the Denorian capital of Salemouth. Still and Pem ran roughshod over the crew, approximating threats they had no real way of carrying out, charming them with smiles and begging for sailing lessons by turns.

I'd arranged with Gerlene for my siblings to be moved to a furnished house in a better neighborhood. Gerlene would give them sufficient funds to live more comfortably and stop stealing. It was only with great reluctance that the eldest four agreed, but given Rylain's apparent tyranny and the possibility of the temple connecting them to me, it was in their best interest to keep a low profile.

Brenna and Chase hadn't been eager to see Pem and Still go, but the girls had wheedled and cajoled until they got their way. Even so, Brenna made Swinton and me promise that we'd keep the girls out of trouble at least a half dozen times before she finally agreed. Just before we climbed aboard the ship, I'd pressed my letters to Vi and the Whipplestons into Gerlene's weathered hands and kissed her on the cheek. Days later, her parting words still echoed in my head.

"You go, and you find a way to take back your throne. Make Runa proud. She didn't spend all these years laboring just to let it all go to pot the moment she let go the reins."

I'd been silent in response. More than anything, I wanted to erase that entire day, to keep Runa alive, to find a way to give myself and Vi more time. But in the icy predawn darkness, my feet planted on the rocking dock as frigid waves crashed beneath me, I could only nod and hug Gerlene fiercely. In the time since, I'd searched my brain for the right words, the right way to thank this woman who'd stepped in to become Runa's silent partner, her helpmeet and support as well as mine. There was just one thing I could imagine that would be enough to honor Runa's memory and thank Gerlene at the same time.

I would find a way to take back my throne. And I would rule Alskad as my grandmother would have done.

I gripped the railing at the bow of the ship and let the cool spray wash over me, a baptism and a benediction from Hamil as I watched the lighthouses on either side of the Salemouth harbor grow steadily closer. Swinton appeared, silent as the shipboard cat, and leaned his back against the railing, elbows resting on the polished wood.

"You'll have to get those younglings under control before we dock, elsewise folk'll think *we're* the attendants and they're the wild nobility."

I looked over my shoulder and up at the rigging, where Pem and Still were battering each other with wooden swords. They'd found the armory our first night at sea, and Pem had been on the verge of losing an arm to Still's clumsy use of a broadsword when the captain found them. The woman and her first mate had—with many beleaguered sighs toward the girls and winks directed at Swinton and me—agreed to give Pem and Still a few lessons in swordplay, using a set of wooden practice swords. And, if they were good, she'd promised to gift each girl with a sword of her own when we arrived back in Alskad.

I'd have to find a way to thank her for her generosity.

"Let them wear themselves out today," I said. "Otherwise they'll be up all night, too excited to sleep before we disembark tomorrow."

"Nervous or scared?" Swinton asked, and I knew that his question was really about my state of mind, rather than the girls'.

"Both." I started to chew on my thumbnail, but Swinton gently moved my hand away from my mouth. He laced his fingers through mine and waited while I worked out what to say next.

None of it was anything new. The worst possible scenario ran through my head over and over again, varying each time in the details of my failure—failing to persuade the queen to join my cause, failing to even get into the palace, failing to keep my sisters safe in this new foreign country, failing, failing, failing.

"You have the perfume?" I asked for the thousandth time.

Swinton, mouth set in a tense line, patted the breast pocket of his jacket. "One on my person at all times, the others safely packed away belowdecks."

"Aren't you worried that it might break? That you might accidentally dose yourself? We've no way of knowing how strong this mixture is, compared to the temple's serum. We don't even know if you were somehow dosed before now."

Swinton pulled me in close and touched his forehead to mine. "Is any of that within our control?"

Brows furrowed, I shook my head.

"Then there's no point in worrying about it. What we *do* have to worry about is how to get a dead prince into a palace."

I chuckled and leaned in to kiss him. He was right. It was rare for the journey between Denor and Alskad to take less than a week, but favorable winds and a fast ship would have us in the city's harbor in just over five days. Even still, that wouldn't be fast enough to beat the news of Runa's death— and my own.

It had been nearly ten years since I'd last seen Queen Noriava, and—aside from the small details I'd gleaned from the polite correspondence required by birthdays and holidays—I knew almost nothing about her. I knew that she thought Alskad's food was too bland, that she hated green beans, that she was an excellent shot and that she'd kept an owl as a pet when she was a girl. Beyond those facts, everything I knew about her was based on rumor and speculation.

"I don't have any idea what to expect, or what to say. 'Hello, Noriava. My, how you've grown since you were a twelve-year-old terror chasing me through the garden. Would you mind lending me your army so I can take back my throne? Oh, and by the way, I'm not only a bastard, but a twin as well, and I'd like my sister, who happens to be a thief and a fugitive trying to take down the extraordinarily corrupt temple that's more or less taken over my empire, to rule beside me.' Think that'll work?"

Swinton snorted. "It's a bit of a mouthful, but it's the truth."

I hated showing up like a beggar at the foot of another sovereign's throne, but it wasn't as though I had much of a choice. The Suzerain had no doubt made Rylain replace every member of the guard with those loyal to their cause. Without the support of another army, without the support of another sovereign, I had no hope of taking back my throne.

"We should have gone to Samiria," I groaned. "At least the Samirians aren't opposed to the idea of a twin in power. Abet and Jax were elected the same year I was born."

"And Alskad relations with Samiria have been just grand ever since. You know they'd see it as a ploy, and you'd be dead before you were allowed to set foot on the docks. Save reparations with Samiria for *after* you and Vi are both safely on the throne."

I gritted my teeth. "I know you're right."

Swinton's smile seeped into his words. "You just hate it."

Still dropped from the rigging and into a roll, coming up just in front of us, wooden sword clenched between her teeth. A rope dropped from the sail overhead, and Pem slid down it to stand beside her sister, brandishing her sword at Swinton.

"What do you hate?" she demanded. "Tell us, or we'll run you through!"

I hid my snicker with a cough.

"That's no way to be a spy," Swinton said. "The best spies are never seen, never heard. They're like the air, always around and never noticed."

Still and Pem nodded thoughtfully, drinking in his every word.

"When'll we get there?" Still asked.

"Will we get to stay in the palace?" Pem's question came

so quickly on the heels of her sister's that their voices blended into one chorus.

"We'll be in the harbor on the evening tide, but we'll wait until tomorrow to dock," I said. "So you two had best make sure you've got your livery all neat and tidy for our meeting with the queen. What're the rules?"

Pem's and Still's hands both flew into the air, two fingers pointing up like the masts of the ship. In unison, they said, "One. Mouths shut. Eyes and ears open. Two. Little girls with sticky fingers become little girls without fingers."

"And…" I led.

"No fighting." They sighed in unison.

"Good. Now go see if the cook will give you something to eat. Scat."

The cliffs surrounding Salemouth harbor rose out of the water like curtains of stone, their smooth, sun-bleached folds and pleats home to birds that dove in and out of the water, squawking endlessly to one another when their beaks weren't stuffed with fish. Tiny islands dotted the wide harbor—nothing more, really, than grass-covered boulders too steep for anything other than grazing goats and shacks that looked liable to blow away in the first passing storm. A constant drizzle left the whole city damp, but the air itself was the perfect temperature. The chill of Alskad had long since faded, and Denor wasn't nearly far enough south to match the suffocating heat of Ilor.

But it was the bright, shocking green of the landscape that took me by surprise as we sailed into the harbor. Even in the jungles of Ilor, I'd never seen this kind of verdant vibrancy. It was as though every blade of grass, every leaf came from the youngest, freshest, most thoroughly fertilized plant in existence.

I smiled to myself. Gerlene would love it here.

"City's not half–bad–looking, is it?"

Swinton nuzzled my neck, and the prickle of his stubble against the delicate skin there sent chills up and down my spine. I leaned into him and kissed his cheek.

"You need to shave."

"Not on a damned ship. Not if you'd like me to live to reach the shore."

I laughed, suddenly remembering the beginnings of a beard he'd sprouted on the trip from Ilor back to Alskad. "I managed."

"But you have all the grace of a cat, and probably the nine lives, as well. I'm not taking those kinds of risks." He nodded at the quickly approaching city. "Have you been here before?"

"No." I shook my head. "Under normal circumstances, I would've visited Denor and Samiria after gaining my maturity last summer, but... Well, you know what happened."

"You'll do well. You've already half put on your kingly mask. Just remember that's what you are. A king."

I grimaced. "I'll worry about Noriava just as soon as I manage to haul myself up those stairs."

Like the cliffs around it, the city rose sheer out of the water. Staircases and wide walkways were carved into the white cliff face, and merchants hawked their goods from brightly painted carts parked along the walkways. People rushed up and down the stairs, going from the docks to the city at the top of the cliffs and back.

It was no great wonder that Salemouth hadn't been invaded and pillaged in the years after the cataclysm when the leaders of Alskad, Denor and Samiria were scrambling for power. Built at the top of the highest cliffs in the bay, the only way into the city by sea was up the daunting expanse of steps and walkways. An impressive black stone wall rose from the top of the cliff, and guardhouses equipped with enormous cauldrons meant to dump boiling oil on invaders were evenly spaced along the top of the wall.

Approaching Denor by land was just as daunting. The country was ringed by a range of some of the highest, most impassible mountains in the world. And though it was a small country, the rich soil in the countryside surrounding Salemouth produced a greater volume and better quality of food than twice the same amount of space in Alskad.

The bounty and safety in Denor had allowed for the kind of improvements that were unheard of in Alskad and Ilor. While we were still relying on hunting and the meager harvests our land could produce, Denor was rebuilding an education system, focused on science and the understanding of what happened during the cataclysm that had nearly destroyed our planet. Denor's citizenry had never looked to the temple for comfort, like the people of Alskad, or closed themselves off from the world, like the Samirians. Instead, they looked to science for answers—and I hoped that logic would sway Noriava to my side.

"Weigh anchor and haul in the rigging!" the captain roared, and the crew sprang to life, scrambling up the ropes and across the deck.

I scratched at the stiff collar of my starched silk jacket and ran an eye over the rigging, looking for Pem and Still. I caught sight of them perched above the captain's quarters, barefoot and missing their vests and jackets. I sighed and set off to find their things and force them into something that resembled order before we got into the rowboat that would take us to shore. There wasn't really a good reason for me to try so hard to make them presentable—they'd probably destroy their fin-

ery long before we ever set foot in the palace—but I was determined to put in my best effort.

Before we'd climbed even halfway up the cliffs, my heart
was pounding from exertion and I was struggling to catch
my breath. It was all I could do to keep my eyes on my boots
and myself from falling ass over elbows down the stairs, as
Vi might say. I finally had to stop a few flights later, bracing
my hands on my knees and panting.

As I fished in my pockets for a handkerchief, Pem came
bouncing back down the last set of stairs she, Still and Swinton
had climbed. She held up the handkerchief I'd been searching for, plus a fistful of coins.

"Can we buy a juice?" she asked innocently. "There's a
juice cart just up ahead, and they've got fruits we ain't never
seen before."

"Pem, what did we tell you about stealing?" I snapped, irritated more by the sweat that would inevitably stain my jacket
than by Pem's sticky fingers. I unbuttoned the irksome gar-
ment and threw it over my arm.

"It ain't stealing if it's from you," she said, her voice all calm
assurance and logic. "You're our brother, so what's yours is
mine and mine yours."

"That'd be a more convincing argument if you had, well,
anything." I laughed. "Go ahead. Buy the juice. One for
Swinton and me, too, okay?"

"Swinton's gone on ahead to make sure we can get into
the palace to see the queen. Took your letter from Lizzer-
whatshername and said he'd meet us outside the palace gates.
Said to tell you to stop in a tavern and clean yourself up 'fore
that. Don't want you meeting a queen all heaving and sweating."

I rubbed a hand through my sweat-damp curls and swiped all but a couple of Denorian *bodle*, worth roughly the same as a *tvilling*, back from Pem's outstretched hand with a glare.

"Don't be cross with me, brother. It ain't my fault you're so dreadfully rich you can't manage to keep in good enough condition to climb some stairs."

Still appeared at her sister's side, her auburn hair escaping from her braid and curling around her face in deceptively cherubic disarray. Still's deep blue uniform jacket hung open from collar to waist. Somehow, in the short amount of time it'd taken us to climb three-quarters of the steps, she'd managed to lose more than half of the buttons. The state of Pem's wardrobe wasn't much better—her buttons were intact, but the white scarf we'd wrapped around her neck before leaving the ship had disappeared.

"Pem, the juice lady has spiced crabs and dumplings, too. Let's go," Still said. "C'mon, Bo. I'm starving."

"You ate not an hour ago. You can't possibly be starving. Get your juice, but we'll wait for a meal until we find Swinton." It would be no small task, finding a way to make these two presentable even without the possibility of food stains, all while navigating a new city in a language I spoke only passably well. That thought snagged something in me, and I narrowed my eyes at the twins. "How'd you talk to the juice vendor? You told me you didn't know Denorian."

My sisters exchanged a series of looks heavily weighted with meaning. Pem piped up first. "Don't not *speak* Denorian."

"Don't really *know* a language if you can't read and write it," Still added.

Despite the incredible absurdity of Still's statement—which took into account none of the myriad causes a person might have that kept them from learning to read and write—I kept my mouth closed, hoping that by staring the girls down I might get more out of them than by asking the wrong questions. I'd address their prejudice when I had more time for explanation and thoughtful conversation.

The girls shuffled their feet and glanced at the passersby, as though strangers might stop and hand them a way out of the corner they'd backed themselves into. Finally, Still said, "Pem and me, we pick up on languages fair quick. We already knew a bit of Denorian from merchants and the like, and them sailors told us a few things."

"So you were just going to keep that bit of knowledge to yourselves?" I asked, raising an eyebrow.

"Spies keep secrets," Pem said matter-of-factly.

"Not from the people they're spying for. The more Denorian you speak, the more use you'll be in this venture."

"Oh." Still and Pem grinned at each other, and Pem said, "In that case, I can talk Denorian just about as well as I can Alskader. Still, too. And she can read it a bit."

I narrowed my eyes at them. "You just said—"

"I didn't say I *couldn't* read Denorian. Just said you didn't know a language if you couldn't read and write it. Tricky things, words." Still's smile was all the more wicked for the baby teeth she was missing.

With a snort, I started once more up the stairs.

The warren of narrow streets that led to the palace were crowded with signs advertising doctors, pharmacies, herbalists and cure-alls. Groups of smiling, well-fed people bustled up and down the street. The wholesome scent of roasting vegetables and grilled meat wafted from vendors' carts, and we saw children as excited about bags of cut fruit dusted with spices and salt as Alskader brats were about the fried doughnuts coated in colorful crunchy sugar that bakers sold at home. The fashion here seemed to be more invested in comfort and functionality than in Alskad, and much more colorful. Most people wore knit sweaters or jackets with close-fitting sleeves and buttons up the back. The fashion for both men and women seemed to lean toward wide-legged trousers or knee-length, kilted skirts, but I saw more than a few people in the tighter pants that were popular in Alskad.

I kept one hand on Still's shoulder and the other on Pem's, but even still, walking through the streets with them was like trying to walk two house cats on leashes. They were constantly distracted and trying to wander off in opposite directions. When we finally made our way through the city and to the palace, I stopped in my tracks, gaping up at the masterpiece of architecture that was the Denorian palace. This building, with its arched gate spiked with portcullis-like teeth, black minarets and domes gleaming even in the drizzling rain and black stone walls looming high overhead, was unlike anything I'd ever seen. Guards in snowy white coats stood in neat formation outside the gates, which stood open, people streaming freely in and out.

We found Swinton leaning against the doorjamb of a tavern in the shadow of the palace wall. Unlike the three of us, he was still perfectly turned out. His hair was in a neat tail, his dark gray coat remained spotlessly brushed and his snowy cuffs peeked out from beneath his jacket just a finger's width. He grinned at me, and just for a moment, I hated the ease of his beauty.

But by the time he'd crossed the street, mussed the girls' auburn curls and kissed me on the cheek, my irritation had dissolved like spun sugar in a rainstorm.

"Best find ourselves a place to clean up, and make quick

work of it. We're eating the midday meal with Noriava and her court."

"On a first-name basis with the queen of Denor already, are you?"

"Jealous?" Swinton made a wicked face at Pem and Still, who could hardly have cared any less about our conversation.

I had to admit—at least to myself—that I was, a little bit. I grimaced and looked down at my boots, scuffed from the climb up the stairs, despite my having polished them just hours ago. Or, rather, I'd tried to polish them rather inadequately, until Swinton took them from me and patiently showed me how.

He'd teased me only a little in the process, but there were times when I worried about what he must really think of me. I wanted to show him how capable I could be on my own, but I feared he'd always see me as some pampered princeling. And how could he not?

Swinton squeezed my arm. "The woman who owns this place will rent us a room for an hour, so we can get cleaned up. C'mon, then."

"How have you managed to get into the palace, see the queen and rent us a room in the time it took us to walk up from the docks?" I asked incredulously.

"You're slow," Pem said.

"Out of condition," Still added.

"Right shame," Pem agreed.

"Enough, you two. You should be ashamed at the state of your kit. You were clean and tidy not two hours ago." With a grin and a wink that made my stomach drop into my boots, Swinton said, "In the short time I've known you, my dear, I've come to learn that I have quite the way with monarchs."

My guts turned at the thought of meeting another monarch on such uneven terms, but I remembered how Swinton had charmed Runa in a matter of no time at all. With him by my side, I knew I would be just fine.

CHAPTER NINETEEN

Vi

"I can't seem to define bravery anymore. I knew it once, what it was and how it would look on me, but now, it's like a light wavering in the distance."

—from Vi to Bo

I woke to the sound of rain pattering against a tin roof. My eyes were crusted from too much sleep, and I felt as weak as a newborn seal pup. The last thing I remembered was the world falling out from beneath me, and Lei's little fingers crusted in blood. When I tried to sit up, pain shot like lightning up and down my back. I couldn't even speak; my throat was so dry that my voice came out in a rasping croak hardly louder than the creaking of the house's timbers.

Nothing in the room was familiar—not the loose nightgown I wore, not the spare pinewood furnishings, not the tin washbasin and pitcher that sat atop the dresser. The one thing I recognized was the only piece of art that hung on the wall, an image of the goddesses distributed by the temple on the high holy days when folks brought their tithe. Dzallie, the Warrior, stood in the center, her ancient, gnarled hands holding the enormous broadsword of Alskad as she stared up at the broken moon over their heads. On her left, Rayleane, the Builder, presented Alskad's crown, her eyes cast downward at the globe on which the three stood. Magritte, the Educator, with the mantle of Alskad draped across her arms, was the only one of the three who stared straight ahead, her lovely face stern and impassive.

I'd grown up with that damned image in every corner of my life. A copy hung above the cot in the tiny cell I was once allowed to occupy in the temple. Richer versions decorated the living spaces of nearly every one of the anchorites. A copy hung in nearly every shop and home I'd ever visited in Alskad, and it wasn't until now, until seeing it just this minute, that I realized I hadn't seen this depiction of the goddesses in Ilor before. I racked my brain, trying to remember if there'd been a copy at the Whipplestons' or Plumleen Hall or even in the temple, but I couldn't remember having seen it even once.

Panic and bile rose in my throat. Where *was* I? I struggled once again to sit up, to free my legs from the restrictive linens, to get away, but between my injuries and the tight sheets, it was like I was tied to the bed frame. I tried to push away the panic, to calm myself, but no amount of slow breathing could stem the tide of fear as it washed over me. I counted truths with each breath. I'd seen the Shriven fall into the gorge. Curlin and the brats had been around me when I fell.

But not Quill. Quill hadn't been with us. He'd been with the other rebels, still fighting the Shriven.

I pushed down a fresh wave of panic, reaching for logic. There was no way the rest of the Shriven had managed to find and capture me, and then gone on to bind my wounds and take care of me. The Shriven wanted me dead. They'd been shooting at me. My memories of the end of the fight were punctuated by pain and fog and moments of bright, golden focus.

Footsteps outside the little room sent my heart into my gullet, and I fought even harder to wrench myself out of the bed. My eyes shot around the room, looking for anything that I could use as a weapon, but there was nothing within reach, nothing I could use unless I could get out of bed. Even then, I didn't know if I'd be able to stand. Every muscle in my body was loose and weak. Even keeping my eyes open was a struggle, despite the adrenaline coursing through me.

I'd managed to get one foot free and pulled myself half-way up on one elbow when the doorknob turned and the door opened with a great rush of cool, damp air. Frantic tears blurred my vision for a moment, and the shadowy shape that came through the door turned my veins to ice. The shaved head, the black outline of tattoos snaking from scalp to fingertips, the thickness of a belt crowded with weapons.

I heaved my other leg out of the sheets and swung myself around, battling through the pain. I refused to let the Shriven take me without a fight. I wouldn't let them use me against Bo. The second my feet touched the bare stone floor, pain shot through me like a bolt of lightning, and I screamed. The world went black and my head spun.

"Vi, don't worry. It's okay. You're okay." I knew that voice. How did I know that voice?

Hands at my shoulders steadied me and laid me gently back on the pillow, and I didn't have the strength to fight. When I managed to open my eyes, I saw a familiar face, twisted in concern, leaning over me.

"Curlin?" I asked.

"And Aphra," she said.

"Where in Dzallie's name are we? Are you hurt? Where's everyone else? Where's Quill?"

Curlin grimaced and looked behind her. Aphra, standing in the doorway, gave a brief shake of her head. The dog we'd saved from Aphra's estate pushed her way into the room, followed by her gangly offspring, now half-grown. They nosed around the bed before settling themselves in a pile on the floor.

"You need rest," Curlin said. "We'll bring you some more pain medicine, so you can sleep."

I pounded my right fist on the mattress, making the pups' ears prick and their mother huff. "I don't want to bloody sleep. I'm fine. Tell me what happened. How long have I been out?"

Aphra leaned against the footboard, her arms crossed over the plain rail. "Four days. We got you here three days ago, and you've been in and out ever since. This is the first time you've been awake for more than a minute or two. The healers didn't know if you'd ever truly wake up—they still can't figure out what that Shriven bitch drugged you with. You were hallucinating and half-dead when you got to the bridge. You need to *rest*."

Curlin shot Aphra an admonishing look. The terror I'd felt on waking was giving way to a splitting headache. I wasn't so sure that my skull wasn't cracked. Curlin handed me a glass of water, and I took a grateful sip.

"Just tell me two things," I pleaded. "Where are we? And more important than that, how's Lei?"

"She's dead, Vi." Curlin's voice was strained with the effort of holding back tears. "She died last night. She fought like hell, but she was gut shot. There was nothing we could do. Maybe if we'd had a Denorian healer... But there's no use in wishing."

Before I could react, Aphra spoke up. "And there's something else we need to tell you, Vi."

Curlin cut her off. "Now's not the time."

"She has the right to know," Aphra countered.

"Know what?" I asked, fear rising in my blood.

Aphra bit her bottom lip and stared at her hands, clasped in her lap. "I don't know how to tell you this. It's...about Bo." Aphra paused, looking at me, her eyes full of concern. "Vi... he's dead. He and the queen were both shot during the queen's birthday celebration in Penby. I'm so sorry, Vi."

Darkness punched into me. It wasn't sadness, or anger, or even emptiness I felt. With sadness, there is grief. With anger comes action. Even emptiness is a lack, a void that needs to be filled. This was something else entirely. This was poison that rushed through my veins, filling me with shadows, taking away my hope, my joy, my passion, my fight. It took everything with it, leaving only a miserable darkness that was at once deafening and silencing. Darkness that threatened to pour out of me if I so much as opened my mouth. Not that I would—the darkness had taken with it my words, my power to form sentences, thoughts, anything.

Bo had been stolen from me. Lei had died on my watch. I had failed, so miserably and utterly, and now I would be the thing I had always thought myself to be. Diminished.

I curled in on myself, turning away from Curlin and Aphra and pulling the covers up over my shoulders. I stared at the blank wall, only dimly aware of the world around me. The world that so blithely went on—birds singing, sun shining, people laughing—in the wake of all this darkness.

The bed shifted as someone sat down beside me. A hand

stroked my hair, an attempt to comfort me, but I was stone. Stone cannot be comforted. Stone doesn't feel. I was endless dark, heaviness, cold. I was nothing. I heard Aphra's voice, Curlin's, but their words were nothing. Meaningless.

Curlin's calloused hands pulled me onto my back, tried to make me sit up, look at her, pay attention. I was dimly aware of pain in my arm where she grasped me, but as soon as I noticed it, it was gone again.

Then Aphra laid cool hands on either side of my face and gently moved my head to look at her. She was a blur of red and gold, freckles and milk-pale skin, green and violet eyes. Just as I was nothing, she was nothing. My darkness seeped into her, pushing, emptying.

"Listen to me," Aphra said, and for a moment, she almost seemed to glow. "Hear me. You will not disappear into despair. We've held off the Shriven for the time being. According to our people, they've retreated to the temples to regroup. We have very little time to act, but we think we've come up with a plan that will allow us something of an advantage. And we need you, Vi. Don't let your brother's death stop you from doing what you'd both set out to accomplish. Bo wouldn't want that. He went back to Alskad because standing up to injustice and hate was more important to him than anything—even you. Don't let his sacrifice be for nothing. Find your fight. Find your *anger*."

As Aphra spoke, that strange golden light slipped from her fingertips, from her eyes and from her mouth, weaving a picture of Bo, sitting on a faraway throne, fire and fight in his eyes, a crown on his head. He reached out, offering me a knife. Asking me to fight.

The golden image faded, leaving me staring at Aphra. She

smiled sadly at me and said, "We have too much work to do to lose you to grief, Vi."

Curlin put her hand on Aphra's shoulder and squeezed. "We talked about this, Aphra. Not too much. Not too often. It's manipulative to use your magic that way."

Aphra nodded. "You're right, of course."

I tried to gather my thoughts, but thinking was harder than running headlong into the surf. The darkness was gone, but left in its wake was confusion and gutting, heart-wrenching anger.

"Listen to me. Hear me. Come back to yourself, Vi."

The world snapped back into focus. The anger was still there, as was the sadness, but it wasn't all-consuming. It didn't break me the way it had moments ago.

"What have you done to me?"

Aphra and Curlin traded looks. Curlin pulled a chair across the room and settled it next to the bed. "Aphra finally found her magic. The magic of the amalgam. She's..." Curlin gave Aphra a wry smile. "...still learning how to use it appropriately. After the bridge collapsed, we, along with Quill's rebels, found our way back to one another. Quill brought us here, and we sent someone to fetch the folks who were left in our camp."

I breathed a sigh of relief. Quill was safe. "Slow down. So what exactly did this so-called magic of Aphra's do to me?"

I wasn't sure I believed in magic, despite the golden light that flooded from her mouth, or my own inexplicable behavior after the fight with the Shriven.

"When I say those words, in that order," Aphra began, "*listen, hear*, the whole bit—something happens to me. I can paint pictures with my words, and people do just as I say. Well, not *just* as I say, but their interpretation of it. After that Shriven nearly brained you, I told you to get to safety. I didn't know a way around it. Just now, I saw your grief consuming you, so I tried to get you to focus on something other than Bo and Lei, but I didn't think carefully about my words." She looked sheepish, an expression I'd never thought to see on her face. "I'm still not entirely sure how it all works."

I digested that for a moment, then took a breath and moved on. "Magic aside, where are we? I feel like I've asked a thousand times."

"Oh," Curlin said. "Of course. Quill brought us to Williford so that you could be tended by a healer, but he couldn't find a way to get us into his house without being noticed. Mal knew a pair of sisters who had a few rooms to spare and owed him a favor. They brought in the healers, and thank Dzallie they did. You wouldn't have stood a chance without their help."

The way my body felt now, I didn't doubt it for a moment.

"I am so sorry about your brother," Aphra said. "He would have made a good king."

Something niggled at me. The small, distant thrum that had always been in the back of my head, the cord that tied me to Bo...it was still there. It hadn't severed. The thinnest line of connection still ran between us, like a strand of a spider-web across an ocean. It was still there, and I trusted that more than I trusted anything else.

"Bo isn't dead," I said, my voice calm.

The blood drained from Curlin's face, leaving her cheeks ashen. "Vi. It's true. Quill's uncle Hamlin had it from his wife. She was in the park when it happened. She heard the shots."

"He's not dead."

"How do you know?"

"I'd know if he was dead, and he's not. I would feel it."

Curlin's sigh held a note of exasperation. "They've appointed a regent. They've had funerals. The news is in every paper and letter written since the day it happened. The whole world is talking about it."

"The whole world is mistaken."

"Vi—"

I cut Curlin off. "Look, I lived most of my wretched life thinking that my twin was dead. I felt that connection, and I thought it was to my dead twin, that she was trying to pull me into the halls of the gods. And I've seen people whose twins have died. I know what it looks like when the tie is severed. So trust me when I tell you—Bo isn't dead. We'll be hearing from him soon enough."

Aphra studied the bedspread, jaw tight.

"Trust me. Bo's not dead."

"And if you're wrong?" Curlin asked. Neither of them would meet my eyes. "If he is dead? What then? Doesn't that change everything?"

"I'm not wrong."

Curlin's hands knotted into fists at her sides.

"But say you're right. Say Bo's dead." Even knowing they were blatantly false, the words felt like ash in my mouth. "Does his death actually change anything? I don't think it does. The way laborers are treated here is still deplorable, and it has to change. The temple is still using the fruit of this land to control the people of the Alskad Empire, and I still think that we can put a stop to it. So I'll stick to the plan, no matter what happens. I'm going to leave this world a better place than I found it."

Curlin sighed and shrugged. "Believe whatever you need to believe. Just know that denial will only make the grief stronger when you finally let yourself feel it."

"So what's next?" I asked, brushing Curlin's comment aside. "What do we do now?"

Curlin and Aphra exchanged a look.

"We talked to Biz and Neve and Quill, and we came up with a plan. We're going to take over the government."

I stared at them, baffled. I couldn't tell if the pain was addling my wits, or if I'd simply misunderstood. "Ilor is a colony of Alskad," I said slowly. "How the hell do you plan to take control of the government of an empire?"

Aphra laughed. "No one is taking control of an entire empire. Just Ilor."

Curlin rolled her eyes, but couldn't control the smile tugging at the corners of her mouth. "She's going to use her magic on the governor. That's how."

I lay back on the pillows and studied the ceiling, thinking through all the dangers and problems with their plan. There was no part of me that thought Bo was actually dead, and he wouldn't be pleased about losing a whole colony when he found out. But if everyone else believed the news, the colony would be in chaos, and that would make a coup just that much easier.

Finally, decided, I looked at Aphra.

"Well, you won't be doing it without me."

CHAPTER TWENTY

Bo

"Denor is like something out of a fairy tale. It's the most beautiful place I've ever seen. I don't know if its most striking feature is the carefully planned streets and promenades, or all of the incredible, shocking green, or the fact that it seems to preside over the harbor like the home of some formidable giant."

—*from Bo to Vi*

Where the outside of Noriava's palace was all elegant lines and black stone, the interior was bright with warm, gilded wood and sleekly designed and polished furniture. It was breathtaking and overwhelming and somehow immediately comfortable. A pair of white-coated guards led us through the maze of halls, finally stopping in front of a pair of vast bronze doors.

From a pocket deep inside his jacket, Swinton produced the Circlet of Alskad and placed it gently on my head. He swept a few loose curls to the side and gave me a solemn nod and a wink.

"You're a king, meeting a queen to warn her of a threat to you both," he whispered. "Despite her advantage, you must remember that you're equals."

I squeezed Swinton's hand and managed to give him a pale imitation of a smile as he resumed his place by my left shoulder. A panel just to the side of the doors slid open, and a round, bearded face appeared in the window. A moment later, the doors swung open, and the guards stepped aside. Just like we'd planned, I entered first, followed by Swinton and then the girls.

The vast hall was practically bare compared to the rest of the palace. Bright, harsh sunlamps hung from the high ceiling at odd intervals. Cylinders of colored liquids bubbled along the walls, lit from beneath. A steel table long enough to seat nearly a hundred people ran the width of the space, flanked on either side not by chairs or benches, but black-cushioned metal stools spaced evenly. And at the very back of the room, an enormous throne of black stone sat framed by the most complex bronze and glass stills I'd ever seen.

We were nearly a third of the way across the room before I was able to make out the woman seated on the throne. She had long, fiery red hair, skin as pale and wan as skimmed milk and a murderously feline grin. Her simple black silk gown was entirely the wrong color for her complexion. The closer I got to the throne, the more familiar the woman seemed. When we were just a few strides away from the dais, an enormous black cat, seated on her lap, lifted its head and regarded us with wide yellow eyes. In that moment, I knew where I'd seen this woman before.

"You came to my birthday party," I blurted out in Alskader. For a moment, I loathed myself—not only had I thrown away any advantage I might have had from speaking first on a thought-less comment, but I'd started our conversation in Alskader, no less. The least I could've done was manage to speak Denorian. I sounded like a child.

The queen's condescending, haughty mask fell away for a moment, and she broke into a wide grin.

"I came as a guest of your cousins, Patrise and Lisette." Her Alskader held just the slightest hint of the lilting Denorian ac-cent. "I'm surprised you recognized me. It was quite a day for you. Named the heir to the Alskad throne and coming of age, all at the same time. And to lose your mother so soon after, and now poor Runa. I am terribly sorry for the horrible year you've had."

She ran her fingers along the length of her cat for a mo-ment, pondering its thick, twitching tail. "I must say that I'm shocked to see you here, though, so far from the halls of your own palace."

"And alive," I added.

Noriava's smile didn't touch her green eyes as she inclined her head ever so slightly. "Fair. I'd given more than a little weight to the rumors that you'd been assassinated alongside Runa. What I couldn't believe was that the council would appoint that boring nobody—Rylain, is it?—as regent. So when your man brought Lisette's letter this morning, I had it in my mind that the person who walked through those doors would be some sort of scheming impostor."

"I may be many things, but I am still the rightful heir to the Alskad throne," I said solemnly.

Beside me, Pem giggled, and Still punched her in the arm. I shot them a glare, but neither of them saw my warning look. When Pem pinched Still in retaliation, I grabbed Pem by the collar and pulled her to my other side, separating them. Noriava chuckled, and I felt the heat of a blush creep up my neck. Only the weight of the crown on my head kept me from running my hands through my hair and shattering the last shards of the illusion that I was some kind of capable ruler.

"Little ones can be so troublesome, can't they?"

I inclined my head in response, trying to regain my equilibrium, and gestured toward Swinton. This meeting couldn't possibly get any worse. Either I could take back control, or I could resign myself to failure—and I couldn't allow myself to see that as a real option.

"Queen Noriava, allow me to present to you Swinton, of Ilor. He has been a most thoughtful adviser and guide to me for some time now."

Noriava offered Swinton her hand, which he kissed with the slightest bow. As he rose, Swinton winked at the queen. "I'd best warn you now, Majesty, that I'm a dimmy, so if you find yourself frightened by those who've survived the most dreadful kind of grief, I'll take my leave of you."

One of Noriava's perfect eyebrows twitched, and her eyes slid from Swinton to me and back again. Despite the pit of anxiety in my stomach, I kept my eyes locked on hers until she looked down at the cat purring in her lap. "Of course not. Denor doesn't ascribe to Alskad's biases against the diminished. You are welcome in my home."

"What about us?" Still asked, her voice an octave higher and significantly louder than anyone else in the room.

Swinton cleared his throat. I struggled for a moment, looking for the right words, but before I could think of a way to dance around the twins' impropriety without losing any tactical ground with the queen, Noriava stood, unsettling her cat, which gave her a spiteful look and stalked off. Noriava swept past Swinton and me and knelt in front of the girls.

"I am so very sorry to have waited to introduce myself, young ladies. I am Noriava Suchill, Queen of Denor, Duchess of Salemouth and Ladderhorn, Countess of Middlebrookhaven, Baroness of the Riverlands, Protector of the Cascadian Mountains and the Queendom of Denor."

Pem's mouth hung open, just a little, as Noriava offered her a hand. The queen smiled knowingly and added, "I know, it's a bit of a mouthful. You can call me Nori, if you'd like."

Still reached out and took the queen's hand. "I'm Stillness, and this is my sister, Patience. We're King Bo's most trusted valets."

I exchanged a horrified glance with Swinton. King Bo? Noriava would certainly know that something was off about my relationship with the girls now.

"King Bo?" she repeated, a laugh in her voice.

Pem's cheeks went bright red, and Still studied her boots.

"I've never really been one for the formalities," I said, trying to sound nonchalant. "I told them to call me Bo some time ago. I'd be honored if you'd do the same."

Noriava stood. "Then you'll have to call me Nori. I'm not much in favor of formalities, either. Are you hungry? I'll send for something for us to eat, and you can tell me what's brought you to my humble queendom. Would your valets like to join us, or would they rather go down to the kitchens to be doted on and spoiled by the cook?" She smiled at the girls. "You didn't hear it from me, but my cook is particularly impressed with tales of travel and ships. I imagine that she could be persuaded to give you some of her famous steamed sweet buns if you told her about your journey to Denor."

The girls' eyes lit up, and they nodded eagerly. Noriava gestured to a servant in the corner, who waved to the girls and whisked them away through a set of hidden doors. Noriava took a seat on one of the stools in the middle of the table. I sat across from her, and Swinton settled onto a stool beside me. A moment later, a number of servants had silently set our places and poured icy water, bright pink juice and golden Denorian wine into a set of queer glasses. Unlike the stemmed glasses I was accustomed to seeing in Alskad, these were simple crystal cylinders etched with the triangular crest of Denor.

Noriava raised her wineglass and swirled the golden liquid, studying it in the bright light of the sunlamps. Multihued light played across her face like a miniature kaleidoscope of rainbows.

"To the future of Alskad. May it be brighter under your leadership than it has ever been before."

"And to the future of Denor," I replied. "A more capable leader, she couldn't possibly find."

I raised my glass and brought it to my lips, letting the wine lap against them, but not past. There was something in Noriava's eyes that I didn't trust, and I wasn't fool enough to be the first Alskad ruler in three hundred years to be poisoned in the Denorian court. Those sharp green eyes followed my every movement, appraising, calculating. Her small smile as I set my still-full wineglass back on the table was disconcertingly smug, and I blushed.

Swinton drank deeply from his glass and sighed with pleasure. "It's been too long since I've enjoyed a glass of Denorian wine. I thank you, Your Majesty."

"Nori, please," she said. "Now that we're comfortable,

why don't you tell me why you've come to my humble little queendom."

I refused to cede another step of advantage to the queen. I'd come crawling to her court to beg for her help—the least I could do was try to match her bravado and assurance. Under the table, I clenched my hand into a fist to stop its shaking, then lifted the glass of wine to my lips again and drank. The taste was full and round, like grassy meadows and sunshine and sweet summer fruit. As it slid down my throat, I felt the warmth of the alcohol rush through my veins, and I did my best to let it wash away my terror. I reminded myself that I was a king, sitting before a queen, and I had every right to ask for her help.

"I'm curious about what you said before," I deflected. "Do you not experience the same level of violence in the diminished here in Denor?"

A trio of servants appeared carrying steaming glass bowls on wooden platters, which they settled in front of each of us with a flourish. The creamy soup studded with chunks of vegetables and shards of white fish smelled heavenly, but I waited for Nori to respond. She dipped her spoon into her soup and took a bite before shaking her head.

"It happens from time to time. Someone's twin dies, and the other either follows or is overtaken by grief and fury for a time. We have retreats in the country where those who need the space may take the time to act out their grief before rejoining society. Perhaps one in a thousand becomes…" She searched for the word in Alskader, then finally shrugged and said in Denorian, "…a *drægoner?*"

"Diminished?" I asked.

"No. When a person becomes violent with grief. We call them *drægoner*. Like the stories about dragons."

The cat reappeared in Nori's lap, and she absently fed it a bit of fish from her spoon. "For you in Alskad, it is more of a problem, yes? You have your— What are they called? Shriven?"

I nodded. "The Shriven are an arm of the temple, and by extension, the Suzerain. They control the population of the diminished in Alskad, though many of them are themselves among the diminished. In the last six months, I've learned that the Suzerain have been experimenting with the properties of various plants for nearly a hundred years, looking to find something that will trigger, as you call it, the *drægoner* response in the diminished. They've only recently discovered something that consistently works, and they're using it to slowly gain control of the Alskader population."

The queen leaned forward, her eyes locked on me. "You say that the Suzerain have some sort of poison that triggers a violent impulse in the diminished?"

"Not just in the diminished," Swinton cut in. "The effects of the drug are the same on anyone."

"But why?" she asked.

"It's a power grab," I explained, unable to keep the disgust from my voice. "They want control of the people, so they've found a way to control what makes them afraid as well as the force that keeps them safe. Alskaders are turning more and more toward the temple and the Suzerain for guidance and safety, and away from the monarchy. Now they've managed to put a fanatical regent on the throne. Rylain has called for all of the diminished in the capital to be brought to the temple 'for the safety of the people.'" My hands were shaking with fury, with fear, and, I realized, a deep sense of responsibility for the well-being of the people of Alskad.

I looked up from my trembling hands and directly into Noriava's shrewd, cool eyes. "I came to you because I need help. Will Denor stand behind the king of Alskad and help me win back my throne?"

The servants reappeared, whisking my soup away untouched, and replacing it with a salad of tender young greens, sprouts and shaved ribbons of bright carrots and beets. Noriava regarded me silently, sipping her wine as the servants bustled around the room. Swinton's mouth was stuck in an amused half smile, but there was a telltale hint of furrow between his brows. At last, a servant carried a large platter to each of our seats and piled slices of red, rare meat on top of the salad, drizzled it all with a bright green dressing and disappeared once more.

"Why not approach the Samirians?" Noriava asked. "Their army is larger, and they have something to gain from an alliance with Alskad."

"What's that?" I asked, curious. To my knowledge, apart from some fur and smoked fish, Alskad didn't have very much export trade with either Denor or Samiria.

"Ships, of course. Alskad's shipbuilding technology is the most advanced in the world, and you've the mines and ore to make shipbuilding into a lucrative business. Runa, of course, was opposed to sharing technology and trade in general, but if it's an army you need, Samiria would have been the wiser choice by a long shot, even with the difficulty of getting an audience with Abet and Jax. With the right offering, even the Samirian Symposium might have seen fit to open their doors to your pleas." Noriava studied me intently. "So, I'll ask you again. Why Denor?"

I knew I had to tell her, but the idea of revealing such a dangerous secret to a woman I didn't trust at all made my skin crawl. I looked at Swinton for support, and he nodded and gave me a tight, encouraging smile.

"While I am the true heir to the Alskad throne, there is a slight barrier to my asking for assistance from Samiria," I began hesitantly. "Are you a religious woman, Noriava?"

She narrowed her eyes at me, petting the cat in her lap. "I believe in science. I believe in the ability of science to teach us about the world in which we live, and its many complexities. I, myself, don't ascribe to the temple's blind faith in a higher power that is at once forgiving and vengeful. I believe in my own power, in the power of the mind, and in proof. I see no proof in the temple—only willful ignorance. What you've told me today about your problem with the diminished only stands as further proof of that ignorance."

I took a deep breath. "I came to you rather than the Samirians because I am a twin, and I want my sister to rule alongside me with equal power. But I think that Alskad might have some trouble adjusting to the idea, and the support of a singleborn ruler would go a long way. Runa knew, and we were trying to find a way for my sister and me to sit on the throne together. But Runa was murdered, and now, here I am." I looked Noriava straight in the eye. "I need the Denorian army to fight for me. But more than that, I need the Denorian scientists to find a way to stop the temple's poison. I need *your* help, because Samiria can't give me what you can—the support of a singleborn monarch, and the brains of your brightest scientists."

Noriava pinched a piece of meat between her fingers and brought it to her mouth, leaving her fingers smeared with blood. She let the cat lick her fingers as she chewed.

"A twin." She chuckled, a small, private sound. "Leave it to Runa to put a twin in line to rule Alskad." She shook her head ruefully. "You're right in thinking the Samirians wouldn't help you. They'd murder you outright before they'd allow a pair of twins to ascend the Alskad throne. Abet and Jax are only in power because there were no royal singleborn left in Samiria—and because they've convinced the Samirian people that they both hold some sort of amalgam magic."

A regretful expression crossed Noriava's face. "But though I would very much like to help you, Bo, I'm not sure I can. My courtiers may be more liberal than the Alskaders, but they would never agree to stand so firmly against the Suzerain. Even the small tendrils of influence the Suzerain enjoy here are more powerful than you might think, and I cannot risk my throne or the safety of my people on a venture that's so likely to fail. I'm so very sorry, Bo."

My heart sank as she spoke, and I looked down, trying to keep the tears from my eyes.

"You're welcome to stay here as long as you like, naturally," she continued. "In fact, perhaps that would be best. It wouldn't be unprecedented for a dethroned ruler to spend his exile in the court of another country. Your sister could join you. You could be happy here, I think."

It was tempting. The idea of living in this gorgeous country, safe, with Vi by my side. But I couldn't just think about what I wanted, what would make me happy. I had all of the people of Alskad to consider.

"I thank you, Your Majesty, but no. I have a duty to my people. Though if you don't mind, I would love to accept your hospitality for a few days while my ship is resupplied, and I try to formulate a new plan."

Noriava nodded. "Of course. I truly am sorry I can't do more." Then she smiled at me and reached for her wineglass. "For now, let's talk of more pleasant things. Perhaps you can tell me about your time in Ilor. I hear that it's the loveliest land."

Swinton smiled and began to charm Noriava with tales of his childhood in Ilor. As they talked, I stared into my wineglass, thoughts swirling with the possibility—the probability—of failure without the help of the Denorian army.

My throne felt a little further away with each passing moment.

CHAPTER TWENTY-ONE

Vi

"Healing is exhausting, Bo. It makes me feel outside myself, like a stranger in my own body. I'm so ready to leave this bed, this room. I want to be out in the world, doing things, rather than cooped up here with my thoughts and my memories and all the ghosts of my mistakes."

—*from Vi to Bo*

At my request, the painting of the goddesses was removed from my room, but sunlight had faded the paint on the wall around it. Now, a square of cerulean watched me from a sea of pale blue, a reminder of my abandoned faith. The healers tried their best to ply me with medicines to make me sleep, but my dreams were full of the Shriven's screams and Lei's bloodied hands. At least if I stayed awake, I could force myself to think of something other than my failures. Or, at the very least, I could try.

I needed a distraction. So every time the healers saw fit to leave me alone, I hauled myself out of bed and forced my body through the training exercises I'd learned from Curlin. I hated the way I wobbled around, as unsteady as a newborn lamb, but not even the healers' admonishments about the temple's poison and my body's need to heal could keep me in bed.

Sweat dripped from my forehead and landed in fat drops on the wooden floor as I ground through a final set of push-ups. The squeak of a loose floorboard outside my room sent me scrambling back to the bed. I hastily wiped the sweat from my face with a sheet as the door swung open.

"Taking the healers' advice seriously, I see."

I gave Quill a wry smile and patted the bed. "They're overly cautious ninnies. I'm fine."

Quill sat down next to me and reached out to rest his hand on my knee. When I flinched, he pulled back, looking stung.

"I'm sorry," I said, staring down at his hand, as if the words I needed were clenched between his fingers.

"Why are you sorry?" he asked. "You've done nothing wrong."

"Nothing wrong?" I spit, astonished. "Lei is *dead* because of me. And we've got nothing to show for that fight. We accomplished nothing. Nothing except death."

"That's not true," Quill countered. "We got our people off the mountain. We lost fewer than the Shriven. Lives were saved, Vi."

Elbows on my knees, I held my head in my hands. "I don't know if I can do this, Quill. I don't know if I can live with the guilt and the grief and the horror of it all."

Quill put a tentative hand between my shoulder blades, just above the bandaged wound that was my constant, aching reminder of how badly I'd failed. "You've lived with much worse for far longer. You're stronger than you know. And, what's more, you're a natural leader. Those brats would walk through fire for you, and the rest of our folks aren't far behind. We need you, Vi. *I* need you."

I scrubbed my hands over my face. "I don't know if I can be the person you need. I don't know if I'm enough."

The bed shifted as Quill moved to kneel on the worn planks of the floor before me. Gently, he lifted my chin and fixed me in his amber gaze. "I've never once felt like I was enough to face the challenges set before me, but I've always managed. The most anyone can ever ask of you is that you try."

"But these are people's lives, Quill! *Your* life. There has to be someone else. Someone better."

"Vi, I worked so hard to keep you out of this fight, but I was wrong. We need you. Not someone else. You."

I swallowed hard, feeling tears sting my eyes. "I feel broken, Quill. I don't know how to find my way back to myself."

Quill climbed onto the bed, pulled me into his arms and held me close against his chest. I froze there, stiff and swollen with tears held back, until finally, I gave in and cried. I wept and wept, shedding tears for Lei, for everyone we'd lost. For the part of me that'd died in that battle. And for our terrifying and uncertain future.

As I cried, Quill rubbed my back, careful to avoid the bandaged wound, and murmured softly in my ear. When I'd at last cried all the tears I could, Quill handed me a handkerchief.

After I blew my nose, I looked into his kind, compassionate eyes, my heart aching. "I don't know how you can love a wreck like me."

Quill traced my jaw with his finger and leaned in, kissing the skin just below my mouth, my eyelids, my cheekbones. "I wish you could see the version of you that I see. You're fierce and empathetic and giving, and I've never met anyone like you. So long as you hold on to those things, you'll never be a wreck. And even if you don't, I'll still love you."

I flung my arms around his neck and squeezed, ignoring the pain shooting up my back as my wound protested. "I love you, too, Quill. You know that, right?"

Quill nodded, and we collapsed back onto the bed, our fingers laced together and our legs entwined. I kissed him, desperate to sink into the deep abyss of pleasure and freedom that coursed through our bodies like a river, the current pulling us together. I tugged at his shirt, wanting his skin against mine. He pulled my nightdress over my head, and his long, elegant fingers traced my hips, my rib cage, my collarbone. He laid a row of kisses down my stomach and wrapped his arms around my waist.

I lost myself in his touch. Melted into him like so many candles burning through the night. Over and over, he asked, "Is this all right? This?"

And over and over, I breathed the word "Yes."

His fingers trailed up my thighs, and he whispered, "May I?"

In his arms, the pain and the fear and the looming knowledge that I was not, nor would I ever be, enough—everything disappeared. It was just Quill and me, and our skin and our lips and the endless insistence of our need. I took his face in my hands, looked deep into his eyes and kissed him, my *yes* rising and swelling like a wave, flooding us with lust and impatience and desire.

The next morning, when the healers burst into my room, they found Quill and me tangled up in my sheets—me blushing hot as the sun itself, him all smiles and easy confidence.

The healers' eyebrows soared up their foreheads as they eyed the pair of us. I reached for my nightdress, hanging off the narrow bed's wooden frame, but one of the healers clucked her tongue and the other shook her head.

"If you're well enough to do *that*," she said, "I feel confident that you're beyond need of our help. Both of you be sure to drink your contraceptive daily, hear?"

"But don't push yourself too hard," the other healer admonished. "You lot tend to get so antsy to be healed and on your feet that you wind up back in bed because you refuse to take it slow."

Before I could ask what, exactly, she meant by "you lot," they'd vanished back the way they came. I'd spent my whole life judged and feared for being one of the diminished, but now everyone—at least, all of the rebels—knew about Bo, and all of them believed that he was dead. Once more, I'd been cast back into the role of the diminished, despite what I knew in my gut to be true.

Then again, the healers might've only meant that I was one of the rebels. There was no reason for me to get my hackles up.

I pulled my nightdress over my head and glanced at Quill. "Breakfast?"

Laughing, he pulled me back into his arms and kissed me. "Myself, I was hoping they'd tell you to stay in bed another week."

I swatted at his arm, unable to keep my own grin off my face. "If I don't get out of bed soon, Aphra and Curlin are going to take over the government of Ilor without me. I can't let them have all the fun, now can I?"

Quill flashed me a ridiculously exaggerated frown as he hauled himself out of bed. "Fine," he said, "but you are going to listen to the healers, aren't you? You'll take it easy?"

Rolling my eyes, I found a robe and a pair of slippers and put them on. "I'll take care of myself. Promise."

His stomach growled, audible from halfway across the small room, and I quirked an eyebrow at him. "Looks like you're just as ready for something to eat as I am."

We found Mal and Hepsy together at the kitchen table, poring over a thick ledger, their chipped cups of tea and plates of toast forgotten. Hepsy looked up as we entered the room and started. "You're supposed to be in bed!"

"They said I'm well enough to get up. What're the two of you working on?"

Mal and Quill exchanged a look heavy with meaning and understanding before Mal turned his dazzling smile on me. "Hepsy here was kind enough to volunteer her knowledge of the intimate household workings of some of the wealthier Ilorian families, so that I can decide who should bear the financial burden of my brother's revolution—*your* revolution."

I plucked a piece of toast from one of the platters and smeared a thick coating of butter onto the browned bread. "So, what?" I asked, leaning against a counter. "You're going to rob them?"

Hepsy glowered at me. "Of course not. Don't be ridiculous."

"We're just going to sell them things they don't really need at incredibly high markups," Mal said mischievously. "As I'm sure we're all aware, Hepsy isn't exactly suited to the whole 'battle thing' any more than I am. So we've decided to do what we do best."

"Pander to rich idiots?" Myrna's voice came from the doorway behind me, and I spun around and flew into her arms, nearly losing hold of my toast in the process. Myrna hugged me gently, and over her shoulder, I saw Curlin and Aphra waiting in the hall, grinning.

"I hardly think it's pandering," Hepsy protested with a pout. "What're you doing here, anyway? I thought you lot were going to the Whipplestons' warehouse or some such thing."

"We thought, with most of the Shriven out of the city, that we might make a little stop at the bank beforehand." Aphra plunked a large purse onto the table, coins clinking inside. "And it's terribly dangerous to travel with this kind of wealth on your person. You know that."

Grins spread like wildfire through the room, and Hepsy leaned back in her chair, hands covering her face. "We can feed everyone. Good glory, Aphra. We can afford to feed everyone."

"That and more," Aphra replied with a hearty laugh. "As soon as it's safe, we'll rebuild the estate, get the young people teachers, make sure everyone is well taken care of."

"They'll finally get to start the new lives they deserve," Curlin said, her smiling eyes trained on Aphra. "That said, this is only the beginning. We still have so much to do. Vi, are you sure you're ready to be out of bed?"

I poured myself a cup of tea from the pot on the table and sat down. "You can't very well keep me cooped up in that room forever. How can I help?"

Myrna, Aphra and Curlin settled themselves on the benches, and Quill perched on the counter behind me. Together, the seven of us talked through the plan they'd concocted while I was laid up. Each time one of us managed to find a weak spot, the rest banded together to patch it. And by the time the cook came to shoo us out of the way while she put together our supper, we were as ready as we'd ever be.

I didn't notice until we'd all gone our separate ways that none of them, not a one, had mentioned Bo. I wondered if their care, the tender way they'd been treating me, had more to do with his purported death than my actual injuries. Just the thought of it sent a shiver of fury through my veins. I knew in my heart that he wasn't gone, but my heart had been wrong before.

A sliver of doubt, as minuscule and devious as a splinter, niggled at me, asking if I wasn't deluding myself. If they weren't right after all. If, Dzallie forbid it, Bo really had been killed.

CHAPTER TWENTY-TWO

Bo

"I wish you could see the enormous cliffs that surround the Denorian harbor at Salemouth. They are as stark and fearsome as the throne their leader occupies. Where Alskad's cold is buffered by our furs and rugs and the fires roaring in every hearth, Denor is a place of quiet. Of clean lines and frigid stone and a society tightly controlled not just by their own will, but by their eyes on each other."

—from Bo to Vi

On our second evening in the Denorian palace, Swinton answered a sharp knock on the door of our rooms. A liveried servant offered Swinton a thick sheet of folded paper held closed with a silver clasp. Before Swinton could finish unwinding the long, lilting Denorian phrase for thanks, the servant was already halfway down the dim hall.

Noriava had given us a generous suite of rooms in a remote corner of the palace last night. The wide windows looked out over the mountains, and we'd spent most of the past two days settling in, recovering from our travels and trying to regroup.

In addition to a sitting room, dressing rooms and a bath chamber, there was a small, elegant bedroom for Swinton and one decked out in cream and gold that Pem and Still were given to share. My room, on the other hand, was far too large to be comfortable, sparsely decorated in navy and forest green. It wasn't a homey space, with its stark, austere furniture and minimalist design, but it was elegant and befitting a visiting regent, and for that, I was grateful.

I looked up from my book as Swinton closed the door and Pem and Still tumbled out of their room like a sudden storm. Swinton, immune to their antics at this point, flicked open the silver clasp to read the message, then glared down at the piece of paper. "It seems we've been summoned."

"Summoned where?" I asked.

"Can we please come?" Pem whined, clinging to Swinton's arm like one of the small Ilorian monkeys we'd seen in the jungle.

"You don't even know what we've been invited to," I said, rising to my feet.

Still launched herself onto Swinton's shoulders as he strode by the couch where she'd been crouching. He handed the invitation to me with a grin before walking out onto the balcony, where he took hold of each of the girls by the backs of their vests and held them over the low railing. Our rooms were on the second floor, above a deep fountain, so while they were never in any danger, the girls shrieked and squawked with delighted terror until Swinton set them safely back on the stone tiles of the balcony.

"You two aren't fit for royal company," Swinton said, laughter singing through his words.

Pem flung herself onto one of the long couches. Still, leaning against the doorframe, cocked her head and fixed me in a quizzical glare. "If you're our brother, and you're royalty, doesn't that make us royal, too?"

"Not…exactly." I looked to Swinton for help, but he simply smirked at me. "We have different fathers, see? And my father was the one who was royal. But honestly, someone being royalty or not? That doesn't matter at all. It's not even a real thing. We're no different, you and me." Seeing Still's skeptical expression, I added, "Queen Noriava was a little girl once, too. I remember her tearing through the halls of the palace in Penby when I was just a boy. This was before her parents passed away. It was some sort of diplomatic visit, and Patrise and Lisette were teasing her mercilessly. Rather than curling up in her room and weeping, which is what I would've done at that age, she plucked an ornamental sword off the wall, chased the two of them down and made them play with her. She was a lot like the pair of you, honestly."

Still narrowed her eyes. "When we get home, I think you should make us royalty. Maybe not the whole family. But Pem and me, definitely."

"I think you missed the point of Bo's story, scrapling," Swinton said. "Now scoot, the two of you, and find something to entertain yourselves with. We've a party to attend."

Hand in hand, Swinton and I followed the rush of servants and the low hum of conversation and music through the dim halls of the palace, hoping they would lead us to Noriava's party before we were unforgivably late. Because the invitation was written in Alskader, and neither of us spoke Denorian well enough to ask for directions, finding our way to the atrium took far longer than I'd expected.

When the servants flung open the doors and announced us, the room was already filled with a sea of courtiers. They all turned to study the pair of us, staring unabashedly, taking in every detail of our appearances before turning back to pick at canapés and snipe at each other.

"What do we do now?" Swinton murmured into my ear.

I squeezed his hand and sized up the room. The atrium was twice the size of the throne room where Noriava had first received us. Moonlight filtered in through the glass ceiling, and tiny solar lights twinkled along the beams, mimicking the stars. Clusters of architecturally ambitious settees and chairs sat beneath trees in wide stone pots, some heavy with fruit, others hung with night-blooming flowers. Servants glided along the black stone pathways carrying trays full of wineglasses and bite-size delicacies. Beside a fountain, a group of musicians played soft music on string instruments.

"I think we should start making friends," I said.

"You know how dogs can sense the alpha in whatever new group they encounter?" Swinton asked.

I looked at him, eyes narrowed. I didn't see where he was going with the analogy at all. "What do dogs have to do with anything?"

"We need to find the alphas and befriend them first," he explained. "That's how we make them care about you. We make you an alpha. Who do you think the most powerful person in the room is?"

"Aside from the queen?"

"Obviously."

Everyone in the room had begun to studiously ignore us almost as soon as we were announced. I looked from group to group, searching for the person who drew their eyes.

"There," Swinton said, nodding toward a bright corner of the atrium where a knot of Denorian courtiers draped in Samirian silk and glittering with jewels sat, their rapt attention focused on a small, bright-eyed woman in neat military uniform. She sat, back straight as a sword, in one of the most uncomfortable-looking chairs I'd ever seen. She was speaking in low, soft tones and animatedly illustrating her words with her hands. Nearly everyone in the room glanced her way from time to time.

"You're right," I said, but before we could make our way over, Noriava appeared in a cloud of perfume and chilly air, her cheeks bright with cold, and swept me into her arms.

"I'm so pleased that you came!" she exclaimed.

"Thank you for having us," I said courteously.

Swinton bowed over her hand, the picture of elegance and graceful manners. Laughing, the queen stopped a passing waiter and plucked three glasses of wine the color of sunrise from his tray. She raised her glass to Swinton and me.

"To leadership," she toasted.

"To friendship," I countered.

Smiling wickedly, Swinton said, "To negotiation."

Noriava sipped her wine and laced her arm, wrist heavy with silver and gold bangles, through mine. "Bo, darling, may I interest you in a game of Caulixian?"

I managed to keep my internal grimace off my face and let Noriava lead me away. I hated board games, and Caulixian, with its overly complex rules and strategies, was the worst of them. Swinton gave me a little wave and wandered down a flowerbed-lined path toward the woman we'd seen before.

Noriava and I found a Caulixian board set up under a pergola draped in thickly perfumed vines of night-blooming flowers. Noriava settled herself on a precarious-looking stool. Her cat appeared, as if from nowhere, and pounced into her lap. I eyed the board, trying to pull the rules of the game from the murky depths of my memory. I'd played as a child, of course, but when it became achingly clear that I didn't have the interest or attention it would take to master the game, my father had given up and played instead with my mother, or with Rylain when she came to visit.

"You can take the opening move, if you'd like. You are my guest, after all."

I slid a piece from the left side of the board forward three spaces and drew a card from the stack. The Tower. Destruction or liberation, depending on Noriava's draw.

"An unfortunate start, I think," she said.

"I'll admit that it has been ages since I sat at a Caulixian board and peered into the future."

"Do you believe in the divination power of the game, then?"

I sipped my wine and swirled the orange liquid, peering down at the unusual color washing the crystal bowl of the glass.

"My father did, I think. He played often."

Noriava's long fingers traced a line down her cat's spine, drawing furrows in its thick fur. "He's the one who taught my parents, you know. Your father's the reason I know how to play."

I looked across the table at her, and for a moment, I saw the mask of the ruler fall away, revealing the vulnerable young woman underneath. Alone. An orphan with a country to protect and adjudicate and defend. The responsibility of nearly a million souls like a weight around her neck. Smudges of sleeplessness darkened the delicate skin beneath her lovely eyes and deepened the hollows of her cheeks.

Then she straightened her spine and smiled, and the lonely girl I'd seen disappeared, replaced by the queenly mask once again.

"I didn't realize your parents knew mine, but of course they would have."

Noriava took one of the knobby pawns and tapped it twice, moving diagonally across the squares of the board to meet mine. She drew a card and stared at it for a beat too long, a slow smile spreading across her lips, which were painted a red as bright as her hair.

She set her card on top of mine. The Queen of Swords.

"An apt card, indeed," I said, relinquishing my pawn to her.

"Some people interpret her as cold or malicious," Noriava said. "But I like to think of her as discerning, driven. Her card is about power and relationships. She's searching for the right partner, not just the most easily accessible."

It was an odd interpretation, one I'd not heard before, but I could see the steps that led her to it. The gilded queen looked out over a mountain, hand outstretched, as if welcoming or seeking. If you looked past the spikes of her crown, the sword in her hands and the blood-soaked bag at her feet, you could perhaps interpret her expression as wistful.

"Do you find yourself pressured to choose a spouse?" I asked.

"The laws of succession in Denor are significantly more stringent than your Alskader traditions. The rulers of my country must be the singleborn child of royal blood born to the current monarch. If I don't produce an heir soon..." Noriava paused, her lips compressed. "Well, to put it simply, my continued presence on the throne is closely tied to the succession." She gave me a wry smile. "But let's not talk about such serious things. It's a party, after all."

Noriava's cat bristled and leaped off her lap to go stalking through the bushes. A ways down the path, I caught sight of the deep, tawny gold of Swinton's hair. He was striding toward us, his dazzling smile firmly in place. Noriava followed my eyes and sighed. "Perhaps we should continue our game another time."

I glanced up at Swinton as he ducked under the curtain of vines at the edge of the pergola. "Swinton won't mind if we finish the round—will you?"

Swinton kissed the top of my head. "I wouldn't dream of interrupting. I just needed an excuse to extricate myself from the world's least interesting conversation with some wool trader who refuses to believe that I'm Ilorian."

"Ilorian? Not Alskader?" Noriava narrowed her eyes. "That's quite a statement to make in front of the Alskad heir."

Swinton grinned, squeezing my shoulder. "Bo knows my politics."

Noriava looked between us, a small smile spreading across her lips. "Do tell me how you met, won't you?"

I launched into the story as Noriava pondered the Caulixian board, glancing, from time to time, between Swinton and me. I felt for her. It was difficult enough to carry the responsibility of a nation on your shoulders. To have that responsibility contingent upon finding a partner and producing an heir as well? It was enough to give a person hives. I hoped, for Noriava's sake, that she found someone soon.

After an evening of Caulixian and uncomfortable small talk with the Denorian gentry that stretched almost until dawn, Swinton and I dragged ourselves back to our suite of rooms. I poured two tall glasses of water from the pitcher on the sideboard and handed one to Swinton, who was propped against a doorframe, slowly shedding his party-going frippery in a pile of embroidered wool, saturated silk and lace on the floor.

"I'm exhausted," I said, pecking him on his slightly scruffy cheek. "Sweet dreams. I'll see you in the morning."

"It is the morning," he groused.

"Then I'll see you after a few hours of rest, yeah?"

Swinton caught my hand and brought it to his lips. "Come with me. We haven't been alone since we got here, and there are things I'd like to say to you."

Despite the weariness that weighed on my very bones, the feeling of Swinton's lips on my skin sent a shudder of need from my heart to my toes and back again. Gooseflesh rippled up my arms as he wrapped one hand around my waist and pulled me close to him. "I miss you, Bo. I know it's been awful, but I feel like we've barely had a moment alone together since we got here."

I wanted to go with him, to slide beneath the thick coverlets on his bed. I wanted to tangle my fingers in his hair and wrap my legs around his. I wanted to kiss him until the whole world fell away and there was nothing left except his lips on mine, his hands on my body and the sweet breath of desire as it passed between us.

"Pem and Still will probably be up and about at any moment," I cautioned.

"And they've no idea what's between us," Swinton teased. "Is that it? You're afraid for the innocence of those wild things?"

"No. Of course not. I just…"

Swinton took my hand. "Come on."

I didn't have a good reason to say no. It wasn't as though we hadn't shared a bed a hundred times before. The only difference now was that we were in a foreign country, and my only chance of regaining my life, my purpose, my throne, was through the goodwill of the queen who was our host.

And I'd seen the way her mouth went hard when Swinton's fingers brushed my skin.

Too tired to try to find the words to capture the apprehension seeping through my veins, I followed Swinton into his bedroom, leaving a trail of our clothes from the door to the bed.

I crawled between the sheets, luxuriating in the cool, soft linen. The Denorians may have been known for their wool, but the linen they produced was just as fine, if not finer. Swinton pulled me into his arms, my back nestling against his warm, firm torso. He nuzzled my neck, sending shivers of delight through my body and clearing a path through my exhaustion.

"I think Noriava will help us," I said.

Swinton made an interrogative hum against my ear.

"I think she'll help. We just need to find a way to make it worthwhile for her."

Swinton flopped onto his back and sighed. "What was it you said about being tired?"

"I just wish I knew what she might want. How, exactly, does one bribe a queen?" I sat up and pulled a tasseled pillow onto my lap.

"Aren't you supposed to be the expert on royalty, bully?"

I shrugged, fingering one of the tassels.

Swinton propped himself up on one elbow and fixed me in his gaze. "You can't trust her. It doesn't matter what you give her or what she promises—the only things Noriava cares about are herself and her country. And unless you can come up with a way to please both her and her country, you're shit out of luck. I think it's well on time to cut our losses, make our way back to Ilor and see if we can't wrangle some help from Vi and her rebels."

"Don't you think they have enough on their hands?" I asked. "Plus, I already wrote to Vi and the Whipplestons. Once they accomplish what they've set out to do, perhaps they'll come to our aid. But we've no idea how long that will take, and the clock is ticking."

"Noriava is a liar, Bo. You'd see it in her eyes if you'd just open your own."

"And what about all those people in Ilor and Alskad, Swinton? The rest of the diminished who've been used and poisoned by the Suzerain? What about them?" I could feel anger cutting through my voice, but I was too tired to stop it. Too tired to care. "Even if we do as you say, and wait for Vi to come and save us, what then? We still need Noriava. We still need her help to find a cure. I'll not go home empty-handed. Not with so many vulnerable lives on the line." I curled my fists in my lap, not sure if I wanted to scream or kiss Swinton or both. "So if we can't trust her, how, exactly, are we supposed to get her help?"

Swinton grinned at me, his smile brighter than the sunlight streaming in through the curtains. "We trick her, of course. But you're going to have to trust me, little lord, because I can guarantee that you're not going to like my plan."

I grimaced, but lifted the coverlet and patted the bed beside me. "If you're going to insist on our doing something horrible, I must insist that you kiss me while you tell me about it."

Hair loose and wild about his shoulders, Swinton pulled me into his arms, laying kisses along my neck and shoulders as his hands strayed across my body and he told me about his plan.

CHAPTER TWENTY-THREE

Vi

"I sometimes forget that there are times when it is better to have a friend by your side than an entire army. I spent so much of my life with only one or two people I could call a friend, and now it is as though the sheer bounty of people I call my friends threatens to break me into pieces from time to time."

—*from Vi to Bo*

Curlin settled into the alcove bed across from where I sat and watched as I tried to unsnarl my tangled curls and cursed under my breath. It was hard to do anything with the stitches across my back. Every time I moved in the wrong direction, they pulled and sent spikes of pain right into the center of my chest.

"So."

I looked up at her. "So?"

"How're you holding up? With everything?"

"What do you mean, 'everything'?"

She looked uncomfortable for a moment. "Well, with Bo's death—"

"Bo's not dead."

Curlin sighed. "Vi…"

"Leave it," I snapped, then changed the subject. "How many did we lose in the battle with the Shriven?"

"Of our thirty that went in? Ten. The brats are all safe at our camp with everyone else. Biz and Neve's group lost more, but they went in with more. Our numbers right now are just over a hundred. Once we take control of the governor's seat, we'll start filtering them into town. It'll be harder for the Shriven to challenge us outright with Aphra in the governor's mansion, especially now that she has access to her money. We'll start using guerrilla tactics to pick them off a few at a time. It's not efficient, but we need their numbers down and their morale low before we try to face them head-on again."

"Do you really think it's a good idea to give Aphra that much power?" I swallowed, looking for a delicate way to say what needed to be said. "I know you two seem to have agreed to a truce, but she's got a fair uncommon sense of what's right and what's wrong."

Curlin snorted. "The woman doesn't have anything close to a conscience, and you know it. She's not evil, not by a long stretch, and there's something in her that I've grown awfully fond of, but she's certainly not perfect. She murdered her husband in cold blood, after all. Now, that's not to say she'll go slaughtering the innocent or enslaving anyone. She's well fixed on being a savior to the people of Ilor, and she'll do anything it takes to put herself in that position."

"That's what I'm worried about," I muttered.

Curlin nodded knowingly. "So, no, I don't think it's a good idea to hand everything over to her on a platter. She needs someone around to check her, and remind her not to use her magic too much or too often. To help her remember where the lines between right and wrong rest, and where she can cross them. That's where Hepsy will come in handy. She's not fully committed to the cause yet, but she's coming to see just how awful the temple can be, and Aphra respects her. It helps that Hepsy's not afraid of Aphra in the slightest, too."

"Do we know anyone who remembers the difference between right and wrong?" I asked. "Because I'm not sure that I do."

"You're far too hard on yourself. Everyone feels like they've crossed a line after a battle."

I bit the inside of my lip and pointed to a zigzag tattooed on the inside of Curlin's wrist.

"What's that one?"

We'd started playing this game when Curlin and I'd been hidden away in the Whipplestons' house while our injuries healed. It seemed like a lifetime ago now. Each of the Shriven's tattoos had a different meaning, and the black lines that trailed over every inch of her skin told the story of her training and service to the order. I'd always thought that the Shriven's tattoos had just made them look doubly vicious, obscuring the lines of their faces and highlighting the scars that crisscrossed their skin. But as Curlin had explained the stories behind her tattoos, I'd come to see the beauty in the practice.

Curlin gave a short, humorless chuckle, and ran her finger along the tattoo. "Sawny gave me that one."

I took a sip from my mug, trying to cover the pang of grief that hit me every time I heard his name, and waited for her to tell me the rest of the story.

"You must remember. You were there."

"I'm fair certain I'd remember Sawny giving you a tattoo."

"No, knot-brain. He broke my wrist. I've a line like this tattooed over every bone I've ever broken."

My eyes flashed to the ring finger on my left hand. One

of the temple's foundling brats had caught me unawares in a hallway and snapped it like a twig when I was eleven.

Curlin sighed. "Remember? Sawny bet me that he could steal more sweets from the queen's birthday to-do than I could."

I smiled. "And you, featherhead that you were, stuffed cakes down your shirt in full view of the guards, tripped over a step on the way out of the park and fell ass over elbows in front of the queen's carriage. I do remember, though how you count that as Sawny's fault, I'll never understand."

Curlin didn't bother to hide her grin. "It was his terrible idea in the first place." She paused, sobering. "I miss him, too, Vi. You know that, right?"

"Of course," I said, then looked down at my hands, thinking. "Do you know how to do it?"

"Do what?"

"Tattoo."

Sitting up in bed, Curlin cocked her head at me. "Why?"

"I want one. A few. I don't see any reason why the Shriven should be the only people who can tell their stories on their skin."

"It hurts. A lot."

I rolled my eyes at her. "Can you do it or not?"

Curlin looked me up and down, considering. "Sure. Let me see if I can find the things I need."

An hour later, I was flat on my stomach, trying not to writhe around as Curlin drove ink into my skin with a tattooing stick she'd cobbled together. In an effort to distract myself from the searing pain, I tugged on the thread of our earlier conversation.

"If someone needs to stay with Aphra, to tame her, shouldn't you be the one to do it?"

"That's never the point of a friendship, at least not one I'd want any part of," Curlin said. "Besides, *you* need me right now. Every one of the Shriven in Ilor is looking for you. You need someone to watch your back. I've been Shriven, and I know how they think." She paused for a moment, then added, "What about Mal? Think he could help keep Aphra in line?"

"Only if she had something to lose by not paying attention to them," I said, gritting my teeth as Curlin went to work on a line that looped around the back of my arm and down close to my armpit.

"Breathe, Vi. It's just pain. It's temporary."

An idea struck me. "What about the governor? We need the governor to either step down or put a plan in place that will enforce the rights of the contracted laborers, right? In addition to stopping the production of the philomena tincture, of course."

Curlin, bent awkwardly over my arm, grunted in assent.

"And we need someone to keep Aphra on task. So why not combine the two? Rather than just deposing the governor, we can show her how powerful Aphra is instead—Aphra can use her magic to make the governor sign the new labor laws. Then we can promise that she'll have the chance to run out her term as governor under Bo's rule, but only if she agrees to Aphra being her cogovernor. If they don't come to a unanimous decision, no action can be taken. That way if one of them is killed or steps down, the other loses their authority. The governor will understand how Aphra's magic works and check her, and Aphra can play the role of savior and leader."

I let the silence hang between us for a few minutes as Curlin continued to work on my arm.

"I won't manipulate anyone, Vi. Not when they're on our side."

"I didn't—"

"I know," Curlin interrupted, "and you might have a good idea here. Aphra needs a check, and we need a figure of authority on our side. But we need to tell her from the first what we're about. And we need to suss out this governor's priorities. Won't be worth a damn if she's only in service for her own gain."

I nodded, and Curlin smacked the back of my head lightly. "Don't move."

Hours later, in the deep, quiet part of the night, Curlin pronounced me finished and brought me a mirror. She'd tattooed lines and symbols up my arm and across my shoulders, just above my healing wound. It was a gorgeously intentional convergence of looping, swirling beauty and stark geometric design. I moved my arm, examining each line, each symbol.

"You'll have to tell me what it all means," I breathed.

Curlin smoothed ointment over the tender skin. "These symbols only show the parts of your life I know. I'll do more as we see how the rest of your story unfolds."

She tapped a pair of overlapping circles she'd tattooed on the back of my arm, just above my elbow. "This, though, is for us. It means I'll always be next to you, guarding your weaker side."

"Thank you," I said, fumbling for the words to tell her how much her gesture meant to me. Even after the whole world had done its best to tear us apart, we had found our way back to each other. Back to our friendship. To being family for each other.

The governor of Ilor was, as Aphra put it, "disinclined to grant us an audience." Irritated, Curlin strapped on her most terrifying collection of weapons and paid the governor a visit in the middle of the night that quickly changed her mind. The next day, Curlin, Aphra, Quill and I strode over to the governor's mansion, dressed in the most ferociously elegant clothes we'd been able to come up with on short notice.

The Ilorian temple had recently entrusted the Whipplestons with transporting some goods back to the main temple in Alskad, unaware of their connection to the resistance. We'd plundered the temple's shipment and come up with all sorts of gems and jewels to outfit ourselves, and a bit of coin besides. Mal and Hepsy made a great show of disapproving of the theft, but they didn't do anything to stop us, and so we'd gleefully walked away from the warehouse with heavy pockets.

Tattoos still healing, I'd adapted an old black Ilorian gown to fasten over just one of my shoulders. The dark silk set off the black ink of my new tattoos, and I'd used borrowed makeup to line my eyes in black, as well. With a thick belt of woven gold taken from the temple's hoard, I'd fastened a set of wickedly sharp ceremonial knives to my waist. I left my hair curling loose and wild around my shoulders.

The result was more than a little fierce. The finishing touch was a golden cuff, much like the one Bo wore about his wrist, the symbol of his place in the Trousillion line of the singleborn. When I came across it in the temple's trunks of finery and jewels, I'd stared at it for a moment, wondering where it'd come from, then slid it onto my wrist and locked it into place. It was the only piece of jewelry I wore.

Aphra and Curlin had outfitted themselves in loose trousers and sleeveless silk tunics that no doubt hid myriad weapons. They dripped with so many gemstones that calling them gaudy would have stopped woefully short of the reality, yet somehow, they managed to appear the height of elegance.

Quill, in deference to his brother, had refused to kit himself out in stolen wealth. He'd simply taken a pile of cash and bought himself a new set of boots and a shirt that hadn't been soaked in mud, blood and smoke. But when Curlin, Aphra and I'd appeared in the Whipplestons' sitting room, he'd looked me up and down slowly, a grin spreading over his face. When he started to whistle, I threw a pillow at him.

When we entered the governor's office, we found her sitting behind an enormous gilded wood desk, hands clasped in her lap and jaw clenched. Aphra went to stand behind her and picked up a folder, flipping it open. Quill threw himself into a chair and settled his new boots on the desk. I grinned, realizing now why he'd paid no mind to the muck we'd walked through on our way to the mansion.

"What do you want?" the governor, Ysanne, snapped. "I'm a busy woman, and I haven't time to waste with a bunch of rabble-rousers."

I flicked my eyes over the woman, assessing. "This position. Is it appointed or inherited?"

Ysanne narrowed her eyes. "Appointed."

"Then if I were you, I would listen very, very carefully to what my friend Aphra has to say. Otherwise, you'll be out of a job, a home and any sort of power you now enjoy before the year is out."

Ysanne started to speak, but Aphra laid a finger on the governor's lips and said, "You'll put in place a plan that will enforce the rights of the contracted laborers. You'll also announce today that any person who has been serving as a contract laborer will be entitled to back wages for the term of their contract they have already served. Should they wish to remain with their employer, their new contract will include a fair wage and an at-will termination of the contract at any point in time, with severance, should the employer be responsible for the termination. Further, new labor laws and a minimum wage meant to ensure the rights of the workers will go into effect immediately." Aphra turned to me. "What did we say, Vi? A hundred gold *ovstri* a year, plus room and board?"

I studied the lavishly decorated office. "Two hundred and fifty, at least. If Governor Ysanne's office is any indication of what they can afford."

"Absolutely out of the ques—"

"Aphra, care to explain yourself to the governor?"

"Happily," Aphra said with a grin. "You see, Ysanne, I'm an amalgam." The governor paled. "For a long time, I didn't think that really meant anything. Recently, though, I've learned that if I say five little words, all put together neatly in a row, you'll be compelled to do exactly as I tell you. Would you like a demonstration?"

The governor shook her head, clearly terrified.

"Best show her anyway," Curlin said, handing Aphra the sheaf of papers we'd drawn up.

"Listen to me. Hear me, Ysanne," Aphra said, and the faint glow of golden light shimmered around her body like waves of heat coming off a fire. "You will sign these papers, and you will uphold the law you make by doing so. Do you understand? In addition, you will put a stop to the production of the philomena tincture and cancel all the temple contracts in Ilor."

Ysanne picked up the pen lying on her desk, dipped it into the ink and began to sign, tears running down her cheeks.

"Don't be sad," I said. "Think of it this way. You're finally getting to do some good in the world. That should thrill you."

"I'm not crying because I am sad," Ysanne hissed. "I'm crying because I'm furious."

"Oh, well," Curlin said. "So much for making her a better person. Should we execute her and put someone else in her place?"

"I imagine that wouldn't go over well with my brother," I replied. "He does hate to see members of his government put out of work."

"Your brother?" Ysanne asked.

"Oh, yes," I said smugly. "You wouldn't know. My brother, Ambrose Oswin Trousillion Gyllen. King of the Alskad Empire, the Colonies of Ilor, the Great Northern Waste, blah, blah, blah. You've heard all the titles a million times."

Ysanne's eyes narrowed. "*Prince* Ambrose is an only child. And he's dead."

"Wrong on both counts, my friend." I perched on the edge of her desk and studied the gold cuff I'd locked on to my wrist. "I'm going to let you in on a little secret. Before the year is out, you'll be swearing your allegiance to King Ambrose, and you'll do it knowing he has a twin. A twin who broke the Shriven force in Ilor, sat on your desk and forced you to make history by doing the right thing for once in your godsforsaken life."

"Where's your proof?"

I drew a folded piece of paper out of my pocket. Along with his first letter to me, Bo had sent a document, signed and sealed by himself, Gerlene and a witness, which stated in clear terms what his relationship was to me—and his wish that should anything happen to his person, I should take the throne of Alskad in his stead. Quill and Mal had kept the document in their safe until I'd asked them to retrieve it this morning.

I slid the paper across the table. Ysanne studied it carefully, taking a moment to look at the seals under a magnifying glass.

When she handed it back to me, her mouth had gone tight and her deep brown eyes were calculating behind her spectacles.

"The Shriven cannot be broken, and you're stupid to think they can. The moment they catch wind of your plans, they'll do what they came here to do and ensure the profit and safety of the Ilorian people."

Curlin gave a dark chuckle. "Aphra, did you notice how she put profit before safety?"

"I did. That's just the sort of thinking we need to change, isn't it, my dear?"

"No one is going to rescue you, Ysanne," Quill said. "The resistance isn't just in the mountains. They're everywhere. They're on your staff. They're in your shops. They're walking your streets. And they all report back to us. Don't think that you can do anything unseen. We are always watching you."

Aphra spun slowly around, studying the room. "There seems to be plenty of space here, Ysanne. I think I'll move in. Better to do the business of governing with you that way. Don't you think? Your cook, Ezra, already knows me fairly well, and I'm sure the other staff won't mind adjusting to a few more residents in the governor's mansion."

The blood drained from Ysanne's tawny face. "Promise me that you won't hurt my wife or our children. I'll agree to all of your terms, so long as they stay safe."

I laid a hand over Ysanne's. "You misunderstand us. We don't want to hurt *anyone*. We want *everyone's* spouses and children to stay safe. That's the point of this whole endeavor—to stop treating some people like they somehow have more value or worth than others just because of the uncontrollable circumstances of their lives."

"Expect to meet the new force of Ilorian peacekeepers this

evening," Curlin said. "Until then, I think Aphra might like to pick out a suite of rooms?"

Ysanne stood, but before she could speak, Aphra looped an arm through the stout governor's, grinning.

"I think we're going to be able to do a great deal of good together, you and me." She smiled brightly at the rest of us. "Why don't you all join us for supper tonight here at the mansion? Perhaps Ysanne's brother Tandy and his family can come, too? Nothing like breaking bread to celebrate a new beginning, eh?"

Smirking, Quill rose to his feet and offered me his arm. Before we left the room, I turned back one last time.

"Governor Ysanne, were things here and at home not so very dire, we wouldn't have come up from under you like this," I said apologetically. "Curlin and I'll explain more thoroughly over supper why we had to do what we did today. I think you'll find that sharing power with Aphra is not so terrible. She's wickedly cunning and has a good mind for business. And she, like you, only wants what's right for the people of Ilor. I'll thank you ahead of time for agreeing to work with her."

Ysanne nodded her head jerkily, and I gave her a sly smile in return. "And just remember, you know how her magic works now. She can't use it on you again unless you let her."

Aphra stuck her tongue out at me, then grinned.

CHAPTER TWENTY-FOUR

Bo

"I feel as though I must write of cheerful things. My letters so often bear too much of a burden to place on your shoulders. So I will give you news of Pem and Still, who have been of enormous help to me here in Denor. I truly don't know if I could manage without them. And to think, when they asked to come, I thought I was the one doing them a favor."

—from Bo to Vi

Small hands jostled me out of my sleep in the gray, predawn stillness several days after Noriava's party, and it took me a disconcerting few minutes to remember that I was in a borrowed bed in her palace in Denor. Every night since we'd arrived, I'd dreamed of Vi. They were grim, desperate dreams, fogged with oppressive heat and punctuated by the shrill calls of birds. I fumbled in the blankets for Swinton's warm hand, the pain and fear of my dream still clinging to me, but the mattress beside me was empty.

Before I'd disentangled myself from the sheets, a lamp flickered on, and I found myself face-to-face with Pem. In the dim light of the single lamp, her sharp cheekbones and wide eyes were so much like Vi's that I wondered for a moment if I might still be dreaming. But then Pem's mouth split in a snaggletoothed grin, and she shoved a robe into my lap.

"Best come with me. There's a conversation in the works, and me and Still think you'll not want to miss it."

"Pem," I said wearily, "my head is pounding, and if you're hauling me out of bed to hear some drunken butler drone on and on about the long-forgotten days when murderous bandits and thieves roamed Denor's roads and waterways, I will actually throw you off the nearest cliff and into the sea. Do you know where Swinton is?"

"Ain't stupid enough to do that twice," Pem muttered, ignoring my question. "Hurry up. Still's got a fair good memory, but she was getting sleepy."

She took my hands and hauled me, grumbling, to my feet. I slid them into a pair of soft-soled slippers waiting by the side of Swinton's bed, wrapped the thick woolen robe tight over my pajamas, warding against the bite of the winter air wafting through the palace, and followed Pem into the hall. She slid through the shadows, up narrow flights of stairs and down dark, empty corridors where dust swirled through the air, telling the tale of how seldom these passages saw use.

"We've not been here a full week yet," I grumbled. "How have you already found your way around the bowels of this castle?"

Pem stopped and turned to glare at me, a finger to her lips. She hissed, "I ain't been sitting around feeling sorry for myself. You gave me a job, and I've been doing it. Now hush. We're almost there."

We snuck through a small door and Pem tiptoed down

a frighteningly steep spiral staircase. An unexpected wave
of fear washed through me as I leaned over the railing and
peered into the darkness. At the base of the stairs, light slatted through an ornately carved screen, and muffled voices
echoed up the stairwell. Pem leaned in close to the screen
and gestured furiously for me to follow her. I began to descend, but before I'd even reached the bottom, I recognized
the voices and ice filled my veins.

"He'll never agree to it." Swinton's voice came through the
screen as clearly as if he stood next to me. His soft Ilorian accent was strong, the way it got when he was tired, and I edged
closer to the screen, trying to see beyond.

Still and Pem moved out of my way and pressed themselves
into a corner of the tiny alcove. Through the holes in the thick
wooden screen, I could just make out a sleek, opulent room,
all beautifully carved blond wood and elegantly upholstered
seating bathed in the glow of dozens of sunlamps. Swinton
sat on the edge of a long, low sofa, his head in his hands and
his long hair in wild disarray. Noriava lounged on a chaise
in a loosely draped robe, lazily plucking berries from a bowl,
dipping them into a cloud of whipped cream and devouring
them one by one.

"You keep saying that," Noriava said, "but I simply don't
agree. He's a reasonable, albeit misguided, young man, and
he's clearly committed to his people and his throne. He'll do
what's right for them, and this *is* right."

My mind raced, trying to piece together the possibilities
hidden within her words. How had this conversation even
come about? I'd hardly seen Noriava in the last few days, much
less had time to think through the ideas that Swinton and I
had discussed. It wasn't supposed to go like this. I was meant
to be the one to convince her. Swinton wasn't supposed to

be involved at all—he was supposed to keep himself safe. So why was he up in the middle of the night, apparently negotiating with Noriava?

"It's *not* right. You're asking him to do the unthinkable. Marry you, someone he barely knows, *and* give up the secret to the serum that's essentially turning his citizens into violent murderers? And it isn't as though he doesn't have other options."

"We can go round and round about this as long as you like," Noriava purred, "but we both know he really doesn't have another choice. You're only standing in the way because you're in love with him. But if you really cared, you'd do whatever it took to put him back on the throne. You would make sacrifices for him."

I was frozen in place. Horrified, and waiting for what Swinton would say next. I couldn't let him get caught in her trap. I looked back at Pem and Still to find them watching me, eyes wide. I pointed at the screen and mouthed, "Can I get in?" Pem shrugged, but Still knelt at my side and began to silently feel the wall, her mouth set in a thin line. I turned back to the heated discussion in the room.

Swinton looked up, his eyes narrowed at her. "Why do you want the poison? Aren't Denorians supposed to value human life above everything else?"

"Human life first, certainly. But profit is a close second. Imagine for a moment that your Ambrose does succeed, and he manages to expose the fact that the temple has been slowly using poison to control the people of Ilor and Alskad. Now, imagine if a small country like Denor held the only cure. Even better, imagine that the queen of Denor was also recently married to the king of Alskad. The rulers who provide the antidote—at a reasonable price, of course—will be seen as the most beatific pair to take the throne in recorded history. You want that for Ambrose, don't you? Power? Justice? The love of his people?" Noriava's expression turned sly. "I'll even allow you to remain in your role as his companion. We'll grant you land, titles, wealth—anything you desire— as our thanks for your role in negotiating this partnership."

"You're sidestepping the question," Swinton said accusingly. "You have no reason to reproduce the temple's poison. No reason to need the formula. You can make the cure without it."

"My reasons are my own," she replied. "You cannot argue that this isn't the right move for your king. He'd be foolish to try anything else. Even if he decided to go to the Samirians for help, there's no way they'd be able to produce an antidote. They don't have the technology or the knowledge required."

Noriava stood and walked to a sideboard, where she poured two glasses of a deep red wine. She offered Swinton a glass and perched on the edge of the low table between the two couches. Swinton took a long draft of the wine and set the glass on the table next to Noriava. Her large black cat twined around her ankles.

"Which matters more to you, the profit or the marriage?" Swinton asked.

I dug my fingernails into my palms as Noriava regarded him critically. "Neither is more important. They're both vital."

"How good are your scientists?"

"The best in the world. Why?"

"Because you'll have to compromise, as well." Swinton pulled a glass vial out of his coat pocket. The fluted glass held an emerald liquid, and the top was corked and sealed with wax. "There are fewer than a dozen people in the world who know how this is made. By the time Vi is done in Ilor, that number will be halved." A calculating expression filled Noriava's face as she eyed the vial. "I'll give your scientists this sample with the understanding that they use it only to create a cure. But you must promise me that the knowledge of how this poison is made will die with this generation. In addition, Denor will provide the cure to everyone who wants it in Alskad and Ilor for free for the first three months after it is produced. Do this, and I'll guarantee you an alliance with Alskad."

My mouth hung open. It wasn't supposed to happen this way. This was my country, my throne, my life. I had to be seen making the decision, at the very least.

Still tugged on my robe. She pointed to the screen and shook her head, then pointed to the stairs and mimed running. I nodded, and she sprang silently to her feet. As I reached the door at the top of the stairs, Noriava's voice came drifting through the screen.

"Fair enough. I'll agree on one condition..."

Still took off, and I raced after her, letting the heavy door slam behind me.

I slid through the halls and down staircases, chasing Still as quickly as I could in my soft-soled slippers. Pem caught up with us in no time at all. I kept expecting to run into a maid or to be stopped by a guard, but the halls of the Denorian palace were entirely empty. I rounded a corner at top speed and ran headlong into a tall table. I managed to right the table, but as I did, the potted plant atop it wobbled and crashed to the ground, where it shattered into hundreds of pieces.

"Hamil's eyes," I cursed under my breath as I stumbled

over the mound of damp earth, broken shards of pottery and fallen leaves.

The girls skidded to a stop in front of a set of double doors, their faces bearing expressions of wariness that edged on fear. Despite how badly I wanted to comfort them, I strode forward, jaw clenched, and heaved open the heavy doors. A set of four low stairs led down into an antechamber and a darkened hallway. I sped toward the end of the hall, where a doorway was ringed in soft, golden light.

Noriava glanced over her shoulder, one eyebrow raised, when I stormed into the room. But the moment she recognized me, her eyes widened, then darted back to Swinton. My gaze followed hers, and I gasped at the sight of what she'd done to him in the few minutes it had taken me to race across the palace.

Every muscle in his body strained against thick leather straps that crossed his body at wrist, ankle, chest and waist, keeping him seated in a sturdy wooden chair. A pair of muscular guards stood on either side of him.

"What in Gadrian's name is going on here?" I demanded. I rushed to Swinton's side and reached for one of the buckles at his wrist, but his head snapped up, startling me.

He snarled, "Get your spoiled, rutting face away from me."

I stumbled back in shock, staring at him. His face was the same. The same thick tawny waves of hair; the same dark stubble along the same square jaw. There were deep, dark smudges under his eyes, but it was the middle of the night, and he'd been up since dawn.

"Swinton…" I started.

"I don't need your godsdamned pity, and I don't need your godsdamned help. You're the one who got me into this fucking shit-show of a carnival ride, but I can get my own damned self out of it. I don't ever want to see your fucking face again."

My chest was tight. I couldn't breathe. I looked up at Noriava, at her placid, curious face, and hate like I'd never felt before in my life coursed through my veins.

"What did you do to him?" I bit off each word like a chunk of ice.

"*I* didn't do anything at all," she said. "He merely chose to drink the wine I poured for him."

I clenched my fists and straightened my spine. I was taller than Noriava, but only just. She lifted her chin imperiously and stared me down, fire in her dark green eyes. "And what, exactly, was in that wine?" I asked.

"It seems that the perfume produced by the philomena flowers is somewhat more potent than the serum the Suzerain produce." She smiled and held a familiar, cut-crystal perfume bottle up to the light—one of the bottles we'd brought with us from Alskad. A finger's width of the emerald liquid was missing.

I gaped at her in horror. "Where did you get that?"

Noriava raised one eyebrow and gave me a pitying smile. "You aren't the only one who employs spies with sticky fingers, Bo, dear."

She set the bottle down on a side table and crossed the room. She reached into Swinton's breast pocket and plucked out the vial of the temple's serum he carried there, calmly ignoring his snarls. "My scientists will begin work replicating the serum immediately. In the meantime, I suppose it's only fair that I send a portion of my army with you to Alskad. You're more use to me on the throne than off it."

Swinton's muttered curses grew just a hair louder, and I glanced at him. He stared intently at his knees, and his hands were held in a white-knuckled grip on the arms of the chair. I'd never seen him this angry, in this much pain. Pem and Still stood frozen in the doorway, staring at him as they clung to each other, both looking terrified.

Noriava's words played over and over in my head, and I gritted my teeth as the meaning beneath them became clear. "Replicating it?" I asked.

"That was my agreement with Swinton. I would be given the drug in exchange for my help with your political situation."

I seethed. "Don't test me. Swinton did not agree to allow you to replicate that poison."

Noriava smiled. "Prove it."

"I heard you!" I said. "And I have two witnesses who heard you, as well. The moment Swinton recovers, he'll verify what I heard, as well."

"Darling, you are a deposed king. Your so-called *witnesses*—" she looked over my shoulder, disdain writ large across her pretty face "—are two children, who are also serving as your valets. As for Swinton, I wouldn't expect a recovery anytime soon. The best thing for him will be to send him off to the countryside, where the good doctors in charge of the homes for *drægoners* can see that he isn't allowed to hurt anyone."

"You told Swinton that you would find a cure—"

Swinton's furious howl cut me off. He struggled at his bonds. His brows knit together, and his glazed eyes fixed on Noriava. Ignoring him, she poured herself another glass of wine and draped herself over one of the couches.

His voice was raw with a rage I'd never heard from him before, and each word seemed as though it had to claw its way out of his throat. "You. Promised. Me. A. Cure. You. Bitch."

Noriava's eyebrows climbed, and she looked past Swinton—

ignoring him as thoroughly as she would have were he nothing but a piece of furniture—to fix her eyes on me. For the first time, I saw that her eyes were two very slightly different shades of green. I swallowed. What if she was an amalgam? What power might she secretly possess?

"You really don't see it, do you?" Noriava asked, shaking her head in disgust. "I owe you *nothing*. You have absolutely no leverage over me, and I already have exactly what I want from you. The only reason for me to do anything more to help you would be if it were to benefit me or Denor. A cure might do the Alskaders and Ilorians some good, but how does it help me? How does it help Denor? Much more profitable would be a poison that could take down any leader, any merchant—ruin lives, and make even the most sterling reputation vulnerable. With this poison in hand, Denor will control not only its own lands." She smiled coldly. "I will have power over the entirety of the livable world. Samiria will bow to me. Ilor will renounce their loyalty to the Alskad crown. Even you will be forced to listen to me, little king."

Her words came like a punch to my gut, and it took every fiber of my strength to keep myself upright. How was it that this woman, just a few years older than me, could lounge there in her nightclothes, sipping a glass of wine and plotting the violent extinction of an entire population? I searched my mind for anything that would help me, anything that would give me a foothold in this argument.

"Your people would never agree to this," I said desperately. "It's the Denorian way to value and protect life above everything else. Your scientists won't replicate a poison. The values of your people won't allow it. And you shouldn't allow it, much less advocate for it. Please, Noriava."

Noriava laughed, a quiet little giggle that gained strength

and power and grew into a wicked cackle. Another sound joined her laughter, a disjointed, terrifying sound like metal on rock. I knew without looking that it came from Swinton.

He started to sing, a familiar tune we'd heard time and again in Ilor. "I have a way with monarchs. I have a way with kings. They shower me with diamonds and golden rings, but show me a farmer, and my heart will sing."

I couldn't look at him. I couldn't look anywhere. Empty desperation filled me, like a ship taking on water, pulling me down, down into the depths of despair.

"I'll do anything you want," I said miserably. "Just don't do this to anyone else. Find a cure. I heard you with Swinton. You can turn this into a profitable venture. More profitable than a poison you can sell only to the most immoral people on the planet. Even better, make something preventative, something that everyone can take, dosed or not. Just find a cure for him."

"Why should I?" she sneered. "You don't seem to understand, Ambrose. You have no more power in this conversation. You've got nothing to offer me. You don't get to tell me what to do."

I glanced back at Pem and Still, watching silently from the doorway, their mouths compressed into thin lines. I met Still's eye, and she started shaking her head violently, as if she'd already heard the words that were about to come out of my mouth.

I looked away and took a deep breath. Vi would call me weak, a coward. She'd find a way to call Noriava's bluff. But I wasn't Vi. I wasn't as brave or as smart or as strong as she was, and the only thing in the world I wanted in that moment was to take away Swinton's pain.

"There's one thing I have that you want," I said, resignation filling me. "My hand in marriage. I'll agree to marry you if you agree to set your scientists to finding a cure. The day that Swinton is cured, I will stand before my people and yours and agree to a union between our two nations."

Noriava popped out of her chair and crossed the room quickly, and I could tell that she'd been expecting and ready for my response. She ran her fingers along my shoulder and tilted her head to look at me with gleaming eyes. "You'll marry me?"

I nodded.

"And have children with me? Heirs?"

The idea of being in bed with the heartless, horrible woman who stood in front of me made me cringe, but again, I nodded.

"Bo, don't," Pem said, her voice quavering. "You don't have to. We can find another way."

But as I turned my gaze to Swinton, I knew that this was exactly what I had to do. The veins on his forehead and arms bulged as he fought against the leather straps holding him to the chair. His muttered curses damned everything and everyone from me to his mother and the sea to the stars. It was as though rage and aggression had washed away the wit and charm and mischievous joy that made him the person I loved.

I couldn't let him stay this way. I couldn't let this happen to anyone else. I would do whatever it took to find a cure for the temple's awful poison, even if it meant tethering myself to Noriava for the rest of my life. Noriava was a liar, and seemed to be entirely lacking a moral compass, but at least I could see what a life with her would look like. At least I knew what I was in for.

Noriava's smile grew wide and wicked. Her lips were

stained blackish by the deep red wine, and her teeth were tinged with crimson, as though she'd been drinking blood.

"I will perform all of the duties of a royal consort and hus-band," I said. "But, before we are married, your scientists will produce an antidote to the temple's poison, and Swinton will be cured. Should anything happen to him in the meantime, our engagement will be nullified."

Noriava's smile dimmed ever so slightly.

"Further, should I learn that your Denorian scientists have been working to replicate the poison, our agreement will be void. Denor will produce an antidote and a preventative. And the entirety of your army, apart from a detachment large enough to protect the people of Salemouth, will sail with me to Alskad. They will be sworn to my service as the royal consort of Denor."

"Royal consort?"

"That's my final condition. You will have no power over Alskad or Ilor. In exchange, I will cede my right to the governance of Denor and its people."

"And if something, goddesses forbid, should happen to you?"

"Then I suppose the Alskad throne will return to the hands of the current regent, Rylain."

Noriava studied me, her venomous eyes moving up and down my body and darting around the room, appraising, deconstructing, testing. I stood still as death, waiting, forcing myself to meet her eyes each time they settled on me. The muscles in my jaw ached from the tension I held there.

"No."

"No?" I asked, my blood gone suddenly cold.

"No. I'll not go to all this trouble to be some sort of impotent consort. Alskad calls itself an empire. With this marriage, it can finally begin to live up to that name. Our nations will be truly joined, or I walk away." Noriava's gaze fell on Swinton. "If you feel half as much for the citizens of Alskad and Ilor as you do for him, you'll agree to my terms. We'll be married when I deliver the antidote. At our wedding, you will name me the heir to the Alskad throne until such a time as we produce an heir."

I paused, thinking of Runa. Thinking of all the work she'd done to preserve the Alskad throne and our place in the world. Could I really sacrifice all of that just to take back my throne? I wondered what Vi would have to say about this. Would she tell me to go ahead with it, or would she toss her hands in the air and find another way?

"An heir!" Swinton's voice cracked through the air like a whip. "An heir! An heir! I can see it now—bully and the bitch and their black-hearted babe."

I swallowed. There might be another way to take back my throne, but I knew in my heart that Noriava was the only person who could make Swinton himself again.

"Agreed," I said, and my fate was sealed.

CHAPTER TWENTY-FIVE

Vi

"I wish you were here. I wish I could tell you my worries and fears and hopes face-to-face, instead of in letters you may never see. They say you're dead, and while I know in my heart that you aren't, the repetition of it makes it feel almost real. I don't think I could stand for my heart to break over losing you again."

—*from Vi to Bo*

The next day, I perched in a window seat of the governor's mansion, fiddling with the cuff I'd locked around my wrist as I listened to the governor of Ilor address the Ilorian people from a stage erected just outside. Dozens of dispatch riders sat on their horses at the edge of the stage, ready to race from town to town, delivering copies of her speech the moment she finished.

With her wife and children on one side of the podium and Aphra and Curlin on the other, Ysanne spoke about freedom and justice. Reading from a speech we—Ysanne, Quill, Mal, Aphra, Curlin, Hepsy, Myrna and I—had spent hours arguing over, she addressed the rumors about the philomena farms, the distilleries and the temples. She spoke to the rising discontent among the laborers, and as the sun broke through the gray drizzle, setting off the lush bushes and flowers planted throughout the square like boxes of sparkling gems, Ysanne declared that all contracts with the temple had been nullified, a dozen new labor laws had been put into effect and anyone who wished to walk away from their contract had that right.

I wanted to be happy that the governor was a reasonable person and not entirely opposed to the changes we'd forced upon her government. But I couldn't shake the memory of the battle I'd fought and the fear of everything we'd yet to accomplish. It still wasn't safe for me to walk the streets. A cluster of the Shriven stood at the back of the crowd, their white robes stark against the green of the plants that grew in every unoccupied inch of Ilor.

Ysanne's voice, amplified by a copper horn, echoed over the crowd. "Further, every person in Ilor, including those who have been previously held by an unfair contract, will now earn a minimum of two hundred and fifty *ovstri* a year."

I drew back the curtain. The wealthy landowners, seated in the front of the crowd, made no attempt to control their disbelief and anger. Some exchanged furious whispers. Others stood and stalked to their waiting carriages in a huff. I smiled to myself as a stout, red-faced woman—Constance, who'd made every effort to buy my contract what felt like a lifetime ago—fanned herself furiously. When she saw that no one was watching her, she fluttered her hands and feigned a dead faint.

"As the minimum wage mandate may be a great burden on those who have not budgeted for it this year, the offices of the governor will be open every day to those who wish to apply for a government stipend to fund their employees—based, of course, on need. Those who wish to leave their contracts or are currently unemployed will be eligible for jobs funded by the government that will aid in expanding our system of roads and conserving the natural resources of Ilor. We, the Ilorian people, will be free. Each and every one of us."

The landowners who'd been making a great show of their distress calmed, and a great cheer rose up over the back of the crowd. I sighed my relief and sat back on the cushions.

Curlin, sitting beside me, patted my leg. "We've accomplished a lot, Vi. You should be proud."

I shushed her and went back to watching through the open window. There was still so much left to be done.

A couple of days later, Quill led us to an abandoned estate, a place Bo had told him about before he left for Alskad. The main house was burned, but many of the outbuildings remained more or less intact. We gathered everyone there— Quill's resistance fighters, the folks who'd flocked to Aphra after Plumleen burned and the people who'd come out of the woodwork after the governor's announcement—so they'd be outside Williford and safe. At least for the moment. We piled ourselves into the servants' quarters and barn, with four, sometimes six, to a room meant for one.

There, we plotted our next move. Our last chance. We didn't have long before the Shriven would find us.

The idea had come from the land itself, and the more we talked it over, the more it curdled my blood. Quill stood in a corner of the room we shared with Curlin, Aphra and two other women, arms crossed over his chest. Curlin leaned across me to pull the curtain aside, and all of us stared through the glass, our minds chewing over the same horrible thoughts. Through a gray drizzle of rain, I looked out over rolling fields where jewel-green bushes dotted with white flowers grew together in endless, tangled rows.

Philomenas.

The plants the temple used to make their mind-altering serum. On the far side of the field, all but invisible through the sheets of rain, an enormous windmill hulked, blackened and charred, but standing.

"It's less predictable, but the smoke has almost exactly the same effect as the serum," Quill said. "There are a couple of folks here who fled Alskad after being tasked by the temple to study the effects of the philomenas. They think they've got a way that we can light the fires and get out without being affected by the smoke. We should be okay."

We had every able-bodied person working around the clock to get the equipment we needed built, and a former farm manager planning how to light the fields for a strategic, controlled burn.

"If the wind is with us and we manage to set the fires correctly, we'll incapacitate the entire Shriven force in Ilor," Quill explained. "Even if we manage to take out just half of them, we'll have significantly evened the odds."

I chewed on my bottom lip, unwilling to meet anyone's eyes. Despite my desperate, aching need for revenge, and my desire to see them suffer in equal measure to the suffering they'd caused, I couldn't get over the slithering wrongness of it. "It's not right," I said finally. "We can't do to them what the temple has done to us."

"We can't what, Vi?" Curlin snapped. "Go to war? Do what we have to do to take away the temple's power? This is the only way we overcome the odds. This is the only way we win."

"At what cost?" I snapped. "You were one of them. They

forced you to be one of them. Had things turned out differently, you would be on that side of the battlefield. You would be the one poisoned."

"How is this any different from any other fight?" Aphra asked. "You'd kill them in battle, but you won't do to them what they've done to hundreds of people like you and me?"

"At least in hand-to-hand combat, someone chooses to hit you, chooses to shoot at you, chooses to accept the consequences of their actions. This is…" I searched for the right words. "Not one of the Shriven will walk into this fight thinking that they're going to lose themselves. Lose everything that makes them who they are. That's not fair."

Curlin's eyebrows knit together, and she scowled at the fields and the drizzling rain. "I think you're right. But I'm also not willing to lose the advantage this gives us."

"So what do we do?" Aphra asked.

I pulled a white blanket up over my bad shoulder and stared down at the fabric in my hands. "I have an idea."

We rode out under a white flag in the lavender light of predawn the next morning. Beetle snorted unhappily each time I turned in the saddle to look behind me, expecting the Shriven to surround us at any moment, but her gait was smooth and steady as she kept pace with Aphra's, Curlin's and Quill's larger mounts. The morning sun had yet to burn off the fog and chill of the night's long rain. Mist hovered above the damp grass that lined the narrow road, and the trees were eerily silent.

We rode for nearly two hours before Curlin spotted the first Shriven lookout. She pointed, all brazenness and courage, and called, "I see you there in the trees. We approach under the white flag. Scurry off and tell your matron."

Before we'd left, Curlin had mimicked the Shriven's customary black paint around her eyes and coated her forehead in a smear of white that made the tattoos across her chin and nose stand out even more starkly. She wore white as well, scrounged from the dressers and wardrobes of the servants who'd fled the philomena farm. Curlin's thick auburn hair had grown into disobedient waves that curled around her ears, and it shone like a newly minted coin in the sun. Her arms were bare, her tattoos telling the coded story of her triumphs and defeats, the secrets she carried, the ranks she'd achieved. I'd covered my newly tattooed arm and the bracelet on my wrist, not wanting to provoke the Shriven any more than we had to, but Curlin wore her history openly, carrying it like a weapon.

Every choice she'd made sent a message to the Shriven: she had been one of them, but now she was free.

Before long, we were forced to rein our mounts to a stop in front of a hastily erected barrier in the road. Four Shriven stood behind it, their weapons drawn and expressions grim.

"We ride under the white flag with a message for your matron and brethren. You will let us pass." Curlin's voice was ice and stone.

The four Shriven shifted and exchanged a series of glances. With a nod from the woman standing in the middle, one of the Shriven turned on his heel and sprinted down the road into the jungle. The others shifted to fill the empty space left by their companion, resuming their stiff, guarded stances and staring into the middle distance. It was like we disappeared the moment they settled back into their places.

Curlin sat back in her saddle, all lazy confidence and quiet power. Aside from Aphra's fingers, which twitched nervously at her reins, she was the picture of reserved, noble elegance.

Her back was straight, her fine clothes immaculate, and her hair, parted in the middle, were twin waves of copper and gold.

"What now?" Quill asked.

"It looks like we wait," I snapped.

The muscles in Quill's jaw twitched. I should have been nicer to the man. After all, he and Mal were the ones who'd found shelter and food for our whole group when we'd had to flee Williford. He was the one who'd come up with our plan. He was the one who had quietly built an actual army.

And he was the only man I'd ever kissed. The only one I'd ever thought I might be able to love. I took a deep breath. My nerves were frayed, but that was no excuse to be an ass.

Aphra and Curlin exchanged a glance, and Curlin glared at me. "You insisted we do this. The least you can do is follow the plan."

I glared down at Beetle's overgrown mane. I needed to pull myself together. I needed to be stone.

A few moments later, a twig snapped, and I looked up to see the path packed with Shriven. They wore battle black, their faces bisected with black paint that covered their shorn scalps. They were disconcertingly silent, standing there with their hands on the long knives at their belts and their wicked staffs. The crowd parted, and a matron, in the flowing orange robes of the anchorites, strode to stand before us. The matrons were both Shriven and anchorites, and they bore the marks of both orders. This woman was tattooed from head to foot, and the pink lines of battle scars cut through the tattoos on her tan arms and face. Her head was shorn but for the crown, which was elaborately braided and pinned.

She regarded our little group critically, and a smug smirk played across her lips. "Curlin, darling, you've let yourself go," she scolded. "Come back to the fold. Your punishment will be gentle, I promise. No more than a few years of hard labor before you're allowed to start working your way back up to your former rank."

Curlin, remarkably, kept her face impassive.

Aphra cleared her throat. "Listen to me. Hear me. Open your minds to Curlin's words."

The Shriven stopped shifting in place and exchanging glances with one another. The weight of their focus landed squarely on Curlin.

"We, the leaders of the fight for reform in the colony of Ilor, come before you to offer you a chance. A choice. A chance that I was given not a few months ago. A choice I resisted." Curlin paused for a moment, surveyed the group of Shriven. "We will meet you on the battlefield in two days, but you do not have to fight. Until dawn two days from now, we will grant complete amnesty to any of the Shriven who come to our camp and willingly surrender their weapons. You will not be asked to fight against your brothers and sisters. We ask nothing of you, beyond laying down your arms."

Curlin swallowed, as if fighting back tears. "I was forced to join the Shriven when I was still a child. I had no option, no other choice. I did terrible things that I will regret for the rest of my life while under orders. It wasn't until my matron left me for dead, and my childhood friend—whom I'd betrayed over and over again—decided to save my life, that I was given another chance. I know that there are those among you who joined willingly, who love what you do, who believe in the original ideals of the order, and I can respect that. But those ideals have been warped and stripped away by the corruption of the Suzerain." Her gaze went hard. "I know you see it. I did. So I'm here to offer you another way. A way out."

Aphra smiled at Curlin.

"Hear the truth in her words, and consider it as you resume your daily lives. You have until dawn two days from now."

Curlin gave the Shriven a four-fingered salute, wheeled her horse around and nudged him to a brisk canter. Quill and Aphra followed suit, but I waited just a moment, looking out into the crowd. Past the paint, the tattoos and the shorn heads, making eye contact with the faces I knew. Making sure they saw me recognize them. Forcing them to see me.

Then I awkwardly turned Beetle's head and followed the others back into the jungle.

CHAPTER TWENTY-SIX

Bo

"I thought I knew what it was to be alone before, but now loneliness surrounds me, envelops me. Even when I am surrounded by dozens of courtiers or hundreds of soldiers, absence follows me like a dark and overwhelming shadow."

—*from Bo to Vi*

Noriava's personal doctor appeared mere minutes after she sent for him. Despite the late hour, the man's salt-and-pepper hair was perfectly coiffed and his white coat pristine. I watched, fighting back tears, as the doctor slipped a needle into Swinton's arm. Swinton fought against the restraints for another moment before he went suddenly stiff and slumped in his chair.

"He'll be out for a few hours. Long enough to get him to the institution in Marvella," the doctor said, bowing to Noriava. "I'll have the transport readied."

I flew off the chair where I'd been perched, watching, and

went to stand in front of Swinton. "You're not taking him anywhere."

Noriava sighed. "Be reasonable, Bo. We have facilities to treat the diminished. He'll be well cared for."

I gritted my teeth. "You think that I would trust you for a single second after what you did tonight? He's not leaving my sight."

"Your Highness, there is no way to keep you safe while he's being treated if he remains here. Please. You must consider your safety and the safety of the palace staff," the doctor said.

"Your Majesty," I corrected stiffly. "It's *his* safety I'm worried about. There's a small servant's room in my suite. It's windowless, and I'm sure there's someone in this godsforsaken palace who can find a way to install a lock on the door."

The doctor looked to Noriava for direction, and she rolled her eyes. "Fine. But the moment he injures someone, he's off to an institution."

"But in the meantime, he'll see a specialist," I insisted. "Starting tomorrow."

Noriava nodded and looked at her doctor. "Send someone first thing, and ring for our guests' butler on your way out. The servant's room will need to be swept for danger. The guards can take him to the king's suite."

"There's no need for anyone else but a doctor to get involved. We can take care of him," I snapped. "Pem. Still. I want you to go through that room with a fine-tooth comb. Remove everything he could use to hurt himself or anyone else."

Pem and Still nodded, their faces grim. "Do you want us to wait for you?" Still asked. "We could help you get Swinton to his room."

I shook my head. "I'll be right behind you."

When the door swung closed behind them, I turned to face Noriava. "I know you think you have all the power in this situation, but I could easily make your life miserable. Don't try to double-cross me again. There will be consequences if you violate the terms of our agreement in any way."

With that, I unbuckled Swinton's restraints, heaved his limp body over my shoulder and carried him out of the room. I had to stop and lean against the smooth stone walls of the palace corridors several times on the way to my suite, but I managed to get Swinton back without dropping him. Pem and Still leaped up when I opened the door, and together, we managed to get Swinton into the narrow bed. I removed his boots, belt and knives, then tucked a down comforter around him.

As I eased the door shut, I saw a pair of thick dead bolts had been hastily installed on the gilded birchwood door. "They didn't waste any time, did they?" I asked, fighting back tears as I slid the locks into place.

"They were in and out before you got here. Guess Noriava ain't real good at listening. We figured we'd take shifts watching him," Pem said.

"I'm going first," Still added. "So that you can get some sleep."

"No. I'll just make a pallet on the floor so that I can be here if he needs anything," I said, a sob cracking my voice. "I don't want him to feel alone."

Pem and Still came and wrapped their arms around me, hugging me between them as I cried. I swallowed hard, wiped away the tears streaming down my cheeks and squeezed my sisters. They helped me drag a pile of pillows and furs and blankets off my bed. We built a nest on the floor outside Swinton's room, and as the first gray light of dawn patterned the carpet by the windows, the girls went to bed, and I settled myself on the floor.

Gentle hands shook me awake sometime later, and though the light filtering in through the windows said I'd been asleep for hours, it felt like seconds. I dragged myself up to a sitting position against the doorframe and rubbed my eyes. The night before came flooding back to me, and through the door, I heard the sounds of muffled sobs. I started to get up, to reach for the door, but a hand reached out and stopped me.

"Before you open the door, may I ask you a few questions, Your Majesty?"

The woman's voice was low and lilting and achingly calm. She crouched on the floor beside my pallet, her smooth brown cheeks flushed, her eyes bright and inquisitive. She wore a long, cream-colored jacket over loose black trousers and a faded blue sweater, and her hair was arranged in long twists that she'd tied back with a cord. Her jacket was fitted with a number of pockets, all bristling with bottles, pens, small pads of paper and medical instruments I couldn't identify.

She smiled at me, and something in her manner put me immediately at ease. "Your Majesty, I'm Doctor Tresley Rutin," she said. "Doctor Loviar said that your friend was in need of assistance."

She offered me her hand, and I shook it. Her long, elegant fingers were cool, but strong. "He's been poisoned," I explained. "From what I understand, the drug mimics the violence of the diminished. I don't know how much help you can give him. Noriava said that the Denorian scientists could make an antidote, but until then..."

Doctor Rutin smiled gently. "My colleagues in the Institute are already hard at work trying to understand the sample you gave the queen. If anyone can find a way to reverse the effects of such a dangerous, potent drug, it's them. Doctor Loviar sent me to you, though, because my life's work has been in the treatment and care for the diminished who become *drægoners*. I've had a great deal of success in helping them learn to control their impulses through a combination of talk therapy and, for some, medication. I'd like to see if I can help your friend."

"Honestly, Doctor—and I do hate to offend—but how can I possibly trust the care of the man I love with someone in the employ of Queen Noriava, when she's the person who did this to him?"

Pem and Still appeared in the doorway, short knives sparking in each of their hands, ready to pounce should I give them so much as a nod.

Doctor Rutin's mouth compressed into a thin line. "Queen Noriava did not send me here. Gracious though she is, she has a country to run and no time to track the whereabouts of a humble doctor. As I said, Doctor Loviar thought I might be able to assist."

"You swear Noriava hasn't ordered you to make him worse?"

"Do you know the Denorian motto, by chance?"

I racked my brain, trying to remember. Our tutors had forced Claes and me to learn all of them in our lessons years ago. They were all in long-forgotten languages that had been dead even before the cataclysm. The motto of Alskad, *In septentrione futura via est*, was supposed to be something about the future being in the North, which just seemed like a way to make the early settlers feel better about having chosen such a cold, dark place to make their home. The Denorian motto had been taken from another dead language and, if our tutors were to be believed, was actually a phrase misremembered from the oath doctors had taken before the cataclysm.

It came to me in a flash, triggered by my negotiation with Noriava the night before. *"Ikke skade når du kan helbrede,"* I said, stumbling over the unfamiliar pronunciation. "Harm not, when you might heal."

I wondered if Noriava had ever learned the phrase.

Doctor Rutin nodded. "I, like my colleagues and many of my fellow citizens, take that very seriously. I am first a healer, second a Denorian and third employed by the queen of Denor. Please let me help your friend."

I swallowed, the sour taste of sleep still thick in my mouth. "Thank you. I care about him a great deal. I will be greatly in your debt if you can alleviate his suffering, even a little."

"Bo." Still crossed the room, thumbing one of her blades in a way that was meant to look menacing, but really just made me cringe. "The queen's sent someone to bring you to see the troops. We can stay and make sure she don't do anything untoward to Swinton."

Doctor Rutin managed to keep a smile off her lips, but she couldn't control the twinkle in her eyes. "I'll certainly keep myself under control with two such ferocious guards watching over me. You go and see to the troops, Your Majesty. I'll be here when you return."

Grateful to have found an ally, I stood and retreated to my room to find something to wear that might impress the troops—or, at the very least, hide the circles under my eyes.

I met Noriava in a wide hall lined with weapons and armor in a mind-boggling variety of styles. There were entire suits made of metal, some polished and shining, some pitted with rust. Mannequins wore black vests thick with layers of metal and padding meant to protect the wearer from weapons long forgotten. Plates of hardened leather adorned others of the faceless horde. It was as though she'd unearthed a collection, a museum that had somehow avoided destruction in the cataclysm.

Noriava herself was decked out in utterly impractical gold armor over a frothy white gown. A thin, delicate sword that even I knew was meant for unarmored shows of fencing skill, not actual combat, was strapped to her side with a gilded belt. Her long red hair was knotted into an elaborate updo and topped with not one, but *two* golden crowns. One looked like a replica of the simple jeweled circlet I wore, the emblem of Alskad, while the other was a heavily embellished spiked tiara with a massively luminous circle of opal in the center.

She looked ridiculous.

"Are you ready to go and meet your troops, my darling?"

Noriava's tone was treacle-sweet and dripping with condescension. The nearby guards shifted and exchanged subtle glances, but I ignored her and stalked up to the double doors at the end of the hall. I shook the golden cuff out of my sleeve and clasped my hands behind my back, fighting the urge to adjust the crown atop my head or check the collar of my charcoal wool jacket. As I approached, Noriava laced her arm through mine, and at her signal, the doors swung open.

Unlike every other day I'd spent in Denor, the sun was bright and there wasn't a cloud in the sky. The Denorian troops stood in neat rows, their pristine white dress uniforms stark against the black stone of the courtyard. The men and women of the Denorian army wore both pistols and swords at their waists and held quarterstaves in the crooks of their arms. A company of crossbow specialists stood with their legs wide, weapons angled at the ground and thick bolts in quivers strapped to their thighs. A line of commanders paced before the troops, stopping to correct even the tiniest mistakes in dress or stance.

The moment we stepped onto the small platform in the far corner of the courtyard, the troops snapped simultaneously into a sharp, four-fingered salute. Before Noriava had the chance to greet them, I moved forward to speak.

I'd been rehearsing what I would say to the troops, trying to remember the right Denorian words for the sentiment I wanted to convey. I knew I would stumble, but the least I could do was try. I cleared my throat. "Someone recently reminded me of the Denorian motto. Though it is, perhaps, a bit ironic to ask a group of soldiers to repeat a pacifist's motto, would you indulge me?"

I raised my hand, and on my count, the voices of the entire Denorian army blended with mine as we called out this idea in a language no one actually spoke anymore.

"Ikke skade når du kan helbrede."

The words echoed off the walls, and I let the waves of sound linger for a moment before I began to speak again. "Out of harm's way. Denor has been lucky. Since the cataclysm—even *during* the cataclysm—your people were protected. You've remained out of harm's way." I shifted and looked out across the silent crowd of soldiers, searching for faces with whom I could connect. "I stand before you today, not as a foreign king deposed, not as the betrothed of your queen, but as a man who has seen great harm done to his people, and who is asking for your support.

"The leaders of the temple in Alskad and Ilor are murdering my people. They have ripped stability and peace from my lands. They've created a poison that makes people unstoppably violent and cruel. The temple has put in place a regent who's called for all of the Alskader diminished to be rounded up and brought to the temple, where gods only know what horrors are being enacted upon them. I cannot stand by and watch this happen. So I've come to ask for your help—to ask you to stand beside me, to keep the temple and its corrupt anchorites and the Suzerain from doing more harm."

I lifted my chin and raised my voice for emphasis. "The Suzerain and their backers won't stop with my land. No place in the habitable world will be safe if they get their way. So I stand before you not to ask you to go to war for me, but to fight *with* me, to help the people of Alskad find their way back to peace. To safety. Will you help me save my people from harm?"

A roar erupted from the crowd, and as the army pounded their staffs on the black stone floor, a chant rose from the crowd.

"Harm not," they cried, "when you might heal!"

Over and over their voices rose, until birds darted out from under the eaves, fleeing the cacophony. But I remained, staring up at the sky, letting the sound wash over me. It should have sounded like relief, like hope. But instead it sounded like chains winding round my body. Like the locking of a prison door.

CHAPTER TWENTY-SEVEN

Vi

"I seem to have lost myself somewhere in the fields of Ilor. The things I once used to identify myself are all gone, replaced with memories of things that keep me up at night and cloud my vision during the day. I keep searching, but I don't know how I'll manage to find my way back to myself."

—from Vi to Bo

Mist crept over the philomenas as we walked between the rows, pouring cans of lamp oil onto the piles of kindling we'd laid between the bushes. The distant beat of the Shriven's war drums grew closer as the first rays of sunlight pierced the horizon. Enormous bonfires were being tended on the edges of the field, and a swarm of activity surrounded a long table by the servants' quarters, where Aphra stirred an enormous trough full of dark mud.

"Quickly, quickly!" Quill called. "There's not much time."

I poured the rest of my can between two bushes, chucked it into the row we'd just finished and jogged back toward the others. Myrna was on the roof of the servants' quarters, peering through a set of binoculars. I glanced up at the person perched atop the windmill. Even knowing that the lookouts would call out the moment they saw movement in the jungle, I still ached to know what they were seeing. I stuck a hand deep into the pocket of my trousers and rubbed the single pearl I'd kept from all my diving back in Alskad—a token of good luck.

Taking a last deep breath, I went to join the chaos.

We'd sent the brats to Mal and Hepsy with our horses and most of our supplies. None of us wanted to risk another of their lives, brave and ready to fight or not, and there were few enough of them that they could sneak back into town under the cover of night without much risk of getting themselves caught. I knew that, for my part at least, I would carry the guilt of Lei's death with me until the day I passed, and I didn't want to think about what another child's death would do to me.

As I walked through the group of rebels—some cheerfully making jokes with one another as they stretched and prepared for the fight, some silent and stone-faced, some openly praying to the gods and goddesses—each person stopped what they were doing to greet me. They saluted, shook my hand, clapped me gently on my uninjured shoulder. With each greeting, each acknowledgment, my throat tightened more and more. I looked for Curlin, to ask her what in Dzallie's name was going on, but she was next to Aphra, conferring with her in low tones. I rubbed my last pearl, sewn into a tiny pocket in my trousers, for luck.

A gentle hand came to rest on my shoulder, and I spun around. Quill's lips quirked in a wry smile.

"What?" I spit, anxious energy about what was to come spilling over into my words.

"I'm sorry. I didn't mean to scare you." Quill smiled down at me and rubbed the stubble on his chin. "I just wanted a moment."

"Quill, we don't have a moment. The Shriven are going to show up at any moment."

"All the more reason to take a breath." His eyes shied away from mine. "And to tell you that I love you, Vi."

He reached out, took my hand and squeezed. I hesitated for a moment—the timing of this conversation felt outrageously wrong to me—but in the end I closed my fingers around his.

"I love you, too. Please be safe today."

I wanted so badly to kiss him. To push him up against the side of the building and lose myself in him. But what we lacked in time, we made up for in the eyes that were watching us, looking to us for direction.

"Promise. There's something else, though." Quill's expression became something far less playful. More serious. "Why're you so uncomfortable with our people taking notice of you?"

"*Our* people?" I closed my eyes and sighed. "I thought they were yours. You're one of the people who started this whole thing. I just showed up here."

"I may've helped organize it, but there's not a person here who's not looking to you for leadership, and you're well ready to give it to them," Quill said. "What you insisted we do for the Shriven? That was nobility itself. You hide a great deal of empathy under that thorny skin of yours."

I narrowed my eyes at him. "Quill, I don't. I can't..." Every idea that tried to form on my tongue was a faltering misstep. Incomplete or irrelevant or both.

Quill laughed, hoarse and throaty and somehow utterly

disarming. "All I wanted was to pay you a compliment and tell you I was wrong. I should have told you earlier. Should have trusted you. You may not have built this army, but you certainly are a leader, and you know I care about you beyond all that. Not many people would grant their enemies amnesty, not after what you've been through."

I looked away, face flushing. "It would've meant more if a single one of them had taken me up on my offer."

"We'll see how many of them show up to fight."

The drumbeats in the south were a constant countdown to the battle we faced.

"And what if they show up with an offer of peace?" I asked. "What if the fire spreads? What if our people are taken by the smoke? I just keep running through all the ways this could go wrong, and I can't seem to see a way this plan doesn't end with each one of our sorry souls dead or taken by unwarranted rage."

"I see them! They're approaching from the west," Myrna called, just as the bell on the top of the windmill began to sound.

That wasn't right. They ought to have just been coming from the south. From the temple. They were too confident in their position to sneak around, and there was no easy way to get from the temple in the south to the road leading west to Williford—only goat paths and jungle.

I looked at Quill. His eyebrows knit themselves together and his face was suddenly grim. "Get your gear," he said. "It's time."

I went. The troughs on either end of the long trestle table were crowded with our people. They smeared mud all over their bodies, over clothes and skin and hair. Not a fingerbreadth of skin was left bare on anyone as they hustled away from the trough.

I shouldered my way in and got to work. Seeing the gold bracelet on my wrist, I paused for a moment, reminded of my brother, but I couldn't make myself take it off. So I took a handful of mud and smeared it over my wrist, bracelet and all. When I was fully covered, I grabbed a rag from the table and dunked it into the bucket of milk. One of the other folks at the table helpfully tied it around my face. The goggles and gloves came next.

It'd taken some doing, but we'd forced our way into the half-burned distillery the day before. We'd found baskets full of old goggles like the ones I'd worn to dive in the Penby harbor and the kind of waxed-cloth gloves that buckled tight around a person's wrists. Fisherfolk used them to keep their hands dry in the depth of winter in Alskad, and Curlin and I figured they might be of some use protecting our skin from the poisoned smoke.

Fully kitted out and covered in a thick layer of mud, I jogged to the nearest fire and grabbed a torch. Without waiting for anyone's word, I ran to my assigned place at the far edge of the field. The others were just behind me, and a moment later, the bell on top of the windmill stopped ringing. As soon as the air went silent, we all bent to light the nearest row of bushes. The oil caught in no time flat, and a line of fire spread across the edge of the field.

Quill's farmers had planned the firing so that it would go up hot and fast and, if everything went our way, burn out quickly. There were deep trenches between the rows and around the field—not much chance of the fire spreading to the jungle, and if it did, it wouldn't get far. There was too much water everywhere. The Shriven should arrive to find the fields surrounding the entire burned-out estate on fire, and before there was a chance for them to put together the pieces of the puzzle, they'd be engulfed in the poisoned smoke. Meanwhile, we'd be on the road to Williford. Or we would've been, had there not been Shriven on that road, too.

I made my way toward the others, lighting bushes along the way. When I stepped out of the field, I found the entire rebel force crowded around the trestle table, on which three people now stood. The smoke was thick and gray, and it hung low over the field, caught under the cover of the thunder-clouds that rolled over the jungle.

"...retreat into the forest," Aphra said. "It doesn't matter that there isn't a path. We can cut our way through."

"And risk vipers or jungle cats or any of the other preda-tors waiting in the trees? I think not." Quill caught sight of me and waved me to the front of the crowd, though how he knew it was me under all the mud, I'd no idea.

The group parted, and I came to stand next to the table, hands shaking. "We should hunker down," I said. "Split into three groups in the distillery, the windmill and the servants' quarters. Wait. The buildings should protect us from the worst of the smoke, and with any luck, they'll inhale so much on their way in that they'll cut each other to shreds, and we'll be free and clear."

Myrna, crouched on the edge of the roof listening, pulled out her binoculars again. "We haven't got much time to de-cide. They're coming from every direction. We stay and fight, or we run."

"Every direction?" Curlin asked. "Are they coming through the jungle?"

"Not that I can see," Myrna said. "But Aphra's right. We

can't move fast enough through the jungle, not this many of us, and we'll leave a path straight to the little ones."

Quill gestured at me. "Vi's right. We should hide. There's less risk in that than any other idea we've got."

I bit my lip, and the taste of rot and mud filled my mouth. I tried not to gag into the handkerchief that covered most of my face. The clouds of smoke billowed up over the fields, spreading like fog and rolling toward us on an errant wind like so many thick gray monsters. "Fine. We stay, but only until we have a chance at the road. Then we run."

I waited until every last one of our people had made their way to hiding places in the half-burned distillery and the windmill before I climbed over a fallen beam and made my way through the distillery to the window that looked out over the burning fields. Curlin, standing next to me, took my gloved hand in hers and squeezed.

"We'll get through this," she said.

"I hope so. I don't like that the Shriven hold the only two roads out of here."

"You know they planned it that way. They're strategists. The only thing you can expect from them is that they do exactly the thing you'd rather they didn't. That's how this works."

"Not long now," Quill called. "Everyone quiet. Ready your weapons. Should they approach the building, stay put. Stay silent. We want to give the smoke time to work. But if it appears that the smoke has taken no effect, we'll have to fight our way out. Be ready."

Aphra's eyes went wide behind her goggles. "If the smoke doesn't take effect? No one mentioned that possibility."

"It will," I rasped, half under my breath. I bit the inside

of my cheek and squeezed Curlin's hand, staring out into the burning field.

Dark figures emerged from the smoky haze that obscured our view of the road just as raindrops began to ping against the metal roof of the distillery. I breathed a string of violent curses. If the fires went out and the smoke dissipated, all of our plans would go to shit, and we'd be left without a chance of getting out alive.

Then the rough sound of coughing came through the smoke, so low and pervasive it felt almost imagined. "Do you hear that?" Quill whispered.

"You see them?" Curlin breathed.

I peered into the smoke as more figures began to appear on the lawn outside the distillery. "Maybe."

"Watch their weapons. Something's off."

The Shriven's metal staffs scraped through the rough earth. A group of shadows, maybe ten of them, had made their way onto the lawn. The smoke grew thicker around them, and they were nothing more than shadows. They were no more than a stone's throw away. Everyone in the distillery held their breath. One of the Shriven doubled over, coughing, and metal screeched against metal as one of the others drew a long blade from its sheath. A sickening *thunk* echoed across the smoke-dampened lawn, and the coughing stopped suddenly as the Shriven's shadow was sliced in two and dropped to the grass. A sound like a pumpkin dropped onto grass was carried to us on the wind, followed by a distant, hysterical laugh that cut through me.

Curlin's grip on my hand became viselike. I hoped with every bone in my body that the groups in the windmill and the servants' quarters were safe.

The relative silence was broken by a single, inhuman scream

that abruptly ended as something essential to the sound gave out in the Shriven's throat. Then, through the thick clouds of swirling gray smoke, we watched as the Shriven began ripping each other apart.

One tore another's arm off their body before burying her teeth in her dead companion's neck. A head rolled across the muddy ground, freed of its body. Shots rang out in the distance somewhere behind the distillery. The Shriven coming up the road must've been taken by the smoke, as well.

I looked to Quill, and he held a gloved hand up, signaling for us to wait, to be silent. I took shallow breaths, trying to stay calm. Even though I knew the damp cloth over my nose and mouth would protect me from the smoke to some extent, watching the Shriven outside sent cold fear spiking into my very soul. This was the nightmare that'd haunted every day of my life, suddenly made real.

Something crashed into the back of the building. Glass shattered, and the thin wooden walls shook. I slipped my knife out of its sheath, whirling to face the source of the commotion.

Another crash. The squeal of splintering wood. I looked around for a way out. Hulking copper barrels stained with soot loomed over us. Tubes twisted this way and that across the beams in the ceiling. The wall on the far side of the barrels was charred, and I could see the gray cloud of smoke and rain through the cracks in the wood.

Thunder clapped overhead, and with it, half of the far wall came down. Gunshots cracked like lightning through the air, and the room erupted in screams. I grabbed Aphra and Curlin and pointed to the wall behind the still. Quill saw my furious gesturing and cupped his hands around his mouth.

"Everyone! Behind the still."

The rebels moved fast, running for cover just before the

Shriven began to stream into the room. As I passed one of the massive copper barrels, someone's shoulder crashed into me, throwing me off balance and into the side of the barrel. It teetered, and I heard the sound of sloshing liquid inside.

The world slowed, and everything snapped into focus. The Shriven's gunshots were going wild, almost like they were firing for the pure joy of it, not with any intention or direction. They raved and ranted, and their words held the same frenzied bloodlust I'd seen in the diminished time and again. Any shred of who they'd been before was gone, replaced by the poison cycling through their veins.

Beside me, the enormous barrel teetered on unstable legs. I grabbed Myrna as she darted past me.

"Wait! Help me push this over."

Myrna cast a dubious look at the barrel but leaned her full weight into it. A few of the others saw what we were doing and ran to help. We pushed, ignoring the shouts of our companions for us to follow, ignoring the bullets flying through the air, ignoring our terror, our pain, our heartache. Together we pushed, and, with aching slowness, the still began to tip. With the great scream of bolts tearing through half-burned wood, we ripped the body of the still out of the floor and sent it toppling over. The liquid inside spilled out in a great wave, and the faint scent of flowers filled the air. The wave hit the closest Shriven at thigh level, and before they could take another step, they were knocked to the ground.

"Run!" I screamed, then turned on a heel and ran with the other rebels all around me.

The air outside was thick with smoke, but the damp rag over my nose and mouth seemed to be keeping it out of my lungs. Rain fell in fat droplets, hissing as it met the flaming bushes. A great many of the fires had given way to the downpour, leaving only the husks of smoldering bushes steaming in the rain. The smoke was thick around us, and the steam coming off the bushes only added to the nearly complete lack of visibility.

The bodies of dead Shriven covered the ground, but more still streamed up the road. Some of our people had been caught up in the fighting as well, their kerchiefs ripped away, leaving them exposed to the poisoned smoke. I froze, staring at the carnage around me—blood everywhere, limbs and heads disconnected from their bodies littering the ground.

A hand closed around my bad elbow, and I had my knife up before I realized it was Myrna. She jerked her head and set off at a run, not letting go of my arm. I followed her to the foot of the windmill, where many of our number had gathered. The rain was coming down in earnest now, pelting us and leaving trails of exposed flesh as it began to wash away our protective layers of mud.

"Both roads are crowded with the Shriven, but I'd put good money on there being fewer of them to the south," Aphra was saying. "Our best chance is to cross the fields and cut behind them. We won't be able to see much, and we'll have to hurry, so we put ourselves at great risk of running into a fight. Or we could stay here, wait for the fighting to die down as they take one another on. Either way, we need to stick together."

I leaned against Myrna, trying to catch my breath without taking in a great lungful of smoke. "Not only is it raining, but we just sent a thousand buckets' worth of some stage of the temple's poison spilling over half of the Shriven," I gasped. "Best case, they're dead. Worst case, they're right behind us, out for blood. We don't have time to argue pros and cons. We have to go. Now."

Quill gave a single, curt nod. "Some of us have to make

it out of this fight alive. Aphra's influence alone could turn the tide among what's left of the Shriven. We'll split into four groups. Biz, Neve, Vi and I will lead. Keep our distance. Protect our own. Keep going until you reach the children, no matter what. Now count off."

The woman next to Quill began the count. As our groups assembled around us, Myrna came to stand beside me, her mouth set in a grim line. Curlin reached out and took my hand.

"I'm right behind you, Vi. Every step of the way."

With a nod, I took off toward the burning field. My group went far to the right, angling away from the road down a path between bushes that would eventually lead us to a ditch that ran along the far edge of the field and back to the road. Moments after we made our way into the field, we were enveloped in smoke so thick I could hardly see where I set my feet. I turned to Curlin behind me, took her hand and put it on my shoulder. She did the same for Myrna, behind her.

Like that, my little cadre inched across the field. The sounds of fighting—metal on metal; screams of pain, victory and fear; gunshots—faded like a distant memory as we passed through the haze. We would be safe soon.

A sudden shot, so close my ears rang, had me jumping nearly out of my skin. A sound, so gutturally painful it brought tears to my eyes, came from just behind me. I started to look back, but Myrna's hand tightened on my shoulder, and she pushed me onward.

My heart raced in my chest, and I did my best to control my breathing. I took short, shallow breaths, just enough to keep me moving forward. I focused on the exercises I'd learned while diving; focused on keeping the poisoned smoke out of my lungs. The kerchief helped, but it could do only so much. I had to do the rest. I could feel the others becoming more and more agitated, so I picked up the pace, hoping they weren't beginning to succumb to the effects of the philomenas.

Then a giant form appeared before us in the fog, and I stopped dead in my tracks. His back was to us, but as one of the people behind me cursed, the giant man whipped his shorn head in our direction.

"Go!" Myrna shouted to Curlin and me. "I'll hold him off. Get the others out."

I leaped into the next row, leading my group at a breakneck pace across the field. The thick, wet sound of an ax meeting muscle and bone floated through the smoke, stopping me in my tracks. A chill went up my spine, but Curlin pulled me forward, and I stumbled as fast as I could move in the thick haze. I kept looking back over my shoulder, hoping to see Myrna catching up to us. Knowing she wouldn't. Knowing she was gone.

A high-pitched scream echoed from the other side of the field. I swallowed hard. I couldn't leave her. I broke away from Curlin and the others and ran back into the smoke, searching for Myrna. My boot caught on something, and I pitched forward, falling into the damp earth. I pushed myself up, looking back for what had tripped me. There, in the blood-soaked earth, lay Myrna. Her throat slit. Her broken limbs at odd angles. One arm torn entirely off her body.

I stood there, disbelieving, until another scream broke me out of my reverie. My kerchief was nearly dry. I had to get out of the smoke or succumb to the poison, too. I drew my knife and ran, but moments later, I stumbled and went down hard into the outer ditch along the edge of the field. I flung my arm away from my body, only just managing to keep from gutting myself.

Rough hands on either side of me pulled me to my feet, and I couldn't help but howl with the pain of it. I sucked in a deep breath and choked, remembering the presence of the poisoned smoke too late.

I felt wild. Out of control. Curlin pulled me forward, forward, until finally, I could see. I looked around and realized that, of the thirty-odd of us who fled together, only five remained: me, Curlin, Leera, Maz and Gret. The others looked as if they were holding tightly to the last shreds of their sanity, and I felt certain they saw the same struggle in me.

As we ran, I yanked the kerchief down off my face, pulled the canteen off my belt and swirled water through my mouth, spitting over and over again. I wanted the smoke out of me. I needed to purge every last particle of that poison from my body that I could.

It felt as though we'd been running for hours when I finally saw someone sprinting down the path toward us. A single runner. I stopped, took a deep breath and immediately began to cough. When the person stopped in front of me, I looked up, holding tight to my last sliver of hope that my people— *our* people—had somehow come out of this alive.

Part Four

"You need not harbor fear, for your bravery is a sacrifice at my altar. Your lifeblood is the truest testament of your love for me. There is no greater wisdom than the realization of your own insignificance that comes in the moment before you give yourself to me."

—from the *Book of Dzallie, the Warrior*

"I am the power in the throne and the truth in the crown, and it is through my will alone that you will achieve victory. The pleasure you enjoy in worshipping me is the true cessation of sorrow."

—from the *Book of Gadrian, the Firebound*

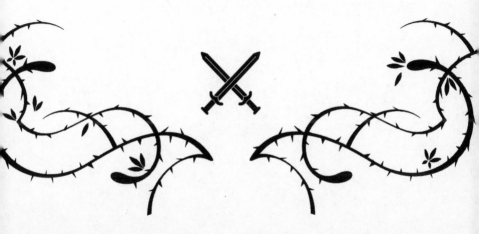

CHAPTER TWENTY-EIGHT

Bo

"I find myself wondering what our lives would be like if we'd been brought up by Ina. I know it isn't a pretty life—the one our siblings lived, and still live—but nevertheless, I find myself wishing we'd always had each other."

—*from Bo to Vi*

It took three days. Three days of prayers to gods I hardly believed in anymore. Three days of fury, of breaking vases and screaming into pillows and crying myself to sleep. Three days of scaring my sisters out of our shared suite with my uncontrollable emotions.

Three days for me to find my way back to the resolve that'd come over me after Runa's death. I was heartbroken, furious and betrayed, but none of that changed what I had to do. None of my emotions excused the responsibility that rested on my shoulders.

On the fourth morning, I pulled myself out of my lonely,

empty bed, dressed and decided that, if nothing else, I ought to find a way to distract myself while I tried to figure out what to do next. Pem and Still were already gone when I emerged from my room, and Doctor Rutin didn't so much as glance up from her book when I opened the door.

"How is he this morning?" I asked in halting Denorian.

She smiled up at me warmly before responding in Alskader. "Calmer each day. This afternoon, perhaps, we will take him for a walk in the garden?"

I nodded. "Thank you." I paused at the outer door of our suite and turned back. "Do you know if there's a library I might access?"

Doctor Rutin furrowed her brows and looked down at her book. "The queen decides who may use the palace library."

I waited, hoping she might give me something more, talk to me, even a little, but she was already absorbed in her reading again. It seemed that Doctor Rutin had very little to say to me if we weren't discussing Swinton and his care. So I took her pointed disinterest as a clear signal and slipped through the door.

I didn't know where I was going, or what I was looking for, so I wandered the halls, hoping that inspiration would find me. Obsequious servants bowed as they rushed past me, all the while ignoring my subtle attempts to flag them down. Polite, but distinctly unhelpful. I heard laughter echoing from the atrium, but the thought of walking into that particular cave of bears made my stomach seize.

Instead, I found myself heading toward the training ground where I'd spoken to Noriava's troops. It had been ages since I'd practiced my swordplay or run through the conditioning exercises Claes and I had done every morning of our youth.

A familiar pang of grief came with the thought of Claes,

the first person I'd ever been infatuated with, the first person I'd ever kissed. At the time, I thought I'd never love someone more than I loved Claes. I'd loved him so much that even in the face of his deathbed betrayal, even though I knew it wasn't what he wanted, I'd clung to the hope that he might recover from his sister's death. But now, when I thought about love, it wasn't Claes's face I saw, but Swinton's. My relationship with Claes had been as shallow as a stream, whereas what I felt for Swinton was as deep as the ocean.

Gadrian's ears, Swinton, I thought. *What have you done to yourself?*

It still wasn't clear to me if Swinton had, in fact, volunteered to taste the poison himself, or if Noriava had forced it on him. Pem and Still had been with me, and none of us had seen what'd actually happened. Once—or Hamil forbid, *if*—he recovered, Swinton would have to tell us himself.

I eased open the door to the practice grounds and entered as unobtrusively as possible. The soldiers were sparring in pairs, grappling barefoot in the grass as officers strode between them, correcting their positions and demonstrating grips and throws. I scanned the field, looking for a familiar face, someone I could connect with, when I spotted her.

General Vittoria Okara was a short, though formidable, woman in her early fifties. Her legs and arms were corded with lean ropes of muscle, and her face was grim as she made her way over to me.

"Your Majesty." She greeted me with a bow. "You know you really don't need to come and inspect the troops every day."

"I wasn't—"

"Quite frankly," she said, her words stepping over mine in a way that would have been unspeakably rude coming from virtually anyone else. But from her, it felt right. Comforting, even. "It's a waste of my time and yours. If you have a question, or if you need something from me, I attend the queen in the atrium most evenings. You may find me there."

"Actually—"

"The gardens are lovely this time of year, as is the queen's art gallery," the general said, pointedly interrupting me again.

I clenched my jaw. I knew that she just wanted me gone, but something inside me railed against the idea. "I came to see if I might be allowed to train with the troops."

General Okara's mouth tightened. "There's no reason for you to risk your health in such a way. That's the whole reason we have soldiers, Your Majesty. To protect you."

"And I, personally, have found that it's better to be prepared than caught with your pants around your ankles."

General Okara looked shocked, and then, a moment later, snorted a quiet laugh. "Fair enough. But these are professionals, Your Majesty. They've been training their whole lives."

"Please call me Bo," I insisted. "And I've had lessons in swordplay and hand-to-hand combat since I was a boy. If I can't keep up, I'll tap out. But I need to *do* something, General Okara. I can't just sit around all day."

She crossed her arms over her chest and looked up at me. "Fine. But here, on this field, you aren't a king. You're just another one of us, and we don't use first names. You'll be— What is it? Gyllen? I can't have it any other way."

"Gyllen is fine. I don't need someone to kiss my wounds when I fall in the dirt," I told her. "I need someone to tell me when I do something wrong. I want to learn to be a real leader, not just some ninny who sits on a throne and plays with his jewels all day."

General Okara clapped me on the back with a grin. "Then

shuck out of that ridiculous jacket and those boots, and let's get to work. You can call me General Okara, General or just Okara. Like the others."

I spent the rest of the morning sweating my way through exercise after exercise. I wrestled. I climbed walls and crawled through the dirt and pushed my body beyond what I'd thought were the limits of my capability. And not for a second did I think about Rylain, or Noriava, or the Suzerain.

It was glorious.

When Okara called a break for the midday meal, the soldiers led me down a long set of stairs carved into the cliff face to a shallow beach, hidden from the harbor by a wide, jutting rock formation. There, on the small beach, one of the men started a fire, a woman hauled a grate from behind a rock and someone else produced an enormous sack of oysters. My offer of help was waved away, so I perched on a rock next to General Okara while the others prepared food for all of us.

"Do you always come down here for the midday meal?" I asked.

She smiled, as if remembering something particularly happy. "Not always, but in light of the fact that we may soon be leaving here with you, I thought I might remind the troops of the things we love about our home."

"I know it's a lot to ask," I said, feeling slightly self-conscious. "To leave your home and defend a foreign king in a foreign land."

The general shrugged. "We follow Queen Noriava's orders. Even when they make little sense to us."

I dragged my big toe through the sand, staring down at the furrow I made. "I doubt she'll follow through, in any case," I said bitterly. "I'm sorry. I know she's your queen. It's just…"

Okara patted my knee. "She doesn't tend to honor her agreements in exactly the way one might expect. I know."

Over by the fire, the soldiers had tucked root vegetables in among the coals and were toasting bits of bread as a pot steamed on the corner of the grate. Then, as if acting on some unspoken cue, two people began tossing oysters onto the grate by the handful. The wind shifted and brought the scents of smoke and brine and the rich tang of cooking wine to my nose. I inhaled deeply, savoring the aroma.

"I wouldn't have come—wouldn't have asked—if it weren't for what it would mean for my people," I explained. "The person who sits on the Alskad throne will determine the lives of thousands of people. You must know what it is to have that kind of responsibility, to have all those lives in your hands. I can't let them down. I won't."

Just then, one of the soldiers appeared with two wide steel plates in his hands, each heaped with a mountain of steaming oysters drenched in a buttery sauce and dotted with chunks of beetroot and sweet potato, the lot of it topped with a heel of toasted brown bread. The general dug in without a word, slurping oysters out of their shells and tossing the empty shells onto the sand. She used one of the oyster shells to scoop up the vegetables and dunked her bread into the remaining sauce. Stomach growling, I followed her example. The beach went quiet as everyone ate, savoring the meal in collective, contented silence. As the soldiers finished eating, they trickled down to the water, squatting to rinse their plates.

Suddenly, a crack like thunder reverberated through the cove, and I looked up just as a cascade of boulders poured off the cliff face, crashing down to the water and sand below. I heard a scream from the waterline, but the only people I could see were looking around, confused.

I leaped up, flinging my plate into the sand, and started running toward the pile of fallen rocks. The closer I got, the louder the screams became. I dropped to my knees at the edge of the rocks and peered into the heap, hoping to catch a glimpse of the person who'd been trapped. More tiny rocks poured off the ledge above, peppering my back like hailstones in a bad storm, but I ignored them. The only thing that mattered was making sure the soldier under those rocks survived.

"Hello?" I called in Denorian. "Can you hear me? My name is Bo. I'm here to help."

There was another loud crack, and, instinctively, I covered my head and neck with my arms as fist-sized stones poured down around me. The scream turned into a wail, but I kept talking, murmuring words I hoped were comforting. As soon as the onslaught slowed, I peered into the gloom and saw the soldier's fingers reaching for me. I grabbed hold and gave them a squeeze before standing to assess the new damage.

Someone laid a hand on my shoulder, and I glanced up to see a group of soldiers gathered around me, seemingly waiting for my command. "Someone go get a doctor," I said hurriedly. One of the soldiers nodded and took off at a sprint toward the palace. "The rest of you, help me. We need to get him out of there. But go slowly. We don't want the rocks to shift and cause more damage."

Moving carefully, we shifted one stone after another. We heaved boulders the size of small dogs off the pile, and we had just uncovered the soldier's face and legs when a team of doctors arrived, screeching for us to stop. I stepped back from the pile quickly, hands up.

"I'm so sorry," I said. "What would you like us to do?"

One of the doctors, a woman in her late middle age, addressed General Okara. "We need to assess the patient before the pressure is relieved. It could be that those rocks are the only thing keeping him alive right now. We'll let you know if we need further assistance."

General Okara nodded and steered me away from the rockfall by the elbow. "What you did, risking your life like that? It was extremely stupid."

I choked back a laugh that threatened to become a sob and gaped at her. "What do you mean?"

"No prince or king should put his own life on the line to save a simple soldier," General Okara admonished. "What's more, the soldiers on this beach are more than capable of seeing to their own."

"They weren't, though," I protested. "No one was moving."

General Okara closed her eyes and rubbed the bridge of her nose. "I'm not making my point well. What you did was stupid and reckless and something I never thought I'd see from royalty. It was brave. It was selfless." She opened her eyes and looked at me intently. "There's more to you than shows up on first impressions, Gyllen."

I pressed my lips together and watched as the doctors extracted the soldier from the rocks and laid him gently on a stretcher. I didn't know what to say to the general, how I ought to respond. I hadn't thought. I'd simply acted as I would've expected anyone to do.

When the doctors had carried the wounded man up the stairs and back toward the palace, I helped the Denorian soldiers clean up the beach and pack everything they'd brought for the meal. We worked in comfortable, companionable silence under the watchful eye of General Okara. And for the first time since Swinton drank the temple's poison, I felt a flicker of hope.

CHAPTER TWENTY-NINE

Vi

"I am lost. There was a time when I thought I knew myself to my very core, to the heart of my soul. But now, when I catch sight of myself in a mirror, the person I see is a stranger."

—*from Vi to Bo*

Rain fell in cold sheets, smearing the mud that we'd rubbed over our skin into dirty streaks down our faces. My throat burned, and the hacking coughs that rattled my bones brought up globs of soot-black mucus.

Someone handed me a flask, and the liquid was halfway down my gullet before the alcoholic burn filled my mouth. I gagged, and my stomach heaved, bringing up a mixture of burning liquid and bile. I collapsed onto my knees in the muddy path, retching again and again as horrible, bloody images flashed in front of me. Bodies left lying in the dirt, broken and empty.

Myrna's face. Oh, *gods*. Myrna's face above her slit throat. Her mangled body.

I threw up into the dirt again. As I knelt there, trembling and gasping for breath, I felt a hand on my shoulder, followed by Curlin's voice.

"If you're finished, we need to move."

She was right. I knew she was right, but I still wanted to wrap my hands around her neck and squeeze until she stopped breathing. The thought startled me—it came out of nowhere. That violence wasn't like me; didn't make sense to me. It felt like someone else forcing thoughts into my head.

Curlin offered me a hand, and I let her pull me up. The pace she set was brisk, and as we walked, all of the aches from the long run and my old injuries flared. Spikes of pain radiated from my feet upward. I wanted to collapse. I wanted to sleep for a thousand years, and before long, I found myself at the back of the group, each step an agony.

Neve and Biz sidled up to Quill and spoke to him in low tones. I was so distracted by the physical pain and worry about Bo, by Myrna's death, by the cloud of death and smoke that I'd created, that I felt only the barest tickle of curiosity about their conversation before the horror of the day washed over me once more. When we finally found what was left of our group huddled in a clearing just off the side of the road, I fell into Curlin's and Aphra's arms, sobs racking my body.

"Hush, hush," Aphra said, petting my muddy, tangled hair. "You did everything you could. You brought your people out of there alive. None of us would have even made it this far if not for your quick thinking in the distillery."

Curlin laced her strong fingers through mine. "Sawny would be proud of you. You chose just as he would've done."

"How will I ever be able to face Bo again? And Quill?

Quill said that he cared about me, loved me, but how could he possibly love someone as violent, as awful as I've been?" I asked through choking sobs. Even though he'd been with me, even though he'd seen it, even though he'd fought beside me, I didn't know how I could possibly face him again.

Curlin's hand tightened around mine, and I fought to get myself under control. I wiped away my tears with my filthy shoulder and said, "I murdered those people. I never should have agreed to the plan. It was vicious, horrible. They lost themselves entirely. We stole their humanity. And Myrna! Rayleane's teeth, poor Hepsy is going to murder me in cold blood, and rightly so."

Aphra took my face in her hands. "Listen to—"

I cut her off. "No. Not like that. You can't just go magicking folks into believing whatever you choose to tell them or taking their guilt and grief away from them. If you're going to use your magic, Aphra, use it to do some good in this world."

Aphra looked helplessly at Curlin, who nodded. "She's right, Aph. You've got to start using a bit more caution. You can't just go around manipulating folks into doing whatever it is that'll please you best."

Though she made a great show of scowling at Curlin, Aphra wrapped her arms around me and hugged me tight. "You made the right choice, Vi. There are no easy choices in a war, and the ones you made today may have turned the tide in this fight."

The rain had let up a bit, and the others in the little clearing were shifting, looking to Quill, Aphra and Curlin—and me, I supposed—for direction.

I crossed the clearing to Quill and asked, "How far to the horses?"

"Not far. Maybe another two hours' walk?" he said with a

grimace. "But it might be a bit difficult, as tired and injured as the group is. I wish there was a way for us to rest safely overnight, but the jungle isn't safe."

"I don't want to split us up again." My stomach heaved, thinking of Myrna lying slaughtered in the field of philomenas.

Quill's full lips compressed into a thin line. I knew the people we'd lost—and that black, guilt-ridden regret—would follow him the same way it followed me, but I couldn't connect that knowing with anything solid. With any feeling. It was like there was a chasm between us, and I wanted desperately to bridge it. Even for an instant.

"No. I won't make that mistake this time," he agreed.

On an impulse, I flung my uninjured arm around his shoulders and hugged him. He, at least, understood the guilt and the horror that I would face each time I looked in a mirror from now on. He would see the same in himself. "It wasn't a mistake," I told him. "It very likely saved the rest of our lives. Magritte's tongue, imagine what would've happened if we'd all been together when that group attacked."

Quill's stiff body relaxed ever so slightly, and he returned my hug briefly before stepping back. "Thank you, Vi. I appreciate you saying that."

"I'm not just—" But before I could finish, he'd walked off to gather the rest of the group.

We walked in a tight clump. No one said much, and everyone spent as much time glancing over their shoulders as they did watching where they planted their feet. I walked beside Quill at the back of the group, and Aphra and Curlin led us. They glanced back from time to time, their eyes seeking mine.

All I could think about was Bo, and how much I wished I was with him. I knew, deep in my heart, that he wasn't dead.

He couldn't be. The missing him was bone-deep, but I knew I would see him again.

What I didn't know was how I'd face him. How I would tell him what I'd done. At least he would never have to see the horror of it, never have those memories playing on an endless loop in his brain. Maybe he'd be able to forgive me without the sickening crunch of metal on bone, the wet rip of teeth tearing into flesh, the agonized screams of the people I hadn't saved playing over and over in his head. I didn't know if I'd ever be able to free myself of those memories. Maybe he'd be able to show me a way to redemption.

But for now, all I could find was hate. I hated myself. Hated the Shriven. Hated the people who'd built their wealth on the backs of the exploited and abused laborers, and the monarchy that'd stood by and allowed them to do it.

Suddenly, I ran dead-on into the person in front of me, who'd stopped short in the road with the rest of the group. I stumbled backward, teeth clenched. I fought down the fury that threatened to overwhelm me, a little taken aback by how quickly my temper rose in my chest. I stood on tiptoe to get a better look over the heads of the people in front of me. Quill, beside me, did the same.

"Shriven," he breathed. "Vi, with me."

He strode quickly to stand beside Aphra and Curlin, and I had to jog to catch up. The Shriven stood in the middle of the road in perfect rows, their spotless white ceremonial dress in stark contrast to our mud-smeared, blood-spattered assembly. There were dozens of them—five or six times our total numbers at least. They must have made up at least half of the Shriven's total fighting force in Ilor.

As we watched, they unbuckled their belts and laid their

weapons at their feet. One of them, a woman with rich brown skin and wide dark eyes, stepped forward.

"Though your offer of amnesty only extended until this dawn, there was no way for us to remove ourselves from the others without raising the alarm," she said. "We hope that you will accept our surrender now, and our offer to aid your cause. We were each forced into this service in one way or another, and your generosity and compassion even in the face of the overwhelming odds you faced was extraordinary. With your permission, we will formally renounce our association with the Shriven and dedicate ourselves to the cause you serve."

Before any of the others could speak, I stepped forward, just a pace away from the other woman.

"You offer to dedicate yourselves to the cause we serve, but you've no idea what that cause is."

A ripple of whispers and shifting weight traveled through the group behind me. The metallic scrape of weapons hauled from their sheaths made me turn and glare at Quill, who signaled his people to stop.

I forced myself to take a deep, calming breath before speaking again. "We've set ourselves two fair impossible tasks. We mean to stop the production of the philomena serum in Ilor, but in order to do that, we have to take down the Suzerain. And we have to go back to Alskad, to see my brother take the throne."

I hadn't consulted with Quill or Aphra. I hadn't asked if they approved. We needed more political clout, plain and simple. And for that, we needed Bo.

If everyone in Alskad thought he was dead, there must be a reason for it, and he was probably in danger. I had to get back to Williford and wait for word from him. I knew that he would write me, and the moment that letter came, I would bring my army to him.

I felt a shift inside myself at those words. *My army.* It was a place I'd been coming to for a long time, a power I'd needed to find my way into. And now, I would lead this little army as far as they would follow me.

"We can't just destroy the temple here in Ilor," I told the Shriven. "Though that *is* critical. We have to put an end to the practice of using the philomena serum to turn dimmys. If I do nothing else with my life, I'll see that the Suzerain pay for that crime. It's unconscionable to exploit the fear of dimmys in order to build the Suzerain's power, and it's even worse to use the dimmys as tools. My work—the work that Curlin and I promised to do—is to defend the people of Ilor and Alskad against exploitation and ignorant hate. Will you help me?"

Curlin stepped forward to stand beside me. A moment later, Quill and Aphra joined us. The Shriven woman, without turning to look at the ranks behind her, gave me a four-fingered salute and dropped to her knee. Another of the white-clad Shriven saluted, then knelt. One by one, the rest of the co-hort, a hundred or more of them, followed suit. Tears welled in my eyes, and my heart surged with hope.

I went to the woman and offered her my hand.

"Thank you," I said, tears making my words wobble and squeak. "I cannot tell you how much this means to me."

"My twin died when I was eight," she told me. "There aren't words to explain the fury I felt when I learned that I'd spent years dreading a change that would never come—not so long as I did as my commanders told me, anyway." Rage filled her eyes. "There's not a person in my company that doesn't have a story much the same. We share the same story, and I trust that you will lead us to victory in this fight."

I gave her a watery smile. "I'm Vi Abernathy. Pleased to meet you."

"Ji. Jihye Elias, at your service."

Ensconced at a table in the corner of Swinton's mother's inn, I tapped my nails on the table and waited anxiously for Mal and Quill to arrive. For the first time in days, I was clean and full, and there was a pitcher of hot, spiced wine resting on a warmer in the middle of the table.

It had taken three days to get the Shriven and rebels set up in a camp just outside Williford. Quill had gone ahead of us to collect the brats and see them safely settled in borrowed rooms all over the city. Thanks to Curlin's tireless coaxing, the two groups had come to an uneasy sort of peace. There were still wary looks on either side, but each night more of the Shriven had joined the rebels at the fires. And each day, more of them had walked beside us as we made our way toward Williford.

We'd gone to the governor's mansion first, to find Hepsy and tell her the news of her sister's passing, but we'd arrived too late. Ysanne told us that she'd succumbed the same day as her sister. Despite how different they'd been, their connection had been so strong that Myrna's death had pulled Hepsy with her into the halls of the gods. A part of me was glad. Glad that she'd not suffered. Glad that she'd not had to bear the grief and burden of becoming one of the diminished.

Curlin put a hand over mine, drawing me back to the present. I shrugged away from her touch.

"I'm fine," I snapped.

"You don't have to pretend."

Lucky for Curlin, Mal appeared, saving her from pushing her comforting routine too far.

"You two look flat awful. Gaunt, battered and bruised." He glanced around and called, "Someone bring these women something to eat! They look starved."

I jumped to my feet and pulled Mal into a ferocious hug, my heart in my throat. "Always trying to take care of people, aren't you? We're all set. Mulled wine and food on the way."

When I finally let him go, Mal kissed the air beside Curlin's cheeks, an affected gesture she barely tolerated, and settled himself onto a stool. I looked at him expectantly.

"Oh, right. Of course," he said, and pulled a battered envelope from inside his jacket.

The handwriting on the envelope wasn't Bo's. The spidery, staccato script belonged to Gerlene, Bo's solicitor. Tears flooded my eyes. Gerlene wouldn't write me unless...

I shook the idea off like cold water. I couldn't be wrong. Bo was fine. He *had* to be fine.

Mal, seeing the look on my face, rushed to reassure me. "No! She wrote us, too. Bo was in a hurry, so she addressed the envelope, but he's fine. Not to worry."

"See?" I gave Curlin a tart look that was spoiled by my relief. "I told you he was okay."

I tore open the envelope and scanned the letter. Eyebrows raised, I passed it to Curlin, who gave a low whistle as she finished reading.

"You go from dimmy to twin more than any other person alive. Why don't the two of you just settle the hell down?" Curlin covered her smile with furrowed brows and poured a mug of spiced wine, then slid it across the table to Mal. "Where's your handsome brother?"

Mal winked at her. "I am the handsome brother."

Curlin's mouth twitched. "Not my cup of tea, darling."

I grinned. "So..."

Curlin cut me off. "Will Quill be here soon?"

Mal shook his head. "He was away as soon as he got the brats settled. Gone to meet Uncle Hamlin up the coast to off-load some of the ship's inventory before he reaches harbor here. We do still have to make a living, you know."

I grimaced into my mulled wine, then forced a smile onto my face and batted my lashes at Mal.

"Speaking of..."

"Vi, my dear," Mal said dryly, "have I ever told you how much I hate it when you get that look on your face?"

I dropped the act. "We're going to need your uncle's ship."

"His *what*?"

"His ship. You know. The big iron thing that inexplicably floats in the ocean? Takes people from Alskad to Ilor and back again? We're going to need that. Most of it, anyway, though once he sees who we're bringing along, he might want to go ahead and let us have the run of the place."

"You'll arrange it, and, of course, Vi'll pay for it," Curlin said.

"Just as soon as she gets her hands on the family money Bo's set aside for her."

"Better, charge it to the temple's account." I shot Curlin my wickedest grin. "It is their people, after all."

Mal threw his hands up and pushed his chair back from the table. "I honestly don't want to know. Uncle Hamlin is due back in port sometime in the next week. I'll leave the negotiations to you."

"Sit down," Curlin snapped. "We've things to discuss with you yet."

Mal sank back into his chair with a sigh and poured himself another steaming mug of wine.

The next morning, I took a pot of milky tea into the crisp air of the garden at the governor's mansion. The first tendrils of winter's chill had appeared, as if overnight, and I shivered with the memory of Alskad's frozen landscape. Somehow, in the space of a year, I'd managed to take myself from Alskad's frozen tundra to the indolent heat of Ilor's summer, and now, as the promise of the first mild winter of my life dangled in front of me, I'd somehow contrived to get myself back to Alskad.

I sipped my tea, kicked my feet up onto the bench and leaned my back against the armrest, feeling more content than I had in ages. In just a few short weeks, I'd be reunited with my twin.

A part of me rejoiced at the idea, but every time I thought about Bo, I saw the faces of the Shriven as the philomena extract rained down on them in the distillery. Whenever someone tried to talk to me, I heard the screams of the people I'd left behind. Every little thing infuriated me, and I was haunted by a kind of anger I'd never felt before in my life. Something in me was broken, and it was all I could do to keep pushing myself forward, day after day.

The screen door at the back of the house whistled shut. I glanced over my shoulder, but wide leaves and bushes thick with late-season berries hid most of the house from my view. I kept my eyes trained on the path until I saw the knot of locks atop Quill's head bobbing over the bushes and heard the dogs' jangling collars as they trotted alongside him. Stomach heaving with sudden nerves, my eyes flicked down to the mug of tea cooling in my lap.

With each day that had passed since the battle with the Shriven, I'd felt my connection to him slipping away. I couldn't imagine indulging in any kind of romance right now, not after everything that I'd seen and done. After everything we'd done together. Not when the horrors of the last few weeks were only the beginning of the fight.

When I first met Quill, I'd fallen for a man who was gentle and funny and kind. But that was only part of him. As much as he was all those things, I'd seen a new side of him these last few weeks—a darker, more vicious side. And that didn't frighten me, didn't lessen my love for him a bit. But I didn't know if I was ready to show him the person *I* was becoming.

"May I sit?"

A thread of tension tied Quill's voice to the fear in my gut, and I drew my knees up to my chin by way of assent. Quill perched on the far edge of the bench, planted his elbows on his thighs and dug the heels of his long, elegant hands into his temples.

"Denor, is it?"

"Bo needs me."

Quill's golden eyes flicked to me, and he lifted an eyebrow. "It wasn't an argument, Vi."

I scrubbed a hand through my curls and stared down at the gold cuff wrapped around my wrist, searching for the right words, but nothing came to mind.

"Not for nothing," Quill said, "but I think it's a good call. Like you said, your brother needs you, and the situation in Alskad is far more dire than it is here. Aphra and Ysanne can keep the temple under control now that we have the Shriven on our side. With their help, she really won't even need most of our people. I assume you've already asked them to go with you?"

I let the question hang in the air. I hadn't asked *him* to go with me. Hadn't even considered it. He had to make a living, after all. After a long, uncomfortable minute, Quill took a deep breath.

"Mal and I would like to go, too. It's a good opportunity for us. We can make connections in Denor for trade." He paused, flicking an invisible piece of lint from his trousers. I could almost feel the tension in his shoulders, same as mine. I wondered if either of us would ever find the words to bridge the immense space between us, or if we'd be forever staring at each other across this chasm of our shared horrors.

"Of course," I said, rising to my feet. "It's your ship, after all."

I started back toward the house, but paused at the edge of the bench, tempted to lay a hand on Quill's broad shoulder. He looked up at me, his brows furrowed, and I stuffed my free hand into my pocket.

"We'll leave as soon as we can provision the ship," Quill said.

Nodding, I hurried into the house before the pain and anger coursing through my veins was writ as plain on my face as it was on Quill's.

Over the next few days, Aphra managed to explain the influx of Shriven defectors by the means of a newsletter, printed and distributed to all the citizens of Ilor at the government's expense. She explained the hard choices they'd made and why, and she asked that the people of Ilor welcome them as their own. To try to see past the tattoos and shorn heads, and see instead the people who'd given up everything they'd worked for and believed in to protect the well-being and safety of the citizens of Ilor. The reaction of the folks I saw was reserved, but no one fingered their weapons as we passed, no one yelled, and most seemed willing to give the Shriven who'd decided to stay in Ilor a chance.

As I walked through Williford toward Hamlin's ship, I was overwhelmed by the number of people who'd crowded into the streets to see us off. While the citizens of Williford stood on the docks and stared, I walked behind the hundreds of folks who, until very recently, had served the temple as Shriven. They handed fruit and sweets to the children gathered along the docks, stopping to speak to those who looked most scared and generally making the best impression they could upon leaving. Some of the Shriven were staying behind to train the peacekeepers and rebels who'd decided to stay in Ilor. Others would serve as intermediaries to the anchorites holed up in the temples. A few simply wanted to make new lives for themselves in Ilor.

Most, however, had agreed to come with us and finish what we'd started. To see an end to the temple's abuse. To see a twin on the throne.

It hadn't been hard to convince Hamlin to take us to Denor. I'd promised him a prince's ransom in gold—some from Bo's accounts in the colonies, some stolen from the temple's stores—up front, and more yet in shipping contracts plus a promotion to admiral once Bo was settled on the throne. He'd happily closed his ticket offices and delayed the passengers already set to travel to Alskad aboard his ship to the next month, then filled his hold with the Ilorian seeds, dried herbs and flowers most valued by Denorian scientists.

But Curlin had been the one to talk to the Whipplestons, not me. Since our encounter in the garden, I hadn't been in a room alone with Quill. I'd slipped away from the countless short minutes he'd tried to steal in the days we'd spent preparing for the voyage, afraid to talk to him again. Afraid to let him see the cracks, the deep oozing rents where I'd torn myself apart in those two battles and stitched myself back together again. He'd fallen in love with someone beautiful, determined and as healthy as one of the diminished could be. But I'd put that person between two rocks and ground them together until all that was left was dust.

Curlin and I were the last people to climb aboard. She clapped me on the back as we scaled the gangplank. "Take a second and look at that."

I stopped and turned to look out over the dock. There were hundreds of people—Shriven, Ilorians and the newly empowered contract laborers. Some had just arrived in Ilor; others had been there longer than I'd been alive. And they were standing together, talking to each other. No one looked scared. No one looked sidelong and distrusting at anyone else.

They looked comfortable together. Happy.

Aphra, at the front of the crowd, caught sight of me. She touched four fingers to her heart, then her forehead, and raised her hand over her head, grinning. She'd taken the Shriven's salute and added a touch to her heart. As I returned the gesture, tears welling in my eyes, I saw Ysanne look between us and follow suit. Soon her wife and their two young children did the same. I wasn't sure if I was more concerned by Ysanne's good behavior or Aphra's, but I would have to let it go, at least for the time being.

"We did it," Curlin said.

"We made a good start," I said, hastily wiping the tears from my eyes. "But there's still a long way to go."

CHAPTER THIRTY

Bo

"I feel so very alone, Vi. I wish our paths didn't keep us so very far apart."
—*from Bo to Vi*

My days in Denor quickly took on a routine. I spent my mornings with the troops learning their drills, practicing my own fighting techniques and mapping out a detailed plan to take back the palace in Penby. General Okara drilled alongside her soldiers, faster and deadlier than anyone on the training field despite her age and size. She was precise in her language, and formal almost to the point of being stiff, but there was something about her that was inexplicably appealing. It felt as though we were becoming something like friends.

"It's an odd thing, to command the army of a peaceful nation," she said one morning, wiping the thin sheen of sweat from her brow with a damp cloth.

Head between my knees and wheezing after the tortuous, seemingly never-ending run she'd led us on that morning, I gratefully accepted the cup of water she offered me and forced myself to stand.

"What brought you to it?" I asked.

"I never had much of a mind for sciences or theory in school, but I loved strategy and sport," the general mused. "Before the queen's mother's time, the army was more of an honor guard for the ruler than anything else. I came up with Noriava's mother, Dextera. We saw the Alskad Empire expanding under Runa's rule, not to mention the threat the Samirians posed. As I was promoted through the ranks, Dextera leaned more and more heavily on my judgment, and we sought to expand the army. It's still not much compared to the Samirian forces, but it gives our younglings a path other than the sciences, agriculture or the scant trade and business a city like Salemouth can support."

"And Noriava? She approves of your work?"

General Okara gave me a discerning look. "I'll say naught of the queen but that she's got double the ambition of her mother and father put together."

A group of soldiers walked past us toward the grappling grounds, their uniforms soaked with sweat despite the cool air of the midwinter morning. As they passed under the general's hawkeyed, assessing gaze, their conversation petered out and they drew their spines up straight. She was the kind of leader that drew the awed respect of her troops without any derision, harshness or cajoling. They simply wanted to do their best work for her.

"I wonder if I might convince you to join me for a cup of tea tonight after supper?" I asked tentatively, knowing she'd likely say no. "I'd love to pick your brain and learn a bit more about Denor and her history."

General Okara gave a slight nod. "It would be my great

pleasure, though I might convince you to offer me something a bit stiffer than a cup of tea."

And with that, General Okara and I began a tradition. Each night, after a painfully tense supper with Noriava, the general would appear in my doorway, proffering a tin of tea imported from the hills of the Samirian mountains, a bottle of Denorian wine or a flask of the heady, smoke-laced spirit the Denorians made in their own stills. And each night, we would talk into the late hours, sometimes nearly until dawn.

General Okara—Vittoria—had known my grandmother more than just a bit, and her stories about Runa were like a balm to the raw grief just under the surface of my anxiety. Most nights, after her steel grip on propriety loosened a bit, Vittoria would tell me a little about Noriava. It was becoming clear that despite our differences, the young woman was an excellent queen, which made it all the more difficult to endure her infuriatingly callous negotiation of our impending nuptials.

Most afternoons, I took Swinton for a walk through the lush palace gardens, under the careful supervision of Doctor Rutin. Swinton was like a volcano. Some days he was calm, almost himself again, but I could see the fury boiling like lava under the stone of his control. Other days, it was like I was walking with a boiling inferno, and I kept myself coiled tight, waiting for him to erupt.

On those days, he terrified me.

"What're you thinking, little lord?"

The question came out more as a sharp command than as a query posed by a lover, but I swallowed hard and did my best to keep my voice light. "Only hoping that Vi's gotten my letter by now. I'd hate for her to hear that I've been killed and be left thinking she's a dimmy. Especially after all she's been through."

"Vi can take care of herself."

"I know. I just—"

"You're the one who needs looking after. You cannot believe that I'm going to let you marry that awful woman." Swinton's hand tightened on mine, squeezing the bones together so hard that I was afraid they might break. I gently pulled my hand free of his, and the moment I let go, he slammed his fist into the nearest tree trunk.

"Swinton..."

Doctor Rutin stepped between us, already pulling the vial of sedative from the pouch at her waist. "Best not. He's been worked up all day."

Swinton pounded the tree, grunting and cursing, oblivious to everything but his fists against the wood. He was, I knew, focused on hitting anything but me. She slipped a syringe into the vial, pulled up to fill the barrel, pushed the first bit of liquid through the needle to clear the bubbles, then plunged it quickly into Swinton's backside. He slumped into my waiting arms, and Doctor Rutin went to fetch the guards who would carry him back to the locked room in my suite where he spent most of his time.

I sat heavily beside him and ran my fingers through his long, dark gold hair. We kept having the same argument. We went round and round in circles about the wedding, about Noriava, about how I ought to have left him and taken my chances against Rylain and the Alskad nobility without the help of the Denorian army.

That was on the days when he was lucid. The rest of the time, he simply lunged for me. It was as though his only goal was to rip the limbs off any person stupid enough to get within range of his hands. Doctor Rutin had started Swinton on the medicine the Denorians had created to help the violent diminished, and we'd seen some slight improvement in his ability to cope with the rising tide of his anger, but not much.

The lush, green beauty of the Denorian royal gardens was made even more striking when contrasted against the sheer black stone of the palace walls that enclosed it. But though the place itself had a loveliness that forced its way into a person's very soul—a hungry, demanding sort of beauty—it did nothing to quell my increasing sense of dread. I hadn't felt the strong tug of Vi's emotions in nearly a week. It was as though she was a deadweight on the end of a very long rope: still noticeably there, but blank, almost numbed. Guilt washed over me as I realized how long it had been since I'd given her or her work in Ilor even a moment's thought. I sent up a brief prayer to the gods that she was safe, and had received and understood the letter I'd sent before I left Alskad.

The soft *thump* of bootsteps in the thick, neatly trimmed grass brought me out of my reverie, and I looked up to see a trio of guards trailing after Doctor Rutin, their white coats billowing out behind them like the sails of an armada.

Doctor Rutin spoke to the guards in Denorian, but all I caught were the words *gently, please*. My Denorian was improving in fits and starts, but I really didn't have much of a head for languages, and it took a great deal of focus to switch my thinking from one to the other.

My mother and my tutors had worked endlessly to try to force me to be fluent in Denorian and Samirian, but despite years of trying, I was still barely competent. After weeks of immersion in Denorian, I found that I understood more than I could say, but that still wasn't much. Each time I wanted to speak, I had to carefully translate each phrase, almost like flipping a card in my head as I considered each idea I wanted to convey.

Annoyingly, Pem and Still had taken the pidgin Denorian they'd learned from merchants and traders in Alskad and quickly become nearly fluent in the language.

One of the guards offered me a hand. Behind him, a bush shook, and I saw a flash of white linen as one of the twins, Pem or Still, darted into the garden's underbrush. Thanking him in my halting Denorian, I allowed myself to be brought to my feet and stood back, biting my lip as I snuck a glance at the lush undergrowth. Doctor Rutin put a hand on my shoulder in a kind, if not somewhat untoward, gesture as the guards hefted Swinton up into their arms and carried him quickly back toward the castle.

The bald truth escaped from my mouth before I could think to measure my words. "He's getting worse."

"You must give the medicine time to work, Your Majesty."

"None of that," I said with a sigh. "Please just call me Bo, Doctor Rutin. And please forgive my abruptness. It's only that I'm worried. He's got no impulse control at all, and his mood swings come out of nowhere."

"I know that seeing him this way is distressing, but you must understand that we rarely see an improvement in a subject's demeanor before they've been in treatment for at least a quarter of a year," she replied gently. "And this is a rather unusual case. To my knowledge, I've never treated someone who was transformed by a poison rather than the natural course of grief. We cannot expect things to progress normally."

"Do you have any word from your colleagues about their work on the cure?" I twisted the gold cuff on my wrist. "The longer I leave Rylain on the throne in Alskad, the harder it will be to establish myself as a ruler there once more."

"Nothing yet, but I am sure they'll have something to test soon."

"Test?"

"Well, yes, of course. You cannot go straight from theory to dosing human beings. There must be testing done in the interim to make sure that the medicine is safe."

I blanched at the thought of still more time spent in Denor with my hands tied, waiting.

"It won't take long," Doctor Rutin said quickly. "As soon as they've come up with something that might work, they'll begin first on animals before moving to human subjects."

My dismay must've been written clear across my face.

"Everyone they'll test the drug upon will give their express and lucid permission, of course, before taking part in the trial. They will be well-informed of the risks before they undergo the therapy."

How I'd not realized the need to test the medicine on human subjects before, I'd no idea, but the idea made me queasy. I needed to talk to Pem and Still. They'd taken to their spy craft a bit too well for my taste, and the reports they'd brought me could only've come from sneaking into dangerous places any decent brother would've certainly kept them from even thinking of visiting. I'd put good money on their having gathered more information than the good doctor was willing to share with me.

"Thank you, Doctor," I said. I hoped she'd take the hint and cut the conversation short.

"May I walk with you back to your rooms? I'm going that way."

I ducked my head to hide the irritated blush that crept up my neck, all the more heated now that I'd allowed myself to acknowledge it. "Thank you, no. I believe I'll just walk a bit longer."

With a nod and a squeeze of my hand, Doctor Rutin turned and meandered back down the path, drawing her notebook from her pocket and scribbling notes in her close script. As soon as she disappeared around a turn, Pem crawled out of the bushes, dried leaves and twigs clinging to her hair and clothes.

"She's a rutting liar," Pem spit without so much as a hello.

"Why do you think so?"

The girls were unabashedly judgmental, so I generally took their pronouncements with all the caution they deserved.

"Me and Still both've seen them up in the labs, already giving drops of this and that to little dogs and wee beasties. Every time they do it, the poor creatures drop dead, too. They spend more than a little time going on about how much easier it'd be if they knew what plants'd been used to make the stuff. They're the ones what are talking about the dimmys, too, so don't go saying it's something else."

I kept my mouth shut, a little shocked by how well she knew me now, and considered her for a moment. "Can you manage to keep an eye out without being noticed?" I asked.

Pem laughed. "Those folks have their heads so far up their own asses, they wouldn't notice me or Still if we bit 'em, and only then if we weren't in uniform. So long as we keep wearing their white coats, acting like the students they got skittering all over the place, and talking to 'em in Denorian, we won't have no trouble at all." She sent me a sidelong glance. "Want us to look in on the other science folks once in a while, as well? I might be able to steal some of their notes, if you wanted to know what they were up to."

"Actually, I want to see it for myself. Is there a way I could get in there with you?" I asked.

"You think you could see something we don't?" I shrugged, and Pem studied me thoughtfully. "Sure, we could get you in there. You just couldn't say nothing. Your Denorian's atrocious."

"I've never had much of a mind for languages."

"Never had much of a mind for languages?" Pem gawked at me. "It ain't as though it's hard, Bo. It's just learning a new vocabulary. You've got to learn how to talk to people, elsewise they're likely to get the best of you. You sure you're cut out to be king?"

I looked up at the darkening sky as yet another cloud front of chilled, drizzly rain rolled across the bay toward us.

"No. I'm not sure at all."

"I don't mean to be awful, you know." Noriava settled herself on the green velvet settee, a glass of amber-colored wine held precariously in one of her elegant hands, her dark green eyes settled contemplatively on my face. "I would vastly prefer to find a way past the challenges of our early relationship and find some common ground."

We had retired to a room just off the atrium after yet another meal through which I remained cut entirely out of the conversation, due to my stumbling Denorian and reticence to engage with the queen. Noriava's guests, still visible through the wide double doors, engaged themselves in various card games and heated debates in highly elevated, intellectual Denorian.

I perched on a low bench, a glass of bubbly mineral water slowly warming in my hands, despite the chill of the palace. As a precaution, I'd stopped drinking anything alcoholic. I didn't want to be caught off guard or agree to any of her seemingly innocuous prenuptial requests without a clear head. I knew, on some level, that I ought to make at least some effort to cultivate a relationship with my fiancée, but I could find neither the energy nor the will to go to such lengths to placate her. Instead, I stared at the patterns in the thick Samirian carpet beneath my feet.

"Doctor Loviar tells me that he's begun your companion on a medication he has great confidence will do some good for the young man."

I forced myself to keep my face still, though it was by no means easy. I'd neither seen Doctor Loviar nor heard his name since that first awful night when Swinton had drunk the temple's poison. I wondered if she was mistaken, or if this was a calculated move on her part, though her intentions were not at all clear to me.

"I'm grateful to you for offering Swinton the care of your medical practitioners," I said, offering my response in Denorian.

I sipped my mineral water and forced myself not to look for Noriava's reaction. My insistence on speaking her language, despite my stumbling lack of fluency, seemed to be a source of endless frustration to Noriava, which in turn fueled the fire of my determination. It was perhaps a bit childish, but the tiny spark of joy I found in irritating Noriava alongside the added benefit of practicing my Denorian was enough to keep me trudging mulishly forward.

Noriava's cat, Tipswallis, leaped up onto the settee and turned three tight circles before settling down to glare at me. Noriava petted him, her dark stare a double of her cat's. He began to purr, and the sound was like a chunk of wood being scraped against rocks. I glanced at the party in the adjoining room, wondering just how long I had to stay before I could make my excuses and retire.

"I was thinking," Noriava said in flawless, only slightly

accented Alskader, "that we might, perhaps, take a bit of a break from the wedding plans and try to get past this barrier we've erected between us. We will, after all, be married within the month."

I bolted upright and stared at her. "You've had news of the cure?"

The small muscles in Noriava's jaw tightened, and her eyes darted to the doorway.

"For once, could you manage to go a full hour without mentioning the godsdamned poison or its fucking cure?" she snapped. Her cat's tail flicked back and forth, and its large green eyes glared out from beneath its lowered brows.

"I would have thought that your interest would at the very least equal my own, given what you have to lose if your scientists fail," I retorted. "Imagine what Denor could do with a fleet of ships and the ability to seek out new habitable land. Finding a cure is in your best interest, as well as Swinton's."

"I'm not the idiot who drank the stuff in the first place, and you'd do well to remember that you have just as much to lose as I do, if not more."

My fingers reflexively tightened around my glass at the implied threat, but I forced myself to relax my grip and set the glass aside as I rose to my feet. "Then I'll take my leave of you, before one of us says something we might regret."

The cat hissed at me, but before I could turn to go, Noriava reached out and took my hand.

"I'm sorry. You have very little reason to like me, and less still to open up to me." Her voice wavered, and tears welled in her eyes. "But a marriage between our two nations is a smart choice, Bo, and I'd very much like it if we could at least try to learn to trust one another."

"How can you possibly ask me to trust you when all you've

done is manipulate me and mine, and try to negotiate every ounce of power away from me?" I yanked my hand away from her. "You've done *nothing* to earn my trust."

Noriava took a long sip of her wine and studied my face over the rim of her glass. "Before anything else, I'm the queen of Denor. Surely you understand that. I have to take care of my people and their well-being before I can even begin to think of myself. It's only natural that I'd do my best to secure the most advantageous position for Denor and her people. That's who I am. That's what I do." Her expression turned sad. "It breaks my heart a little to see you so thoroughly committed to that man, that you put aside what is best for your people. You should be there now, fighting for them, for your throne, but instead you wait here like a schoolboy aching to be praised by a distracted professor."

Her words echoed my own secret fears, and I stuffed my hands into my pockets to keep her from seeing them shake.

"Patrise and Lisette told me that they believe in you, in your ability to rule the people of Alskad fairly and well. They told me that our ideas and personalities would align both personally and as rulers, but to be frank, the fact that you've so thoroughly exposed your weakness in your love for Swinton gives me great pause."

"Your Majesty..." I started, but she cut me off.

"It isn't the relationship itself, or even that you intend to maintain it after our marriage, Ambrose. It's that you are letting it get in the way of your ascent to the throne. So long as you need something from me—need a cure for Swinton—I can take anything I want from you, ask for any power in our negotiation. I know that I have the upper hand." Noriava shook her head. "It's no way to rule. It's irresponsible."

I tried to keep the volume of my words low, so that the

people in the next room wouldn't hear me, but my voice still shook with rage. "At the very least, I'm not the one who considered the manufacture and sale of a poison that steals minds, steals lives."

Noriava's expression settled into one of calm disdain. "Once again, my dear, you show yourself to be entirely clueless. Of course I wouldn't ask my scientists to replicate the poison your temple created. Even if I did ask them to do such a thing, even if I lied to them and told them that the formula was something else, they would surely find the truth in their testing and immediately remove me from my throne. But you believed me, and because you were so gullible, I've gotten what I wanted out of you. A marriage contract. One that you cannot easily back out of, unless you want to lose your man and my army."

I spun on a heel and stalked toward the door, as much to hide my deepening blush as anything else. I'd fallen so thoroughly into her trap that there was nothing I could possibly do to redeem myself.

"I can teach you, if you'd let me," Noriava said, her voice low and so close it startled me. I turned and found myself face-to-face with her. The queen's expression was somber and oddly kind, something I wasn't accustomed to seeing in her.

"Everything I do, I do for Denor," she said huskily. "If we are going to be tied to one another, I hope that you'll allow me to show you how to be the best ruler you can possibly become. You have it in you—that indefinable quality that makes people want to do as you say. Makes people want to follow you. All you need to do is get past your squeamishness and decide what kind of king you want to become."

Noriava took my hand again, and this time, I didn't pull away. "Will you be a pawn of people like Patrise and Lisette, seeking all of the glory and fame with none of the hard work?

Or will you be like Abet and Jax, cut off from the world and isolated by their fear and magic? Now is the time to decide, young Ambrose."

"You're not even five years older than I am," I growled.

"Age is nothing but a number," she said, a sad smile playing across her lips. "I've been a queen for more than a decade now. I've written laws to protect the rights of my citizens and staved off not one, but *two* attempts at invasion. I've negotiated treaties and funded research. I've spent hours reading through security briefings and historical texts to understand the international politics that affect my people. And despite my personal feelings on the matter, I've been forced to uphold the convictions of people I deeply loved after they committed human rights violations."

Noriava paused for a moment, and I was shocked to see that there were tears in her eyes. I wondered whom she had sacrificed in order to enforce the laws of her kingdom, and for the first time, I began to see past the ruthless, calculating front she'd always presented to me.

Her voice was quiet when she spoke again. "I am a queen first, Ambrose. I am the voice of my people second, and a woman only distantly third. You may not have to make the choices I have made, Ambrose, but you *do* have to choose. Who will you become?"

With that, Noriava bent and gathered her cat in her arms before settling herself back on the velvet settee. I sketched a bow and fled back to my room.

CHAPTER THIRTY-ONE

Vi

"I wonder if you'll recognize the person I've become. You met me scarred and terrified. So much has changed since then. I barely recognize my-self anymore."

—*from Vi to Bo*

The Denorian harbormaster didn't have any idea what to do with the arrival of an unexpected—and enormous—ocean liner stuffed to the brim with tattooed Shriven and grim-faced Ilorian rebels. Captain Whippleston was made to drop anchor outside the harbor itself while the harbormaster fled back across the short, choppy waves to Salemouth, where he might consult the will of the queen.

When we were eventually allowed to let down a small boat and row toward the towering cliff face and the city that sat atop it, Curlin and I emerged from the cabin we'd shared on the journey, kitted out in the same finery we'd worn to see the governor of Ilor. We found Quill pacing the ship's deck as Mal looked on with an amused smile.

"Are you ready?" Quill asked, his voice thin with tension.

I furrowed my brows at him. "Of course. Whenever Hamlin says we can go."

I crossed the deck and leaned against the railing next to Mal. His eyes briefly flicked over to me, and then back to Quill.

"What's he so worked up about?" I asked quietly.

"He's gone all territorial and paranoid. Thinks the Denorian guard will sweep you up and cart you off to prison the moment you set foot on the shore," Mal whispered, the barest tickle of a laugh playing through his voice. "But he does have a point. You are fair worthless at keeping yourself in one piece."

I rolled my eyes and nudged him with my elbow. "Don't be an ass."

"Honestly, Vi," Mal said, sounding exasperated. "Neither of you have been the same since that battle. It's like you're both a breath away from murderous rage all the time."

"I'm fine," I snapped, but the truth in Mal's words sank like a knife into my gut. Had the smoke affected us?

Curlin, on the other side of Mal, flicked open a small knife and picked at the dirt under her fingernails. "If you'd been there, Mal, I don't imagine you'd be calling these two out on their anger so readily."

Quill turned a sharp glare on Curlin, and she gave him a sweet smile. "This has nothing to do with Vi—"

At the same time, I said, "Really, Curlin, it's like you *want*—"

Quill met my eyes, and for the first time since the battle, I felt like I might be able to return his smile. But just then, Captain Hamlin cleared his throat, and everyone turned to him. I heaved a sigh and rolled my head slowly around on my neck, enjoying the release as the vertebra cracked.

The captain's face was implacable as he stood by the skiff, which was already over the side and ready to be lowered. "Curlin, Vi and Jihye, with me, if you please," he instructed. "Quill? Mal? I'd be mightily obliged if you'd take another skiff into town and see what you can do about getting some fresh food, weapons and fabric for new clothes onto the ship. Use however much coin you need."

Quill's eyes narrowed. As I walked past him toward the skiff, his fingers closed around my wrist. Panic surged in my veins, followed quickly by throat-clenching anger. I whirled on him, blazingly furious, free hand on my knife, and yanked my wrist out of his hand. Anger ballooned inside me, filling up all of my empty space and taking over everything else until there was nothing left but red.

"You'll not touch me again without my permission," I snarled. "Do you understand?"

Quill took a step back, hands raised and mouth wide with surprise. Guilt flooded through me, washing away the fire of my rage. Why had I reacted like that?

"I didn't mean any..." His words trailed off, lost in the noise of the crashing waves below.

"I'm sorry, Quill. I just..." I shook my head, unable to find the right words. "We'll talk when I get back to the ship with my brother. I promise. But until then, just...please, don't touch me."

With that, I turned away, tears burning in my eyes as I fled from him.

The staircases that led up the sheer cliff faces and into the city of Salemouth were busy. Merchants hawked food and drink from brightly painted carts. Fisherwomen skipped down to the docks with empty baskets and climbed back up carrying loads of lobsters, crabs and glossy scaled fish.

We traveled in a bubble of silence and gaping stares. Only the white-coated soldiers guarding each landing managed to keep their faces from betraying the blend of fear and fascination that seemed to envelop every other person we passed, and then only barely. But despite the squirming feeling in my stomach each time a person gasped or whispered as I passed, I kept my head up and the muscles in my face relaxed.

These people, with their safe, stable lives and their warm, comfortable houses, had never been made to fight. Even the soldiers had rarely seen actual hand-to-hand combat. The defenses that surrounded the city, with its high cliffs and towering ring of mountains, had kept even the greediest of the Alskad and Samirian rulers from making any kind of real attempt on the small country.

I was jealous of their safety. Jealous of the version of me, now lost, that had existed before the battles. Of the straight and easy path their lives took. Of the myriad ways their government stabilized their lives.

At the top of the cliffs, I looked over the chest-high wall down at the water far below. The docks were all clustered in a single small inlet, and the rest of the harbor gave way to sheer cliffs plunging into the water, so deep it was nearly black. Curlin, careless of her finery, collapsed on a scrap of lawn at the edge of the promenade and groaned, sipping water from her canteen.

"It's a long way down," Jihye said, leaning against the wall next to me and peering over the edge.

"Scared of heights?" I teased. The breeze tickled the slightly raised edges of the newly tattooed lines on my arm, and I pulled back to stretch against the rail. The air in Denor was damp and smelled of plants and growing things, but in a different way than Ilor. Here, it was the dark musk of fertile earth and an undercurrent of moss and mushrooms. It was cool, slow growth and secret things hiding in the shade of ancient trees that had somehow survived the cataclysm.

"I'd not say that I'm scared," Jihye said, seeming to choose her words carefully. "It's only that I have an appropriate respect for the ability of a fall from a great height to break a person's neck. And seeing as how I've managed to put myself in a position to risk my neck a dozen different ways this year—and that's not too likely to change anytime soon—I plan to do my best to keep myself from inviting unnecessary risk whenever possible."

"And I'm over here wondering how cold the water is," I replied.

Jihye snorted, and Curlin sat up. "If you two are done philosophizing, let's get on about our business, yeah?"

"Let's," I agreed, grinning. "Bo's close by. It shouldn't take long to find him."

Jihye pointed behind me. "Were it up to me, I might start looking for a lost king in the palace."

Together we made our way through the winding streets and narrow closes toward the black stone palace. Its domes and spires loomed over the city like something a jealous goddess might build in worship of herself. When we finally arrived at the public entrance to the palace, however, we found the portcullis down and a bevy of guards in tight formation outside the gates. The square around us gradually emptied as people noticed our arrival, and in a matter of moments, we were alone with the guards.

I stepped forward, suddenly realizing that I spoke no Denorian at all. I hoped at least one of them knew a bit of Alskader.

"I'm here to see Ambrose Trousillion, the king of Alskad. Will you let him know that Obedience Violet Abernathy has arrived?"

The guards exchanged a series of pointed looks, and from the back, a woman's voice, high and clear, called in a lilting Denorian accent, "There is no Alskader king here. Go back to the temple, Shriven dogs."

Curlin's hand tightened on her staff as she surged forward, but I put a hand out to stop her.

"There's an Alskad ship in the harbor flying the king's colors," I said. "Tell me again how he's not here."

The woman raised her hand, and a line of slatted openings slid open above the portcullis. A moment later, the barrels of a dozen rifles were trained on the four of us.

"Get gone, scum, or get dead. And if I or any of my soldiers see you in the city again, it'll be your gods' judgment you face at the bottom of the harbor."

Jihye laid her hand on my shoulder in warning, but I was already backing out of the square, hands up. Fury seethed like a boiling cauldron inside me as various plots and plans twisted themselves together like coils of rope in my head.

I wouldn't let some self-righteous twig of an untested soldier keep me from my brother. Not in this life or the next.

CHAPTER THIRTY-TWO

Bo

"Sometimes the monarchy feels like a gift. Other times, like a punishment. But it is always there, like a weight around my neck or an unruly beast tethered to my waist. I'm never without it."

—*from Bo to Vi*

Noriava's words hung like a chain around my neck. I didn't know if I could take her approach to the monarchy, much less want to. It seemed to me that she'd given up everything, even her own sense of self, to become her idea of the best monarch. Looking back on our conversations, I had to admit that she was exceptionally dedicated to her people. But with all of her sacrifices, she'd put aside something else that should have truly mattered: herself.

She wasn't really Noriava anymore. She was the living manifestation of Denor. Since our argument, I'd spent innumerable hours contemplating that sacrifice. Was it really the best thing for a country if its monarch lost herself so completely, even if it was for the good of the realm? Was I right to admire her dedication to her crown? Should I do the same?

I wondered what Runa would do—what she had done.

I wanted to talk to Vi, as my intention all along was to share the power of the monarchy with her. And to Swinton as well, because articulating the issue to him would crystallize the clarity of my thoughts and ideas. But as things stood now, I had only myself and the unfocused attention of my increasingly absent little sisters to rely on.

Late one afternoon, as I was mentally preparing myself for the rigors of supper with Noriava and her court, Still burst through the doors of the sitting room, a wide smile on her face and a scrap of paper in her hand.

"You'll never guess who I found skulking around the gates of the castle," she crowed with a laugh.

"If I'll never guess, why don't you go ahead and tell me," I replied tiredly. "I'm supposed to be downstairs for supper in just a few minutes."

Still snapped, "We'd never've agreed to come if we'd known all you were going to do was yell at us all the damned time."

"I'm sorry, Still," I said with a sigh. "I don't mean to be so irritable. I've got a lot on my mind. Who did you find outside the castle? Just so that you're warned, though, if you tell me you've spent more money on useless trinkets for our siblings back home, I'll be forced to wring your neck."

Still looked guiltily at her boots and bit her lip. "That's not what I've come to tell you," she said, then, regaining her arrogant swagger, continued, "but if you're going to be a snot about it, I'll just go on about my business and leave you right here in the dark with your head up your ass."

I cringed at the image and stuck my tongue out at her by way of apology. "Well, who was it?"

Still shoved the paper into my hand with a grin. Unfolding it, I at once recognized the familiar hand.

Bo,

I've been in Salemouth for three days but can't get the guards to let me into the palace to see you. Still says that you've gone and gotten yourself engaged to the queen. Which is bloody stupid, by the way, but we can discuss your horrible decision-making later. Look, I've got a ship full of the Shriven—long story—ready to fight for you in Alskad, but the captain won't wait forever. Either get your ass to the harbor or find a place to house them, and fast. No one here in the city will do business with any of us, and we're running out of stores on board to feed ourselves.
—Vi

PS: Of all of our siblings, you chose to bring these two thieving weasels with you? I wonder how you'll manage the folks at court if you let Pem and Still have their way with you, and them only children.

PPS: On second thought, it might be good practice.

PPPS: I cannot believe I've been in this city for three days and you've not come to find me yet. Obviously, you have a lot on your mind, but to not notice me at all?

I ran a hand through my hair, relief and terror flooding my veins in equal measure. Vi was *here*, and now that I thought of it, I didn't know how I could've managed to ignore the thrum of our connection these last few days. Hers was a vibrant shifting river of feeling that tugged at me. The more I thought of it, the more it edged uncomfortably close to fury, and I pulled back from the connection, dazed by the intensity I felt in her.

"Where is she?" I asked Still. "How does she look?"

"I told her to go to a place me'n Pem found by the harbor and gave her enough coin to bribe the barkeep to serve her a drink or two whilst she waits." Still made a face.

"What is it?"

"She's with two of them Shriven. Nasty-lookin' pieces, too." Still pressed her lips together and stuck her hands deep in the pockets of her coat.

"What aren't you saying?"

Still glanced at the door, where Pem stood, staring at her sister. "You go on with Bo and make sure no one sticks him with a knife or nothing. I'll stay here with Swinton."

Pem nodded and ran into my bedroom, returning just moments later with my old, dull traveling clothes and a pair of scuffed boots.

"There hasn't been a stabbing in Denor in almost a hundred years," I said, but my words fell on deaf ears.

"Don't want to go looking like a fancy nobleman, anyway," Pem said. "Still will make your excuses to the queen."

Still grinned. "I'll tell her you got the shits."

I groaned internally, but recognizing that Still would come up with something even more vile if I admonished her, I shrugged out of my silk jacket and into the sturdy—if a little musty—wool Pem held for me.

Pem studied me a moment, then nodded her approval and said, "There's a hat in the pocket. Put that on. Don't think you'll be recognized, but better safe than sorry, yeah?"

"Lead the way," I said, sliding the deep hood over my curls and pulling it forward to cast my face in shadows.

We snuck through the back passages of the palace and out

through a hallway stinking of rotting fruit and refuse. The day was cool, and the sun cast the streaks of clouds in shades of blood and fire as it sank below the horizon. I pulled my coat tight around me, thankful for the thick wool as the cold wind coming off the sea whistled through the back alleys and winding closes that Pem led me down. My stomach roiled with a queasy mix of excitement, anxiety and hunger.

The tavern was built on stilts over the water, more an extension of the docks than a part of the city itself. Men and women of questionable repute, their cheeks bright with cold and drink, lounged against the posts and on the benches, calling out to potential customers as sailors and fishermen walked by. I looked quickly away, hoping Pem hadn't noticed them, or if she had, that she hadn't put two and two together.

"Seems strange that folk'd turn to whoring, what with the queen's big talk about the crown making sure each citizen has a warm bed to sleep in and a roof over their heads," Pem commented.

I grimaced.

She yanked on the narrow door, swollen with the damp sea air, and held it open for me. "After you."

As my eyes adjusted to the dimness inside the tavern, it took every ounce of my will not to recoil from the stench. The miasma of unwashed bodies, fatty stewed meat and sour ale permeated the room. A haze of smoke hung low over the greasy heads of the tavern's patrons, bent over their drinks or their hands of cards, oblivious to everything but what lay directly in their path. A woman stumbled past me, hand clapped over her mouth, and Pem leaped back and out of the way only moments before the contents of the woman's stomach spilled out the open door and onto the wide slats of the dock.

"Vi should be in the back," Pem said with a grimace. "I'll catch up in a moment."

"You absolutely will not leave my side," I hissed. "Not in a place like this."

Pem rolled her eyes at me. "This place is safer than the house I grew up in, brother mine."

And with that, she slipped away. Tense, I made my way through the crowded room, scanning for Vi's familiar face, so much like my own. There were people with skin and hair in all variety of color and cuts; people with scarred and painted faces; people wearing Denorian, Alskader, Samirian and Ilorian clothing in jarring and decidedly strange combinations. But nowhere in the crowd did I see my sister's freckled face and black curls. I approached the bar, thinking the barkeep might've seen her, when a hand reached out of nowhere and pulled me into a dark corner booth I'd not even seen during my inspection of the tavern.

"Took you long enough," Vi snapped.

We were sitting on opposite sides of the booth, but I flung my arms around Vi anyway and pulled her half over the table into a tight, awkward embrace. She held herself stiff and rigid in my arms for a moment. Then, with a deep breath, she relaxed and held me tight in return.

"I missed you, you great oaf," she whispered.

"Missed you, too, stubborn wretch. Kept you waiting, did I?"

When we finally let go, I glanced around the table. Curlin scowled beside me and an unfamiliar woman sat next to Vi. Her head was covered with a scant inch of spiky black hair and a new, pink scar marked her upper lip. A patient smile twinkled in her dark eyes as she met my gaze. Her tattoos and

shaved head marked her as a Shriven, which only brought a
slew of new questions to mind.

I put my hands across the table, palms up, and when Vi laid
hers in mine, I gasped.

"You're…"

"Yes, tattooed. I know. Curlin did them."

"Did you…?"

"Join the Shriven?" Vi raised her half-empty glass to Curlin. "You owe me a drink."

"You fed him the line. It doesn't count if he didn't say it
himself."

I smiled and poured myself a glass of the thick brown ale
from the pitcher in the center of the table. "To be fair, it is
what I was going to say."

"You're her twin. Of course you'd take her side," Curlin
grumbled.

Vi snorted. "To answer your question, no, I didn't join the
Shriven. Curlin's been telling me about the meaning behind
her tattoos, and I wanted a way to commemorate everything
I've been through. Do you like them?"

I looked at the patterns crawling over Vi's hands and arm.
The swirls and symbols and geometric designs were so deeply
reminiscent of the Shriven's tattoos that they made my stomach turn circles at a glance, but as I studied them, they began
to take on a kind of fascinating beauty. There, on her tattooed wrist, was a golden cuff almost the mirror of mine.
When she saw me looking at it, Vi tried to cover it, looking
a bit embarrassed, but I brushed her hand away and fingered
the filigreed gold.

"It suits you," I said, smiling at her.

Vi raised an eyebrow, but a moment later, her smile met
mine. "I've missed you, brother."

"I've been rude," I said, and offered the woman next to Vi my hand. "I'm Bo. Vi's twin brother."

She took my hand with a warm smile and a raised eyebrow. "I've heard there are some other titles that go along with that. I'm Jihye Elias. The Shriven in Ilor who defected to Vi's cause follow my leadership. Apologies, of course, for the impact on your imperial concerns there."

"Um?" I looked to Vi for answers.

She grinned. "We may or may not've liberated Ilor from Alskad's control just a bit. We can talk on it later."

Snorting at the absurdity of the situation, I took a sip of the ale. It was bitter and smooth and went down a bit too easily. "I appreciate that someone so thoroughly trained by the temple might come over to our side," I told Jihye. "It gives me hope. As for Ilor, the people will always come first. We can discuss next steps when all is said and done. I hold no grudges on that account at all."

"So what's this about you marrying the queen of Denor?" Curlin interjected. "And where's Swinton?"

I shifted uncomfortably. "The two are rather intrinsically entwined."

Just then, Pem and Still appeared at the end of the table, their faces matching pictures of concealed mischief.

"If the two of you are here, who's with Swinton?" I asked, panic rising in my throat.

"Snuck one of Vi's folks into your suite and hid her in the drapes," Pem said. "Bribed a kitchen boy to wear my clothes and lie on the pallet and scream like hell if one of Noriava's people came close. We've got a thing to do."

"What thing?" Vi asked, her voice brimming with suspicion.

"Don't you go worrying your pretty head about it, sister," Still said.

"We're spies now," Pem said. "Won't Ma be proud?"

Vi scowled at them. "Doubt it."

"We'll see," Pem chirped. "Anyway, that's not to do with anything. Maybe—"

Still elbowed her. "Sorry about treating you like a dimmy for so long, Vi. Glad you're okay."

Pem punched her twin's arm and gave us a pained look. "We'll see you in a bit."

With that, they were gone nearly as quickly as they'd appeared.

"I cannot believe that you brought those two along to spy for you," Vi said. "More than that, I can't believe Brenna let you."

"It wasn't as though they gave her much of a chance to argue."

Vi laughed and nodded. "Fair enough there. Care to tell us how much trouble you've managed to get yourself into since you left Ilor?"

As I recounted the details of the last few months, I watched Vi's face grow more and more still, as though she was putting on a mask, inch by careful inch. By the time I got to the part about my command of the Denorian army, Vi's mouth was a thin line and her eyes were all steel and reserve. Jihye's eyebrows had climbed so high on her forehead it looked as though they were trying to escape, and when I finally ran out of things to say, Curlin snorted.

"I think you've mayhap made your situation even worse than it was before you left Alskad." Curlin swirled the ale in her cup. "I'm beginning to think that perhaps it's not such a good idea to have the both of you in the same place at the same time. Seems dangerous."

"'They two are chaos, and they will pull great evil from

the land.'" Jihye stared down at the battered, scarred wood of the table as she spoke. Her voice was velvet smooth, with the careful accent of a Penby merchant. "'When finally the dust settles, and everything is still, they two shall build this earth anew.'"

Curlin gave Jihye a thoughtful, assessing look. "Hamil. The Book of Songs. That's an obscure one, even for me."

Jihye gave her a wry grin. "The Shriven's training isn't all tactics and combat. We are devotees, after all."

"Are you diminished?" I asked.

Jihye nodded. "I've spent my whole life waiting for the grief to overtake me. I thought being one of the Shriven might save me somehow. When I learned about the poison, everything changed. I just didn't see a way out until Vi came riding up on her stout little pony, waving a white flag."

"I wish I'd been there to see that," I said with a smile. "Well, I appreciate the sacrifice you and yours have made in joining the cause. And I promise to do everything in my power to see you protected."

"So all we have to do now is figure out how to get you and the Denorian army onto a boat without marrying you off to a woman who is both power hungry and seemingly lacking even the barest hint of a conscience," Curlin quipped, then shrugged. "Can't be any more difficult than anything else we've tackled recently."

"You forgot Swinton," I reminded her, my mood darkening. "We have to find a way to cure Swinton, too."

Vi smiled grimly, raised her hand to call over the barkeep and ordered another pitcher of ale.

CHAPTER THIRTY-THREE

Vi

"It's time."

—*from Vi to Bo*

I paced the length of the ship as the sun came up. My nose was tingling with cold, and my fingertips were numb as they ran along the wooden rail for the umpteenth time that day. I had to find a way to get Bo out of the castle. Some distraction. A trick. Something.

Quill emerged from one of the doors at the other end of the ship and waved to me. I quickly looked down, pretending I hadn't seen him. I knew I needed to talk to him, to tell him why things between us had shifted, soured. I needed him to know that it wasn't his fault. I needed him to see that the poison I'd inhaled was spiking me through with barbs of fury. I needed him to know that I didn't want to push him away. But how could I possibly tell him how broken I really was? How could I make him see how much I'd changed, when every time I spoke to him, I was lit aflame with anger for the girl I'd lost?

I wasn't the same reckless girl who'd thrust her heart into his hands and run away to fight a war. These last few weeks, the battles with the Shriven—they'd changed me. And not for the better.

Quill deserved someone undamaged. Not someone as raw and frightened and broken as me.

"Vi," Quill called. "Stop running away from me. At the very least, you owe me a conversation."

"I don't owe you anything, Quill," I snapped, and turned to stalk down the deck away from him.

"You don't, do you? When did you become such a coward?"

I froze at the accusation, furious and gutted in the same moment.

"Even when you were pushing me away, afraid that you'd hurt me when you finally snapped, you were braver for it. Why go back to the same defensive walls you worked so hard to pull down? What are you so afraid of?"

I whirled on him.

"Afraid?" I seethed. "I've crossed oceans and won battles with the deadliest fighters in the world. I've killed people in cold blood and sent them hurtling into the same violent fury I've spent my entire life waiting to descend on me. You've every right to call me armloads of names, Quill Whippleston, but the one thing I'm not is afraid."

"What is it, then?" he insisted. "We were in love. We were planning a life together. What changed?"

I gaped at him, astonished. "Didn't you hear me? I am responsible for inflicting on others the same horrors I feared for myself. You saw what I did on that farm. You know what

I'm capable of. You deserve better than me—someone who isn't so broken. You deserve someone who can stand by your side at supper parties and charm the owners of foreign enterprises. You deserve more than me."

The shock on Quill's face was as real as if I'd punched him in the gut.

"I'm sorry," I said, my voice too soft to stand against the shrill wail of the wind whipping all around us. "I loved you. I love you still, but I'm a shell of the person I was when we first met, and you deserved more than me even then."

"You don't get to just decide that, Vi!" Quill exclaimed. "Don't I get a say in who stands beside me? In who I choose to love? With whom I spend my time? My life?" He shook his head, looking exasperated. "I love *you*. Pain and flaws and bruises and all. I love you."

"How?" I cried. "How could you love someone like me?"

Tears cut like ice picks down my cheeks, and all I wanted was to fall into his arms, but I couldn't let myself burden him that way. It wouldn't be right. And I knew in my heart that even if his arms were the only shelter I wanted, I had to find another way to make myself whole. On my own.

"Quill," I said, heartbreak picking its way into my every word. "You may get a say in who stands beside you, but so do I. And as much as it isn't what I expected, as much as it isn't what we planned, you and I don't make sense anymore. I don't think we'll ever make sense again. I don't think we can. I don't deserve to be loved."

"Obedience Violet Abernathy." Quill shook his head and stepped toward me.

I took a step back, chest heaving with barely contained sobs.

"When are you going to learn that I don't love you because of what you've done or not done?" he asked gently. "I love you because of who you *are*. Again and again, you sacrifice yourself for the greater good. Again and again, you make the most difficult choice, even when there are options that would hurt you less. All because you believe in the causes and people you champion." He came to stand beside me, and this time, I didn't move away. "I'm not afraid of the things you've done."

I so desperately wanted everything he said to be true—to believe it myself. But I knew in my heart that I was making the right choice. "Your being afraid or not doesn't matter, Quill," I whispered. "It's a question of fit. We don't fit anymore."

Quill sighed and closed his hands around the railing. "Do you forget that I was there, too? I made hard choices that day. I fought beside you. I lost pieces of myself, as well. What makes your actions so much more unforgivable than mine?"

I wanted him to be right. I wanted to see myself the way he saw me—strong and worthy and capable. But my wanting and his believing wouldn't make it true. It wouldn't make me into something I wasn't. He was a hero, the best person I knew. And I was nothing.

I put my hand over his and squeezed. "I'm sorry, Quill."

Before he could try once more to argue with me further, I fled back to the rooms I shared with Curlin. She looked up from the book propped open on her lap and raised her eyebrows at me.

"You look a right mess. Who'd you tussle with this time?"

"I don't want to talk about it," I said, pulling the thick down blanket off the bed.

I flopped onto the couch and flung the blanket over both our legs. Glaring, Curlin put down the book she'd been reading and poured me a cup of tea. I doctored it with an abundance of cream and sugar and plucked half of a sandwich off the plate Curlin'd balanced on the back of the couch. Curlin pretended to go back to reading but kept glancing up at me. When I unthinkingly reached for the other half of her sandwich, Curlin slapped my hand away with her novel.

"Forget it. You come in here and disrupt my perfectly nice afternoon with your sighing and tearstained face, and now you're trying to steal my food, as well? Either tell me what's going on with you or get out."

"It's nothing," I lied.

"Then for the love of all that's good in the world, go get your own food and stop bothering me."

I bit my lip. "It's just that…well, I've broken things off with Quill. I think."

"You think?" Curlin asked. "How do you not know for sure? You'd think it'd be quite obvious."

"I didn't exactly plan it!" I said defensively. "He's just got no idea who I am anymore. No one does, really. I feel like the weight of everything that's happened these last few months is haunting me. It's turned me into someone different, someone I didn't expect."

Curlin's brows knit together. "And that's a bad thing? Why not figure out who you could be with him after all this is over?"

"If he really saw me, he'd think I was a monster," I said, gloom filling me. "And the worst part is that it's not just Quill I'm worried about. It's Bo. I've no idea what I'm going to tell Bo."

I paused, remembering how wonderful it had felt to see him again yesterday—how bittersweet, when I'd realized that I'd eventually have to tell him the truth about myself. "How will I face him once he learns everything I've done?" I whispered.

Curlin rolled her eyes. "If you're a monster, then so am I,

and I'm fair certain that's not true for either of us. You inhaled more than a little of that philomena smoke, Vi. Don't you think that might have something to do with how you're feeling?"

I shook my head. "No. You know how that feels. It's rage and fury and overwhelming contempt. That's not what I feel right now. I'm just looking at myself, at the things I've done, and acknowledging who I've become."

Curlin sighed. "You've lived through trauma—not just what we endured when we were brats, but everything these last few weeks. What you're feeling is real, sure. But that doesn't mean it's right. Your mind is twisting itself in knots, trying to explain away the things you've seen. The things you've done. But you're shouldering blame where you shouldn't. Someday you're going to have to address it."

I sniffed, not wanting to believe her, but hearing the truth in her words regardless. Everything I did felt bad; everything I thought felt wrong. The only comfort I could find was in blaming myself.

"I've been there with you for every step of it. I know the things you've done, and no matter how you're beating yourself up about it, none of it is as bad as you think. Quill, too. You act like he wasn't there, but he's seen all you've done and been there beside you the whole time." She shook her head in disbelief. "We *all* see you, and I, for one, don't think you're a monster. As for how you'll tell Bo, why not practice? Tell me."

I looked at her, considering, and reached for her sandwich again. She smacked my hand away, laughing.

"Go on, then," she said. "Convince me that you're a monster, and I'll give you the rest of my sandwich."

So I told her everything. I laid bare every moment that haunted me, every detail of the battles I'd fought, every memory I wished so desperately was just a dream. I held nothing back. From Lei's death to the Shriven's screams as the poison in the still twisted their thoughts to violence... I told Curlin my every sin.

When I finished, the tea gone cold in my hands, I sat beneath her unflinching gaze until she nodded and rose.

"See?" she asked. "That wasn't so very bad, was it?"

"It wasn't a walk through the park," I snapped.

"But it's done, and I'm not even shocked. If Bo is, come get me. I've done all that and worse."

I gaped at her, unable to find anything else to say. She shrugged and said, "Now, I'm going to go get us some food. You need to put something more than my snack in your belly before you go save your brother from his bride."

Without waiting for my response, she strode out of the room. As the door's handle clicked into place, something inside me shattered. I put my face into a pillow and screamed. Howled. Cried until my cheeks and throat were raw. Not for the loss of Quill's affection—I'd counted that gone since the moment I'd felt my blade slide into another person's belly in the first battle with the Shriven.

No. I cried for myself. For the futures I'd lost the moment I stepped into that fight.

Each life I'd taken had taken something of me with it. Each swipe of my blade, each drop of blood, each splash of poison had nudged me further and further away from the girl who'd spent years cultivating pearls in the vain hope that they might one day buy her a quiet life by the sea.

But that girl was dead. And after I wept my last tears for her, I dried my eyes and stared out at the waves. I was not the same girl who'd left Alskad all those many months before, but perhaps this new Vi was better, stronger. Perhaps I really was the person Quill saw when he looked at me.

Perhaps I could become something great.

CHAPTER THIRTY-FOUR

Bo

In the days after my reunion with Vi, I found it nearly impossible to sleep at night. So, instead, I walked. I paced the city and watched as the shell pink-and-lavender light of early dawn was beginning to encroach on the deep navy of the night, pushing the darkness out of the way of the sun. The obsidian walls of the palace loomed over the city, its spires reaching up like birds taking flight into the sunrise. The guards, in the last hour of their nightlong watch, gave the cuff on my wrist—proof I was who I claimed to be—a lengthy assessment with tired eyes before waving me through a narrow door to the side of the portcullis.

On the third night, still without any word from Vi, I trudged through the palace as the sun was rising, managing to avoid most of the servants, and when I finally made it to my chambers, I peeked through a crack in Swinton's door to see that he was still sleeping. Relieved to find him safe, I shuffled into my bedroom, pulled my boots off and fell face-first into the cloud-soft warmth of my bed. There were mountains to move and an endless list of nearly impossible tasks ticking through my brain, but first, I had to sleep.

A gentle hand on my shoulder and a kiss on my forehead pulled me, unwillingly, from the black depths of dreamless sleep. I shrugged the hand off and rolled to the other side of the bed, curling myself around a pillow. The bed shifted, and a weight dropped down beside me as I did my very best to push away the wakefulness creeping into my brain and dragging a headache along with it.

"Go away," I groaned.

Someone lifted the down comforter, sending a shock of cold air down my body. I swatted at the weight on the side of the bed. Then stubble and soft lips brushed against my cheek, and I sat bolt upright, startled.

To my utter shock, it was Swinton sitting on the edge of the bed, a giant grin on his face. I scrambled back and off the bed, eyes trained on him, heart pounding and hands fumbling for the club I'd leaned against the nightstand.

Swinton raised an eyebrow. "Now, really, that seems excessive. Not even at my worst did I try to kill you, bully."

I gaped at him.

"I thought you'd be happy to see me back to myself," he mused, "but Still and Pem tell me you've gone and gotten yourself engaged to be married to that wretched bitch of a queen, so perhaps I was wrong in thinking you might've kept the torch burning for me for longer than a minute."

"How...?" I stuttered, not even sure what the right question might be.

"We thought they was taking an awfully long time to find a cure for the temple's poison when they've already got medicine what helps the dimmys," Pem piped up. I glanced over my shoulder and found her and Still cross-legged on the floor with a platter of half-eaten pastries between them.

"Plus, much as we liked Doctor Rutin," she continued, "it didn't make sense as she'd just be sticking Swinton with needles full of drugs to make him sleepy when all the other dimmys take a pill every day, talk to one of the scientists once a week and then go on with their lives. Happy as a sloth bear in a flower shop."

Still picked up the narrative. "So when we was in the labs looking at how the cure was coming, we come across some papers what said that they were nearly done with trials on a new drug for dimmys that was supposed to work a lot better than the old stuff."

"And 'cause it were made from a plant, like the poison..." Pem shrugged. "Me and Still, we figured, why not steal some for Swinton?"

I gritted my teeth. "What if it had made him worse? What if it had killed him?"

Pem made a face. "But it didn't, did it?"

"We read all the notes about it and everything first," Still added. "This one didn't kill no one. Plant just made every-one a lot happier for a while. Seemed to give folks a chance to fix what was broken inside them for themselves. One of the doctors wrote... What was it, Pem?"

Pem pulled a scrap of paper from her pocket and read in a dry monotone. "'The effects of the plant seem to allow the patient to see and repair broken neural pathways rather than rerouting and masking them like drugs of the past. Studies show great improvements among the diminished, and the potential for other afflictions is nearly endless.'"

"They were right," Swinton said. "I feel better than I have in a very, very long time. Since Noriava poisoned me, I don't even know how much time has passed—I've been in a haze. I've either been so angry that nothing made sense, or I've been too tired to do anything but sleep. I've never felt hatred like that. Never felt anger so blazing that it made me insensible. I was too mad to be scared. Too furious to do anything but seethe."

"And now?" I ventured. The bed was still between us. My fingers were white-knuckled around the club, waiting for him to lunge at me.

And then he smiled, in that charming, irresistible way only Swinton could. All the terror and tension of these last few weeks melted away, and I was left with tears pricking the corners of my eyes. Until this moment, I hadn't realized just how desperate I'd been to see that smile again.

"It's really you," I said, voice choked with emotion.

"Yes, it really is," Swinton said softly. "And now, I would very much like to kiss you. After that, I suppose we can tackle the issue of your engagement."

He opened his arms and I leaped across the bed toward him, wrapping him in a ferocious embrace that held all of the misery of the last few weeks and the joy of seeing him restored to me. Then, to the groans of mock dismay from the twins, I kissed him. And despite everything—despite the exhaustion and horror and endless worry—for a moment, everything melted away. It was just his lips and mine. His arms around me, and the exhausting, gripping fear finally loosening its grasp on me.

When we eventually came up for air, Swinton grinned at me and took my hands in his, a mischievous gleam in his eyes.

"Seems to me that we have some scheming to do, my dear."

In the waning light of the evening, while I endured another agonizing supper with Noriava and her court, Pem and

Still snuck Curlin, Vi and Quill past the changing guard and into my room, where they would hide until Doctor Rutin finished her nightly visit with Swinton.

"How has he been?" I asked, as she walked back from supper by my side.

Doctor Rutin pursed her lips. "He's had a difficult day. He didn't require sedation, but it was a near thing. I hope to begin seeing continuous improvement in the very near future."

I furrowed my brows, feigning a look of concern. "You've been saying that since the beginning, but I've yet to see any real improvement. When he's not sedated, he's raving. Whatever you're doing, let's double it."

"That wouldn't be prudent," Doctor Rutin said. "Give it time, Your Majesty. I have a great deal of experience treating cases like Swinton's. I swear to you that this will work in time."

The guards swept open the doors with respectful bows. Inside, Pem and Still were stationed outside Swinton's door, absorbed in an enormous book laid open on the floor between them.

"He's sleeping," Pem said, without so much as a greeting.

I eyed her warily. I needed her to act normal, so that Doctor Rutin wouldn't think anything was amiss. Not that I expected her to pay much attention to the girls, but I also couldn't afford to be too careful. She was likely a spy for Noriava, after all.

"I'll just go in and check on him," Doctor Rutin said, setting her bag on the floor next to the girls as she went to unlock the door.

Still propped herself up on her elbows and winked at me.

"I'll join you," I said. "Perhaps there's something stronger we could try with Swinton?"

Doctor Rutin slid open the bolts, her eyes fixed in the

middle distance as if in thought. "I'll speak to my colleagues tomorrow and see if they have anything they might recommend."

I looked over my shoulder at Still, who'd silently undone the clasp on Doctor Rutin's bag and had half her arm inside already. I yanked a sunlamp off the table beside Swinton's door and followed the doctor inside. Swinton rubbed his eyes blearily at the sudden light and sat up in bed.

"What do you want?" he snapped, fury lacing his words.

"I just wanted to check on you before I left for the evening and give you your medicine," Doctor Rutin said. "How are you feeling?"

"Like someone decided it was a great night to wake me up in the middle of the first good sleep I've gotten since we arrived in this godsforsaken country. Give me my pills and get out, bitch." Swinton glared up at me. "What are you staring at, little king?"

"I...I just wanted to see you," I sputtered, surprising myself with the pain in my voice.

"You've seen me. Now get the fuck out," Swinton spit. "Give me my pills and leave me the hell alone."

Doctor Rutin handed Swinton a pair of white tablets and a glass of water. He tossed the pills into his mouth and downed the water in one gulp. Doctor Rutin snatched the glass away from him just as he raised his hand to smash it on the floor. She'd learned his tricks quickly.

The doctor wished Swinton a good sleep and quickly exited the room. I paused at the door. "Good night," I said, my voice tremulous. "I love you, Swinton."

He winked at me just as I pulled the door closed behind me. He'd done it. Or, at least, I hoped he had. He'd gone the whole day without setting off her suspicions.

Doctor Rutin scooped up her bag, set the glass on the side table and gave me a small nod. "I'll see you in the morning, Your Majesty. Girls. Sleep well."

I followed her to the front door of the suite and, once I'd closed it behind her, let out a huge sigh of relief.

"We got it," Pem said. "Or at least we think we did."

I looked back at them and nodded. "Good. That was slick work of you."

"It weren't hard," Still scoffed. "She always puts her bag there."

"We're not done yet," I said, crossing the room to unlock Swinton's door.

Vi, Curlin and Quill spilled out of the girls' room just as Swinton emerged, squinting, from the darkness of his room.

"Well," he said. "That was fairly painless."

I narrowed my eyes at him. "Was it?"

"I'm sure you were brilliant," Vi said, swinging herself over the back of a sofa and tucking herself into the corner.

"When does the general usually show up?" Curlin asked.

I glanced at the clock on the mantel. "In the next hour or so? Would anyone like kaffe? A drink?"

Quill wandered over to the buffet with Swinton on his heels. When Swinton held up a bottle of ouzel, Quill shook his head with a grin and squatted to open the cabinet beneath the buffet. He pulled out one of the rare bottles of Denorian wine kept there and handed it to Swinton, whose brows soared up his forehead.

"You've been here for, what, half an hour? How'd you know where they keep the good stuff?"

Quill laughed. "Rich folks are the same everywhere. It's no great secret that the best stuff is always at hand, but always out of sight."

Swinton clapped him on the back, opened the bottle and handed glasses of golden Denorian wine to Quill and Curlin. Vi shook her head when Swinton offered her a glass, and I asked Still to run to the kitchens for a pot of kaffe. Pem poured the vial of the sedative she'd stolen from Doctor Rutin into a half-empty bottle of top-shelf spirits, then settled it into a rubbish bin littered with wadded bits of paper and a broken glass.

"Ready?" she asked.

I nodded, and she slipped into the hall to demand, in an imperious tone, that the guards posted outside our suite do away with the trash. If everything went according to plan, they would slip the bottle of spirits out of the bin and be well on their way to oblivion by the time the general arrived. We couldn't risk being overheard.

I settled in next to Vi on the sofa. She was paler than usual and the expression in her eyes was determined, if a little distant. When I reached for our connection, I felt an unexpected brittleness in her, a vulnerability I'd never experienced before.

"How are you?" I asked, doing my best to keep the concern out of my voice. I'd seen how prickly Vi could get when she was cornered.

Vi tucked her hands under her knees and avoided my gaze. "Fine. Ready to get you out of this mess and back where you belong."

"You don't seem fine," I said tentatively.

Curlin, on the other side of the sofa, reached out and poked me with the toe of her boot. "Not the time," she admonished.

"It's all right," Vi said, her voice soft and strained. "He's my brother. He gets to ask."

Curlin shrugged and went to wait with her ear to the door next to Pem. I looked back at Vi. "So?"

"It just took a lot of doing over there," she said. "I did things I'm not proud of, saw things I'll never unsee. I don't know. It was awful, but it's done. I was glad for your letters."

"And I was glad for yours," I said, reaching out to squeeze her hand.

"We left Aphra in charge," Vi said. "So that'll be something to deal with when you get your throne back."

Unease filled me when I remembered that night at Plumleen, when Aphra had murdered her husband right in front of me. "Was that really the best—"

Pem flung open the door, interrupting me midthought, and Curlin pulled Vittoria into the room. For a tense second, it looked like the general and Curlin might come to blows, but I stood and crossed the room as quickly as I could.

"General Okara, we're sorry for the ambush, but we weren't sure how else we could have this conversation."

General Okara's eyebrows soared up, her usually tightly controlled expression betraying her shock, just for a moment. "Well, Your Majesty," she finally said, "you certainly have surprised me."

I smiled apologetically. "You understand the necessity, yes?"

The general nodded.

"Then would you allow me to introduce my friends—and my sister Vi?"

Vi rose to greet the general. "My brother tells me that he trusts you, and that I must, as well. I hope you understand what a rare honor that is."

General Okara bowed over Vi's hand. "I do. And I am very happy to meet you. Your brother has more than earned my respect, and I am happy to make myself of use to him."

Glowing with the general's kindness, I went around the room, making introductions and outlining the roles each person would play in my plan to take back the throne. When everyone had been introduced, we settled in to talk logistics.

"So, let me see if I have this right," Vittoria said. "You're asking me to defy the orders of my queen, encourage my soldiers to defect and help you take back the rule of a foreign land that doesn't believe in the ability of a twin to rule justly."

Vi pressed her lips together, fighting back a smile.

"Or," I said, "you could think of it as though you're fulfilling a promise your queen made in good faith and subsequently has reneged on, encouraging your soldiers to assist a wrongly deposed foreign monarch and helping the legal heir to the Alskad throne take back his rightful place."

Vittoria gave me a wry smile. "I'm not opposed to the idea, but it does require rather a lot of ethical gymnastics." Her expression turned thoughtful. "But I'll not leave the harbor undefended, and there are fewer soldiers I can trust with a mission like this than I'd like," she said, sipping a cup of kaffe. "It'll mean taking fewer troops than I'd originally planned, but I think we can still manage to take Penby with the help of the Shriven."

"They're not Shriven anymore," Vi reminded her. "I don't mean to offend you, General Okara, but you'll be a lot less use to us if one of them cuts you stem to stern for offending them. Why not just call them the Legion?"

Vittoria nodded. "A fair point. We'll have to coach the troops as we load them onto your ship. How many can we take?"

Quill sketched a few quick sums on a scrap of paper. "With two hundred and fifty or so of ours aboard, plus crew and supplies—if Mal can convince anyone to sell to us—I think the vessel can hold another five hundred soldiers and their gear."

Vittoria snorted. "If only I had that number to offer you. There aren't but fifteen hundred soldiers in the whole of the Denorian army, and those spread out across the country. There are perhaps seven hundred and fifty here in the city. I might trust three hundred of them with a mission like this, and of those, only two hundred can actually keep their mouths shut."

Curlin let out a low whistle. "It'll be hard to take Penby, much less all of Alskad, with a force that small."

"You forget," Vi said. "There aren't that many Shriven left in the whole of the empire. A huge number of them were sent to Ilor because of—well, me. And we saw what happened there."

Curlin grimaced. "The sooner we set sail, the better. I don't want word of what happened in Ilor getting back to Alskad much before we do. The less time the Suzerain have to plan, the safer I'll feel."

Vittoria nodded. "I'd like to leave tomorrow. I'll inform the troops and have them ferry themselves out to your ship in small groups. We'll try to keep it as inconspicuous as we can, but we'll have to move fast. If Noriava finds out about your plan, there's no telling what she'll do."

The kaffe soured in my stomach at the thought, but Swinton squeezed my hand reassuringly. "It's not exactly outside the bounds of the sentiment of your arrangement," he said.

"I'm sure she'll see it that way, too. Sounds like she's quite the reasonable one," Vi quipped.

Vittoria shot me a narrow look over the rim of her steaming kaffe cup, and I shrugged even as a wave of irritation passed over me. Vi must have felt it as well, because she knocked me on the shoulder.

"Don't be like that," she said. "I'm not the one who went

and tied myself to a queen just to get hold of some soldiers that would have fought for you either way."

Before I could stammer out a reply, Vi grabbed a pastry from the plate in the center of the table, thumbed the jam filling out and rubbed a sticky glob of deep purple jam onto my nose. The tension in the room broke, and everyone burst into laughter, distracted, for a moment, from the dangers we'd yet to face.

CHAPTER THIRTY-FIVE

Vi

We didn't make it back to the ship until the small hours of the morning, and I fell into a deep and blessedly blank sleep as soon as I reached my berth. When I woke, the sun was already high overhead and streaming in through the windows of our cabin. I dressed quickly and tiptoed out of the room, trying to avoid waking Curlin. Seeing Bo the night before had been harder than I'd expected, but I didn't feel like hashing through my feelings at the moment. The task that loomed before us was overwhelming enough without giving voice to the demons of depression that curled in my belly like snakes waiting to strike.

I searched the ship, my face a hard mask that kept everyone, even Jihye, from saying a word to me, and I was grateful for their silence. After nearly an hour, I finally found Mal deep in the bowels of the hold, sorting through one of the stolen chests of the temple's treasure. Our horde was dwindling quickly, and with hundreds of mouths to feed, if we didn't manage to restore Bo to the throne in short order, the cause would be lost entirely. All the more reason to get Bo and Swinton out from under the thumb of the Denorian queen and on our way back to Alskad as quickly as possible.

Mal peered up at me in the dim light of the solar lamps. "You don't look like you slept at all."

"What of it?" I snapped.

"Just an observation." He shrugged. "Quill's in quite a temper. What happened between you two?"

"We're in the middle of a war. How anyone has time to think about romance is beyond me."

"That doesn't answer my question." Mal stood, brushed his hands off on his trousers and looked down at me, assessing. "But seeing as you're well-set on being a prickly beast about it, I'll leave off. What're you looking for?"

"You," I said. The truth of his name-calling stung. I was working at it—at the feeling of inadequacy that clung to me like a film of oil—but I'd not yet managed to wash it away. "And whatever you've got squirreled away down here that might distract a queen enough for her to take her eyes off her fiancé for a few minutes during her weekly open audience."

Mal's brows knit together, and from his calculating expression, I could tell he was going through an inventory of the ship in his mind. A slow grin spread across his face, and a moment later he dove behind a stack of chests, shifted them this way and that, and came up with a box, long and flat and nearly as tall as I was.

"This'll do the trick. Now, she's not yet met you, has she?"

I shook my head.

"Perfect. Do you trust me?"

There was a maniacal gleam in his eyes that I *definitely* didn't trust. I bit my lip, then said, "Not as far as I can throw you."

He laughed. "Well, seeing as I'm twice your size, I'd suggest you get over it. How long do we have until the audience?"

I shrugged. "Maybe three hours?"

"Long enough. Get word through Pem and Still. Tell them to make sure everyone is ready to go before sunset."

Getting the Denorian soldiers onto the Whipplestons' ship was no small task, but General Okara's troops were disciplined and quick-witted, and they managed to disguise themselves and their weapons quite thoroughly. They were hardly noticed among the comings and goings of the merchants who'd deigned to deal with Mal and Quill as they restocked the ship's ravaged stores.

Getting Bo and Swinton out of the palace was another matter entirely. We'd puzzled over the problem, turning it this way and that, upside down and sideways, and every time it came up all wrong. Ever since Noriava discovered that Bo had been wandering the city at night, she'd put a guard on him around the clock. They stuck to him like glue, standing outside every entrance to his rooms while he slept, trailing him like puppies as he went from once place to the next and even pacing beneath the windows of his rooms, despite the fact that they were on the fourth floor of the palace and only someone with a death wish would try scaling the smooth black stone of the palace walls.

We hoped Mal would be able to distract the queen long enough to get Bo free of the palace. We just had to keep her from recognizing me.

My tattoos and the gold cuff on my wrist were completely concealed by many layers of fine Denorian wool cut in the latest fashion. I'd used dark makeup to disguise the shape of my eyes and brows, and my curly hair was oiled and slicked back into a tight chignon at the base of my neck, rendering me entirely unrecognizable, even to myself. Mal also wore something of a disguise—rather than his usual blend of casual Ilorian and Alskader fashion, he had decked himself out in the finest Alskader clothing he could lay his hands on, and his short, tight curls were trimmed close to his head.

As I followed him meekly into the grand palace hall, my eyes immediately sought out Bo. My hand unwittingly drifted toward the small silver box in my pocket as I pushed down the anxiety roiling my belly and pulled hard on the feeling of connection between us. Bo's gaze drifted through the crowd, passing over me several times, the picture of indolent boredom. Though I felt the moment he recognized me, nothing in his outward manner changed.

The moments crept slowly by as we waited for Mal to be called before the queen. Finally, after listening to dozens of requests for research funding, minor property disputes and personal quarrels—which Mal had to translate from Denorian to Alskader for me—we were announced and summoned to the throne. Heaving the long, heavy box with its intricate carvings and brass fittings onto his shoulder, Mal stepped before the queen and my twin brother.

"Your Majesty, as the date of your nuptials quickly approaches, you must be in the market for an appropriate gift for your new spouse, and I am sure he searches for the perfect gift to present to you. My partner and I have with us two very rare items that we believe will suit your needs most perfectly."

Mal beckoned me forward, and I executed the queer, intricate bow he'd made me practice all morning. A large black cat shared the throne with the queen. Its green eyes followed me knowingly, and its tail twitched like a jungle beast about to spring for the kill. I kept my own eyes lowered—they were so like Bo's that even the most casual observer couldn't help but make the connection, and from everything I'd gathered, Queen Noriava was anything but unobservant.

"You cannot imagine that I would buy a gift for my future husband whilst in his company, Master..." Noriava trailed off.

"Whippleston, Your Majesty. I would hate to impose upon your time in any way, but perhaps I could take you aside so that you might examine my wares, and let my associate do the same with your fiancé? Under guard, of course. What I've brought you..." He paused, a secretive, charming smile bringing out the laugh lines around his golden eyes. In moments like this, Mal was utterly, disarmingly appealing. "...is incredibly rare and valuable. It dates from before the cataclysm. Shall I go on?"

"And the gift that you, in your infinite wisdom, believe would appeal to me?" she asked, a note of flirtatious teasing in her lilting voice.

"What can a man give a monarch as powerful and beautiful as you?" Mal flattered. "I would hate to spoil the surprise, but I will tell you that the object my partner carries with her is, perhaps, the most exciting item I've had the pleasure of procuring in my entire career. I assure you that you will be most pleased, and if you are not, I will do everything in my power to amend my error in judgment."

Noriava's foot, in its delicate sandal, tapped once, twice, three times on the floor before her skirt swished and she stood.

"Very well," she said. "Come with me. King Ambrose, use the second chamber on the right. Be sure to take your guards, darling."

Bo stood, and three guards formed an arrow around him— one in front and one on either side. After they swept by me, I hurried to follow in Bo's wake. As we walked out of the hall and down a short corridor, I surreptitiously opened the box in my pocket, and my fingers closed around the object inside. Once the door to the small chamber closed behind us, I pulled my hand from my pocket.

"Duck!"

The guards whirled on me. I took a deep breath, aimed the bottle at the nearest guard and pressed the top of the antique atomizer Mal'd dug up for me. The scent of flowers filled the room, the last of the perfume in the bottle having mixed with the sedative Pem'd stolen from one of the labs. I spun on one heel and sprayed the other guard in the face just as the first dropped to the ground. The third managed to land a punch on my ribs, but I was too quick for her, and as soon as the spray hit her nose, she was down.

As an advancing guard reached for my neck, Bo grabbed him from behind. He struggled to hold the squirming man as I carefully aimed a spritz into the guard's face, and he went down, taking Bo with him.

Feeling a bit woozy myself, I pulled Bo to his feet. "We have to go. Quickly."

"But Swinton—"

"Pem and Still have him."

"What about Mal?"

"He'll delay the queen as long as he can and then slip out through the kitchens. He's got a scullery maid hooked around his little finger and a uniform already waiting for him in one of the pantries."

Bo nodded and squeezed me into a tight hug. "Thanks for coming to get me, sister."

My jaw tightened at the sudden affection, but the genuine warmth of his feelings came over me in a wave, and I hugged him back ever so briefly.

"Come on. They won't be down for long."

I shrugged out of my long jacket and handed it to Bo. As he dropped the heavily embroidered robe he wore and traded it for my jacket, I pulled my hair loose, then removed the Circlet of Alskad from Bo's head and mussed his hair. I tucked the circlet into one of the deep inner pockets on his jacket and scrutinized him carefully. The fabric was a bit tight around his shoulders, and no one who looked carefully at us would be fooled for a minute, but the disguise would have to do.

Opening the door, I glanced quickly up and down the corridor. Thankfully, it was empty, and we sprinted away from the palace hall. We slowed around corners and kept our heads down as we passed servants with piles of linens and trays of food heaped in their arms, and in a matter of minutes we were out a side door and blinking in the unusually bright light of the late winter afternoon.

"Dzallie's tits," I hissed, scanning the grounds around us. We'd somehow managed to emerge on entirely the wrong side of the palace—opposite the main gate nearest the stairs that led down to the harbor. On the queen's audience days, that gate was left open, its portcullis up, and the guards were lackadaisical about scanning the people coming and going. Here, there wasn't any way out that I could see.

Bo raised an eyebrow at me.

"We have to get out before the queen notices you're gone."

Bo nodded. "I know a shortcut to the front gate through the gardens. Follow me."

We raced through the lush green gardens, crashing into bushes and sending flocks of small songbirds whirling into the sky. When we finally burst through the last clump of trees and into the wide outer courtyard, dozens of people turned to stare. Before they could get their bearings, we sprinted through the gates. Behind us, I heard a cacophony of angry voices yelling in Denorian.

"Faster, Vi!" Bo gasped. "They're calling for me to stop."

As we dashed through the city, my feet kept slipping on the cobblestones, and I felt like I was always one wrong step away from losing my balance and crashing to my knees. I half raced, half stumbled down the first flight of the stairs leading to the harbor, but skittered to a stop on the landing, Bo crashing into my back. A startled pair of guards stared blankly at us for a moment and began to step aside, but then the enormous brass bells inside the castle clanged.

They exclaimed something in Denorian and lunged for us. Bo grabbed a handful of my sweater and yanked me back up the stairs and away from them. When we reached the top, I heaved a juice cart away from an unsuspecting Denorian merchant and sent it hurtling down the stairs. The tumbling cart caught one guard in the leg, sending him sprawling backward. Bright, sticky juice sloshed out onto the white stone steps, staining them bright red and purple. The other guard looked between us and his partner and yelled what sounded like curses as he dashed down the sticky stairs to rescue his partner.

"This way," I panted, grabbing Bo by the hand.

A plan was beginning to form in my head. A stupid, dangerous plan, but a plan nonetheless. I fled away from the stairs, weaving between the vendors with their carts, the baffled Denorian citizenry and the street performers that traced the line of the stone wall at the top of the cliffs, looming over the Salemouth harbor. The guards, having gathered their wits, raised the alarm behind us, but it did them more harm than good, as curious citizens peered after us, impeding the guards' ability to give chase.

When we were close to running out of wall and would soon be forced to turn back into the city, I slowed and turned to Bo.

"Do you trust me?" I wheezed.

"Are you about to do something particularly stupid?"

I nodded, clambered onto the wall and looked down. The cliffs sheered away below us, and though it might have been an illusion, it looked like they angled slightly inward, giving way to deep water below. I offered Bo my hand.

"No," he said, gasping for breath. "The drop will surely kill us both, and even if it doesn't, I'm a terrible swimmer."

"You'd rather stay and marry Noriava?" I demanded. "Give her the keys to the empire and sit in her lap for the rest of your life?"

Bo's face was pale. He pressed his lips into a tight line, then sighed. "I suppose if I have to die doing something breathtakingly risky, it stands to reason that I'd do it with you."

He took my hand, and as I pulled him up onto the wall, I saw a squadron of the queen's guards just a few strides away, their white coats flapping as they ran.

"Stay as straight as you can, take a deep breath and start kicking as soon as you hit the water," I told him. "Get to the surface and I'll take care of the rest." I took a deep breath. "On my count. One. Two…"

A guard's gloved hand grabbed the collar of my coat, and I squirmed out of it while pulling us into the open air.

"Three!" I yelped.

The wind whistled in my ears, and beside me, Bo screeched as we fell to the ocean below. The water hit me like a wall of ice. Even with my long years of experience in the frigid water of the Penby harbor, panic threatened to send me reeling as the black water closed around me like a coffin. I forced my feelings aside and treaded, keeping myself suspended in the water until I managed to catch sight of the column of bubbles where my brother had crashed into the water. He was completely still, sinking fast. Pushing away the panic that threatened to steal my breath and my focus, I launched myself through the water toward him. Fool hadn't kept his arms by his sides. He'd be lucky if he'd only broken an arm.

By the time I reached him, we were deep under the waves, and the current tugged us out and out toward the open ocean. I grabbed Bo around the chest and kicked us to the surface.

The moment our heads broke above the waves, Bo coughed, and relief washed over me like a crashing wave. Thanks to the strong current, we were already far from the base of the cliffs, and the guards were like ants on the wall.

"Can you swim?" I asked, treading water for both of us.

Bo coughed some more before he replied, his voice tremulous with pain and perhaps a little fear. "I can manage."

"Don't be a hero," I scolded him. "If you can't, just tell me. I'll do for us, but you'll have to lose your shoes and jacket."

I'd already kicked my boots off, but the heavy Denorian wool sweaters I still wore were weighing me down. "Float on your back, and I'll pull your jacket off. Can you manage your shoes?"

"The circlet," Bo panted. "We can't lose it. It's been a symbol of Alskad's power for as long as the empire's existed."

I pulled the jacket off Bo's shoulders, ignoring his whimper of pain as the sleeve caught on his wrist, and shoved my hands into the inner pockets, but came up empty-handed.

"It's gone."

Bo clutched his wrist to his chest and sighed. "I suppose it's just a symbol. No reason to be so attached, really."

But his grief pulsed through our connection, and as I pulled us back to the Whipplestons' ship, tears coursed down my cheeks, mingling with the salty water of the bay.

CHAPTER THIRTY-SIX

Bo

Noriava's few naval vessels gave us chase only as far as the outer islands just north of the Denorian border. I would undoubtedly be forced to endure some exceedingly uncomfortable meetings the moment her ambassadors got word of what I'd done, and I expected that the concessions I would have to make in the inevitable negotiations to follow would be dear indeed. My leverage—that she'd withheld the cure from Swinton—was nothing but conjecture, after all. But for the moment, at least, I was free of her clutches and on my way home with an army at my back and my sister at my side.

Vi was quiet and distant during the voyage, and as the ship sailed into the harbor at Penby, I found her leaning over the railing at the back of the ship, staring into the water.

"Scared or nervous?" I asked.

She gave me a half smile, tracing a curving line of the tattoo etched along her wrist. "Both?"

I waited for her to continue.

"I just don't know where I fit in the scheme of this world," she confessed. "I don't know the rules. I won't get the jokes, and I'll surely be the laughingstock of court. And that's even if they accept you with me tagging along."

"Gerlene says—"

"I know she says that the paperwork is all legal and in place, but wouldn't it be easier if I weren't around? If I weren't an everyday reminder of how strange this whole thing is?"

I studied her as she gazed out over the vast expanse of the gray sea. She'd grown leaner in the months we'd been apart. The hard lines of her cheeks and jaw cut against her freckled skin, and her mouth seemed to be perpetually frowning. Vi moved with an athlete's grace now, muscles rippling under the plain clothes she wore, and she was never without a weapon. A cloud of wariness hung around her like a fog. Her black curls, having escaped from the thick plait that hung over her shoulder, whipped around her face, the only piece of her that hadn't been transformed during her time in Ilor.

"It might be easier," I conceded. "But I haven't spent these last few months cultivating allies and pushing against the Alskad gentry's ideas about the temple and the throne just to maintain the comfortable ignorance of the Alskad people. I don't plan to land a foreign army on the shores of my own country just for the sake of my vanity. Our grandmother wanted to shift the ideas of rulership in our empire, and I see it as just that, Vi. *Ours.* I want you to share the responsibility and power of the throne with me. I thought you knew that."

"But I never said I wanted that. You just assumed that because you were raised to the crown that I'd want it, too, but you never *asked* me."

"Well," I said, doing my best to make my tone measured, patient. "What do you want?"

"I don't bloody know," Vi spit. "I'm fair certain I've no business stuffing myself into silks and jewels and pretending to be royalty, when everyone and their mother knows well and good that I'm not."

I bit my lip, irritation building in my gut, and reached out to touch the gold cuff, so like mine, that she wore around her wrist. "But you are. At least as much as I'm royalty, you are, too. If I have every right to be king, you have every right to be queen."

"It isn't about my right to anything, Bo. It's about who I am, who I've become. You've grown more and more a king through all this, and I've become more...something else. But I don't feel like a queen. What's more, I think you have to love a place to rule it, and I don't have any love for Alskad. Nothing good has ever come from my being here, and no part of me yearns for it. I'm not driven by the will to make it better like you are."

"But you're here. You're fighting for these people."

Vi furrowed her brows, her frown deepening. "I'm here because of you, Bo. I'm fighting because I think that you'll protect Alskad from the temple, and because I think you should be the person making decisions for the empire."

"But it's not just about me, Vi," I insisted. "If it were just about me, you wouldn't have stayed behind in Ilor when I came home. You would have kept yourself out of danger."

Boots clicked on the deck behind us. As I turned, one of the Denorian soldiers gave me a salute and said, "We're approaching the docks, sir. Would you like to speak to the troops?"

I gave Vi's shoulder a squeeze. "We'll talk more later?"

She gave me a sly grin. "Let's go talk to your soldiers, little brother. I'm not running off on you yet."

A small boat tugged the great iron ship into one of the

many berthings along Penby's great harbor, and after Captain Whippleston had a brief discussion with the harbormaster, the gangplanks were lowered and the work of off-loading the cargo we'd brought from Ilor and Denor began.

We met Swinton at the ship's stern. His long golden hair was neatly plaited and clubbed. He wore a new, dark wool jacket over close-fitted trousers and a Denorian wool sweater. In the simple, elegant clothes, he looked to me more like a prince than I felt, but his expression was somber.

"Are you ready?" I asked.

"I don't suppose there's a 'go back to Ilor and let the rest of the world burn' option, is there?"

Behind me, Vi chuckled grimly. "If there were, I'd be on that ship with you in a heartbeat, Swinton. Especially if Bethesda's cooking is at the other end of the journey. I have dreams about her meat pies."

"Don't go telling her that. She's got a big enough head as it is." Swinton grinned. "But it's the thought of her mango and lime tarts that keeps me up at night."

Curlin thumped Vi's shoulder hard enough to make her snarl and gave a disgusted snort. "There are dimmys being rounded up in the streets and the temple's set to poison half of Alskad to get their way, and the two of you feel like it's all well and good to go on and on about Bethesda's food? What's broken in you? I, for one, am ready for the fight."

Vi stuck out her tongue at Curlin as I gently moved Curlin's hand away from the hilt of her knife. "We're hoping that we won't have to fight, remember?"

Glancing down the length of the ship, I saw Quill already halfway down the gangplank. He raised his hand and waved at us. The Ilorian troops on the deck were already in formation, and the Denorians were waiting to take up our flank.

I'd not yet grown used to seeing General Okara out of uniform, but she'd insisted that, as the Denorians were operating outside the bounds of their official capacity in the Denorian army, it was inappropriate for them to wear the Denorian uniform. In hopes that it would foster a sense of unity, all of the forces—the former Shriven and the Denorians—wore a band of violet cloth, the color of the Alskad flag, wrapped around their upper arms.

"I wish I had a more elegant speech to give," I said. "But thank you. Thank you for being with me. Try to remember that the Alskader soldiers are my citizens, too, so the less we can engage them, the better. Ideally, Rylain will step down the moment we enter the palace, and we'll be able to focus our attention on untangling the issue of the High Council. But in the meantime, I'm eternally grateful to you all for volunteering to serve with me as we take back Alskad, for the safety of her citizens."

"From your lips to Dzallie's ears," Curlin muttered.

CHAPTER THIRTY-SEVEN

Vi

Before we took the troops to march on the palace, there was something else we had to do. Something I'd been dreading since Bo first brought it up.

I had to meet the nobility.

The singleborn who could either support or oppose my brother's claim to the throne had made it very clear that their support of Bo's ascension would depend a great deal upon whether or not I would be an embarrassment to the monarchy.

I didn't feel at all certain that I could hold my own in this challenge. For the first time since we'd left Aphra in Ilor, I wished that she was with us. At least if I bungled everything with her around, she could fix it. Plus she knew how to act around the fancy nobles.

I sighed and stepped onto the gangplank behind Bo. We'd outfitted ourselves in plain clothes—though finely made—so as not to draw too much attention as we passed through the streets of Penby. Since we suspected Bo's house was being closely watched, Bo sent word to the members of his royal council, instructing them to meet us at Gerlene's.

"How's it feel, being back here?" Bo whispered as we slid through the crowds on the docks.

My life had been turned on its head and rewritten so many times in the months since I left Penby, but somehow, the streets were the same, if a bit smaller than I remembered. The docks still smelled like fish and salt tinged with rot and smoke. The same vendors hawked their wares from the same carts.

I pulled my sleeve down farther to cover the tattoos that climbed my wrist and bit the inside of my cheek. "It's strange," I said. "I never thought I'd be back here. When I left, it was supposed to be for good. Forever."

We walked in silence for a bit. Bo's curly black hair was hidden by a knit cap, but he still carried himself like a king, all shoulders and straight spine and jaw set to take on the world. Suddenly, a familiar smell snatched me out of my reverie like a riptide, pulling me into the past. The scent of Bene's spiced pigeon pies wafted on the breeze, and I grabbed Bo's elbow, making him stop as I searched the square.

I knew in my heart it couldn't be Bene—I'd seen her die at Skalla's hand with my own eyes—but there, in the place her bakery had been, was an identical shop, down to the name etched in the window where Bene had died.

"What is it?" Bo asked.

"Do you have any money?"

"A few *tvilling* and a handful of *drott*. Why?"

I took him by the hand and pulled him across the square, careless of the fact that someone might recognize me, or worse, Bo. I pushed open the shop door, and a bell chimed in the back. A young man appeared, barely older than Bo and me, with an expectant look on his familiar face. Bene's son.

"Can I help you?" he asked.

Tears welled in my eyes at the familiarity of the bakery, the knowledge that I could now afford anything in the display case, the strangeness of being greeted without the fear and terror I'd always known because I was a dimmy.

"Vi?" Bo asked, his voice as gentle as a lamb. "We're going to be late."

"Two pigeon pies, please," I said. Then, on a whim, added, "And a slice of spice cake, please."

"Gerlene will feed us if you're hungry," Bo whispered.

I ignored him.

"You're in luck," the boy said. "Pigeon pies just came out of the oven. They're still warm. That'll be eleven *tvilling*, please."

He handed us each a pie wrapped in waxed brown paper, then set the cake in a small box and tied it with a purple ribbon. I elbowed Bo, who dropped a handful of coins into the boy's waiting hand.

"What's all this about?" Bo asked as we left the shop. "I'm sure Gerlene will have food."

"Not this food," I said, taking a bite of the pie. The crust flaked into my mouth, all butter and salt. The filling burst with spice and fat and chunks of savory meat. It was everything I remembered and more. Bo took a tentative bite of his own pie and closed his eyes, smiling.

"Fine," he admitted. "That was a worthwhile detour. But we should hurry. We don't want to be so late that everyone leaves before we get there."

We finished our pies as we walked and pinched bites of cake from the box I carried. By the time we'd reached the quaint row of houses and Bo knocked on the green door, the only thing left was crumbs. I tossed the box and waxed paper into a trash bin and climbed the stairs two at a time to wait with Bo on the stoop.

The door flew open, and a woman in a moss green sweater and olive trousers wrapped her arms around Bo and me, hugging us close. When she drew back, she cupped our faces in her hands and grinned.

"The two of you. Together! I never thought I'd see the day. Come in, come in."

She ushered us into an elegant foyer, decorated from ceiling to rugs in more shades of green than I'd ever seen in one place, including the Ilorian jungle. Bo grinned at me, and I realized my mouth was hanging open.

"Vi, I'd like you to meet my—our—solicitor, Gerlene Vermatch. Gerlene, this is my sister Vi."

Gerlene took my hands in hers and squeezed, smiling at me. "I am beyond pleased to see you, my dear. Now, come with me, please. Everyone's waiting in the great room."

"They all came?" Bo asked, tension clipping his words short.

"Patrise and Lisette, of course. And Olivar, Turshaw and Zurienne, as well. They're eager to hear your plans."

Bo swallowed hard and reached for my hand. "They won't bite, Vi," he said, almost as if he were comforting himself more than me. "For all that they're self-involved and snobbish to a fault, they care about this country and these people."

"And they respected Runa. They'll respect her wishes now," Gerlene added.

My stomach was in my throat, and I managed to nod, but all I could think was, *What if I'm not enough? What if they refuse to support Bo because of me?*

Bo squeezed my hand. "You are enough. More than. Remember that."

My heart tumbled over in my chest, warmed by the reminder that Bo knew me as well as I knew myself—better
at times.

Gerlene looked from me to my brother and back again,
smiling, before turning on a heel and leading us down the
hall. "This will be great fun, I think," she called over her
shoulder.

The great room went still as we entered, and five expectant faces looked up at us, assessing. Calculating. Then one
of the women, young and startlingly beautiful, stood up, a
brilliant smile transforming her face. She held out her arms
to Bo and, not the least bit subtly, kicked the handsome man
who'd been sitting next to her on the couch in the shin. He
rubbed his leg, glaring up at her, but didn't move.

"Bo, darling," she crooned. "We're ever so delighted that
you've returned to us unscathed."

Next to me, Bo held his ground, and I could feel the irritation pouring off him as if it were my own. "Lisette. Lovely
to see you. I am honored to present my sister Vi Abernathy.
Vi, this is Alskad's singleborn royal council—Lisette, Patrise,
Olivar, Zurienne and Dame Turshaw."

The elderly woman seated next to the fire looked at Bo
aghast, and the others didn't do a great deal to cover their
shock at the introduction. Surely they'd been warned? Surely
they knew about me already?

"I am truly appalled at your manners, child," the older
man said.

Bo smirked. "Because of the order of my introduction?
Olivar, please. Surely you know that, as my sister, Vi out-
ranks you by a wide margin, singleborn or not."

Out of nervous habit, I touched the gold cuff I'd worn
since I left Ilor, and immediately regretted the gesture as all

the eyes in the room followed my hand to the bracelet, so like those they wore. Lisette coughed and plopped back onto the couch from which she'd risen.

This wasn't going well.

"Look," I said. "The reason we're all here is so that you can see if I'm going to be a total embarrassment when Bo takes the throne. I can assure you that I will not. I have no interest in taking a leadership role in your government. I'm here to support Bo, nothing more. He's the rightful heir, and he'll make a brilliant leader. He cares so much about this country and its people. Why else would he have risked so much to save it from Rylain and the Suzerain?"

"Pretty words, darling," the handsome man—he had to be Patrise—said, "but why should we believe you?"

"Because as many times as I've asked her to rule beside me, she's said no." Bo's voice was clenched, emphatic.

Zurienne tapped out a rhythm on her knee with long, brown fingers, then looked up at me, considering. "We are, after all, in the house of a solicitor. She could sign something that testifies to her intentions."

I said, "Of course," in the same breath that Bo said, "Absolutely not."

I turned to glare at him. "We want you on the throne. If this will make these vultures back you, then let's do it. You know being queen isn't the life I want."

Patrise clapped his hands giddily. "Look, Lisette, they're alike as a pair of earrings. Let's make them argue more."

Bo shot Patrise a deadly look, and Lisette preened at him, fluffing her auburn hair. By the fire, Dame Turshaw snorted and cast an indiscriminate glare about the room.

"It's an idea worth considering," Olivar said. "Gerlene, could you draw something up? A document stating that His

Royal Majesty's sister and her offspring would have no claim to the throne? So on and so forth? You understand, of course."

Gerlene glanced at Bo, who gave a tight-lipped nod. "Of course," she said. "I won't be a moment."

Bo collapsed onto a settee with an exasperated sigh and put his head in his hands, mussing his already out of control curls. I sank down beside him and eyed the members of the council from under my lashes.

"So," Lisette said brightly. "Things here have been particularly terrible since you left. Rylain's a tyrant, and she told the whole of the empire you were a twin just as soon as you left—trying to cast you and Runa as traitors to the crown and the empire's traditions and all that. What's more, the Suzerain are using the Shriven to push the lot of us to attend adulations every day. *Every day*, Bo. I simply cannot go on like this."

I raised an eyebrow. "You're upset because you have to attend adulations? What about all the people they've imprisoned? Those they've killed?"

"Well, obviously that's terrible, too."

Patrise cut in. "How was Denor? Isn't Noriava just wonderful?"

I could just see Bo gritting his teeth, head still resting on his palms. "It wasn't exactly the easiest of negotiations," I said.

"That's putting it lightly," Bo quipped.

Gerlene appeared in a flutter of green cloth, a piece of paper in one hand, a pen and ink pot in the other. "All this says, my dear, is that you will not take a leadership role in the governance of the Alskad Empire, and that any children you bear would be ineligible for the throne." She glanced at Olivar. "Is there anything else?"

He shook his head and sipped from a steaming teacup.

"Then, if you would, Vi, sign here." She set the paper on

the low table, along with the ink pot and pen. I read through the document quickly and signed my name.

"That's all settled, then," I said. "Let's hope things with Rylain go just as smoothly."

Lisette pursed her lips, and Bo straightened up beside me. There was steel running through his spine, and resolve seemed to radiate off him in waves. The others in the room sat up straighter, too, their eyes trained on my brother.

"When will you go?" Zurienne asked.

"This afternoon. We'll go back to the ship and assemble the troops and then go on to the palace," Bo said. "I'll need you ready to use what power you have on the council. I hope that Rylain will step down, but I don't think it's likely."

The councillors shifted uncomfortably, and every one of them avoided looking at Bo. Finally, from her place by the fire, Dame Turshaw spoke up. "We'll support your ascension as the first twin king of the Alskad Empire, should it come to that, but it is deeply immoral for us to promise you votes on a topic not yet brought before the council."

Zurienne and Olivar nodded their agreement.

"We will, of course, do what's in the best interest of the empire," Zurienne said. "But who's to say what that will be?"

"And after you made Vi sign away all her royal rights," Bo snapped. "You lot are worse than any pirates I've ever met!"

He stood and, with a sour look at Dame Turshaw, stalked out of the room. I rose as well, cringing.

"Look," I said. "If you won't do it for Bo, at least think about all the people who've been affected by Rylain's rule. Think about the families ripped apart, and the people killed. Bo may not be your idea of a perfect leader, but he has to be a hell of a lot better than Rylain."

The front door slammed. With a half-hearted bow, I fled

the room, Bo's anger and disappointment flooding through me from outside. I took a deep breath as I tripped down the front stoop and ran to catch him up.

He needed to be calm. We had a regent to depose.

CHAPTER THIRTY-EIGHT

Bo

We drew more than a few stares as we made our way through the city with a regiment of heavily armed warriors, and I tried to let go of my anger at the singleborn. I understood their need to be careful, but I hated that they wouldn't simply take my side. It made everything I was trying to do feel so much more tenuous, so out of my control.

The sun was just past its zenith when we arrived at the palace gates, the light harsh and blindingly reflecting from the snowdrifts piled on every corner and against every wall. The scent of kaffe carts and roasting nuts came sharp and bitter on the chill wind, and yet they were somehow also comforting and familiar. I'd not been gone but a handful of weeks, and yet everything was at once entirely unchanged and achingly foreign.

As we approached the palace, I stiffened upon seeing the enormous wooden doors that served as the major entrance and exit to the palace grounds. Not once, in the span of my memory, had they ever been closed—until today. The imposing stone walls were lined with guards, their weapons trained on our party, standing between us and the only way into the palace.

I straightened my back and stepped forward through the ranks of the Ilorian and Denorian soldiers. Many of those who'd formerly been Shriven had continued to shave their heads, and some, before leaving the ship, had painted their foreheads and scalps. Others had painted symbols of peace and justice on their exposed skin. It surprised me to see that some of the Denorians had shaved parts of their scalps as well, and as I walked through their ranks, I saw the reddened lines of new tattoos peeking out from collars and shirtsleeves. I was astonished by how quickly the three factions—the former Shriven, the Ilorian rebels and the Denorian soldiers—had rallied together and coalesced into a prodigious and intimidating force.

I approached the captain, a woman I recognized from my time in the palace with Runa. "Captain Devi," I said politely. "Please inform my cousin that I've returned to reclaim my throne."

The captain fixed her eyes somewhere in the middle distance over my left shoulder. "The regent grants audiences on the third day of every month, sir."

"Your Royal Majesty," I corrected, my jaw tightening.

"No, sir. The crown prince and Queen Runa were murdered by dimmys on the queen's birthday."

Vi sidled up beside me. "Trouble?"

"Apparently I've been murdered," I snapped.

"Heard about that," Vi said. "Tricksome thing, being dead. Were you snatched up to the halls of the gods to feast with

Hamil and Magritte and all the rest? Get bored of all the fighting, fucking and feasting, did you?"

Captain Devi's control over her face slipped just a hair at Vi's sacrilegious and, frankly, coarse remark.

Vi went on, circling Captain Devi like a shark considering its next meal. She kept her voice loud enough that even the guards on the wall could hear her without straining. "Thing is, brother mine, if you're dead, then I'm a dimmy. And I just don't see the appeal in ripping out anyone's throat at the moment. I'd hate to get blood all over my nice new trousers. What's more, I see you standing here in front of me, plainly not dead. So mayhap all Captain Devi here needs is a good slap upside the head so as she can see what's clear in front of her. What do you think?"

Vi draped an arm around the captain's stiff shoulders and traced a finger along the hilt of her sword.

"I'm sure Captain Devi is just following orders," I said smoothly. "She had no way of knowing that Rylain's been lying to everyone this whole time. But then, so have I, I suppose." I looked up and addressed the guards standing between me and the palace. "I am the rightful king of the Alskad Empire. Ambrose Oswin Trousillion Gyllen. Duke of Nome and Junot, Count of Sikts, Baron of the Kon, Protector of the Colonies of Ilor and the Great Northern Waste. Queen Runa, my grandmother, chose me to succeed her in ruling Alskad. It was her firmly held belief that the singleborn were no better than those with twins, no better than the diminished. She knew, when she chose me, that I had a twin. *Have* a twin."

There was an uproar from the guards along the wall, and those stationed before the great doors shifted and looked to one another, visibly uncomfortable.

"I tell you this now," I continued, "because I want to begin my reign the way I intend to conduct its entirety—honestly. Now, Captain Devi, if you will oblige me, I would be grateful to be allowed into my palace."

Anxious energy thrummed through my veins as I watched the captain's eyes flick from me to Vi and back. She made no attempt to disguise her emotions. Anger, dismay and confusion played across her open features.

Finally, she turned to her second and barked the order. "Open the gates. Notify the regent."

The guards, though clearly well seasoned and trained to mask their feelings, paused for a moment, gaping before they managed to pull themselves together and follow her orders.

Vi grinned at Curlin, who scowled back at her. Rolling her eyes, Vi turned to me. "Didn't expect you to go and declare yourself a heretic before you'd even taken the throne, brother."

"I can't say I believe it's a particularly intelligent move," Quill said.

Curlin, eyes narrowed against the bright sun, scoured the square. "We're not going in there without your solicitor and papers to back us up. The High Councillors will demand proof of all your claims, and you can bet your ass they'll do everything in their power to stop you getting those papers if they're not in your hand when you walk through those doors."

I nodded, willing Pem and Still to appear with Gerlene with every fiber of my being. Vi, gray eyes flashing, strode over to confer with Jihye. I stared straight ahead, spine stiff and face impassive. The appearance I presented to these guards would travel through the barracks and the halls of the servants like an avalanche, and I couldn't afford to let even the barest hint of the fear and anxiety roiling through my guts show on my face. If I did, it would as much as hand Rylain the throne on a silver platter.

After a delay so long I'd begun to believe time stood still, Gerlene flew into the square, emerald coattails flying behind her. Pem trotted in her wake, lugging a stack of books under each arm and a leather satchel bulging with papers.

Gerlene was talking before she'd even made it past the first of the Denorian soldiers, her eyes gleaming behind her spectacles. "How are you, my boy? Excited? I can barely contain myself, even after the spectacle you made of yourself this morning. I've been waiting for this moment for the entirety of my career. Your grandmother would be so proud." She straightened the collar of her jacket. "Shall we?"

I nodded, though I was a little frustrated at her mention of my losing control of my temper.

"Wait! Wait!" she cried. "Where's your sister? Where's Vi? I assume she won't want to miss all the fun."

Vi, having slipped farther into the soldiers' ranks, radiated caution, but she was all ferocious charm when she strode up to Gerlene and embraced the solicitor. Then she moved to my right side, and we strode into the palace together.

We found Rylain in the throne room, seated on Runa's throne. *My* throne. The Suzerain stood behind her, flanked by three anchorites on either side, all their faces impassive. Their fine silk robes were embroidered with gold thread, and they were laden with jewels that sparkled in the dim light of the sunlamps.

Just as I was opening my mouth to greet Rylain, someone in Shriven white stepped forward, and my mouth went dry. For a moment, I felt as though I was seeing a ghost.

"Claes." I breathed the name, hoping against hope that my eyes were deceiving me. If this man in Shriven robes standing before me really was my first love, then were *his* whispers what had been driving the atrocities of Rylain's reign?

The man's eyes flickered to me, and he gave me a triumphant smile, freezing my guts. It *was* Claes. He was alive. And now he was one of the Shriven.

From time to time, I'd imagined what might have happened if Claes had survived his sister's death, but the thought of him joining the Shriven had never even crossed my mind. Though my love for him had died the moment he betrayed Vi and me, the shock of seeing him alive shook my resolve more than a little.

Claes was soon joined by eleven more, most of their faces worn with age, but nevertheless possessed of the same catlike intensity that all of the Shriven seemed to inhabit. I knew that at any moment, they could spring forward, slit my throat and be back in their place before I even realized I was bleeding. More frightening than the promise of violence, though, was the light in their eyes that told me they yearned for blood in ways I couldn't ever manage to dream up. And if Claes was one of them now, they knew my every insecurity, my every weakness.

The room was cold, the hearths swept and empty, and we had only been allowed a phalanx of ten of our soldiers to accompany our core group of leaders and Gerlene. Though I had hoped we might meet Rylain in front of the greatest possible number of witnesses, it seemed this would have to do. Beside me, Vi was a beacon of self-possessed fury, and I drew strength from the power of her emotions.

"Cousin Rylain." I projected my voice loudly enough that even the servants with their ears pressed to the doors outside the room would have no trouble hearing me. As I spoke, I tried to keep my eyes trained on Rylain, but I could feel Claes's steady gaze boring into me. "I appreciate the great sacrifices you've made in caring for our empire during my absence. But as you can see, I have returned, and I will, from this point forward, take on the duties of the king and emperor as my grandmother intended."

Rylain's gaze flicked to the Suzerain before she regarded me with a critical eye.

"You are quite bold, young man, to appear before me impersonating my much beloved and murdered relative. I ought to have you arrested and tried before the citizens of Penby for treason. But, as you've caught me on a merciful day, I'll simply tell you to go back to whatever hole you crawled out of and stop wasting my time."

I clenched my jaw and pushed up my jacket's sleeve. My cuff, the same one Runa had locked on to my wrist when I was declared her heir, glinted in the dim light, and the metal glowed with the soft warmth of genuine gold.

"There is only one key in the whole kingdom that can unlock this cuff, and unless you've managed to find and move it, it is in a secret compartment in the seat of my throne." I paused, an eyebrow raised. "The throne upon which you sit being mine, in case that was, for some reason, unclear to you."

Rylain's face remained implacable.

Claes scoffed. "Anyone could re-create that cuff, and the key's location is no secret."

"In that case, show us where it is," I said mildly, spreading my hands wide. "Unlock my cuff, and you may be relieved of your duty as regent. You can go back to your books."

Jaw tight, Rylain said, "I'll thank you to stop wasting my time. Be gone. Guards! Take these pretenders away."

Gerlene stepped forward. "Madame—"

Rylain cut her off. "Queen Regent, if you please."

"No, madame. I'm afraid not. You see, the law of the empire clearly states that there may be no regent if the monarch is both of age and present."

Fists clenched on the arms of the throne, Rylain started to speak, but Gerlene plowed on ahead. The mouths of both the Suzerain had compressed to twin lines, and Claes, standing just behind Rylain, glowered at me.

"Speaking as the official solicitor to the crown, I may assure you that this young man is, in point of fact, Ambrose Oswin Trousillion Gyllen. King of the Alskad Empire, Duke of Nome and Junot, Count of Sikts, Baron of the Kon, Protector of the Colonies of Ilor and the Great Northern Waste. Should you further wish to confirm the veracity of my statement, do as His Majesty has commanded. With the key, you should find a sealed envelope, which contains the inscription made upon the interior of the cuff by the jeweler. Since the jeweler is the only person who has ever seen the interior of the bracelet, aside from our dear, departed queen, a quick glance at the inscription on His Royal Majesty's cuff should suffice as proof of his identity, should you wish to continue this charade of pretending he is not exactly who he claims to be."

Pure, unabashed admiration warmed me through and through. I couldn't possibly have a better advocate, a better scholar of the law, on my side. And the fact that she had the gall to talk over Rylain, when the woman's position was backed not only by the strength of the council, but by the High Council of the temple as well… Her bravery lent strength to my resolve.

"Well?" I asked. "Are you going to sit there and pout, or are you going to let me prove my point?"

Rylain rose and felt along the arms of the throne, looking for the switch that would open the secret compartment. Vi grinned at me. I'd told her about the compartment during our journey from Denor as we'd talked through all the possible reactions Rylain might have to my return. Vi tapped her boot on the stone floor, and Rylain's back twitched at the sound.

"Need a hand with that?" Vi asked.

"As if a common mercenary would have any idea about the secrets of the Alskader throne," Claes snapped.

Amler, the female Suzerain, put out a hand, and Claes stepped back, cowed.

Vi started to saunter toward the dais, and in a blink, three of the Shriven were in her way. Curlin's reactions were just as quick, though, and she was beside Vi, palm flat against the chest of the Shriven in the center of the formation.

"Step aside, Sakira," Curlin snarled. "On my honor, she'll do the pretender no harm."

"What honor could a traitor and defector possibly claim?" The Shriven flicked the end of Curlin's hair, grown to chin length and braided away from her face in glossy, auburn twists.

Curlin grinned savagely. "More than a bitch who uses bribe money to fund her gambling and defends a slubbering mold-wort like Rylain Trousillion. Out of her way, or I'll lay you out. You're not nearly quick enough to take me on anymore, old woman."

Vi muscled her way past the Shriven, who stood their ground, glaring at Curlin. They made no move to stop her, and in a matter of moments, Vi had elbowed Rylain out of the way, found the switch and opened the hidden compartment.

The Suzerain watched her with unreadable looks on their still faces as Vi pulled out a stack of envelopes, each one more yellowed than the last, and a familiar set of golden keys on a long chain. Vi riffled through the envelopes, her bottom lip caught between her teeth.

"Ooh, look," she said. "Here's one for you, Rylain. Care

to see what the inside of your cuff says? I'll bet it reads, 'Turns out she's a surly, fundamentalist traitor with no sense of humor at all.'"

"Vi," I cautioned. "Let's get on with it."

My sister rolled her eyes, obviously enjoying peacocking around in front of Rylain and the Shriven. I didn't know how she could be so blasé about the Suzerain, though. Their mere presence in the room made me nervous, and all the more so with Claes watching me, suddenly back from the dead. It wasn't the history of our romance that made my blood go cold, but all the years he'd spent scheming for me, getting to know every last detail about me and my life. If anyone in the world knew my every weakness, it was Claes.

"Fine. Here's yours, Bo. Shall I open it, or would you like to do the honors?" Narrowing her eyes, she tossed me the chain of keys. "Actually, you know what? No one's ever given me any jewelry, so I'm going to do it. Fair's fair."

She stuffed the sack of envelopes under one arm, ripped open the one in her hands and pulled out a single sheet of paper. Her face split into a grin as she read, and she handed the stack of papers to Gerlene.

"Bo, this really is too good. Turns out Granny was a fire-cracker."

Behind her, Claes's jaw went tight and his eyes narrowed—a look of irritation I knew all too well.

I thumbed through the keys until I found the one bearing my initials, then slid it into the lock on my cuff and turned the key. The cuff snapped open, and I held it up to the light, trying to see the inscription. I had to turn the thing over in my hands twice before I caught the right angle and was able to read the words my grandmother had chosen.

"The First Twin King. Champion of Justice. Harbinger of Peace."

I crossed the room and showed the inscription to both Rylain and the Suzerain before locking the cuff back on my wrist. I wasn't about to let Rylain get her hands on the thing. Claes snatched the paper away from Vi and scanned its contents, then thrust it at the Suzerain.

Castor and Amler exchanged a glance, and after a long moment, Amler spoke. "So it's true. Not even singleborn, and yet you claim the right to be king."

"I do," I said, keeping my voice even.

"And where's this twin of yours?" Rylain snapped. "Do you plan to share the throne with her, then?"

Vi tapped Rylain on the shoulder and offered her a hand to shake.

"Obedience Violet Abernathy. But don't let the name fool you. I'm not known for being particularly agreeable." She jerked her chin at the Suzerain standing on the dais. "This lot keeps trying to have me killed, or locked away, or made into a dimmy with their poison— Oooh, look at her face, Bo! I told you she had to at least know about the vile stuff. All that to say, I haven't exactly rolled over and let the temple do what they will to me, so I wouldn't go expecting that to change anytime soon."

Rylain, Castor and Amler stared down at Vi's hand, their faces twisted in disgust. Claes exchanged a look with one of the Shriven standing beside him.

"But say you're willing to do the right thing," Vi mused. "Say you're willing to put your obviously enormous ego aside and allow my brother to take his rightful place on the throne? Then I do believe that you and I might be great friends. We're

family, after all, and I've always wondered where the scheming, backstabbing part of my personality came from."

No one in the room moved. My breath caught in my throat,
and I wondered if Vi might've gone too far. For the first time
since I'd met her, I was genuinely worried for her safety. There
was something reckless, something akin to but so far past anger
that it was unrecognizable. It scared me.

"Is it the tattoos?" Vi wiped her palm on her trousers. "It
must be. I'm not Shriven, but I just couldn't let you lot go
having all the fun, now could I?"

A vein on Claes's forehead bulged. He took a step forward, fists knotted, but once again, a gesture from Amler
stopped him.

Rylain, clearly fuming, shoved past Vi and resumed her
seat on my throne.

"A twin does not, nor will they ever, have the right to rule
Alskad," she spit at me. "However, I'll allow you to go back to
your estates in the North and live out your days in peace. I'll
see that the High Council doesn't prosecute you for the crim-
inal deceit you've committed against the Alskader people."

Gerlene stepped forward, already flipping through a leather-
bound book as thick as the palm of her hand.

"Actually, if you'll refer to the third amendment to the four-
teenth law passed by Her Royal Majesty, Queen Emerezine,
in the year 207, you'll see that the succession is, in fact, passed
down through contractual obligation as well as the ritual that
the temple oversees. Both elements must be completed and
affirmed by witnesses."

Rylain exchanged a glance with Claes, who shook his head.
Gerlene, seeing the look, handed the book of laws back to
Pem and bent to shuffle through the leather satchel at her
feet. She came up with a sheaf of papers and riffled through

them. In a powerful, booming voice that was surprising coming from her slight frame, Gerlene launched into a fast and impenetrably complex diatribe that, from what I understood, drew together the laws and precedents that would allow for my ascent to the throne.

Despite several attempts by various anchorites and the Suzerain, as well as Rylain and Claes, to interrupt, Gerlene hardly paused for breath for nearly ten minutes. When she finally finished, she looked up from her papers, her face aglow.

"And so, you see, while the custom of the guiding religion of Alskad may frown upon the idea of a twin king, there is, in point of fact, nothing illegal about the ascent of King Ambrose. Rylain is, according to the law of Alskad, a pretender to the throne." She quirked an eyebrow at my cousin. "No offense, of course. That's just the legal terminology."

In a low, powerful voice, Amler said, "It may be that the High Council finds all of these laws, contracts and details in order, but it will take time for us to review the records and decide how we must proceed. In the meantime, it is in your best interest that you, Prince Ambrose, be kept under the supervision of the temple, along with your sister."

"King Ambrose," I corrected. "And while you may believe that I am a naive child who may be swayed to your whim, I will remind you that I was raised to lead this nation and will not be told where to go and what to do. Under no circumstances will my sister or I give ourselves over to temple supervision. The throne is mine, Rylain. Get off it, or I will remove you by force."

Castor said, "In that case, we will have to assume that you do not actually believe the lies you are spewing about your ascendance to the throne, and we will not waste our valuable time reviewing your claims."

Rylain stood. "Seeing as you've just more or less admitted to falsifying your claim of being singleborn, and you've threatened my person and my right to rule, I see no other option than to arrest you for treason." She gestured to her guards. "Seize them!"

Claes couldn't keep the smirk off his smug face as a squadron of royal guards stomped toward us, a phalanx of Shriven just behind them. Claes had obviously planned this gambit, and I'd walked right into it, ego and bravado on full display. I looked at Gerlene, whose brow was furrowed in concentration, as if she was scanning the pages of her law books in her head.

The guards closed in around us. Sweat trickled down my back. Then Vi stepped in front of me, her hands in the air.

"Wait," she said. "If I agree to give myself over to the temple's supervision until the High Council has made a proclamation about Bo's ascendance, will you let him go safely back to our ship to collect his companions, and then on to his home in the country?"

The Suzerain simultaneously put up their hands, and the guards stopped. Claes scurried toward the throne, where he conferred with Rylain and the Suzerain in low whispers.

"What do you think you're doing?" I asked.

"Saving your ass," she whispered back. "You can't do anything from inside the temple, and they're not about to let both of us walk out of this room. You worry about your crown. I'll take care of myself."

Claes resumed his place on the dais behind the throne, and Rylain cleared her throat.

"We will accept Obedience as collateral, but only if the deserter Curlin agrees to give herself over to the temple's custody, as well."

Vi glanced at Curlin, wide-eyed. "That's not part of the deal," she said. "I won't bargain her life away, too."

Amler put a hand to her chest, clutching the pearls that hung there. "We would never—"

"Shut up," Curlin spit. "We all know you would. But I'll go with Vi."

"It's settled, then," Castor announced. "Take them to the temple. The rest of you may go."

Vi flung her arms around me and pulled me in for a rib-cracking hug. "Get your throne back, Bo. Don't worry about me. I love you."

"I'll have you out of there in no time at all," I promised, blinking back tears.

The Shriven, led by Claes, wrenched her out of my arms and dragged her to the door.

I would kill him. I'd loved him and mourned him and forgiven him for his betrayal, but now I hated him. He'd held on to life for one reason, and one reason only—he wanted, more than anything, to be the power behind the throne.

And now he had my sister.

The last thing I saw as the door closed behind them was Vi kicking one of the Shriven savagely in the back of the knee. I started to pray for her safety, but quickly stopped, gritting my teeth.

None of this was up to the gods. It was up to me and me alone.

CHAPTER THIRTY-NINE

Vi

The Shriven shoved Curlin and me through a door that immediately clanged shut behind us. The key screamed in the rusty lock, and then we were alone, but for the low moans coming from the cells around us. The stone walls were slick with grime and mold and condensation, and moldering hay was heaped in the corners of the room. Curlin used the toe of her boot to push a rot-scented bucket as far away from us as the cell's scant space would allow.

"It's not so bad," Curlin said. "At least the rats in this part of the dungeon don't try to chew your fingers off while you sleep."

I glared at her. "How'd we not see this coming? We got so cocksure taking out the Shriven in Ilor that we didn't think they'd have the gall to haul us off? And us walking into the palace just like we owned the place."

Ignoring me, Curlin picked up a half-rotted blanket. "Look here. They even left us blankets. We've come up in the world,

Vi. A year ago, there's no way they'd have stuck us in the fancy cells. It's good to be rebelling with the king's sister."

A large section of the blanket fell away as Curlin held my gaze.

"Shut up," I snapped, unable to share Curlin's forced amusement at our dire situation. "What do you think they'll do to Bo?"

Curlin shifted from foot to foot, both of us being careful not to touch the mold-slimed walls. "Too many people saw him on his way through the city. They'll have to let him go back to his estates. If he's smart, he'll find a way to take the rest of our people with him."

I bit my lip. Thoughts raced through my brain half-formed and jumbled. The awfulness of the room weighed on me— the stench of rot; the darkness; the high, looming ceiling; the skittering chirps of the rats. It grew together into something massive; something living and unconquerable and real.

I couldn't catch my breath. I'd come all this way, done all this work, just to die in the same fucking dungeon that'd waited for me my whole life.

I gasped a short, squeaking sob. Another. My heart pounded in my chest, so hard it felt like it was going to beat its way out of my rib cage and onto the cold, damp floor. Pain shot through my limbs, circled the scars I'd gathered in the time since I left the temple, squeezed my lungs. I couldn't breathe. I couldn't think. I just gasped like a dying fish as tears coursed down my cheeks.

Curlin let out a string of curses, but she seemed unreachable, as distant as if she were on another continent. Her hands closed around my shoulders and she pulled me to her, my back against her chest, her arms wrapped tightly around me.

"Shh, Vi. We'll be fine. Everything will be fine."

"Fine?" I heaved. I had to fight for each word. "Our bodies'll be burned with the trash before the week's out. And that's *if* they decide to go easy on us."

The cold air seized my throat, and great, shuddering coughs racked my body. Curlin still held me tight to her chest, her warmth seeping into my cold bones.

"Breathe, Vi."

"I am breathing."

"You're not. Breathe in."

It took three short, gasping tries, but I managed to take a deep breath that filled my nose with the smells of rot and mold and human waste. I gagged, and Curlin rubbed my back, doing what she could to ease my sobbing panic.

"Once more."

When my breath came slow and steady and my heart had stopped racing, Curlin turned me around to face her.

"They can't kill us outright without a confession of some crime, and with Bo and Gerlene fully aware they've taken us, they can't just make us disappear."

A bell rang far overhead, and its faint echo reawakened the moaning in the other cells on our level.

"They'll do their best to make you confess to something, anything," Curlin told me. "All you have to do is keep your mouth shut. Admit nothing. If you can manage to do it, say prayers. It'll make them spitting mad, and it'll buy you time. Can't very well say a prisoner is committing treasonous sacrilege if they spend their interrogation praying. But don't look them in the eyes," she warned. "Don't provoke them in any way. When they hurt you, cry, but don't curse. You can't retaliate. If you raise a hand to them, if you say an aggressive word, they'll have cause enough to trump up charges against you."

Heavy boots clattered on the stone steps, and a door's hinges squealed in protest as someone forced it open.

"How do you know all this?"

"Every Shriven initiate has to train as an interrogator," Curlin said sadly. "They'll be coming for us soon." She put her hands on my shoulders and looked me square in the eye. "I love you, Vi. You're the best friend I ever had. Thanks for giving me a second chance."

I threw my arms around her and squeezed. "You're more my sister than my own flesh and blood."

With a grin, Curlin squeezed my hand. "Don't let Pem or Still hear you say that. They're right loyal to you and Bo."

The key scraped into the lock with a sound that set my very bones to screaming. I laced my fingers through Curlin's and steeled myself.

"We're going to get out of this," she said.

"By the headsman's block or the holy fire."

Curlin punched me in the arm just as they flung open the door. "Promise me you'll stay strong, Vi. Promise me you'll try."

Six strong Shriven piled into the dank cell and pulled us apart. As they hauled Curlin out through the door, I shouted after her.

"We'll show them. We'll show everyone. I didn't come this far to die in that same fucking square that's been soaked in the blood of the diminished."

One of the Shriven knocked me in the head so hard, I would've collapsed if the other two hadn't already taken bruising grips on both my arms. They dragged me up flight after flight of stairs to a room I'd never seen, not in all my explorations of the temple as a brat. Slim windows high on the wall let in slivers of crimson evening light that sliced across the scarred wooden floor. The room, lit by a crackling fireplace, was mostly bare, save for a plush upholstered chair and a table that held a wide, shallow chest.

The Shriven slammed my back into a pillar and strapped me to the thing with thick leather straps. They pulled my arms behind me and chained them to the floor, so I was pulled down by my wrists and held up by the straps across my shoulders and torso. Splinters ate into my exposed skin.

They left me there without a word, icy wind whistling through the open windows. I did everything in my power to push down the panic that threatened to creep back into my lungs as I watched the last light of the sunset fade across the floor. Finally, when the room had been fully dark for some time, and my eyes had grown heavy, the door slammed open, and bright sunlamps burned my eyes.

"Obedience Abernathy." The slow, drawling accent crawled over my name like a slug. "You've been a very naughty girl."

My eyes adjusted, and I saw the mouthy Shriven who'd been standing behind Rylain in the throne room leaning against the doorway, a cluster of Shriven on either side of him.

"I'd rather you called me Vi, thanks very much. And you are?"

He rubbed his back against the doorjamb, like a massive bear scratching itself on a tree. Regarding me with cool, calculating eyes, he smiled. "You are so like him. My Bo. Who would ever have guessed he was so common?"

"*Your* Bo?" I asked, pushing as much disdain into my voice as I could stand.

"My Bo," he confirmed. "That sweet lamb has been in love with me his whole life, ever since my mother foisted my sister and me on his mother and ran off to the colonies. I'm Claes. Surely he's told you about me."

I shrugged, a mask of nonchalance on my face as I racked my brain, trying to place the name. Claes was his cousin. The one who'd died. The one who'd betrayed him. Us. "Can't say as I have."

"You know, not in a thousand lifetimes would I've guessed that Bo wasn't singleborn. Myrella did an incredible job disguising the unfortunate influence of his maternal blood. It's a pity, really, that you didn't have her good guidance."

I gritted my teeth. I didn't have much use for my shit of a mother, but that didn't mean I was happy to let him drag her through the mud. I wanted to ask what had happened to him, why he'd joined the Shriven, why he'd place himself in direct opposition to someone he'd once loved.

But I knew why. I'd seen it a dozen times or more. He was afraid. His sister had died, and he was terrified that he would lose himself. So he ran to the Shriven, and once there, he did what he did best. He sought power. And apparently, he'd been quite successful.

"You know something?" He pulled himself off the doorframe and sprawled into the thickly upholstered chair just in front of me with a deep sigh. "This means we're related."

Claes poured wine the color of amber into a tall water glass, filling it to the brim, then took a sip.

"Oswin was our third cousin twice removed, in addition to our mother being Myrella's sister, which makes you... Oh, it doesn't matter. What *does* matter is that you've sinned against the gods and goddesses, and until you free yourself of the burden of those transgressions, it will be impossible for the temple to accept you back into her warm embrace. Back to where you belong." He set down the glass. "Now. Let's begin with the pearls. Anchorite Bernadine told us that you hoarded some of the temple's pearls while you were still a ward of the Penby temple. The anchorites who protected you have been punished according to our will.

"Were you always drawn to thievery and lies, or were you corrupted by the trash you grew up with?" Claes asked. "I understand you were close to a pair of wretched orphans who left you for the allure of Ilor—Lily and Sawny, weren't they?" He shuddered and flicked an invisible piece of lint from the sleeve of his sumptuous silk robe. "Even if you are an unacknowledged bastard, you shouldn't have been forced to associate with that kind of trash."

"Eat shit, you scum-sucking mold cock." I spit at him, my blood boiling. It didn't matter that he was Shriven, and Bo's cousin and first love to boot. He'd stepped over the line.

He easily sidestepped the glob of spit and flicked his wrist at one of the Shriven. The black paint around her green eyes made them sparkle as she flipped open a leather case and laid out her implements of torture. She grinned up at me, her smile revealing teeth shaved to points, and fingered a pair of bloodstained pliers. Claes shook his head and pointed to a silver cup that held a fistful of delicate silver needles. The Shriven woman snatched them up and crossed the room in a single stride. Claes followed and yanked at the gold cuff on my wrist.

"Look at you, wearing the symbol of royalty like you own it." He sneered. "I don't want to hurt you, Obedience, but it's time someone taught you a lesson. Just admit to the ways in which you've violated the goddesses' trust, and we'll see that you don't rot in a cell for the rest of your life."

He nodded to the woman. She ran a fingertip lightly up my arm from wrist to clavicle, prodded the soft flesh above my collarbone until I flinched and then drove a cluster of the needles into my flesh. Pain shot up and down my arm, and despite myself, I screamed.

Claes kept talking between sips of wine. "Perhaps you'll make a good anchorite? Or one of the Shriven, even. You do have that sort of animal ferocity they look for. Not to mention the tattoos. It would make the most sense for you to disappear into the Shriven after your confession." He surveyed me over the rim of his glass. "Are you ready to confess, Obedience?"

I glared.

At Claes's signal, the needles were yanked from my clavicle, and relief washed over me. The pain disappeared as quickly as it'd come.

"You may begin in your childhood, if it would be easier," Claes said. "Tell me the origin of your thievery. Was it food? It's always food with brats like you."

"Perhaps if the growing children in the temple's care got more than thin porridge morning, noon and night, there might be less theft in their kitchens." I gritted my teeth. "Not, of course, that I'd ever confess to stealing from the temple." I sighed and feigned a pitying look. "Just let me go. My brother'll see you jailed for this."

"Jailed? By the time I'm done with him, Bo will be begging for me to share his bed once more." Claes shook with controlled laughter. "My dear, if you don't start talking, you will lose your mind from the things I've planned for you. And that's before you're sentenced to death. I see being broken on a wheel in your future."

He considered me for a moment, then clapped his hand over his mouth, gleeful. "No! No. I have it. We'll stake you out in the harbor and let you drown. They used to do that to the sea thieves in the old world. Before the cataclysm. How perfect for you! You can wait for the tide to take you as dozens of eels and crabs and sharks eat chunks of your flesh in the cold winter harbor." Claes's face took on a cajoling look. "Or you can confess to your sins. Wouldn't that be better? Wouldn't it be easier?"

I shook my head, and the needles plunged once more into my flesh, sending waves of agony down my left side. The pain caught like fire and washed down over my breast, across my abdomen and down the other leg, like molten metal being poured through my body. I tried to breathe through the pain and the horror and the crippling weight of anxious terror that shrouded me.

"You may think that you'll break me, Claes, but there's nothing you can do to me that I haven't already imagined a thousand times worse." I swallowed the bile that rose in my throat and glared at him, letting all the hate and anger that'd built up inside me flood out and wash over him and his grinning, dogmatist, vile body. "You can't touch me, Claes. You can't touch my brother. We are stronger than you'll ever be, and he is the rightful king of Alskad. Mark my words—"

"Stop her!" he shouted. "Do something!"

A heavy blow landed in my gut, but I kept talking. "Mark. My. Words. You'll kneel before my brother and me before this is done, and you'll pay for your greed."

Knuckles rammed into my cheek. My mouth filled with blood, and I spit. "You'll pay for your hate. You'll pay for the bigotry that's eaten away your soul."

Claes drained the tall glass of wine and pushed himself to his feet. Swiping a handful of thin wooden strips from the table, he strode across the room to stand over me. His sour breath washed over me in fast, forceful gusts.

"You will confess, girl. Even if I have to make you do it myself."

His large, calloused hand closed over my left wrist, and before I could take a steading breath, he shoved one of the wooden strips under my thumbnail. The pain shot through me, electrifying my nerves like lightning pouring through my body. The room dimmed. I screamed and screamed, and despite Curlin's warning, I cursed the goddesses every way I knew how. Tears poured down my cheeks. The room spun. And all the while, Claes loomed over me, the scripture tattooed up his arm seeming to writhe with his flinching muscles.

When I was finally able to speak, I ground out, "You'll admit that we were right before you ever make me confess."

Claes backhanded me across the face, his rings opening welts over my cheekbone. He raised his hand again just as the door swung open. An acolyte, a boy who couldn't have been older than ten, entered the room, his eyes fixed on the floor.

"Sir, the Suzerain are asking for you."

I could see Claes struggling to regain his composure, to rein in his rage. "Put the bitch back in her cage," he sneered. "I've an appointment I can't miss. We'll see her broken yet."

A hand closed over my mouth, and I bit down as hard as I could, but my teeth closed on damp, bitter cloth rather than flesh. The leather straps across my body rendered my struggles ineffective, and the room began to darken. I knew in a moment I would be unconscious, but I never took my eyes off Claes's pallid face, and I saw the fear beneath his mask.

When I woke again, I was on the hard stone floor of the dungeon, and Curlin was next to me. One of her eyes was swollen shut, and her fingernails were black and bloody. Long, thin, blistering burns marked her arms, and it almost looked like some of her tattoos had been deliberately marred. Her tunic had been rucked up when they dumped her in the cell, and a deep purple, ugly bruise blossomed across the top of her exposed hip.

My own body was a map of pain, and despite the dry rasping ache in my throat, I couldn't force myself onto my throbbing hands and knees to crawl to the bucket of scum-slimed water by the door. I turned my head and let the chill from the stone seep into my bruised cheek. Tears ran down my face, and I tried not to think about any individual injury for too long.

"No use getting yourself all dehydrated with pointless weeping. You're not a brat anymore." Curlin's voice was ragged and torn, and she heaved herself up to sit with her back against the stone wall. "My hands are wrecked. Mind dragging that bucket over here?"

"Shut up, Curlin. There's no point." Gloom overwhelmed me. I'd let the temple take me to save Bo, but it was becoming more and more clear to me that I'd let them get exactly what they'd wanted.

Control.

The trap they'd laid for us was even more clever than I could've imagined. The moment I escaped—if I could manage it—they would go after Bo with all the lethal force of the Shriven. They wanted any excuse to see him dead and keep their pawn in power. The only thing for me to do was wait until Bo's machinations landed him back on the throne…or until they came to take me to my execution.

"Dzallie's tits, woman," Curlin said tiredly. "Please tell me you didn't cart me all the way back across the ocean and away from Aphra just for you to give up in a temple dungeon. You need to drink and clean your wounds. So do I. Then we need to find a way out of here."

"I promised to stay," I countered. "If I escape, they'll go after for Bo. My being here protects him."

I rolled onto my side, my back to Curlin. A rat skittered out of the pile of moldy hay in the corner, across the filthy flagstones and through the iron-barred door.

Curlin kicked me in the spine, making me groan in agony. "Don't be a rutting fool. You aren't keeping him safe by staying here. You're allowing these asses to use you as leverage. Bo would never do anything that would put you in danger, and as long as you're here, the temple can force his hand."

I sat up and faced her, my body screaming in protest. "There's no way out of here, no way out of this. Acting like we're suddenly going to find a key or somehow pick the lock is wishful thinking. We've got no allies. We've got no friends. We're alone, and we're trapped. Even the rats have more freedom than we do."

"Well..." A thin voice, wavering and quiet and eerily familiar, came floating over to us from the darkness just outside our cell. "That's not entirely true."

CHAPTER FORTY

Bo

After the disastrous meeting at the palace, we retreated back to the ship, where we found Patrise and Lisette waiting on board. Not, as I might have guessed, preemptively celebrating our victory—they hadn't expected that outcome for a moment—but ready to plot our next move. Or, rather, putting themselves in the room where our next action would be decided. Neither of them had made a single suggestion in well over an hour.

"You truly mean to say that you didn't think it was important to tell me that Claes had survived? My sister just handed herself over to the temple. To him. There's no telling what he'll do to her."

Vi's pain, her fear, were like bells ringing in the far distance. I forced myself not to focus on the cord of awareness that ran between us. I would get her out of there. I had to.

I glared at Patrise, lounging on the sofa. "We've all but declared war on both the temple and Rylain, and if the two of you

have spent these last few months drunkenly gallivanting around
Penby rather than bringing the singleborn over to our side and
actually paying attention to what's been going on here, I honestly can't promise that I'll be responsible for my own actions."

Patrise sighed and took a sip of his kaffe. He made a face and
turned to Lisette. "Darling, get me a bit of ouzel, would you?
I don't know that I can face this conversation entirely sober."

Lisette snickered and passed Patrise the cut-crystal decanter.
"No reason to change your reprehensible opulence now. I
doubt you've faced an entire day fully sober in your adult life."

"If you two don't focus, I'll throw you bodily off this
ship," I said.

Swinton snapped, "Who's to say I won't either way? Looks
to me like they could use a good, cold dunk, the rutting in-
grates."

I laid a calming hand on his arm and forced my attention
back to the papers and books on the table in front of me. We
would have to talk about Claes, but not in front of these two.

"Gerlene, is there anything we're missing here? Anything
at all?"

She drummed her fingers on the table, shaking her head.
"In the history of the empire, there's never been a transition
of power this complex, but as I said to the rest of the singleborn, I cannot see any legal reason that you should not ascend.
Rylain's newly formatted council is another matter entirely,
as she's changed the rules without legal precedent. We can
question the legality of it, but it would be better still if we
could simply force a majority vote."

"If I understand it correctly—" Quill spoke slowly and
deliberately, his brows furrowed "—Rylain's new appointees
doubled the size of the council, filling it out with temple
flunkies. Correct?"

"That's right," Gerlene agreed.

"But by law, there's a clear limit to the number of voting members allowed, whether Rylain changed the size or not."

"Yes, but she has the majority," I said, sighing.

Patrise flung his booted feet off the table and stood. "I do believe I may see where you're going, you delectable bite of rebellious perfection. Brilliant. It's simply brilliant."

Quill's jaw clenched, but he went on. "Bo has a seat on the council, and any person voted onto the council after him has no legal right to participate. Therefore—"

Patrise cut him off. "With the help of the other singleborn, we should be able to force Rylain to step down."

Lisette's sour look blossomed into a wry smile. "Well, that'll be no trouble at all. We've got three of the six votes in the room already. And the others all but said that they would support Bo's succession the other day. Plus Olivar's got a dimmy daughter who was taken up by the Shriven not a week after Rylain took power. He's not seen or heard from her since. He'll be with us, certainly. Zurienne is a bit more difficult, but I do believe that somewhere in our little collection of blackmail we might have something on her if she tries to double-cross us. Dame Turshaw is the real beast."

"It would be in everyone's best interest if she would just do the right thing and die already," Patrise said.

While Patrise and Lisette sniped, Gerlene's face had taken on the blank, dreamlike quality that it did when she was in the midst of working through a complex problem in her head. But at the mention of Dame Turshaw, her eyes snapped into focus.

"There's been more tragedy in that woman's life than you'll ever know, and she's much stronger for it," Gerlene said coldly. "I'll thank you to speak of her with the respect and admiration that her long service to this empire rightly deserves."

Patrise slumped back into his chair and filled his delicate porcelain kaffe cup with ouzel before sliding the decanter down the table to a pouting Lisette.

"That said," Gerlene went on as she gathered up her papers, "I might have a way around the question of the temple's seats at the council table. I'll need to consult my books. I'll be in touch as soon as I have a concrete answer."

With Gerlene gone, the rest of the group disbanded, and I sank onto a plush sofa next to Swinton.

"So," he said, "Claes is alive."

I nodded and reached out to lace my fingers through his. "You know I don't... I couldn't... You are..."

He snorted. "You really think that after everything we've been through... After all you did for me in Denor—after everything that bastard did to you and Vi that I would, even for a second, imagine you'd go running back to him?" He brought my hand to his lips and kissed my palm. "Call me arrogant, but it would have never crossed my mind."

I let out a breath I felt like I'd been holding since the moment I recognized Claes. "I haven't got feelings for him," I said. "I haven't for a long time."

Swinton grinned at me, a look that contained more confidence than I'd often felt in my life. "How could you with me by your side? I'm a far better catch."

He leaned in close, his breath sweet with spiced tea, and kissed me. The scent of the sea clung to him, salt spray and adventure, and the scent reminded me of all the hours we'd spent on the decks of ships, talking about a future that felt impossible and just within our grasp at the same time.

I let myself fall into the kiss. Into him. Into the future we'd imagined together. And as I pressed my body into his, everything else—the stress, the fear, the sheer impossibility of what we were trying to do—receded into the back of my mind. And we were just two people. In love.

"Do you think it's even worth it?" I asked sometime later. "Should I just let Rylain take over, and to hell with the empire? Save Vi and walk away? We could set up a house somewhere in the mountains in Ilor. Fill it with books and animals and children. We could be happy."

Swinton, who'd been stroking my hair, froze. "Bo, these people..." His voice was determined, confident. "They're your responsibility. Your endless compassion, your dedication to this enormous task that Runa set in front of you, your optimism, your hope—all of those pieces of you, all of those things I love about you—they're what will make you a great king. You can't give up now. Alskad is in your blood. You'd never be able to live with yourself if you walked away now."

Exhaustion ate at my bones, gnawed at me until I felt raw. The conviction I'd felt not so long ago was a well long dry. I wanted to see a way out. Any way out. "Rylain's not so bad. Without the ability to make more of the poison, the temple is basically harmless."

I knew the words were lies even as they formed in my mouth.

"If you believe that, you're not the man I know."

Swinton shifted my head out of his lap and stood abruptly, pulling me to my feet.

"I don't. Of course I don't. I just feel so helpless. I don't know what to do."

"You can go see your people," Swinton suggested. "Remember who you're fighting for. Come on."

Swinton and I followed Pem through the winding streets of the neighborhood by the docks and into the End. People rushed past us with their heads down. No one made eye contact. Gone were the fisherwomen hawking oysters and clams. Gone were the vendors with carts of tea and pastries. The people we passed were afraid, though of what, I couldn't quite guess.

By the time we reached the house where my siblings still lived, curiosity and fear had seeped into my bones. Pem climbed the steps, cautioning us to stay back. She knocked a complex rhythm on the thick wooden door. The windows were shuttered, even on this mild day, giving the house the look of something abandoned, forsaken. The door finally opened, just wide enough for the barrel of a rifle to slide through the crack at head height.

"It's me, you slivering hair ball," Pem said. "I've brought Bo and Swinton."

I heard a muffled cry, and then the door flew wide. Brenna raced down the steps to us and flung her arms around our necks, pulling us all together into a tight embrace.

"Come on, then. Let's get you inside before someone sees you."

Brenna pulled Swinton and me into the foyer, and Pem and Still hustled in behind us. The moment we were inside, Chase and Tie slammed the door shut, bolted all the locks and shifted a heavy iron bar into place across the door.

I glanced at Swinton, but his face was an impassive mask. "Has it gotten so bad as all that?" I asked.

Tie and Chase just stared at me, their jaws nearly hanging open. "Best come into the kitchen and have a bite," Brenna said. "We've clearly got a lot to talk about."

As she led us through the dim rooms, she pulled Pem and Still close, tugging on their collars and smoothing the flyaway curls that had escaped from their braids. Seeing them in this house, with its shabby carpets, shuttered windows and close, sparsely furnished rooms, my youngest siblings looked suddenly out of place. Though we'd been gone less than a quarter of a year, the two of them had grown taller, with roses in their cheeks and the bright eyes of well-fed, happy children. They looked like different people, especially in comparison to our other siblings. Brenna and Chase had dark circles under their eyes, and Tie's cheekbones were sharp against the new shadow of a beard coming in. Guilt ate away at my stomach.

In the kitchen, Lair was stirring a pot of thin soup. When he saw Pem and Still, he dropped to his knees and wrapped his arms around the girls, wooden spoon still in his hand. He looked up at me with tears in his eyes.

"You kept them safe, brother. Thank you." He looked back at the girls. "And you two. What trouble have you gotten yourselves into, then?"

Pem glanced over her shoulder at me, but before she could speak, I cut in.

"A story for a later time, I think. What's happened here? Has Gerlene not taken care of you? Why've you turned this place into a fortress? Moreover, why are you still here? I thought Gerlene was going to set you up somewhere new. Somewhere safe. And where are Fern and Trix?"

Brenna filled a kettle with water and set it on the stove to boil, avoiding my eyes. Lair dished the thin soup into eight chipped and mismatched bowls, which Chase and Tie set on the table. When everyone was settled, Brenna poured tea and I watched as Pem and Still loaded theirs with cream and cubes of sugar, while the others stared at them aghast. Just a couple of months away, and already they'd seemed to have grown blind to how dear those little comforts were for the rest of our family.

Lair cleared his throat. "Fern and Trix got took up by the

Shriven 'bout three days ago. They went out for an hour to get some things with the money Gerlene sent—"

Brenna cut in. "She's been doing her best. Truly she has, but with the Shriven prowling the streets, and them knowing how we've ties to you? Well, it ain't been easy for us to get in or out or nothing. We've been more or less trapped like rats in here."

Tie went on, "Fern and Trix were the best at getting around them without being noticed, but I guess either they got careless or the Shriven got trickier."

Swinton hadn't touched his soup. "But what do they want from you? What could they possibly do to you? You've broken no laws that I can see."

Tie and Chase exchanged a look. "They don't need a reason no more. They took Brenna in for questioning right after you left. Broke her wrist, roughed her up—"

"You hush," Brenna interrupted. "It wasn't nearly so bad as what they've done to other folks. I got off easy."

The single sip of soup I'd taken turned to stone in my throat. I looked at Brenna, but she was staring into her bowl. Pem and Still were the only of my siblings who would meet my eyes, and they looked as confused as I felt. I waited, hoping that my silence would force one of them to tell me the truth.

Finally, Chase squared her shoulders and put down her spoon. "We didn't expect things to get so bad so quickly after you left. But before your boat even left the harbor, Rylain decreed that dimmys were no longer allowed to walk freely, and all of them had to turn themselves in to the temple, where they could be 'properly supervised.'" Her voice became choked, and she swiped angrily at the tears flooding her gray eyes. "The ones stupid enough to follow those orders were burned on the beach within the week. A sacrifice to Hamil, the temple said. To make up for the evil of a twin having the audacity to take the sacred vows of the singleborn heir to the throne."

Under the table, Swinton's hand closed around mine, steadying me. I took a deep breath. "They're placing the blame for a mass murder on my shoulders?"

"That's just the beginning," Lair said. "Anyone who's not made donations to the temple at a sacrificial level has been tapped for immediate payment or seizure of property. The folks who've not gone to temple have disappeared, and anyone with enough sheer stupidity to speak out against the Suzerain or Rylain is executed. There are executions every evening at the square and sacrifices to the gods on the beach every morning at sunup. Even the children of dimmys, the brothers and sisters of dimmys, have been snatched off the streets.

"Ain't no one safe leaving their house, and gods forbid everyone falls asleep without someone to stand watch," Brenna said. "I never in my life thought I'd be grateful for Ina Abernathy, but the fact that she was always in enough debt to send bill collectors calling at all hours of the day and night has been a blessing. We've found more hideaways, hidden stashes and secret ways out of this house in the last few months than I'd've thought possible."

Chase grinned at her siblings. "Should we tell—"

"Where is Ma, anyway?" Pem's interruption was the first thing she'd said since we walked into the house. "Where's Da?"

Brenna bit her lip. "Ain't seen her since you left, pet. Dammal's been in and out, but we ain't seen him in a week or two."

"Did you check Zinnia's place over by the tanner's?" Still asked, a note of sour hope squeaking into her voice.

"I know you can't stand to see them as flawed, bratlings,"

Lair said. "But we're a right bit better off without them. Don't forget, Dammal sold Bo here out to the Shriven. Plus Ma's never made our lives easier, and we can't afford for them to be any harder now."

"You'll come with me," I said, squeezing Swinton's hand beneath the table. "If we can find a way to get you onto the ship, you'll be safe enough."

Swinton pulled his hand from mine and stood. "It's all well and good to get your family to safety, Bo." His voice shook with barely contained rage. "But what about the rest of your people? What's happening here, it's genocide. It's murder. You can't let this go on. And what about Vi? What about Fern and Trix? What are you going to do about the rest of them? How'll you protect everyone *and* take back your throne?"

Brenna's gray eyes fixed on me, her expression gone cold. "You let them take her? Bo, they'll kill her! The minute she's dead, you're a dimmy, and they can murder you, free and clear."

I pushed back my chair and stood, all the pieces of a plan spinning themselves together into a complicated and unlikely tapestry. I wrapped an arm around Swinton's shoulder and pulled him close to me before he had the chance to shake me off. His rages had been lightning fast and frightening since Denor, but we'd both worked hard to find a way through them without the dreadful fights we'd thrown ourselves into at first. And the medicine helped—it wasn't perfect, but it helped.

"Pem, Still? Are you up for a bit of intrigue?"

Beside me, Swinton moved to protest just as Brenna's and Lair's faces went hard.

"Hear me out," I said. "The girls have more than proven themselves, and the only way this plan will work is with their help."

★ ★ ★

My hands shook as I made my way through the halls of the palace, Swinton at my side. His rage had cooled as I'd explained my plan to get Vi, Fern and Trix free, and by the time we'd managed to sneak the rest of my siblings and their small bundles of goods through the streets of Penby and onto the ship, the tension between us had cleared entirely. If anything happened to either of the girls, though, Brenna had assured me in no uncertain terms that she'd rip me apart, limb by limb, king or no.

I'd never thought having a big family could be so fun.

Swinton took my hand as we passed into the corridor that led to the council chamber. A contingent of the Ilorian and Denorian soldiers—the Vigilant, as they'd taken to calling themselves—stalked behind me. The remainder of our force had split. Half had gone to meet Vi, and the other half was tasked with securing the palace.

In theory, the palace guard would obey whoever sat on the throne, but as the people who'd shot at and killed my grandmother had been in the uniforms of guards, it was hard to know who to trust. Our force was just large enough that, positioned smartly, they should be able to ensure a peaceful transfer of power. If everything went as we planned, anyway. Which it undoubtedly would not, but I couldn't allow myself to think about that. Not now.

Each of the soldiers behind me bristled with weapons, but despite everyone's fervent protestations, I myself had come unarmed. It was one thing to take back my throne, but it was another entirely to show up looking like I *needed* to fight for my rightful place. For me to walk into the council chamber armed would make my position look weak. So I kept my head high and forced myself to make eye contact with and nod at every member of the royal guard as we passed.

"When we move back into the palace, bully, will you give me my own suite of rooms, or will I be forced to keep bunking with this pack of brutes?" He winked at the soldier walking beside him.

"If we move back," I muttered.

Swinton squeezed my hand gently and whispered, "Put on your brave face." Louder, he said, "I was thinking about the green suite just outside the royal wing. I know it'll make Gerlene absolutely incensed with envy, but I like the view of the gardens."

The palace guards stationed outside the council chamber opened the doors. My Vigilant guards all knew they could go no farther. There was a part of me that wished I could send them in my stead, but my time to let others do my work for me was over.

Gerlene came bustling down the hall behind us. "Everyone's been notified?" I asked her.

Gerlene nodded. "Patrise and Lisette should be waiting for you inside. You'll be wonderful, Bo. Remember that this is what Runa wanted. Draw strength from her memory. There's never been a woman so capable of turning an argument on its head. You can't go wrong by doing as she would've done."

The solicitor shoved a green leather folder stuffed with loose papers into my free hand. I looked down at them, puzzled. "Thank you?"

"I made some notes for you. Just in case."

Swinton laughed. "He'll be fine. Never worry. And we'll be right here waiting the whole time."

I took a calming breath and squared my shoulders, wishing I'd managed to save the circlet. I needed something more than the cuff circling my wrist to feel like a king. I wanted a symbol. The thought of Runa's crown, still hidden in Brenna's attic, flashed before me. I wished I'd thought to retrieve it when we'd been there earlier.

With a sigh, I gave Swinton one last hug. "In the worst possible scenario, they kill me in there," I said quietly. "If that happens, I want you to promise me that you'll get Vi and the rest of the family and take them back to Ilor. At least there, they'll be fairly safe."

Swinton sniffed hard and squeezed me harder. "Hush. No one's dying today. Now get in there and take back your crown."

Patrise and Lisette stood up as I entered the chamber alone.

"Please tell me your fairy godmother came up with something," Lisette hissed.

"Please tell me that you convinced the rest of the singleborn to vote for me," I countered.

Patrise collapsed back into his chair with a huff. "Down, you two. We've work to do. Ambrose, darling, didn't you notice that we got you a present?"

I glanced down at the table. Just before the seat I'd taken at my first and only council meeting, a box was waiting for me, tied with a cloth of gold ribbon.

"It isn't my birthday," I said cautiously. With my luck, there would be an angry viper inside, waiting to strike the moment I opened the box.

"Don't be silly. It won't bite," Lisette teased, eerily echoing my fear.

"Think of it as a coronation gift," Patrise said.

I went to the end of the table, untied the ribbon and gently lifted the lid. There, on a velvet cushion, sat a crown. It wasn't an exact replica of the Crown of Alskad, the one I'd hidden in my sister's attic, but it was as though this crown had evolved from that. It was a powerful piece of artistry, all glittering gems surrounded by a knotted pattern of yellow-and-white gold. I lifted it out of the box, turning it over in my hands. The gems were the same kind of gray diamonds that had been used in the crown and Circlet of Alskad. They caught the light and sparked, like thunderclouds brimming with lightning.

I stopped short, breath caught in my throat. One of the gems was cracked down the middle, just as the gem in Runa's crown had been. I looked up at Patrise.

"Your Swinton gave it to us to pass along to you," he said. "The crown itself was irreparable, and we all thought that the symbols of the royal house should reflect this new era in the history of the Alskad Empire. Swinton insisted we include the broken gem, though why, I'll never understand."

My heart fluttered, and I felt the heat of a blush rise up my neck. I hadn't realized he was just as worried about taking care of me as I was about taking care of him. I promised myself that at the first opportunity, I would remind him of exactly how I felt about him. Our relationship had grown and shifted these last few months, and the weight of everything we'd endured had cracked each of us in its own ways, but I knew that together, we could and would get through any obstacle set in our way.

"He thinks of everything," I said softly.

Lisette sniffed and went to the sideboard to pour herself a glass of ouzel while Patrise went on, "The guild of jewelers asked that we convey to you their support and best wishes, and their hope that they will be allowed to continue to offer their services to you during a long and peaceful reign."

"The others will be here any minute. Put it on," Lisette said.

I turned the crown so that the broken diamond would be centered over my eyes and placed it on my head. A peace came over me as the crown's weight settled into place, and I took my seat at the head of the table to wait.

CHAPTER FORTY-ONE

Vi

A dark figure rose out of the shadows outside the cell. At first, in the dim light and through the shroud of my pain and exhaustion, I imagined for a moment that it might be one of the goddesses come to give me a piece of their mind for all the times I'd cursed their names. I coiled, ready to unleash the sharp edge of my tongue. Not even a goddess would be safe from my ire in my current condition.

"We send you all the way across the ocean, give you everything you need to stay safe and under the radar, and yet here you are. Come crawling back to the temple like a beaten cur, begging for more."

The figure stepped forward into the slashes of moonlight let in through the barred grate overhead, and Curlin let out a low, hissing curse. Recognition dawned over me as the woman went on.

"And you, Curlin," she said, clicking her tongue. "We give you one task, and you can't even manage to do that much.

More than that, you break vows you've held for, what—not even five years? Child, do you know how long I've upheld these vows? Do you know how long we've worked from within this temple without having to go so far as to break our sacred oaths? No. Of course you don't. You've no respect for the sacred. Neither of you. Not that I can say I'm surprised. Disappointed, yes. But never surprised."

Sula. One of the three anchorites who'd raised Curlin and me. Who'd been like mothers to us. Cold, distant, punishing mothers, but mothers nevertheless.

Curlin struggled to her feet and bowed her head, grimacing. "Anchorite Sula. My apologies. I did everything in my power to watch out for her, to take care of her, but I failed you."

"Wait just a minute. *You* failed?" I shouted. "What about them? What about the temple? They're the ones who've failed *us*." I turned my gaze on Sula. "You knew about the serum, didn't you, Sula? How could you? How could you allow them to poison us? Not just the two of us, either, but everyone they look down on, everyone who speaks up against them? *Everyone*."

Sula closed the distance between herself and the rust-speckled iron bars. She withdrew her hand from the folds of her robes and reached out to us. "Child, it is so much more complicated than you know."

I stood, summoning every ounce of power I could muster to get through the pain that pounded like sledgehammers against every nerve in my body, and fixed the anchorite in a hard stare. "I'm not a child anymore, Sula. If you've come here just to rub our broken noses in the dirt and tell us all the ways we've managed to disappoint you, I think I speak for both of us when I say that if I never saw your face again, it would be too soon."

I glanced at Curlin. Her split lip curled into a snarl even more ferocious for the fresh blood welling in the cut. She nodded. "That about covers it."

"Surly and churlish from the cradle, both of you." Sula sniffed. "You'd think I'd learn to expect no less, but here I am, yet again, doing everything in my power to save your sorry, ungrateful souls." The anchorite's hand slipped back into her robes. When it reappeared, there was a thick iron key dangling on a chain between her bejeweled fingers.

I reached for it almost unconsciously, but Curlin's hand darted out to stop me.

"What do you want from us?" she asked.

Sula's lips curled into a tight smile. "Ever the cautious one, aren't you, Curlin?"

We stood, the three of us waiting for another to say something and interrupt the symphony of thick drips, rat squeaks and distant chains rattling. The back of Curlin's battered hand pressed into mine, as much comfort as she could manage, given the wrecked state her torturers had left her body in.

Finally, after what felt like a thousand pounding heartbeats, Sula sighed. "The three of us... Lugine, Bethea and I... We believe in Alskad. Not to say we don't stand by our sacred vows and our faith in the goddesses. But we believed in Runa. In her work. I doubt there's a person alive who remembers this, but Runa's mother and mine were the best of friends. So when I learned about the serum, I took that information to Runa. As time went on and we needed more eyes and ears, I brought Lugine and Bethea into our inner circle. And then you came along, Vi."

I bit the inside of my cheek, thinking of my mother, jobless, far away from her family and friends, set up in an unfamiliar city to give birth to some nobleman's cast-off children. And then, a few months later, having to give them up—I didn't know how she'd done it. I'd always felt like a burden to my family; an unwanted, embarrassing burden. I'd spent my whole life grimly anticipating the moment when I would lose control and the rage would take me. At least then my family would have been free of me.

And when Bo'd found me, when I'd been reunited with my twin, I'd felt the cutting pain of being unwanted even more. Bo wanted me, of course, but neither of our parents had cared enough to look after me. To save me from the hellscape of growing up in the temple. Bo'd had two parents who wanted him, and a grandmother who loved him. I'd had no one. No one but Curlin and Sawny and Lily.

Tears stung my eyes.

"Runa brought you to me herself," Sula said. "She charged me with your care, and you wouldn't for a minute believe me if I told you how often she came to see you in secret. You were always in her thoughts. We all so badly wanted to dote on you, child. But it was imperative that no one know you were special. That no one know you were different in any way. *You* were our mission—your safety, your education. We even pushed Curlin into the Shriven so that we'd have someone trustworthy we could use to protect you without suspicion."

Her words did nothing to cool the rage that seemed to run through my veins like blood more often than not of late. If anything, they made it worse. Runa had cared about me, sure, I could see that. But she'd placed a great deal more import on her succession plan. She'd cared a whole lot more about Bo.

Curlin bristled. "Do you have any idea what that training's like, Anchorite? Do you know what you did to me?"

"Of course I do," Sula snapped. "We all make sacrifices. But the time has come. Rylain's gone too far, and the young king is poised to lose the throne forever if we don't rally the people. We need you." Her eyes, shining with determination, met mine. "It's time to stand up. It's time to resist. Will you join us?"

I reached through the bars and took the key. Wanted or not, cast-off or not—hell, royal or not—I still believed in stopping the temple. I still believed that Bo's place was on the throne.

I still believed in the resistance.

Draped in the hooded robes of anchorites, Curlin and I followed Sula through the unfamiliar hidden halls of the temple that had been our home throughout our childhoods. Every footstep sent spikes of pain up my spine, and I could only imagine the agony Curlin was enduring as we sped through the halls. Sula led us through a door, and just like that, we were in the library where she'd cracked our knuckles through hours of mathematics, history and reading lessons. I couldn't remember a door on this side of the room, though, and I turned just in time to see one of the bookcases swinging back into place alongside the others.

"How many hidden doors are there that we don't know about in this place?" I whispered to Curlin.

"More than you'd imagine, but still no more your business than it was when you were brats," a clipped, authoritative voice snapped.

The voice was so familiar that I nearly cried, and I spun around to see Anchorite Lugine emerging from the shadows, tears gathering in the wrinkles around her eyes, her arms spread wide.

"Come and let me squeeze you, the both of you."

I didn't even have to look at Curlin. We went to Lugine, as quick as we could manage, and were consumed in the warm, wholesome smell that clung to her. I breathed in her scent— baking bread, oyster stew and the sharp tang of the whiffle- berry jam she dolloped into her porridge every morning. In a sudden rush, all the resolve and strength and honed-steel nerve I'd layered around myself as a shield crumbled. I was a child once more, clinging to the only comfort I'd ever known. She had bandaged every broken bone, every scraped knee, every oyster-cut knuckle. And while no one would ever call this woman maternal, exactly, she'd been the best we'd had, and I let myself sink into her warm, soothing embrace.

"You can't be allowed to keep them all to yourself, Lugine," Anchorite Bethea said in a quavering, nasal tone.

Lugine released us, and Bethea looked us up and down, leaning heavily on her canes. "Had a rough go of it, I see."

She swung her cane up and tapped gently on my tattooed arm. "Those aren't just for fashion's sake, girly. Are you to have me believe you've earned what's written there on your skin?"

"You think I'm stupid enough to tattoo lies onto my body, to carry around with me the rest of my life?" I asked.

Anchorite Bethea crooked an eyebrow at me. "Fair enough. Come on, now. Quickly. We seem to've collected a whole posse of you Abernathy brats in the last few hours, and I've never seen any good come of having more than one of you in one place at the same time."

I started to ask what she meant, but before I could open my mouth, the anchorites were hustling us down a darkened servants' hall. Overhead, the first bells rang out the call to prayer. The entire temple would be hauling themselves out of their beds and beginning their days. Soon, there'd be no-

where for us to be without raising all sorts of questions we
didn't have any answers for.

"This way," Lugine said.

She opened a door and led us into a long-unused suite of
rooms just off the kitchen. Dust and cobwebs clung to the
stacks of furniture broken and piled in heaps against the walls.
The sounds of breakfast being prepared echoed through the
vents that ran along the wall shared with the kitchen. My
mouth watered at the familiar scents of baking bread, butter
sizzling in skillets and sausage skins popping as they roasted on
skewers over pans of potatoes set beneath them to collect the
spiced grease. Pots clanged, and initiates cursed and chirped in
equal measure, hurrying to finish their chores before prayers.

Through a doorway, a lamp flickered in the interior room.
A figure leaned against the doorjamb, and tears welled in
my eyes as more lamps flared around the room and I recognized him.

Quill took two steps toward me and faltered. "What did
they do to you?" he whispered.

I touched my bruised cheek, suddenly shy. "I never was
much good at keeping a respectful distance between my brain
and my tongue."

He closed the space between us and waited until I wrapped
my arms around him before he pulled me in close. I pressed
my face into his chest, breathing in the complex, familiar
smell of him. The salt air of the harbor clung to his clothes,
and underneath he smelled like spices and rain and the green
jungle scent of Ilor. He smelled like home. His hand stroked
my hair, and for the first time since I'd let the Shriven take
me away from Bo, I let my guard down, just a little, and tears
welled in my eyes.

As if he understood without my having to say a word, Quill

took me gently by the elbow—perhaps the only part of my body that wasn't bruised, battered or scraped—and led me into the next room. Around a wide table, scarred with years of use and still damp from a recent scrubbing, sat my youngest siblings: Pem, Still, Fern and Trix. A steaming pot of tea sat in front of them, and the table was scattered with plates and crumbs, peels and cores, and crocks of butter and jam scraped down to the dregs.

"What the bloody hell are you lot doing here?" I croaked. My knees trembled, and Quill guided me into a chair.

Curlin slumped down beside me and eyed Fern and Trix suspiciously. "More Abernathy brats, I take it?"

"Gerlene swore on her life we could trust this one." Pem jerked her head at Lugine, who ducked her head, but not before I saw the smile dart across her face. "Bo couldn't let you rot away in a temple cell. Not with him as likely to lose his head as wear the crown."

Still punched her sister in the arm. "We weren't supposed to tell her that part, chatterbox."

My fingers started to drum on the table of their own accord, but the shooting pain from where Claes had shoved slivers of wood underneath them stopped me. Quill sat down next to me and took my hand gently. I glanced at Curlin, who was sipping from a chipped teacup. She shrugged.

"We've got a plan," Pem said. "And it didn't hurt that we could get these two out of the clink in the meantime."

"*We've* got a plan?" Quill asked with a sardonic smile.

"Well, Bo hatched it," Still conceded, "and Quill and Gerlene filled in the missing bits. But without me and Pem, ain't none of this'd be happening, and you can bet your ass on that."

"Language, child," Sula said gently.

Bethea settled into the chair next to Quill, and the other two anchorites perched on stools at the other end of the table.

"The girls have already filled us in. We'll get Fern and Trix to the ship where they'll be safe—"

Fern interrupted Bethea. "You won't. If these two little brats can dart about the city unsupervised and stuffed up with their own import, then we're gonna help, too, and ain't nothing you can do about it."

"Fern..." I cautioned. "They've been trained."

"Ain't nothing they know from Bo that we ain't learned picking pockets."

"Weren't you snatched by the Shriven for picking pockets?" Quill asked mildly.

"That's neither here nor there," Trix snapped. "Don't need to pick pockets to make this work. Just need to get bodies to rally to us. Need to make some noise. We can make noise."

"Listen," Curlin said. "Why don't you tell us the plan, then we can decide who goes with and who goes to the ship. Fair?"

Before any of my sisters had half a chance to argue, Quill launched into an explanation. Their idea was smart, albeit risky, and we would have to move fast. But Fern and Trix were right—we'd need all the bodies we could get.

With the help of the three anchorites, we made our way out of the temple unseen. Waiting in an alley behind the temple was a wagon, with General Okara in the driver's seat and a team of four strong horses stamping in their traces. Quill helped Curlin and me into seats on either side of the general and pulled my sisters into the wagon bed.

"You're not coming with us?" I asked the anchorites. "You'll be dead if anyone finds out you've helped us."

Bethea smiled up at me. "There's work to be done from within the temple, too, my dear. We've let our brothers and sisters lean on their wicked poison for too long. It's beyond time that they see their power curtailed."

Lugine interrupted, the barest hint of a laugh coloring her words. "And if we made every decision based on how likely our brethren were to string us up, neither one of you'd be here to argue the point. We'll see you again."

"We pray that the goddesses will keep you both safe," Sula said.

Curlin rolled her eyes at me, but didn't manage to control the edge of a smile that played across her lips. "We've been doing just fine without 'em lately, Anchorite, but I won't say no to the extra help."

Then General Okara snapped the reins, and the horses sprang to a trot.

General Okara drove us into the narrow, winding streets of the End. Familiar faces gathered around us, following the wagon as we went. They were the former Shriven and the Ilorian soldiers, and as we traveled, a chant began, part of a verse that Quill had quoted all those many months ago.

They two are chaos.
They two shall build this earth anew.
They portend great loss,
For those whose greed's rent the world in two.

First it was just Quill, his voice a surprisingly lovely tenor, and then the former Shriven around him joined in. Then the Ilorians, and as their voices called down the sky, doors were flung open, shutters lifted and people from the End began to pour into the streets.

We stopped in a park, and the crowd of our people parted, allowing the folks from the End to press in close. I looked to Quill, to General Okara, waiting for one of them to speak, but their eyes were on me. Curlin nudged me painfully in the ribs with an elbow, and I glanced helplessly up at Quill. This wasn't part of the plan. I had nothing to say to these people. What could I tell them? They'd spent their lives fearing and hating people like us. Dimmys. The Shriven. The other. There was nothing in my appearance that might suggest that these people could trust a word out of my mouth.

Quill offered me a hand. "Tell them the truth. It'll be the first time anyone's done that much for them in a long time. Perhaps ever."

I took his hand and stepped onto a crate in the back of the wagon.

My voice was small and quavering as I spoke. "My name is Vi."

Someone in the back of the crowd shouted, "Speak up, lovey."

"What're you doing, then?" another person cried, and something like relief washed over me when I realized that I knew these people. These were the faces I'd grown up with, people I'd seen every day for most of my life. These were the people whose brothers and sisters, whose mothers and fathers and lovers had been ripped away from them since Rylain stole the throne from Bo. These people were grieving and raw and scared and ripe for a revolution.

I started again. "My name is Vi Abernathy, but most of you know that already. Up until about a year ago, I lived in your neighborhood. I sold you oysters and bought things from your shops. You know me. What you don't know—what I didn't know up until a couple of months ago—is that King Ambrose is my twin brother. And I'm here to ask for your help in putting him in his rightful place on the throne."

A hush went over the crowd. Then someone called out, "Piss off. The prince is dead."

I raised my hand for silence. "King Ambrose is alive, and right now he's fighting to take back the throne so as to help fix all the horrible things Rylain's done in the name of the temple. Queen Runa knew he was a twin, and she wanted him on the throne. She chose him to lead you. Everything the temple's been feeding you all your lives is a lie."

The people gathered around the wagon shifted and murmured to each other. I looked out over the sea of familiar faces. They were the fisherwomen who'd bought the temple's oysters from me for years. They were the bakers who'd looked the other way when I paid them in stolen coin. They were the shopkeepers who'd watched me warily for years, who'd waited for my inevitable violence for so long that they'd almost forgotten about it and made a pet of me. These people had watched my sisters and brothers grow, had talked behind their hands about my mother's drinking and bar brawls, about Dammal's gambling. If anyone had reason to trust my word, it was them.

"Why should we believe you?"

"I've no reason to lie to you. You know me, Irina Hatclove. You gave me a pair of old oyster knives when you found me crying my eyes out behind your shop because I'd snapped the temple's blade. Remember?" I looked out over the crowd, spotting another face I knew. "Thomasin Gretinsk, I see you there in the back. I used to save my pennies just to buy one of your raisin cream tarts. Makes my mouth water just thinking about them to this day. And you, Jemma Twillerson. How many times did you slip me a salve when my knees were skinned, or a mug of tea when I was sniffling? No matter what you think, you all cared about me, and I you.

"I had another life waiting for me in Ilor, but I came back because I believed in my brother," I said huskily. "And because I believe in protecting you. You think I'd be back here, risking my life, just to lie to you? I've nothing to gain from that lie. Only the temple does. They've got a poison, a poison that makes dimmys turn, and they've been using that fear to control you. To keep you down." I paused for a moment, weighing the suspicious looks on the faces of the crowd. "Think about what the temple has done these last few months. Think about all the harmless dimmys they've rounded up. Think about all the people who've disappeared. You can see it. Think about all the violence and horror you've seen in these few short months of Rylain's rule. Bo wants to change all that. He wants you to be free."

I could see the wheels turning in their heads. They didn't want to believe me. Didn't want to upend their lives on the word of a dimmy. It took a lot for a body to change the way they saw the world. I knew that. I'd need to give them something more. I turned to look at Curlin, the question in my eyes, but she was already pulling herself to her feet.

"You lot know me just as well as you know Vi," she said. "You saw us come up together. You watched us with fear in your eyes for our whole lives, waiting for us to lose our grip and put one of your brats in danger. That whole time, though, you cared for us. Each of you, in your own little ways, did things to make our lives easier. You weren't open about it, none of you, but there's not a face in this crowd who didn't, at some point, do something kind for Vi or me."

Curlin shrugged out of the loose jacket that Bethea had draped over her shoulders and let the cold Alskad air send gooseflesh whistling up her tattooed arms.

"You know I joined the Shriven. You know I was one of

them. All of you think you know what the Shriven are capable of, but the brutality you've seen from them doesn't come close to the full scope of the temple's evil. The serum Vi's telling you about is real. I've seen perfectly sane twins lose their grip and rip each other apart. I've helped the temple dose people without their knowing. I've done some truly horrible things on their orders, but I've never changed. I've never become diminished, because the temple's always had another use for me."

I wrapped an arm around Curlin's waist and took up the thread of her narrative.

"Right now, my brother is fighting to take back the throne so that he can protect us from the temple. We need you to spread the word of what the temple has done, rally in the palace square, tell the High Council that the people of Alskad are done with being ruled by fear, done with being ruled by religion. We want a king who fights for his people. We want a king *of* the people. We want King Ambrose!"

The applause started in the back of the crowd, hesitant and quiet at first, but it spread like wildfire, and before a full minute had passed, the crowd was roaring all around us. My knees shook as Quill helped me back to my seat. Curlin and Quill each held one of my hands as the wagon rolled forward once more, and my bones vibrated with the reverberations of the cry that echoed through the streets behind us.

"King Ambrose," they cried. "We want King Ambrose."

CHAPTER FORTY-TWO

Bo

The anchorites that Rylain had installed on the High Council tried, for the most part, to keep their expressions cool and nonplussed as they entered the council chamber and saw me, crown atop my head, seated at the head of the table. Not a one of them made any gesture of respect or so much as acknowledged my presence in the room, but some didn't make even the slightest effort to control their disdain. I had steeled myself against the possibility that Claes would sit on the council, but, mercifully, he was nowhere to be seen.

One of the anchorites tightened her mouth into a hard line, and she refused to meet my eyes. Another, a man I recognized from the ceremony on my birthday, sneered at me, his face contorted into an expression so hateful that he seemed more like a villain out of a novel than a person who'd devoted his life to the temple and the gods.

But then, I reminded myself, it was the anchorites who'd created a serum that induced violence and delusion. It was the

Suzerain who'd used that serum to control my people, and it was the Suzerain who'd murdered my people on the shores of the Tethys. It made sense for them to appear villainous. They *were* villains.

The singleborn entered the council chamber one by one and made a point of giving me the greatest courtesies possible. Each of them bowed over my hand in turn and asked after my health before taking their places around the table. Patrise, grinning, took the seat opposite me at the other end of the long table, surrounded by anchorites. One of them gave him a hard look and started to remind him that his chair was the seat usually reserved for the heir to the throne.

Lisette, in her airiest, most flippant voice, said, "Calm down, you old bat," and dismissed the woman's concerns with a wave of her hand.

Rylain was the last to arrive. She flew into the room, coattails flapping behind her like dark wings. She wore a simple gold circlet over her brow, and the sleeves of her jacket were cropped at the elbow to emphasize the highly polished gold cuffs she wore on each of her wrists.

"Who called this meeting of the council?" she demanded, not looking up from the hefty legal tome in her hands. "I have a great deal of work to do, and almost no time for any of it."

I rose, my hands firmly on the table to hide their shaking, and said, "I, King Ambrose Oswin Trousillion Gyllen, called this meeting of the High Council of Alskad. Rylain, if you would, please take a seat."

"You've no right," Rylain sputtered.

"In fact, cousin, it's you who has stepped beyond the boundaries of the law."

I took a deep breath and launched myself into the monologue of legal gymnastics that Gerlene had seemed to conjure out of thin air within hours of Vi handing herself over to the temple. The gist of it was that the law precluded Alskaders from holding a seat on the High Council while simultaneously serving as a guild master or—thanks be to my wily ancestors who'd built the scaffolding of these laws—as a member of the temple clergy. That meant the anchorites Rylain had installed on the Council would either have to step down as councillors or denounce their vows to the temple. Regardless, until their conflict was resolved, they would be forced out of the council chamber.

One pinch-faced anchorite sputtered and spit and demanded to see the original book of law that set down these rules, thinking it would be impossible for me to set my hands on it, but I was ready for her. As soon as we entered the council chamber, Swinton had gone to the law library to retrieve the book. So the moment Patrise opened the door to summon a chamberlain, the book was in his hands, the appropriate passages already marked.

"With respect to my cousin and the work she's done to maintain order in Alskad in my absence, I would like to call for a vote," I said. "Those in favor of allowing the anchorites to remain on the council, please say 'yea.'"

In unison, the temple sycophants and Rylain voted in favor.

"That's it, then," Rylain said. "They stay. Now I would like to call a vote that will put this pretender's claim to rest once and for all."

I was barely able to contain my smile as Lisette raised her objection in a lazy, melodic voice. "Rylain, darling, I do hate to be a bore, but the trouble is, you're not actually *on* the High Council. The last I remember, you stepped down to allow King Ambrose to take your seat. In the confusion after his death, of course, we all assumed it was right and good that you take back that place, but unfortunately, without the rightful monarch swearing you back onto the council, you don't get a vote."

Patrise looked around the room, his face all raised eyebrows and dramatically pursed lips. "In that case, shall we finish the vote?"

"All those opposed?" I asked.

Every one of the singleborn, even Dame Turshaw, who looked like she'd swallowed a rotten egg, raised their hands.

"And with my nay, the vote carries. I'm afraid I must ask you all to leave." I didn't take my eyes off Rylain's blazingly furious face. "Rylain, as the next vote I call will concern you, you may remain in the council chamber for the time being."

"Should we ask her to stand?" Lisette asked, toying with one of the many rings that decorated her long, slender fingers.

"Don't be a brat," Patrise said, grinning.

"Order," Dame Turshaw intoned. "I demand that the order of this chamber be respected, even by the two of you." She turned to me. "If you'd continue, Ambrose, I'd like this business concluded as soon as possible."

The room went quiet, and I looked at each of the singleborn in turn. These people were, one and all, my family. Each of them had seen me grow up, had known my father, had served my grandmother, had mourned with me when I'd sent my mother and Penelope and then Claes to the halls of the gods, all within a month of each other. I thought of all I'd been through to get to this place, everything Vi had sacrificed, all the planning and careful thought that Runa had put into choosing me—choosing Vi *and* me. I wanted to honor that history, all of it.

"I come before you today much changed," I told them. "I'm not the man I was a year ago when I first made my oaths to

Runa and to the Alskad people. There was so much I didn't know then, so much that had been hidden from me. I had no sense of the scope of the work I'd agreed to inherit. But Runa chose *me* to follow her. She chose me knowing that I had a twin. She wanted to break away from the idea that only the singleborn can lead—an idea that the temple has forced on us.

"I've spent my whole life preparing to be king, but I stand before you now, humbly, to ask for your support. I will not bully my way onto the throne. I will not take this power without your consent." I cleared my throat. "So, with all that in mind, I ask for a vote. All those in favor of my ascension, please mark your agreement with a 'yea' vote now."

The room was silent for a moment, but for the fire crackling in the hearth. Dame Turshaw sniffed and shot Patrise an evil look. Rylain's jaw was clenched tight enough to crack her teeth.

To my great surprise, it was Zurienne who broke the silence.

"Yea."

Patrise and Lisette quickly followed suit. Dame Turshaw gave her curt "yea" a moment later. I looked at Olivar, a distant cousin I barely knew. He was in his forties, with the dark hair, olive skin and piercing eyes that marked the members of the Trousillion line. I met his gaze, forcing down the anxiety and fear that ate at me. I focused on the weight of the crown, my crown, on my brow. On the promises I'd made to Runa and Vi and Swinton. I'd be sure to keep those promises. Even if Olivar said no, I would find another way to help my people. I wouldn't let Rylain stay on the throne, but I wouldn't take it for myself, either.

The hairs on my arm stood in the electrified silence as we

all waited for his answer. Finally, with a great, heaving sigh, Olivar dropped his eyes to the table and said, "Yea."

"The yeas have it. Ambrose Oswin Trousillion Gyllen will take the throne. I move that the coronation take place immediately, to discourage further questions," Patrise said, suddenly paying all serious attention to the rules of decorum. "May I have a second?"

"I second the motion," Lisette called.

"A third," Zurienne finished. "The motion carries."

Rylain threw her hands in the air and popped to her feet. "Nay. I vote nay. Doesn't that count for anything?"

"I'm afraid not, dearie," Dame Turshaw said. "You're not actually *on* the council anymore. Do try to remember that you gave up your seat. You may go now. Thank you for your service as regent."

Patrise went to the door and opened it with a flourish.

"Guards, would you please take Rylain to her rooms and stand guard?" he called. "I believe there may be some charges brought against her in the near future."

The guards outside the room looked at each other, befuddled, but before they could move, the members of the Vigilant I'd brought with me stepped forward and took Rylain gently by her arms, escorting her out of the room.

"This will not stand," she cried. "You'll be punished for your insolence."

Before Patrise could close the doors behind her, Swinton stepped forward, his face clouded with worry.

"Bo," he said in a low tone, "there are hundreds, if not a thousand or more people, gathering in the square outside the castle. They're calling for you. Vi is with them."

I breathed a sigh of relief. "She's safe?"

"From what we've heard, she's battered, but safe. They've

rallied around her, around you. They're calling you the Twin King."

I grinned. "I'll go out to them as soon as our business concludes in here. Thank you, love." I squeezed his hand and kissed him on the cheek, but he still wore a troubled expression.

"What is it? What's wrong?" I asked.

"We've also just gotten word that a Denorian ship has entered the harbor. It's flying royal colors and the flag of the queen."

I blinked at him, stunned. "What does that mean?"

"Noriava's here. She's come to collect on your debt. Your engagement."

All of the blood drained from my face. My mind went spinning off in a thousand directions at once.

"I'll have to tell the council. Will you wait here? Please?"

Swinton nodded and, in a sudden burst, wrapped me in a fierce embrace. "I'm that proud of you. You'll be a king to mark the ages."

I pulled him closer and buried my face in his neck. "I couldn't have done it without you."

My arms still tight around his warm, muscular body, I raised my head and kissed him full on the mouth. The guards, the High Council watching through the door, even the whistling members of the Vigilant, could drag themselves to deepest hell for all I cared. Swinton was hesitant for a moment, his whole body tensed, but then he relaxed. Everything fell away except the two of us, and there was nothing in the world except my arms around him and our lips pressed together.

I drank in that kiss like the first taste of cool, clear water after an endless race through the desert. I let everything go except his lips against mine, his hand on my neck and mine on the tight ropes of muscle running up his back. It felt like it'd been lifetimes since we shared a kiss like this, a kiss that consumed and burned and quenched something inside me I didn't know had been parched. When we finally broke apart, I pressed my forehead to his and looked deep into his eyes.

"I missed you, my love."

"And I you, bully."

I went back into the council chamber, blushing at Patrise's leering grin and slow clap. Lisette's small, vicious smile was nothing compared to the eyes of the rest of the council boring into my skull as I crossed the room and resumed my seat at the head of the table.

"Not, of course, to be indelicate, but this—" Olivar cleared his throat "—revelation does raise some questions as to the line of succession."

I forced back a smile and raised one eyebrow, thrilled that for once I'd found my way to a solution before the question had even been asked. The joy I felt was something more than that, though. It was a pure, humming rush of victorious glee coming from something outside of my control, outside of me. And with a pang, I realized that what I felt was Vi's exhilaration as the crowd gathered in the square, calling for me. Calling for me to take the throne. But before I could go out there, before I could reassure them, I had to deal with the problems in this room.

"I have a plan for the succession," I said. "One that's been taking shape for a long time. And while I may very well have children of my own—frankly, it isn't something Swinton and I have yet discussed—I believe there is a better way for Alskad to choose its next ruler. Runa was deliberate in her choice of an heir, and I would like to honor that legacy, but take it a step further. I've talked it through with Gerlene, and there's nothing in the laws that would stop a change like the one I propose."

"And," Lisette purred, "what is it that you propose, exactly?"

"I firmly believe that the qualities of a ruler are learned, not inherited," I said. "So from this point forward, the crown will no longer remain solely in the hands of the Trousillion line. I propose that once every ten years, each Alskad principality be asked to send three young people between the ages of ten and twenty to Penby for an education. This education will be a privilege earned based on public service, school performance and the inclinations of the children themselves as determined by an interview with the entirety of the High Council. It is from this pool that the next generation of leaders—and the next ruler—will be chosen."

"And just like that, you'll throw away tradition that's been handed down since the cataclysm?" Dame Turshaw sputtered. "What of the faith? What of the temple? Have you no fear of angering the gods and goddesses? It's their law that dictates the singleborn must be the ones to lead the people."

"Has it ever occurred to you that it might just be a fluke?" I asked. "What if there's simply something in our family that doesn't always allow us to produce twins? What if the singleborn aren't so special after all?"

Jaws dropped all around the council table, and even Patrise and Lisette looked stunned.

"Honestly, though, the question of the succession can be debated endlessly for the foreseeable future. We have another problem that needs to be addressed right now."

"And what, exactly, could possibly be more pressing than establishing a clear line of succession, so that what's happened here these last few months never happens again?" Zurienne asked, her expression sour.

"Two problems, actually, at that," I said, my brain scrambling to corral all of the moving parts. "First, I've just learned that a ship bearing the royal flag of Denor and the colors of Queen Noriava has arrived in our harbor. I suspect that the queen herself will be making her way to the palace at any minute."

Patrise's eyebrows sailed up his forehead. "And why, exactly, do you hold that suspicion?"

I grimaced. "I may or may not have promised to marry her and then ran away with half of her army."

Lisette clapped her hands giddily, and the rest of the members of the council turned their glares away from me and onto her.

"What?" she asked. "It's just too delicious for words."

"Do you intend to honor your agreement?" Dame Turshaw asked. "Or will you start your reign with broken promises and shattered alliances?"

I swallowed the sour fury that coated my tongue and took a deep, calming breath. "As Queen Noriava forced me into the engagement using blackmail and a number of other nefarious tactics almost too unbelievable to mention, I don't feel that my honor particularly compels me to stand by the agreement I made. Technically, I was a prisoner at the time. That said, I do think the alliance with Denor is of exceeding importance, especially given the scientific advances I saw during my time there and the rational way their society is structured. We need, more than anything, more rationality in every aspect of the way this country is run."

"What, then, do you propose?" Patrise asked, then smiled. "No pun intended, of course."

Every member of the council simultaneously gave him a withering look.

"Funny you should ask." I beamed. "I was thinking you ought to marry her."

Patrise's smile vanished. "Me? Marry her? Why, in Teuber's name, would your squirrelly little brain go there?"

I rolled my eyes. "Patrise, perhaps refrain from using the term 'squirrelly' to describe your king?"

"Apologies," he croaked. "But the question remains. Why me?"

Zurienne, calculatingly, answered for me. "You're of age, you're single and it's well-known that you and Noriava have behaved indiscreetly when in one another's company for years at this point. The only reason Runa never forced the match is because she didn't want the two of you conniving behind her back." She glanced pointedly at me. "Which, if I may say so, Your Majesty, is a fairly good reason to oppose the pairing."

"True enough," Dame Turshaw said. "But Runa simply wanted to avoid any confusion with the line of succession. With King Ambrose's new succession plan in place, that really ought not be an issue."

It took every ounce of will in my body to keep my jaw from dropping straight to the ground. Never, not once, had I expected Dame Turshaw to agree with me. About anything.

"Do you love the woman, Patrise?" Olivar asked.

Patrise looked to Lisette, who had her chin cupped in her hands, elbows on the table, grinning like a house cat who'd finally caught her mouse.

"That's a fair question," I said. "If you're truly opposed to the idea of becoming the king of Denor, Patrise, please just say the word, and we'll find another way. But if you can find it in your heart to do this service to your country, I would be eternally grateful. We will, of course, have to negotiate a mutually beneficial trade agreement and exchange of technologies, but I think that if I can give Noriava a singleborn Alskader, and one she likes as much as she likes you, we'll be well on our way to a resolution."

Just then, there was a knock on the chamber door. I nodded to Zurienne, who crossed the room and opened the door to reveal the chamberlain.

"Yes?" I asked.

"Apologies, Your Majesty, but there's a woman here who claims she's the queen of Denor. Would you like me to send her away?"

I looked at Patrise. Everyone in the room turned their focus to his face as he considered. Finally, he pushed his chair back from the table and stood.

"Bring her in," he said, all the humor and calculation swept from his voice, and in its place a firm sense of determination.

I stood as well, and a moment later, Noriava swept into the room, looking every bit as radiant as ever.

"Before you say anything, Bo, darling," Noriava began, her voice smooth as Samirian silk. "I know that my methods leading up to our engagement were a bit, shall we say, underhanded. However, I never in my life thought that my very own fiancé would rather jump off a cliff than marry me." She pouted. "You can't imagine the stories flying around Salemouth. A thing like that—well, it's rather a blow to a woman's confidence."

Olivar's mustache twitched, and he settled back in his chair, eyes flicking from Noriava to me and back again. Lisette did nothing to hide her delighted grin. I met Dame Turshaw's disapproving glare with as much calm as I could muster, and Zurienne chose a new chair next to me at the head of the table, where she had the best view of the rest of the room. Through the thick lead glass windows, I saw snow drift from the sky like powdered sugar dusting a cake. This late in the spring, it was likely to be the last snowfall of the season. The first of my reign as king. We all waited, listening to the fire crackling in the hearth, our eyes on Patrise.

"Well?" Noriava exclaimed. "Haven't you anything to say, Ambrose?"

Patrise went to her and took her hands in his. "Nori, my dear." Noriava looked surprised, though not displeased, at his touch. "I wondered…if you might consider taking me. Instead of Bo."

A mask came down over Noriava's face, and she narrowed her eyes at me. "Don't think you're going to get out of our arrangement so easily, Ambrose Gyllen. You agreed to a marriage, to an alliance, and to the fact that our progeny would sit on the thrones of both Alskad and Denor."

"I did think of that," I said. "If you agree to regular inspections of your labs to assure me that you've ceased trying to replicate the temple's poison, and you agree to sell whatever medicines and cures your scientists are able to produce to the people of Alskad, I will allow any children that come from a union between you and Patrise to be considered for the school from which the next ruler of Alskad will be chosen. That is, of course, if they meet the minimum requirements." I met her gaze squarely. "It's the best I can offer. A hat in the ring, and a marriage that's based not on lies, but on a real connection. Is there really a choice?"

"We could declare war," Noriava spit.

"Do you really want to come into my council chamber and make those kinds of threats?" I asked her. "Just because you didn't win? Aren't you the person who told me I should put the good of my people and their needs before everything else?"

Patrise put a hand on Noriava's arm, and there was a light in his eyes I'd not seen there before. "It's the right choice, Nori. Please say yes."

Noriava looked around the room, her green eyes not settling on any one person for more than a moment. Finally, after a long while, she nodded.

"Fine. But we will need to settle the question of your impertinent theft of my army."

I grinned. "Fair enough. You can have them all back—all the ones who'll go back to you willingly, anyway—just as soon as we take care of the one last thing standing between me and a peaceful empire."

"And what is that?" she asked.

"The temple."

CHAPTER FORTY-THREE

Vi

Though a light snow had begun falling in slow drifts, the crowd surged and pulled around me. Their energy buzzed like a hive of bees, but stronger than that, stronger than anything, was Bo, thrumming in the back of my mind. I knew without hearing for myself that he'd done it. Somehow, he'd managed to get Rylain off the throne and the temple's flunkies out of the council chamber, and the confident force of his focus poured through our bond. It was the strongest I'd ever felt his emotions, and his feelings threatened to overwhelm the tingle of wary fear that curdled through my veins as I watched more and more people pour into the square.

I needed that fear. I needed it to keep me safe, to keep me watchful, because right at that moment, I was trapped.

Quill stood beside me in the wagon bed, and I leaned into him, just a bit. Whatever had broken between us now felt healed, and his sturdy presence bolstered me, the warmth of his body keeping the chill of the snow at bay. There'd been

warm, fur-lined jackets and boots waiting in the wagon for
Curlin and me, but the cold ate into my bones nevertheless.
Quill kept one hand settled gently on my waist, its weight a
subtle reassurance.

Curlin perched on the wagon seat in front of us, every
muscle in her body tensed. Despite her injuries, or perhaps
because of them, she was ready for a fight. She'd even bullied
one of the former Shriven who'd positioned themselves around
our wagon to give her their staff. She held the weapon—as
thick as my wrist, metal-tipped on both ends, and as long as I
was tall—across her lap as she scanned the crowd. Beside her,
General Okara leaned back against the wagon's armrest, ap-
pearing more relaxed than a soldier staring down at a square
packed with people on the verge of a riot had any right to be.

Clearly, the plan had worked, and word had spread throughout the city. Everyone in the square was calling for Bo.

Quill pointed to the palace. There, in the center of the second floor, members of our guard—Denorians, Ilorians and
the former Shriven—took up positions on a wide balcony. It
was just high enough for whoever stood there to be visible
to the entire square, but not so high that a crowd might feel
as though their ruler were looking down on them. I craned
my neck for a closer look, but the balcony was too deep for
me to see who stood in the open doorway.

Leaning down to whisper in my ear, Quill said, "If I were a
gambling man, I'd say we have just about even odds of seeing
Rylain or your Bo on that balcony in a moment, but Mal'd
slay me if he knew I'd even joked about playing the odds."

"And I'd say Mal's right to discourage you from trying
to be a betting man, for you've no eye for it. Say Rylain did
manage to throw Bo off somehow," I speculated. "There's
no way that she'd be careless enough to show her face to a

thousand souls calling for Bo. Plus, if you knew anything at all, you'd know there's not a soul in Penby who'll bet against an Abernathy and expect to win. Stubborn as barnacles, to a one. And fancy upbringing and Trousillion father or no, Bo's an Abernathy. Through and through."

A low horn sounded on a distant rooftop, joined by one after another until the sound reverberated through the square and sent a hush through the crowd. A woman, her silver-streaked hair twisted into an elaborate knot at the crown of her head, stepped forward, and she raised a long, twisting horn covered in thin gold filigree to the sky. She blew a single clear note and stepped back. I thought I saw something like pride on her thin, lined face, but she was far away, and it could've just as easily been my exhaustion as anything else.

When Bo stepped forward, a cheer rose up through the crowd. His simple, well-cut suit showed not one wrinkle, not one stain, though it was the same thing he'd been wearing when I'd seen him last, days before. His head was bare, and snow clung to his riot of black curls. Swinton stood just behind Bo's left shoulder, a large wooden box clasped in his arms. Bo raised his hand to wave, and the crowd sent up a wild cheer. When they eventually quieted, Bo's voice boomed out over the square.

"People of the Alskad Empire, my beloved subjects. The High Council has heard your call, and my cousin Rylain has relinquished her place on the throne. I stand before you, humbly, to ask your forgiveness. I should not have left you for so long without the comfort of a permanent and rightful ruler." He bowed his head for a moment, then lifted his gaze to survey his people once again. "In these dark times, I cannot condone the kind of lavish, over-the-top celebration that has accompanied the coronations of my predecessors. To that end, I ask that you stand with me today as I once again reaffirm my vows to you and am crowned."

As murmurs of shock rippled through the gathered crowd, pride surged through my veins. Two servants brought a simple chair cushioned with thick furs and set it at the edge of the balcony. Bo sat, and Swinton handed the box to the silver-haired woman who'd blown the horn.

Bo's voice rang out over the assembly. "By right of law and the choice of my predecessor, Queen Runa Trousillion, I stand before you—as a twin. As a man of both the royal house of Trousillion and the people of Alskad. And I hereby declare my intention to take my rightful place upon the throne of Alskad."

Swinton reached into the box and lifted out a crown. It was not entirely unlike the Crown of Alskad I'd seen as it rumbled by in a glass case all those many years ago, but it certainly was not the same. He handed it to Lisette with a bow.

The gray gemstones glittered in the sunlight filtering through the softly falling snow as Lisette went to stand before Bo, holding the crown up for the entire square to see.

"Do you swear to uphold the honor of the Alskad people?"

Bo raised his chin, his voice booming out over the whole square. "I do."

"Will you guide the people of the empire with your conscience, serving them with justice and grace, putting their needs before your own?"

Bo's smile was brilliant as I laid a hand on Curlin's shoulder. She started and then looked back at me, tears in her eyes.

"We did it," she whispered.

Bo's response came on the tail of her words. "I will."

"Will you wear this crown, its weight a reminder of your duty to your people and your country?"

"I will."

"Then swear that you will serve the people of the empire for the rest of your days."

Bo put his hands over his heart, and the sleeve of his jacket fell back to reveal the gold cuff on his wrist.

"I swear on my honor that I will serve the people of the empire for the rest of my days."

Lisette lifted the crown to the people gathered in the square, then turned and settled the crown on Bo's curls. She held out her hand to Bo, and in a high, clear voice said, "Stand, then, King Ambrose Oswin Trousillion Gyllen Abernathy, Emperor of Alskad."

The crowd erupted into cheers, and all around me, people called Bo's name. He went to the rail of the balcony, scanned the crowd, and for a moment, it felt as though his gray eyes met mine. Warmth traveled both ways along our bond, and I relaxed. Bo was king. It would take next to nothing for him to push back against the temple and their frightening hold on the people of Alskad. For the first time in my memory, the odds were no longer stacked overwhelmingly against me.

Then, at the front of the square, near the balcony where my brother stood, an explosion. A scream. Another. In a wave, people surged back, back, running away from the palace. Away from the square. Away from Bo.

Fear seized me, but I couldn't see through the smoke. I touched the pearl in my pocket, seeking comfort. General Okara was bolt upright, her hands on the reins, her eyes focused on the four horses tethered to our wagon. Curlin shot up, staff at the ready.

I was more prepared when I heard the second explosion. Fire flashed, the horses reared, and I leaped down from the wagon. Focus seemed to pump through my veins, and the pain that had haunted me since my night with Castor in the temple disappeared. Bo was the only thing that mattered, the only thing I could see. I pushed through the crowd, like fighting my way out into the bay through an incoming tide. I heard Quill's voice behind me, but there wasn't time to argue, wasn't time to do anything but find Bo.

I pressed through the last wall of frightened people and stopped short at the scene in front of me. Bright patches of blood and fire were the only spots of color. Fine stone dust and drifting ash coated everything in a blanket of gray. Bodies lay scattered like fallen rag dolls, their limbs at odd angles. A child's bright yellow shoe lay next to the crumbled stone where the balcony had collapsed in the first explosion.

"Vi," Quill cautioned, but I didn't have time to listen. Didn't have time for my stomach to heave or for the crippling memories of the battles I'd fought next to him in Ilor to come surging back. I had to move.

I forced my eyes up, forced my legs to move, and I scrambled up the collapsed stone and onto the balcony. There were others already there—the Shriven, locked in a furious battle with our people. Hearing a pained grunt, I glanced back and saw Curlin right behind me. Quill moved faster than I could manage and heaved her up onto the balcony with us.

Then, like three pieces of the same machine, we entered the fray.

CHAPTER FORTY-FOUR

Bo

The first explosion lifted me off my feet and threw me backward, all the way to the palace wall. For a single, dazed moment, my vision dimmed, but the rain of fire and stone that erupted from the second explosion drew me quickly from my stupor. My first coherent thought was for Swinton. I forced myself to my feet as dozens and dozens of the Shriven poured over the ruins of the balcony railing.

Fear clogging my throat, I yelled his name. "Swinton! Swinton! Where are you?"

The doors, which had been closed last I remembered, were flung open, and my people, the Vigilant, surrounded me, forming a protective barrier that, while useful, blocked my view almost entirely. My focus came back in slow, wavering gasps, and I realized that the Shriven were fighting their way toward me. These were not the people Vi and Curlin had recruited. These Shriven, with their shorn heads and black paint and slick, silent blades, were the deadly tools of the temple. These were people dosed with just enough of the temple's poison to quiet the voices of their consciences.

These people would not stop until I was dead.

There was a yowl followed by the sounds of a scuffle to my right, next to the door. I wanted to shove through the guards, to find Swinton, to fight, but I couldn't. I was un-armed, beyond the knife in my boot. I couldn't promise my people permanency and fair leadership with one breath and risk my life with the next. So I drew my knife, the blade not half as long as my forearm but wickedly sharp, and took up a defensive position by the wall.

The double row of guards around me moved like water, forcing the Shriven back and back, covering the holes where their comrades fell. All the while, my eyes searched for the bright flag of Swinton's honey-gold hair, a flash of his coat. Something. Anything.

The guard around me shifted, and I caught sight of another familiar face. Not Swinton's, but Vi's. Her eye was blacked, and a line of ruby blood trickled down her cheek. She sank her knife into one of the Shriven's bellies with a vicious, practiced ease. Panic tightened around my throat. What the bloody hell was she thinking?

Before I could wrap my head around it, she was moving again, out of sight. Then the guards parted ever so slightly, and Swinton slipped through their ranks. He tossed me a sword, belt wrapped tight around its sheath. I caught it with my free hand, slid my knife back into my boot and threw my arms around him in the briefest of embraces, searching him for wounds.

"Sorry it took so long, bully. Bloody lot of these fellows, and they're all pushed far beyond the bounds of reason."

"What the hell happened?" I asked, buckling on the sword belt.

"They set off some kind of bombs. Two of them at the edges of the balcony. It wouldn't've been half a thing to do, what with all the people and confusion. My guess is that they hoped the bombs would take the whole structure down, kill you and that's the end of it, but they didn't go off at the same time, and the first one threw us out of range of the second. Are you injured?"

I shook my head. "Not really. You?"

Swinton wiped the blood from his two short swords onto his trousers. "Nothing serious. We need to get you to safety. Can you run?"

"Vi's on the balcony. I won't go without her."

A muscle in Swinton's jaw clenched and released and clenched again. "Vi's a wicked beast. You're the king. As soon as you're safe, I'll come back for her."

Before I could respond, a surprised shout rang up from the guards nearest us. One of the Shriven had rushed the Vigilant, but instead of engaging with them, he vaulted over their heads using his staff. The Shriven aimed his landing with Swinton as he crashed down. The weight of the falling Shriven flattened Swinton to the ground, but before the Shriven could rise, Swinton's arm was around his neck as fast as a striking serpent.

"Run!" he shouted.

Then three more Shriven came sailing over the heads of our guards. And just like that, the pocket of calm they'd provided was absorbed into the fray.

I heard Vittoria's voice shouting orders in Denorian over the din of the fight. The air was thick with the shrieking prayers of the Shriven as they fought, low Denorian curses and the screams of the injured and dying. As much as I knew I had to keep myself safe for the sake of my people, there was a voice in my head crying the word *coward* over and over again. A surge of Vi's bloodlust and fury boiled through the bond, and my mind was made up.

Somehow, the fight was louder on the other side of the wall of guards. I saw Vi immediately, whirling around a familiar figure—Claes. My throat tightened. He was trying to kill my sister. He slashed and stabbed at her with a speed and grace that seemed impossible. I glanced over my shoulder just in time to see one of the Shriven, all snarling, razor-sharp teeth, black paint and tattoos, streaking toward me. The Shriven's staff traced a wide arc through the air as it hurtled toward me in what was meant to be a killing blow. I had my sword halfway out of its sheath when the staff slammed to a stop inches in front of my face. It quivered in midair against Vittoria's still-sheathed sword. The general began to buckle under the force of the maddened Shriven woman bearing down on the staff. I freed my own sword, and my swing bit into her shoulder deeply, showing the white flash of her bone. Immediately, Vittoria began to gain the upper hand, and she growled, "Go."

I dashed across the balcony to the edge, where Vi and Curlin were still locked in battle with Claes. I saw Swinton, his swords flying around him like extensions of his arms, meeting one of the Shriven blow for blow. His braid whipped out from behind his head as he turned to catch sight of another assailant flying toward him. Without so much as a blink, he flung one of his swords at his original opponent, and it landed with an unsettling *thunk* in the man's chest. Swinton spun on a heel and planted himself to face the onslaught of his new attacker.

Another Shriven hurled at me, knives flashing, and someone shoved me out of the way. I stumbled, but caught myself, and looked up to see Quill, teeth gritted, straining to hold the Shriven off, even as blood stained his shirt red. He was using every ounce of his strength to protect me, but the blade of the Shriven's knife kept sinking deeper into his abdomen. I moved to help him, to pull the Shriven off him, but Quill shook his head at me.

"Go!" he shouted. "Get out of here."

Just then, I froze, a feeling like an icicle running down my spine stopping me. Suddenly, the strange mental thread that tied Vi and me together flickered and exploded into something huge and powerful and overwhelming. And just like that, Vi's voice came surging into my brain.

I won't let you kill me, bitch. I won't leave Bo alone. Not after all this time.

I shook my head, sure that I'd hit my head in the explosion and was hallucinating, but when I closed my eyes, it was as though I was staring out of someone else's eyes. Vi's. It wasn't perfectly clear, just colors and flashes of images, but in that vision, I saw Amler, the female Suzerain, leering over Vi, and felt hands wrapped around my throat. Vi's throat.

A feeling as sure and natural as breathing overtook me, and I knew just where to find Vi struggling for her life against the Suzerain. I turned on a heel and dashed across the ruined balcony. I raised my sword over my head in a double-handed grip, ready to bring it down on Amler's neck. But just before the blade connected, Amler ducked. The strength of my missed swing staggered me, but, remembering one of Vittoria's lessons, I used the momentum of my swinging blade to aim a kick at Amler's ribs. Amler lifted one hand from Vi's throat and lashed out to grab my ankle without even looking up.

This can't be real, I thought, and tried to kick back out of the Suzerain's iron grip.

Vi's eyes were fluttering. I had to get her free of the Suzerain before she lost consciousness. I raised my sword to hack at Amler's arm when a force like a surging storm washed over me and Vi's voice slammed into my head.

Bo! Behind you!

I dropped instantly to the ground, unquestioning. Amler's hand was still tight around my ankle. A second later, the deadly snap of a kick whipped over my head, and I squeezed my eyes shut in sudden terror. But the world didn't disappear, only shifted, and I saw Castor looming over me. Vi must have seen him approaching.

In a flash of understanding, I realized that the Suzerain must share the same kind of connection. That was how Amler had avoided my initial attacks. An explosion came from somewhere to my right, and Castor looked away. Sensing my opportunity, I swung my sword at Amler's wrist, her hand still tight around my ankle. Finally, the Suzerain released Vi's throat and spun to smack the flat of my blade with so much force that it knocked the weapon out of my hand, sending it skittering harmlessly away across the balcony.

Vi sucked in a breath and sent a booted heel flying into Amler's jaw. The impact bowled her over and she released my ankle, snarling. Vi rasped a victorious laugh and said, "Reap what you sow, isn't that—"

But before she was able to finish, Castor leaped over his sister, arm pulled back, aiming a killing blow. Vi rolled to the side just in time, and Castor's hand slammed into the stone where her chest had just been. The stone split down the middle, and Vi's eyes flickered over the splintered balcony floor, Castor's bleeding knuckles, then came to rest on mine. Simultaneously, we both thought the same word. *Run!*

Vi sprinted just ahead of me. In my peripheral vision, I saw Amler as she dove for Vi's legs. Focusing on the new awareness blazing through my senses, I thought, *Left!* As fast as if it had been her own thought, Vi zigged to the left, and the Suzerain only caught hold of the edge of her coat. Without slowing, Vi spun out of her coat in one motion, and we left the Suzerain behind once more as Amler furiously tossed the coat aside.

A wild, ululating cry split the air, and I saw Castor spot Curlin as she ran, screaming, toward Amler.

"Curlin, no!" I screamed, but I was too late. Amler whirled on her heel, and in a single, decisive movement, grabbed Curlin's head and snapped her neck. I stopped in my tracks, horrified, and in that second, as the battle raged around us, the Suzerain turned in my direction. Amler's fist rammed into my gut, and I doubled over, the wind knocked out of me.

A second later, Vi was at my side, a bloody staff clutched in her hands, swinging wildly at the Suzerain. I pulled a short sword from the hand of a fallen guard and came up slashing. The two Suzerain ducked and deflected all of our blows. My muscles were tight with fatigue, but over Amler's shoulder, I saw Vittoria disengage with her opponent at the same moment Jihye appeared at the edge of the balcony. Taking advantage of my distraction, Castor's leg whipped around my defenses, his foot cracking against my ribs. I recovered just in time to see Amler wrest the staff away from Vi, and a sense of foreboding filled me.

Then bright red blood bloomed over Amler's bright robes,

and a blade sprouted from her heart. As she crumpled to the ground, Castor looked down at her, stunned, and I immediately lunged toward him, thrusting my sword through his neck.

Without his sister's eyes watching for him, Castor never saw my killing blow. He fell beside her, and their blood pooled between them, staining their white robes crimson.

I was still looking down at the fallen Suzerain when Vi's voice came clear through my head. *Knife!* I spun around to see Claes release a throwing dagger. There was less than a blink of an eye to act, and the knife was hurtling straight for Vi's throat.

Without thinking, I reached out to catch the knife, and it buried itself to the hilt in my palm. Adrenaline coursed through my body as I yanked the blade out of my hand and lunged for Claes. Fury overtaking me, I tackled him to the ground and wrapped my hands around his neck, determined to squeeze the life from his deceitful body. My blood pooled beneath him, and he glowered up at me as he bucked and writhed, trying to throw me off.

And then his knife slid between my ribs—a searing, white-hot pain that took my breath away. I blinked in disbelief as my strength began to leave me, and the world went dark.

CHAPTER FORTY-FIVE

Vi

Thirteen Alskader citizens died because of the temple's actions on the day of Bo's coronation. Thirteen names that would forever haunt my memories. Ten families lost mothers, fathers, daughters, sons, brothers, sisters, grandparents and cousins. Four little girls would grow up without mothers. Eight children orphaned completely. Six more left fatherless. All because of the temple. There was no reparation we could pay, no wound we could heal. The temple had gouged something from our city, from our people, that they could never get back.

But the people I loved had paid an even higher price. Curlin and Quill, the two people who knew me best—who loved me, flaws and all—were dead. Curlin at the hands of the Suzerain, and Quill in protecting my brother's life.

Though my grief at their loss was nothing to the pain that Mal now felt as one of the diminished, we steadied each other in our pain. We were seldom apart, leaning on each other for support.

My sadness was an empty thing, a hole inside me so large I thought it would never be filled. Curlin, who'd promised to always protect my weaker side, had been murdered doing exactly that.

And Quill. I couldn't face the thought of the world without him. So I busied myself with the work of helping Mal through his grief as best I could.

Together Mal and I had readied their bodies for their pyres together. We'd stood, hand in hand, on the beach as we released their spirits to the halls of the gods. Then we'd walked, hollow-eyed and empty, back through the streets of Penby to the palace where my brother lay, feverish and unsteady after a surgery we hoped would save his life.

It wasn't hard, after that, to loosen the grip of the Suzerain and their corrupt anchorites on the throat of Alskad's citizens. The people did the great bulk of the work themselves, coming in droves to the palace to demand the High Council examine and prosecute the anchorites of the temple for the evil they'd done to the people of Alskad.

In the early days after Bo's coronation, while he was still unconscious, recovering from surgery, the members of his High Council came to his bedside almost hourly to confer in low whispers. They wanted, inexplicably, to hear my thoughts as we all waded through the murky waters of a country shaken to its very foundation. They asked questions of Swinton, too, and General Okara, and Gerlene. But mostly they asked my opinion, and they listened, full of eager respect, when I told them what it was like to come up in the End, a ward of the temple and a dimmy to boot.

Even Queen Noriava came to sit by Bo's bedside. Swinton, through no great fault of his own, refused to speak to the woman, and spent her visits glaring daggers at her. But still, she came every day, and he let her. Though I'd never say it to Swinton, I was grateful to the awful woman. It turned out to be a boon that Noriava had pursued him across the Tethys. Her royal surgeons had accompanied her, and she'd reacted quickly to the disaster on the balcony. The swift and decisive action of her doctors had been the only thing that'd stood between Bo and death, and even still, it'd been a very near thing.

Lugine, Bethea and Sula came to the palace, as well. For the first time in my memory, they wore plain clothes, not a pearl or an ounce of gold on any of them. Pem and Still brought them through back alleys and secret doors all the way to Bo's rooms. It wasn't safe for anchorites to be on the streets these days, even those so entirely dedicated to the people of Alskad and the service of their vows. They told me in low, hushed tones that in the confusion and panic after the attack, they'd found and destroyed every ounce of the poison the temple had secreted away. They vowed to do anything in their power to aid the High Council in their quest to find justice for the people of Alskad, so I called for Patrise and Lisette and introduced them.

A letter from Aphra arrived two days after the attack. Thanks to the careful, patient persistence that was Aphra's greatest flaw and greatest strength, there wasn't a drop of the evil serum left in Ilor or the rest of the Alskad Empire. Soon, too, the philomena plant would be culled from the hills of Ilor, and access to the flowers would be limited to only a few trusted souls carefully chosen by the High Council.

While Bo recovered, neither Swinton nor Mal nor I left his bedside for very long. When he finally came fully awake, on the third day after his surgery, he fixed the three of us with a deeply troubled look.

"I don't mean to be an ass, but when was the last time any of you three bathed?" Bo croaked.

I glanced at Swinton, confused. Swinton stood and laid a gentle hand on Bo's forehead. My brother sniffed and wrinkled his nose.

"I'm not feverish," Bo snapped. "You stink. I don't know if anything could ruin my appetite at this point, but if anything could, it would be that stench."

I snorted and clapped a hand over my mouth to hide my grin.

"You're not immune, Vi. I can smell you from here. And there's something crusted in your hair."

I raised my hand to my braid but didn't feel anything.

"Not there. On the top..."

Bo raised his arm to point, and I felt the blood drain from my face and the laughter die on my lips as he saw Mal alone, with Quill conspicuously absent.

Swinton took his hand in a gentle grasp. "We lost some of our best people that day, bully."

Bo took a sharp breath in through his nose.

"Mal," he said, his voice a mirror of the pain and sympathy that I felt echoing through me. "I am so sorry. He was a truly wonderful man. I know nothing I can say will be enough. This is such a senseless loss. All of these deaths, all of this violence— it could have been stopped, had the Suzerain... Had I..."

I clenched my jaw and did my best to steel myself against Bo's anger as it radiated through our bond. I wouldn't let him blame himself for this.

"How about the two of you go find something for us to eat?" I asked gently. "Bo and I could use a moment to talk."

"I'm not a child," Bo said. "I can be left alone. And I'd rather like a moment to myself, if you don't mind."

"I mind," I said, glaring at him. I wasn't about to let him throw himself into a sinkhole of despair. Not with so much work to be done, and not because he'd only just seen the cost of his crown. I would grieve Quill and Curlin every day for the rest of my life, and I knew he would, too. But Bo didn't have time to wallow in his sadness. He had an empire to run, and I wasn't about to keep doing it for him.

Tearing my eyes away from Bo, I smiled sweetly up at Swinton and Mal and ever so slightly jerked my chin toward the door. Swinton could come in and clean up my mess when I finished, but someone had to knock some sense into my twin, and today that task fell to me.

"I'm sure Bo would love some soup," I said. "And maybe you can hunt through the cellars for something decent to drink, Mal? I've had about as much tea as I can stand."

Swinton nodded, and when Bo looked away, mouthed, "Thank you," to me before slipping out of the room with Mal.

"You're angry," I said.

"How could you tell?" Bo crossed his bandaged hand over his chest and glowered at me.

"No one ever thought we would get out of this fight without losses." My voice cracked on the word, and Bo reached out to me, sympathy replacing the anger in his eyes.

Bo sighed, biting his lip. "I know. I mean, I can see the fact of it. It's just…"

"We never expected it would be the people closest to us."

"It doesn't seem fair," Bo agreed. "It's *not* fair."

"It isn't. But we aren't the only people who've lost loved ones in this fight. We need you up and well. We need you to be a king."

"Everything hurts. My body. My heart. I don't know when

I'll feel like myself again," Bo said. "I don't know how I'll fix this."

"Well, I've been running your kingdom for the last three days," I said, smiling. "And I can tell you right now that it won't be easy. Cry me a rutting river, but get out of bed and do your damn job. I've no interest in being queen, and there are a thousand and one things that need to be decided."

"Can't I have five minutes to grieve?"

"You can grieve once you put your house in order. And I'll do the same." I knew I was being harsh, but the doctor's cautions—that the best thing for him would be to push himself through the grief and pain of his recovery—echoed through my head. What he really needed, they'd said, was to be thrown off the end of the dock and made to swim. Metaphorically, of course.

"Curlin," Bo started. "I am so sorry, Vi."

I pressed my lips together, once again unsteady as the waves of grief washed over me. "And Quill."

Tears welled in Bo's eyes. "He was trying to save me. Oh, Vi."

As his grief swelled to join mine, I flung my arms around him and wept. We'd lost so much to find our way here, to a place that felt just as hard, just as impossible as the one we'd come from. But below the pain and the anger and the grief, there was a kernel of hope. A promise of a brighter future for the people who would come after us.

CHAPTER FORTY-SIX

Bo

Though Gunnar and Karyta and their pack of servants did everything in their power to keep me in bed for a full week after my surgery, they couldn't quite manage to keep me from my work. And honestly, I couldn't have kept the kingdom at bay if I'd tried. There was too much to be done. The High Council had appointed Gerlene to the newly minted position of Royal Counsel, and she and a handpicked team of the brightest legal minds in the land were hard at work tracking down and prosecuting every crime that had been overlooked because of the temple's influence.

Patrise convinced Noriava—using means I begged him not to detail—to allow some of her scientists and researchers to join the new university we were planning to build outside Penby. The High Council had banded together in my absence and stripped Rylain of her enormous wealth, voting unanimously to use the confiscated funds to build a school that would not only generate the future leaders of Alskad, but also educate any student willing to dedicate themselves to learning. The temple's hoard, accumulated through years of theft, tithing and greed, would be dedicated to the education of the Alskad people, as well.

Patrise and Noriava were a shockingly good influence on each other—he encouraged her to enjoy life a bit more, while she brought out the more responsible and caring side of his nature. Noriava voluntarily came to Swinton and me to apologize for her horrifying behavior, and offered to send as much of the Denorian treatment for the diminished as they could produce. I didn't think Swinton would likely forget what she'd done anytime soon, but at least he'd forgiven her.

As I ought to have expected, I was never, ever alone. People streamed in and out of my bedroom day and night, asking for opinions, answers and thoughts on everything from the color of the drapes in the throne room to the rate of incentivized pay for shipbuilders, now that I'd agreed to sell Alskader ships to Denor. Swinton was constantly by my side, a book in his lap and his feet propped on the bed. The advice he offered was practical and always welcome.

My Abernathy siblings tumbled in and out of the room, bringing me bits of gossip and suggestions for improving the lives of the people in the End. At their request, I'd found Ina and offered her and Dammal a fresh start—a small property near Ina's family, in the town where she'd been raised. But to a one, my siblings had chosen not to join their parents, in favor of staying in Penby.

The only person conspicuously absent was Vi. It wasn't until the late evening on the day Patrise and Noriava departed for Denor that she finally appeared in my doorway.

"Have a minute for your sister?" she asked.

"Always," I told her with a smile.

Vi slid into the room with Mal in her wake and perched on the settee at the end of my bed.

"Mal," I said, my voice grave. "I'd just like to say again that I'm so sorry for your loss. Quill was an exceptional man."

Mal bowed. He'd grown the beginning of a beard, but even that didn't disguise the hollowness of his cheeks and the bags beneath his eyes. "Thank you, Your Majesty. I plan to honor his memory as best I can."

"How are you this evening, Your Majesty?" Vi asked, delicately changing the subject.

I gestured to the piles of paper laid out across my bed. "Just fine. I doubt I'll ever make my way to the bottom of these decrees and memorandums, though. I thought I knew a bit about the role of a ruler, but I've learned there's much more to it than I ever imagined. For instance, did you know that Alskad consumes nearly half a million tons of smoked fish per year? Also, you'll be happy to know that the new goat ranchers subsidized by the crown are producing wool nearly as fine as that of the Denorian sheep."

"I...did not know those things," Vi said, hesitantly.

Swinton rolled his eyes. "Don't encourage him."

I stuck my tongue out at Swinton and grinned at Vi and Mal, but their returning smiles looked forced.

"What's wrong?" I asked.

"We wanted to talk to you about Ilor," Mal started.

"What about it?"

Vi took a deep breath. "We both think that Ilor should be allowed independence, if they want it. We think you should call for a vote."

I glanced at Swinton, looking for his opinion. He shrugged. "It wouldn't have occurred to me, bully, but I think they're right. To keep a colony so far away, with no real leadership on the ground, is its own kind of folly. The people there know what they want, and they know who ought to lead them. That said, I think leaving Aphra in charge without a check is asking for trouble, and if it's not done right, the transition could lead to an oligarchy more dangerous than what's been the case there since it was settled. They still need more than a little help from you."

"That makes sense," I agreed. "But there's so much happening here, I don't know when I'd be able to devote the necessary time."

"It wouldn't have to happen now. The governor has a fair tight leash on Aphra for the time being," Vi said. "Maybe in a year or two. You can send people to start building relationships now and ease them into the idea of a transition."

Mal put his hand on Vi's forearm, and Vi looked up at him, giving an almost imperceptible shake of her head. I could feel her anxiety building.

"What is it?" I asked. "What aren't you saying?"

"Vi should be the one to serve as the ambassador," Mal said. "I'm going back in any case, but the people there look up to Vi. They trust her. She's the right person to lead this…"

Mal trailed off, leaving the room in silence. My hand clenched on the sheets, and tears welled in my eyes. I didn't want to be without her. I'd come all this way, endured all this pain to have my sister by my side. I looked up, to try to read Vi's expression, but her eyes were trained on the sheaf of papers she held in her lap.

"Do you want to go?" I asked.

Vi looked up, her gray eyes the mirror of mine and full of tears. "I want to be of use."

"You can be of use here." But the argument died on my lips. I knew, all at once, that asking Vi to stay would be like trying to keep a wild thing in a cage. It didn't matter where she was—she would always be my twin, my other half. But this place didn't hold the same memories for her as it did for me.

Vi got up, walked around the bed and nudged me over, settling in beside me. Swinton and Mal exchanged a glance, stood simultaneously and left the room.

"It seems like the world is always pulling us apart," I said.

"Does it?" Vi asked, resting her head on my shoulder. "Because to me, it seems like the world is set on bringing us back together over and over again, like waves against the shore."

I touched the battered gold cuff on her wrist, a reflection of mine, and let myself grieve, just for a moment.

"When will you go?"

"Not for a while yet," she said. "Some of the other Ilorians want to get the next ship out, but the Shriven who joined us are doing their best to rehabilitate those who remained loyal to the temple. Mal and I feel like I need to see that through. For Quill and Curlin."

We sat together, not speaking for a few minutes as the fire crackled merrily in the hearth. Finally, I broke the silence with the question that'd been biting at me since she'd said she wanted to leave.

"Will you come back? Not forever, necessarily, but from time to time?"

Vi smiled. "The world is always pulling us back together, Bo. What makes you think it'll stop now?"

CHAPTER FORTY-SEVEN

Vi

The waves were choppy and the wind not yet chilled with winter's edge as the tide pulled us out once more into the sea. Mal and I had booked our passage on the maiden voyage of the smallest, fastest ship to come out of Brenna's shipyard in the last year. The first class of students had just been welcomed into the halls of the new university, and judgment had at last been handed down for the wrongdoings committed by the anchorites. It was a new era for the Alskad Empire, and unlike the last time I'd left Alskad, I felt a pang of sadness as I watched Penby fade into the horizon.

"Will you be homesick?" Mal asked.

I wrapped an arm around his waist and pulled him close to me in a sisterly embrace. "I'll miss Bo and the brats. I'll miss Gerlene. But homesick? No. I don't think so. I don't know that Alskad is really home anymore."

"Where's home, then?"

I rubbed the pearl I'd saved from my hoard, now set on a

gold chain around my neck, and watched the waves churning in the boat's wake as I thought about his question. I loved the ocean, and the answer that sprang immediately to mind was that home was anywhere where the salt air kissed me good morning and tucked me in at night. But I also loved books and good food and having my brother by my side.

But if all of that disappeared, it wouldn't end me. I'd keep going, keep working, keep living. As I watched Alskad disappear, I thought about the choices I'd made and the things I couldn't live without. The little cottage by the sea I'd always imagined would become my home.

It seemed to me that home was more of a feeling than a place. Home was hard work for a cause I cared deeply about. Home was resisting the easy choice in favor of the right one. Home was an honest conversation with someone I loved. Home was every moment of a life I'd learned to never take for granted.

Home was the difference I made in the world.

★ ★ ★ ★ ★

ACKNOWLEDGMENTS

It is important, I think, to acknowledge that I wrote this book in the wake of the 2016 presidential election. I poured my fury at the state of the world into these pages and left poor Vi and Bo to deal with it all. Vi's experience with depression very much mirrors my own, and as I read back over these pages for the last time, my heart yearns to reach out and hug her and everyone else who battles this disease. For those of you living with depression or anxiety, www.depression.org and www.suicidepreventionlifeline.org have some tremendous resources. And, if you can, talk to someone you trust. Depression thrives in the shadows and does its best to keep us silent and suffering alone. Talking about it brings it into the light.

And now, thanks.

Thank you to my editor, Lauren Smulski, for loving Vi and Bo as much as I do, and for helping me bring them to life on the page.

My eternal gratitude to the Inkyard Press team for your support of these books. Y'all are the best.

Thank you to my readers and writer pals and friends and

Fighters. I owe my ability to finish this book and the next one and the one after that and on and on to you.

Thank you to all the booksellers who have embraced and championed my work. I owe you the moon—and not a broken one.

Thank you to Brent Taylor for having a vision for my twin books about twins. I am grateful for your friendship and support.

A big thanks to my family. It means the world to me that you understand when I have to buckle down and put my head into an imaginary world for weeks at a time. I love you the most.

Many thanks to Molly Ker Hawn, a bright light and a steadying force, for whom I am deeply grateful.

To Cody—within these pages is your horse chase scene, one of a multitude of suggestions you've made that make my stories a thousand times better. I couldn't do this without you. I love you more than black holes love warping time.

And to my readers—thank you for taking this trip with me.